MW01224013

UNDER THE STONE ARCH
—BOOK ONE—

WITHIN

Thank you for the support!

To myself—
Despite everything, you did it

TABLE OF CONTENTS

TABLE OF CONTENTS

PART 2: THE WORLD OF DECEIT

I swear—upon my life and my love of it—that I will never work for the sake of another man, nor ask another man to work for mine.

Ayn Rand

PART 1:

THE THEME

CHAPTER I:
HOW YOU FEELING?

"JAY... PLEASE, TALK TO ME," Stacie said. She was crouched in front of a slender brunette, who was sitting on a hospital bed.

Jay's pine-green irises were empty as they stared into Stacie's watery, brown eyes. Her pretty, tan face with angular features was without expression. Stacie was seventeen, a year older than Jay, with long black hair that ran down her back. She wore a yellow top and washed jeans.

"I'm your best friend. You can tell me anything, love." She took Jay's hands, and Jay let out a shuddering breath.

Both teenagers continued to stare at each other in silence as the fluorescent lights buzzed above them and the EKG beeped steadily.

"Do you remember what happened?"

Jay hesitated before shaking her head as she adjusted the blanket that she wore around herself.

Stacie let out a breath. "Good. Well, not good. Good that you're communicating. Not good that you don't remember. Um, do you think...?" She swallowed. "Do you think it had something to do with last night?"

Jay's arm muscles twitched.

"I mean, it must have, right? Can you try to remember? No

pressure, just… Take your time." Stacie gripped her friend's hands tighter. "I'm here for you."

⤙o⤚

THE PREVIOUS DAY…

"You can do this," Jay Dijenuk said to herself as she stared into the smudged mirror. She was standing in a small bathroom, where there was only a toilet and a toothpaste-stained counter. "Just stop thinking so much sometimes. Enjoy the night. Talk to people… Talk to *Stacie*. It'll be fun," she said as she made final adjustments to her shoulder-length hair. Her voice was low-pitched, a mix between masculine and feminine.

She put the brush down and stepped out into the entry hall of her home. It was a short space adorned with a variety of family photos. Her brother, David Dijenuk, was standing by the front door.

"Ready to go?" he asked. The seventeen-year-old David was a muscular, handsome boy with long, swept-back, light-brown hair, a chiseled jawline, and broad shoulders. He was six feet and one inch tall. Jay was just two inches shorter. Although they were siblings, David was noticeably lighter in skin tone.

Jay nodded as she slipped on her black-framed glasses.

"I've never seen you wear so much pink," he said, smiling as he noticed the pink sweatshirt tucked into her jeans. David wore a denim jacket over a yellow-and-white-striped shirt with ripped jeans and black brand-name sneakers.

"Better than wearing the same denim jacket every single

day," Jay said back.

David shrugged. "Fair enough. Come on, though. We don't wanna be late." His voice was bouncy, energetic, and tenor-like, putting it at a pitch similar to Jay's. "You told Mom and Dad about it, right?"

Their parents, Carl and Rebecca Elm, had adopted the siblings fourteen years ago. Their biological parents, Renold and Sarah Dijenuk, had been murdered by a supposed psychopath. Renold and Sarah were the last of their blood relatives, and Carl and Rebecca were the only friends close enough to adopt them.

"Yeah. *Andiamo*," Jay replied. It was an Italian word Jay's best friend had taught her a couple years ago. She wouldn't stop saying it, and so neither did Jay.

David and Jay stepped outside, the mild sunlight touching their faces. The house behind them was a two-story white building with a double-wide garage, cramped between two other similarly-styled houses.

"Huh, it's somewhat cool today. Perfect for the party," David said as they headed down their empty driveway, past their overgrown front yard, and onto the sidewalk.

"I'd prefer it cooler," Jay added, watching a blue butterfly flutter past her.

The late spring air of Oregon carried the chirps of birds and the hums of cars as they made their trek through the Lake Oswego suburbs. The area was composed of large houses and well-kept lawns. Almost all of them had two or three stories. It was quiet, like it normally was in their part of the neighborhood, aside from the occasional dog bark or passing vehicle.

The siblings chatted and laughed as they walked to their destination. After a few minutes, they approached a small river that cut through the suburbs. While it wasn't wide, it ran downhill to a larger river nearby. Another blue butterfly hovered past them. Jay wondered if it was the same one.

"More than halfway there," David said once they crossed the metal bridge. "You know, sis, I've been meaning to ask. I know she's your best friend and all, but… are you sure you wanna go? There's gonna be a lot of people like the last one, and we all know how *that* went."

Jay exhaled. "It wasn't as bad as you think."

"You ran away, and we spent, like, half an hour trying to find you."

"Yeah, I *know*. I was there."

"Just… call me or Stacie or something if you feel weird."

"Can you stop talking about it?"

"Yeah… Sorry." David looked out into the sky. "No matter what happens in life, Jay, I swear to you that the two of us won't split apart. We won't become strangers or hate each other like other siblings do. We'll hang in there. Alright?"

Jay raised an eyebrow. "Where's that coming from?"

"I was just remembering something Josh told me."

"Wait, who's Josh? Is he… the football friend?"

"Nah. He's from my weights class."

"Right," said Jay, pretending to know.

"Well, just promise me that we'll stick through it, both the

4

good and the bad. Yeah?"

Jay smiled. "Yeah. I promise."

"Good. Or I'll find you, even when you're a millionaire and too busy for your brother," he said, giving her a light shove.

"Shut up," she said, smirking and shoving him back. Her attention turned to a nearby woman on her front porch. She was reading from a large book.

It was then that a tingling sensation spread from Jay's fingertips. Her eyelids became heavy, as though her body wanted her to sleep. She let her eyes close, and her entire self became numb. Neither David's footsteps nor the hums of cars or chirps of birds were audible. She couldn't even sense her own body. Jay tried to open her eyes but couldn't. There was only black.

A wooden chest appeared. It hovered in the emptiness. Its lid opened to reveal a book, and on its cover was a golden letter D surrounded by seven dots, each of a different color. Both the book and chest faded away, leaving the golden letter floating there in the void of her mind. Slithering green snakes wrapped around the letter and squeezed until it exploded into a black mist. Something hit the back of her head, and all her senses returned at once. David was hovering over her.

"Jay!" he said, shaking her shoulders.

"I'm alright," she blurted as her brother helped her up.

"Are you sure? Was it another hallucination? If it is—"

"I just fell, that's all. Come on. We don't wanna be late."

"Are you sure you're up for this? Can you walk okay?"

David asked as he held onto Jay's arm.

"I'm alright," she repeated, removing herself from David's grip. "I'm not fragile, okay?"

"Right. Sorry. I just want to make sure you're okay."

Jay nodded. "I know. It's fine."

"Well, we're almost there now."

Their destination was across the street. It was a blue, two-story house with a large lawn, all nested within tall trees. The flat, green lawn was devoid of anything else but neatly trimmed grass. The concrete driveway and the surrounding curbs were all occupied with parked cars. The siblings crossed the street and took a curving brick path to the front door. David rang the doorbell. As they waited, Jay's heartbeat quickened, and her body shook.

David looked to his sister. "You'll be alright," he assured her. "And if things go sour, just talk to me. I'll be looking out for ya."

"Promise?"

"Promise."

The door swung open, revealing a pretty girl of David and Jay's age: Stacie. She wore a sleeveless yellow top with pale-blue jeans and black, casual brand-name shoes. She was about the same height as Jay. Upon seeing them, she showed her glowing smile and immaculate teeth.

Jay couldn't help but notice every little detail in her outfit, like the blue hair tie on her wrist, how the white parts of her shoes were completely unblemished, and how her subtle makeup accentuated her natural beauty. Jay's heart skipped a beat.

"Hi, Jay!" Stacie said, hugging her.

In the brief moment that Jay felt her friend's arms around her, her body began to settle down, the comforting warmth lifting all worries and doubts from her mind.

"So glad you came. Oh, and David! Glad you came, too."

Jay opened her mouth to say something, but no sounds came out.

"Hey, Stacie. How are you?" David said as the girl led them through the house.

"A little stressed, but pumped. It's my birthday, after all. Seventeen!" Her voice was so cheery that it never failed to raise the spirits of others.

"Oh yeah, uh, happy birthday," said Jay, snapping out of her silence.

"Thanks!"

They made their way to the conjoined kitchen and sitting room. It was a cozy, well-decorated space with an unlit fireplace, a set of three sofas, and relaxing, brown colors. Numerous family photos sat atop the mantle, and one of them even featured a fourteen-year-old Jay sitting with Stacie at a football game. There was a sliding glass door leading to the spacious backyard. Both areas were populated with dozens of teenagers. Jay recognized the Janet Jackson song playing in the background. It was loud enough to enjoy, but quiet enough for conversations that didn't require raising one's voice. Platters of snacks filled with fruits, chips, and candy were spread out on the many tables.

Some were emptier than others.

David looked over at her, lips pressed together and eyebrows lowered in concern. She had been standing still at the end of the hall for a few seconds now. Jay gave him a confident smile and walked into the sitting room with him, standing between David and Stacie.

"Yo," greeted a low voice.

"Hey, Josh."

"How's it goin'?" asked the boy named Josh. He was even more muscular than David. His grey tank top added to the effect. His hair had short sides and blond curls on the top.

Other teenagers occupied the sofas. Most of them were familiar to Jay, but not by name.

"Alright," David replied. "You?"

"A bit stressed."

"Just a bit?"

"Yeah, man, those finals were killer. I'm *not* looking forward to the grade report," Josh said, leaning back in the sofa.

"I don't think anyone is. I wish they'd just send them already and get it over with," said a girl. She was a skinny brunette who also wore a yellow flannel. "It's been a tough year."

"Eh, not for Jay. If anyone did well on finals, it's her. And she doesn't even have to try," David said.

The others nodded and mumbled in agreement. Jay's face glowed. *Please stop talking about it,* she thought to herself.

"Oh, *that's* who you are. You get a perfect score every time, huh?" another boy asked, his head tilted.

"I-I mean, I do, b-but I—" Jay stammered as she clutched the fabric of her jeans. *I can't look like some kind of nerd here,* she thought.

"Knew it," said the flannel-wearing girl.

Stacie put an arm on Jay's shoulder. "Well, what do you expect from the smartest girl in school?" she said.

"No, no, no! I am *not* the smartest—"

"Pft, of course you are. Admit it," Stacie continued.

Jay shrugged. "I mean, I guess I'm on the smart side of things…"

Stacie raised an eyebrow. "You guess? Since when does Jay Dijenuk guess?"

Jay's face reddened even further.

Um… What do I say? I need to look like I belong here, Jay thought. As she retreated into her brain, another party guest arrived and the conversation shifted. She stared at the floor as the newcomer and the others discussed a different social event. *And now it changed. Ugh, I missed my chance and now I look like a weirdo for just standing here and not saying anything. Come on, think…*

Jay looked back up and found that Stacie was no longer next to her. She glanced to her right. David was gone, too. Her heart accelerated as she searched frantically around for them. She stopped after a few seconds. *No, I have to look like I belong here. Confidence.* She took a shuddering breath. *Why did they disappear? Was I too awkward for her? Too uninteresting? Probably… Maybe they're outside.*

Jay left the group, exited through the sliding door, and scanned the backyard. There were even more kids outside than inside. The yard was large, allowing tables, chairs, a pool, a fire pit, and a trampoline to fit with ease. She spotted the two sitting at a small table. Its three seats were all occupied, and one of those occupants was a girl named Nancy who was a close friend of Stacie's.

She was a shorter girl who wore a leather blazer over a white graphic tee and denim jeans. Her blonde hair was styled into high pigtails and bangs. The only makeup she wore was blush and pink eyeshadow. Stacie had just laughed at a joke someone told. It was much easier to hear, for the music was quieter than it was inside. Jay's throat tightened for a second, and her stomach dropped.

"Oh, there you are, Jay," Stacie said as Jay approached them.

"Hi, Jay," Nancy greeted.

"Hey," Jay responded.

"Oh, um, pull up a chair or something. We were just talking about summer plans," David said to her. "Specifically Stacie's."

"She's going to Spain and Italy over, like, the entire summer," Nancy filled in. "Pretty crazy."

Jay's heart sank. "The... whole summer?"

"No, not the *entire* summer. Just the end of June through the end of July. We're seeing other places in Europe, too," Stacie corrected.

"That's pretty cool, Stacie." Jay paused. "I didn't know," she added as she took an empty chair from another table. There wasn't any space to put it, so she had to sit awkwardly behind David and Stacie. *I won't see her for an entire month?*

"I didn't really wanna tell that many people about it. But yeah, I'm excited!"

Jay opened her mouth to say something. She stuttered for a few seconds before forming a sentence. "A-and, um, uh, what, um, w-what are you doing after you come back from Europe?"

Stacie's eyes lit up. "I'll be at like a summer science camp, learning cool nerdy stuff, like how computers are programmed and all that."

"Oh," Jay responded. Her heart sank again. *So it basically is the whole summer.*

Stacie frowned. "What's wrong?"

"Huh? Oh, nothing," Jay answered, looking at the grass. Her leg couldn't stop shaking.

"Jay." Stacie's single word was all she needed to deliver her serious, concerned tone.

"It's just, um, I, uh…" Jay hesitated, feeling her throat tighten again. She took a breath and tried again. "It's just that I wanted to hang out with you over the summer, and, um… there was this D&D campaign I kinda wanted to do, but it sounds like you'll be busy, um, but it's cool," she said quickly.

"Oh," Stacie realized. "Yeah, I'll be pretty busy." She placed a hand on her shoulder. "I'm sorry, Jay."

"It's alright," Jay said. She paused. "I'm alright."

"But hey, maybe we can go to Europe next summer after we graduate! Just the two of us."

11

Jay did her best to keep her outward excitement minimal. "Yeah? That'd be really cool."

Stacie smiled. "It's a plan, then. Next summer. Promise?"

Jay smiled back. "Promise."

"So, uh, what about you? What are you doing this summer, Jay?" asked Nancy.

"Me? Oh, um, well, I'm just planning on staying home. I usually don't do much during the summer, sadly. I kinda just wait until school comes back," Jay answered.

"Doing nothing is okay, too, you know," said Stacie.

"So, what do you do at home, then?" Nancy continued.

"A lot of not-very-interesting things, really. I read sometimes, though not as much as I used to. I also write occasionally, but nothing specific or finished. Not much else," Jay admitted.

"You are *really* good at writing. You know that, right?" Stacie said. David and Nancy nodded.

"I dunno. I mean, essays for English are all I can do well. There's not much else."

"What about your poems?" David asked.

"My poems?"

"Yeah, you showed me some of them, and they were really good," Stacie recalled.

"They were a mess," Jay said, grinning.

Stacie shook her head. "If you can't accept my compliments, Jay, then I'll only throw more of 'em at you."

Jay struggled to think of a response. The inside of her chest heated up. "I-I actually just wrote another poem, recently," Jay finally blurted with a low voice. "It's, called, um, 'Fo—"

"Oh, hey, Nancy. Are you still up for that sleepover tonight? I just remembered," Stacie interrupted.

"'Forever and Always…'" Jay finished, her voice even quieter. *I didn't know there was gonna be a sleepover…*

"Oh, yeah, I forgot to call you back about that. Uh, yeah, I think my parents are cool with it."

"Awesome! We just got all kinds of movies."

"Oh, finally. I swear we've seen the same ones twenty times."

I've only rarely seen movies with her, Jay thought. *No, do what your therapist told you to do, Jay. Stand up for yourself! Say something about it.* "Hey, Stacie—"

Before Jay could finish, the volume of the music drastically increased. It nearly deafened her.

"Ooh, come on!" called Stacie. She took David and Nancy with her as they disappeared into the mob gathering on the concrete dance floor.

"Huh? Wait, where are you going? Wait for me!" called Jay, but to no response. She looked for them, assuming they were in the dancing crowd, and failed to find them. It was too dense a scene. She frantically searched the rest of the party, trying to find anyone else she could be with or talk to. Realizing what had just happened to her, she sat at the farthest end of the backyard.

Jay didn't know how long she sat there as she rested on the grass against a tree, staring at her knees. Her body was shaking, her eyes were watering, and her throat was in pain from all its tightening. Her stomach ached, but she wasn't hungry. Tears fell on her pant legs, and her vision blurred.

"What did I do wrong?" she said quietly. "It had to be more than just me being kinda quiet… right?" Jay could barely make out Stacie on the dance floor. She was smiling and laughing. Jay sniffed. "You're the only reason I come to these things… I just wanna be alone with you," she said as she watched her. Jay took off her glasses, put her face in her hands, and groaned. *What am I even saying?*

As the minutes passed, her mind took her on a trip through the memories of the other parties she'd been to. In each of those memories, she had sat alone and ended up crying. But in those instances, like a similar party in the same house a year ago, she had been completely alone. There had been no one to notice her even if they had tried. This time, there was a crowd of people not too far away, and Stacie and David were among them.

It happened again, she thought. *It really did happen again. I was an idiot for thinking it wouldn't.* Her crying worsened. *I'm right over here. Why can't you see me?*

There was a burning in her chest as her body shook again, and it was getting difficult to breathe. Eventually, as her breaths became faster, a tingly sensation ran through her. It wasn't long before she lost feeling in her fingertips, feet, and face. Her vision darkened.

God, I must have looked like an idiot with all my stuttering and pausing. They'll look for me, right? They're my friends… Then why hasn't anyone even noticed me here yet? She gripped her own hair as she sobbed. *No… they hate me, don't they? They secretly hate me, and they pity me. Why else would this happen so many times? It's my fault, it's my fault, it's my fault! But… she's my friend. She does so much for me. So she can't hate me, right? Or maybe she only kinda does? Nancy seemed to know things when I didn't, and she'd do things with her that I never did. Why am I different? Ugh, why do I even care so much? I hate this! I just wanna—*

"Jay!" a voice yelled over the music.

She wiped her tears with her sleeve and lifted her head. She slipped her glasses back on. It was Stacie.

"Where have you been?"

"Just sitting here," she replied. She shrugged and did all she could to hide the shakiness in her voice. The numbness made it difficult to speak. "How long has it been?"

"Like, half an hour. Are you okay?"

Jay nodded.

"How you feeling?"

"I'm alright, alright?" Jay said. She looked right at Stacie.

Stacie frowned. "You sure?"

"Yeah," Jay said, smiling.

"You know I love you, right?"

"Yeah." Jay smiled. "That's all I needed to hear," she said softly.

"Huh?"

"I mean, um, I just wanted to sit. I'm okay, I promise." *So… she doesn't hate me, then… right?*

15

"Cool. You wanna join us? You're sitting by yourself again."

"Oh, um…" Jay sat up straighter. "Yeah. Sure!"

"Hell yeah." Stacie grabbed Jay's arm and pulled her towards the dance floor.

Jay merged with them just as the beat for the song hit. She matched the others in wildness and energy. Her body lost itself in song and dance, the former louder than she'd normally consider healthy. Her mind, however, continued to buzz. *Does she even really care?*

Once again, Jay lost track of time. The sun had set, and in its place loomed a night sky. She was exhausted, but she didn't mind. Between songs, Stacie, David, and Nancy were talking about something together. Jay stared at the group, and her fist clenched. The next song played, and the mob was reignited.

Of course. What was I thinking? Jay took a quick look around. No one was paying any attention to her. She disappeared through the crowd and stormed towards the exit.

"Huh? Jay?"

She forced herself through the crowd. David's voice was barely audible.

"Hey, are you leaving? Hey!"

Jay glanced back. David didn't go after her. Something seemed to keep him at the lively party. "Why?" she muttered, and left through the sliding door.

―<o>―

The teens collectively exclaimed in an "Aww" as the music died down.

"Sorry! Neighbors, ya know?" Stacie said. They all dissipated as they retreated into their circles of familiarity. She rubbed her eyes and yawned. Blinking, she took in her surroundings. "Hey, David!"

"Yeah?" David responded, coming over with a beverage in hand.

"Um… Where's Jay?" Stacie asked.

"I think she left."

"What?! When?"

"A few songs ago."

"Oh. She didn't even say goodbye…" Stacie sat down.

David sat next to her. "I dunno what happened. She didn't say anything to me. She… walked home, I guess."

"In the dark," Stacie added, biting her lip. "Does she have a summer assignment she wants to do early or something?"

David shook his head. "You know her. She already has them all done."

"Then… is it my fault? Is it something I did?"

"I don't think so. Don't blame yourself, Stacie. Jay is just… in her head a lot, and she isn't the best in crowds, ya know? You should feel honored that Jay even came at all," said David with a weak laugh.

"Yeah, I know, I know. But I just wish I had done something to make her feel even a little better here. I checked on her like your parents told me to do, and I even asked her if she wanted to dance with us. She actually wanted to this time, so I thought she was okay after all." They said nothing for a few seconds and listened to the sound of faint music and fainter conversation. "How did she seem when she left?"

"It can be hard to tell with Jay sometimes. I think you and I know when something's up with her, but I can never tell exactly what it is or why she's like that."

"Do you think she's mad at me?" Stacie asked.

"Why would she be mad at you?"

"I dunno. She probably isn't."

They sat in silence again. Eventually, a sound grew in the distance: ambulance sirens.

David's stomach dropped. He closed his eyes, and for a split second he could see blue-and-red lights and hear the whines of the ambulance even closer. In that same amount of time, he felt a sudden urge to cry. His muscles tensed, and his heart raced. There was a pain in his chest. He opened his eyes again, and the foreign senses vanished from his brain as fast as they had come.

"Jay!" he yelled, standing.

Stacie looked up at him. "Huh?"

"The ambulance sirens! Something happened to her, I know it!"

"What? How do you know?"

"I don't know. It's weird. You know that thing we have where we, like… sense each other, kinda? I can't really describe it. I-I just feel it, somehow. I think she was scared. Come on, we gotta find her!" With Stacie following closely, David sprinted into the night, the chill Oregon air echoing with sirens.

⤛o⤜

"Jay… Jay… *Jay*…"

Jay felt cold, crisp air penetrate her skin and bright lights attack her eyes as she began to open them.

"Jay! She's awake. You stay with her. I'll get a doctor!"

She immediately recognized the voice. *Dad.* "W-Where am I?" she asked with difficulty. There was a horrible pain in her throat. "What happened?"

The girl found herself in a hospital bed and gown. There was a funny device clipped to her finger with a wire leading to the foreign machines behind her. Three chairs took up the space to her right, one of which was occupied by her brother.

"You don't remember?" he said.

David. As soon as she saw her brother's face, a series of flashbacks came to her, and her heart sank. *It didn't work,* she thought. *Why didn't it work?*

"You're gonna be fine." David placed his hand on Jay's shoulder. She pulled her arm back. Her lower lip was trembling, and her widened eyes glistened. It gradually morphed into anger as the siblings stared at each other, confused. Jay broke contact and looked to the clock on the wall. It read: 3:34. *I can… see it?* Her hands moved to her face, grasping at the air.

"Oh, your glasses! They're right here." David handed them to her from a metal tray by the bed.

Jay slipped them on. The lenses completely clouded her

vision. Everything was blurry. She took them off. *What?*

"Is there something wrong with them?" her brother asked.

She stared at the glasses in her shaky hands. A rage bubbled within her, juxtaposed by a wave of sadness. *No... this isn't right. Nothing is right. Last night at the party, they...* Jay gasped and let go of the glasses.

The door opened, and a doctor walked in with Carl Elm behind him. Carl, the siblings' adopted father, was a tall, well-built man in his late thirties with dirty-blond hair.

"Good morning, Jay," the plump doctor greeted with an upbeat tone. "How are you feeling?"

Jay didn't answer. She stared at the doctor stoically. Her green eyes had become dead.

"Not much of a talker, huh?"

"She, uh, she's usually pretty shy. It's okay, Jay. Just answer the doctor's questions, alright?" Carl Elm said.

"Let's try again. How are you feeling, Jay?"

No response.

"Jay? Can you hear me?"

"She spoke a little bit earlier," David pointed out. "I dunno what's wrong now."

The doctor turned a paper on his clipboard over to its blank side. He carefully wrote on it, then showed the writing to Jay. It read "Nod if you can hear us" in big letters.

Jay made no motion.

"Does she normally do this?"

Carl shook his head. "Never before. Did she suddenly go

deaf or something?"

Jay's fists clenched.

"No, Mr. Elm. That is why I showed Jay something she could read."

"R-right, of course."

The doctor pulled up a chair right next to Jay's bed. He sat on it backwards. "Well, then, Jay, I'm going to continue speaking to you anyway. I am certain you can hear me but are just choosing not to respond." He cleared his throat. "Someone called 911 and said that a teenage girl was about to, quote, 'do something stupid in the river.' Paramedics found your body about eight miles away from the bridge by that river, unconscious and completely dry. We found no sign of drowning or any other injury. Even your glasses were still on your face, intact. Can you explain what happened?"

Nothing.

"Have you been feeling more sad or down than normal lately? Hopeless? Uninterested in otherwise-interesting hobbies and activities? Sleepy? Angry? Any of these at all, Jay?"

Nothing.

"Does this have something to do with your history of passing out and having hallucinations?"

Nothing.

"Jay, you have to talk to us! We are just trying to help you," Mr. Elm interjected.

"Perhaps it is me whom the girl won't talk to," the doctor guessed.

Carl Elm took a few steps closer to his daughter. "Sweetie, will you talk to me?"

There was only the stable beeping of the heart monitor and a cacophony of noises from outside the room.

"Or what about me, your brother?"

Jay turned to look at David. Her expression remained blank.

"Is there anyone else Jay is close or closer to? Someone who might get her to talk?" the doctor asked.

Carl frowned. "I don't know, maybe—"

"Stacie," David answered. "Maybe Stacie can."

"And Stacie is...?"

"A close friend of hers," Carl said. "She is actually waiting in the lobby with my wife."

"She is? Wonderful. Can you bring her in, please?"

Carl nodded and exited, his pace brief.

David, Jay, and the doctor were left in silence aside from the beeping of the EKG. After a minute, the doctor broke it and asked, "Are you two high schoolers?"

"Yeah," David answered. "We're both seniors, actually."

"Really? Are you two twins?"

"Nah. She just skipped a year in middle school."

"Ah. I was gonna say, you two don't look like twins, let alone siblings," he said with a hearty laugh.

"Yeah, we get that a lot."

Just then, the door flew open, and Rebecca Elm and Stacie both raced inside. Carl Elm was a few seconds behind. Rebecca, the siblings' mother, was a skinny woman with red, curly hair.

22

She was in her pajamas.

"Jay! Are you okay?" Rebecca asked.

Jay sat up, and the doctor moved out of the way for Stacie to give her a tight embrace. "I've been so worried," she said.

"Hey, give her space, please. You're crowding her," the doctor said.

They all backed away except for Stacie, who sat with her hands on Jay's knees. "So, you don't wanna talk to them, huh?" Stacie said. "Well, what about me? Will you talk to your best friend?"

Jay let out a shuddering breath.

"Maybe the rest of us should step outside," the doctor suggested after another period of silence.

Alone with Jay, Stacie asked, "What happened? The doctor thought at first that you jumped into a river and swam far away, but you weren't wet or anything. You were just unconscious when they found you. We're all confused."

Jay continued to stare blankly at her.

"Jay… Please, talk to me." Stacie's eyes began to water. "I'm your best friend. You can tell me anything, love." She took Jay's hands, and Jay took a sharp, panicked inhale.

They continued to stare at each other in silence.

"Do you remember what happened?"

Jay hesitated before shaking her head as she adjusted the blanket that she wore around herself.

Stacie let out a breath of relief. "Good. Well, not good. Good that you are communicating. Not good that you don't remember.

Um, do you think…?" She swallowed. "Do you think it had something to do with last night?"

Jay's arm muscles twitched.

"I mean, it must have, right? Can you try to remember? No pressure, just… take your time." She gripped her hands tighter. "I'm here for you."

Jay closed her eyes, and Stacie watched as she tensed up. She opened them. Her pupils contracted. "Stacie, I… I…" She shook her head and let go of her friend's hands.

"Jay?"

The beeping of the EKG quickened as she closed her eyes again.

"Please remember," Stacie said.

"Grey void…" she murmured.

"Huh?"

"A voice… calling me. It's cold." Jay gasped, but her eyes remained closed. Her muscles twitched faster as the heart monitor sped up.

"Jay? Hey, how you feeling?" The beeping became absurdly fast. "Are you alright? Hey." Stacie glanced at the monitor. The BPM had gone past two hundred, and it was still climbing. "Doctor. Doctor! Something's wrong!"

The doctor burst in with the family in tow. "Three hundred and sixty-six beats per minute," he read, astonished.

Stacie grabbed Jay by the shoulders. "Breathe, Jay, breathe!" Jay was shaking in her upright position, and her eyes remained shut.

"It's staying so consistent…." the doctor said.

"Jay, listen to me! Breathe!" Stacie begged. "Jay? Jay, can you hear me?" She faced the doctor. "Do something!" she screamed.

The heart monitor blinked a few times before going out completely. Sparks flew everywhere. The lights flickered in rhythm with Jay's horrifyingly rapid pulse.

Other doctors entered, and they escorted everyone else out.

"Jay!"

CHAPTER II:
THE OPENING

FIVE MONTHS LATER…

DAVID NOTICED THE NOTE ON HIS BEDROOM DOOR only after he had finished changing into his jeans and grey hoodie. His hand hovered over the doorknob as he read it.

"'If you wish to learn the truth, if you wish to chase what your parents left behind, you will have to make a leap of faith. When the time comes, trust him. For now.' Parents…?"

It was written on a torn piece of notebook paper. The letters were perfectly even and spaced out. He removed the note, stared at it for a few more seconds, and stuffed it into his pocket. He then threw his red gym bag over one shoulder and his black backpack over the other and scanned the bedroom one last time.

It was a small, comfortable room, enough to fit his twin-sized bed with its red bedding, a wooden desk, a dresser, and his beanbag chair. There were a couple of Nirvana and Green Day posters on the wall. He turned to leave, and the sound of thunder froze him in place as his normal morning dread worsened.

David sighed. "Practice in the rain again…" He exited his bedroom into a hallway, where there were three other doors, all of them an identical white. He took the carpeted staircase down.

David entered the living room. It was simple little area with a single grey sofa, a CRT television, and only a few decorations. There was a dying potted plant in the corner, an abstract painting of various bright colors, and a couple of family photos. The small number of objects allowed for the room to remain tidy. On the wall opposite the stairs was a sliding glass door that led to an overgrown yard too small to fit its mucky pool. All the interior walls were painted a soft, cerulean blue.

Sitting on the arm of the sofa was Jay. She sported pixie-cut hair that often got in her face, and her pine-green eyes held an aggressive intelligence that pierced whoever made the mistake of looking directly into them. They were accompanied by lowered, sharp-angled eyebrows. It was the only part of her face that emoted, for she otherwise appeared stoic and unfeeling. Her skin carried few blemishes, although her knuckles were bruised and torn. She carried herself with what others called a 'masculine authority' that was aided by her tall posture.

The girl wore black pants, black combat boots, and a white, tucked-in button-up accented by a black leather belt. A long coat, also black, sat folded on the floor beneath her. She was writing on a sheet of paper.

"Good morning, Jay," David said. He moved to the conjoined kitchen to make himself breakfast. It was messier than the living room, with its clutter of plates and pans. White cupboards and appliances surrounded the center island. Last night's dinner of chicken and rice remained on the stove.

As the boy poured himself cereal, Jay's stare moved from

her writing to the sliding glass door. David asked, "You good?"

Jay twirled her pen in her left hand as she continued to stare at the raindrops pelting the glass. She scribbled down a sentence.

"Don't tell me," David said. "Is that the essay for English?"

Jay joined the sheet of paper with several others and slipped the collection into a brown leather bag at her feet.

"It is, isn't it? Sis, it's due next week and we got it assigned yesterday. I know you're super smart, but, like, going that fast probably means it isn't *that* good."

"Tch. Perhaps for some idiot like you," Jay said as she continued to face away. A muscle in her cheek twitched. "But for someone like me, such efficiency is only natural." Her voice was usually toneless, although, sometimes, her words carried a hint of cockiness with a subtle irritation wavering through it. She picked up her leather bag, put on her slim black coat, and made her way to the stairs just as Rebecca joined them.

"Good morning, Jay," she greeted as she yawned.

"Rebecca," Jay muttered before storming up the stairs.

The early morning passed as they went through their daily routine. Rebecca left for work in her own vehicle as David got in the car with his father. It was a spotless interior without any clutter. The sound of pounding raindrops muffled most other noises.

"What's Jay doing?" Carl groaned as he tapped the steering wheel.

"Probably reading. I'll go get her."

"I'll do it," Carl said. He stepped out of the Honda Accord and made his way back inside. Through the front door, he entered a short hall that led into the living room. There used to be nearly a dozen framed pictures hanging in the hall, including family portraits and photos of the kids with their friends. Less than three months ago, every single photo in the house that included Jay had disappeared, leaving empty frames. He assumed that it had been Jay's doing.

Carl went upstairs and approached Jay's bedroom door. "Jay?" he said, knocking. After waiting a few seconds, Carl opened the door.

It was a small room with green, mostly-empty walls. There was a twin bed in the corner with a matching set of grey pillows and blankets in disarray. Opposite the bed was a shelf, which held only a small cardboard box and a couple of textbooks. On the back wall was a window with its curtains closed, and against the wall was a wide desk made of dark walnut wood. Next to it was a simple wooden dresser. There were no posters, photos, or any other decorations. It was barren.

Jay sat at her desk. She was scribbling in a journal, her hand moving so quickly that it was almost mesmerizing. The rest of the desk was cluttered with all kinds of books, documents, notebooks, and journals.

"What're you doing?" Carl asked. "We have to go."

"No, *you* have to go. I still have another two minutes, assuming traffic is at its worst and taking into consideration my before-school appointment." She continued to write as she talked.

"I have to go to work, Jay. If you keep making us wait like this, then we'll just leave without you."

"No, you won't. You're pathetic like that, and I'm going to take advantage of it."

Carl exhaled as he sat on Jay's bed. "Sweetie, what's wrong?" he asked gently, placing his hand on her shoulder.

Jay swatted his hand away. "Quit asking that."

"Why?"

"It's none of your business, Carl." Her voice began to rise.

Her father said nothing for a few seconds as he listened to the furious scratching of Jay's pen. "Is this one of those teenage phases?"

"A what?"

"A phase. Don't be mad, Jay; it's just an observation. You cut your hair—"

"That was months ago."

"You look like a boy—"

"What does that even mean?"

"And you mistreat all of us. Your poor brother, especially."

Jay paused. "Amazing observation skills. Truly."

He sighed. "Jay, he's your *brother*."

"Is that supposed to mean something?"

Carl paused. "He's your brother," he said, as if he were a broken record, or repeating some kind of spell that he couldn't permit himself to doubt. He sighed again. "I'm afraid I don't understand, Jay."

"I don't care."

Carl stood, running his hand through his messy hair. "If you weren't doing so well in school, you'd be in so much trouble, young lady."

"Perhaps, although not of your doing."

He shook his head. "I'll be waiting for you in the car."

David watched the trees and buildings speed past, quietly waiting in his seat for his destination. The rain drowned out the early-morning hustle of the Portland Metro area. "Hey, Dad?"

"Yes, son?"

"Do you know what this note's about? I found it on my door." He pulled out the crumpled piece of paper from his jean pocket.

"What? What does it say?"

"Something about finding the truth and chasing what our parents left behind. I dunno."

"Er…" Carl tightened his grip on his wheel.

"Does this mean, like, our biological parents?"

"I, um, I don't know," he said with a nervous laugh. "Your mother might, ah, know more, um…"

The rain had stopped, leaving an eerie silence cut only by the scratching of Jay's pen. She was sitting in the back.

"Uh, what are you writing about there, Jay?" Carl asked.

"It is none of your business."

"Ooh-kay, then."

"Oh, I know," David said. "It's that economics class essay or whatever, right?"

Jay stopped writing and raised an eyebrow. "It is. How do you know that?"

"I took a peek at it a few days ago. I dunno, I was curious."

"An essay on a class? So, like, a review?" Carl guessed.

"It's a call to reform it," Jay said. "I will be submitting it to our principal first and, more importantly, to the school district board."

"Oh. Well, that's great, honey. Hopefully they listen to their students."

Jay continued writing. "They'll listen to *me*, anyway."

They reached a stoplight. "You know what'd help, Jay?" Carl asked.

"I don't need your useless opinion."

"If you took a petition from your peers. Include their opinion in your essay, too."

"That's absolutely idiotic," Jay said. "Although that's to be expected, coming from you."

"Why is that?"

"My plan calls for an economics class that actually teaches you something and provokes real thought without bias, not just an easy A. But most students disagree."

David yawned as he leaned back in his seat. "Sounds like you need a new plan."

"Just because they disagree?" Jay responded, taken aback.

"Well, yeah."

"That's not how it should work. As the most intelligent, my input needs to be considered the most," she said matter-of-factly. Her voice dropped to an intense tone. "But those peons fail to understand even the most basic of concepts." She squeezed her fist as she spoke.

"Huh… Well, are you sure about that?" Carl questioned. "You always used to get the opinion of that one girl. Uh, what was her name? Stacie, right?"

David froze in his seat. "Um, Dad…"

"Huh?" Carl looked into the rearview mirror and met Jay's penetrating eye, the other concealed by her hair. A quiet rage burned within her pupil. The glance alone was enough to shut him up.

A large, two-story building loomed closer as they entered their high school campus. It was a roughly rectangular structure, composed of brick walls and large windows. A roof arched over the entrance, with stone steps leading up to it. They looped around the main parking lot and pulled up to the curb. The siblings exited the vehicle.

"Prison…" David sighed as he shut the door behind him.

"Opportunity," Jay corrected.

David snickered. "How are we still friends?"

"We're not."

One of the car windows slid down. "Your mother will probably pick you two up today," Carl said.

"Does she know I have practice today?" David replied.

Carl shook his head. "She always forgets. Have a good day!"

"See you later, Dad," David said as he drove away.

Jay looked up. The overcast had faded away, making the students below squint from the sudden change in brightness. With their bags, the siblings went up the stone steps and towards the main entrance. Around a dozen other students were milling about.

David opened the glass door, and they entered. A pleasant warmth washed over them, as did the fluorescent lights. Other students moved to and fro or hung out in place as they waited for the bell.

"See you soon, Jay."

Jay had already gone. She had turned left and was heading straight for the principal's office. He watched for a few moments as she moved with an abnormally fast pace, weaving through the slower crowd and even forcing a few out of her way. The length of her black coat billowed behind her like a cape.

She'll come back to us one day. I know it. Sighing, David took a flight of stairs.

≺o≻

"Rodriguez."

"Ah, hello, Jay. Come in, come in," the smiling principal said. She was a slim woman in her early thirties who often wore neutral business attire. Her heels, however, changed every day from one bright color to another. Today, they were magenta. She also had curly, shoulder-length brown hair.

Jay stepped into the office and sat down. In terms of furniture, it was a simple room. There was a desk with three cabinets behind it and a couple chairs in front of it, as well as a few shelves. The wall space was covered with the same motivational posters Jay had seen her entire life in public schooling. They spoke of perseverance, the importance of college, bad math puns, and so on. There was a hefty computer, monitor, and keyboard on the desk, matching in their off-white color.

"I am here to present to you my essay on the reform of the district and state's economics classes." Jay pulled ten typed sheets from her bag and handed them over.

Mrs. Rodriguez raised her eyebrows as she skimmed the pages. "While this is impressive and thorough, yes, you must know that I am just a high-school principal. Why give something like this to me?"

Jay scoffed. "I swear, you people have the memory capacity of a goldfish. I told you before that I plan to have this change implemented, but, for a reason that can only be explained as pure idiocy, I need a voice other than mine. At least, for now. It would be greatly beneficial to have someone higher up in the district represent my ideas and back me up. Those idiots who decide these putrid standards would rather trust someone based on position rather than intellect."

Mrs. Rodriguez set down the essay. "Ah, right. You need a representative, of sorts."

"For now," Jay reiterated.

The principal took a breath. "Look, Jay, I recognize that you're one of the brightest students in the school—"

"*The* brightest," Jay corrected.

"But I'm afraid that I can't help you."

She rose. "Why?"

"Calm down, please. When you first told me about your idea, I told some other staff members. We all agree that this change in difficulty and content would greatly upset the students."

"Yes, *most* students, *most* of whom are quite vacuous on matters like these. They're a bunch of incompetent fools moving from one day to the next."

"Jay, other students' opinions matter, too."

Jay slammed the desk, leaning in. The principal flinched. "But mine matters more. This will benefit our education. I know that they hate not having information spoon-fed to them and that they dislike anything resembling a proper education, but we must move away from such a culture. This is a step toward something great. Read the essay," she demanded.

"Jay, I would appreciate it if you didn't slam things or speak to me like that."

Jay leaned back in her chair and crossed her arms.

"No disrespect is intended," Rodriguez continued, "but I have gotten to know who you are in my few months here. You don't have to lie," Rodriguez continued. The girl clenched her teeth. "What are your real motives, Miss Dijenuk?"

Jay's index finger continuously tapped her opposite arm as they remained crossed. "I have no real care for the education that others receive. I truly only care for getting my name out there. A good way of doing so is by making change, whatever that change is," she answered. "Additionally, there are ideas put forth in these current economics classes that are improperly explained and are possibly subject to bias. Specifically, the bias of looter culture. I explain this in better detail in the essay."

Mrs. Rodriguez leaned back in her chair. "There's another problem, Jay." She bit her lip. "Uh... If I were to 'represent' your essay, as you put it, there could be some issues due to certain..." The principal's gaze lingered on Jay's bruised knuckles for a second. "Behaviors of yours."

Jay glared at her. "Behaviors?"

Mrs. Rodriguez leaned forward. "You know what I'm talking about, Miss Dijenuk. Yes, I know about it all."

Jay glanced at the bruises on her knuckles.

"Many students have come to the nurse's office with injuries," Mrs. Rodriguez continued, "reporting that another female student with short hair and green eyes—"

"And so what?" Jay interrupted. "What're you going to do about it? Clearly nothing, since you haven't acted on it after all this time." Her expression was stoic, like always, except for the devilish twinkle in her pupils. "You and the rest of the administration wouldn't dare even to *discuss* disciplinary action against me. You couldn't lose a student as bright and talented as me. This pitiful facility would have nothing to offer then. And I will continue to abuse that fact. Are we clear?"

Rodriguez shook her head, her teeth clenched. "I don't think you've thought this all the way through." Her voice softened. "You're facing a greater risk doing what you're doing. Women who look like you and me—"

"Do *not* speak to me of such meaningless traits. The color of my skin doesn't even have an *iota* of influence on me and my actions. I don't give a single damn about it, and neither should you. I'm not pathetic and piteous. I take pride in my own abilities and achievements rather than what I look like. And my abilities will keep me in the clear from my less-than-desired actions. Are we clear?"

The principal pursed her lips. "We are clear."

"If it helps your 'conscience,' consider the essay for its content, and not the writer. That's why it's imperative that you read it, even if you currently intend to decline."

"…I'll think about it."

Jay brushed her hair out of her eyes. "Don't think about it. Just do it."

"Don't worry. I'll read it." Mrs. Rodriguez glanced at the wall clock. "And while I do that, you'd better head to class, Miss Dijenuk. Hurry along now."

The bell rang just as David entered the classroom for first-period Mythology. It was a dusty old space filled with a few too many desks and not enough bookshelves. Its musty odor and overflowing textbooks made it resemble a library. Most of the seats were already occupied.

Some students were resting on the desks, trying desperately to stay awake, while some were talking amongst themselves. A few others were doing schoolwork.

David took his seat in front of Jay, who was too busy scribbling in a small notebook to pay him any attention. Her black coat had been hung over her chair.

"Hey, Jay."

"What?" she replied, her eyes still focused on her page.

"I tried talking to Margaret today."

"Do I care?"

"You know I'm gonna talk to you about this stuff, anyway."

"So I will continue not to care."

"Well, anyway, the first bell rang and I couldn't really say much. I should've gone sooner but, ugh, I was… scared, to be honest."

"Okay."

"Maybe she walked away so fast because she was uncomfortable. Would it be uncomfortable for you if a guy who you suspect might like you suddenly talks to you even if you've never really talked before?"

Jay looked up. "Hm… Well, yes, but—"

"Ugh, of course. I shouldn't have done that. I'm an idiot!"

"No, David, for me, it's… never mind." Jay went back to her notebook.

"I'm just trying to move on, ya know? Maybe I'm trying too hard."

Jay clenched her left fist. "Move on…" she echoed quietly.

Right then, their Mythology teacher stepped through the door. He was an older man with long grey hair and surprisingly clear skin. His rounded glasses were too small for his face and always crooked. Although he was tall, his height was minimized due to his constant slouching. His teeth were horribly yellowed, and he smelled like an old library. He wore tattered jeans, dirty boots, a black shirt, and a grey cardigan. It was an outfit not unusual for Mr. K. He also wore the same amulet he always did. It was a circular piece of blue glass just a quarter of inch thick, adorned by thin metal vines wrapped intricately around it.

He carried a book about two inches thick with a worn leather cover. It was like nothing the students had ever seen before in person. When Jay's eyes moved to the object, a shiver went down her spine.

"Hey, Mr. K, you a'ight?" a student asked.

Mr. K walked forward with a precise, stiff rhythm. One leg went straight out, then it bent and moved onto the floor, and then the other leg did the same thing. It repeated. His head remained still, and his eyes stared at nothing while his mouth hung open. Even his slouch was completely gone. He would only inhale and exhale on those rigid steps, and his breath was touched with an orange hue.

The teacher made his way to the large, dark brown desk in front of the classroom. Upon that desk, Mr. K set the leather-bound tome. Another bell rang, initiating the start of class.

"Greetings, young scholars," Mr. K said. His voice was egregiously slow and monotone. "On this day, I shall present and teach to you the contents of this tome I have here…" He took a long pause. "Before… me. It is… called… *The Legends*."

His arms stiff, Mr. K picked up the large book and held it in front of the class. The leather cover bore strange symbols on the top and bottom. They were composed of straight lines and basic shapes. Most curiously of all, however, was a gold letter D in the center, surrounded by seven dots of different colors. Jay's arms and legs tensed as soon as she saw it. Her breath stopped for a moment, and her brain pounded against her skull. Something whispered an incomprehensible language in her head, but there were two words she could understand:

"*Seek me…*" It was high-pitched and screechy.

"Mr. K?" said a student.

"Silence, young woman." The teacher's hands gingerly met the leather, his hand gripping the cover one finger at a time. Mr. K gasped out of nowhere. "No, no!" His voice was trembling. The crawling, stagnant voice immediately returned, and he said, "Yes. It begins." Mr. K forcefully jerked the book open as though it were stuck.

Time seemed to pause as everyone's eyes fixated on the tome. David and Jay felt their insides burn for a moment before the book, *The Legends*, flashed a bright yellow light, forcing the students to cover their eyes. David and Jay, on the other hand, had their sights glued on the book. They watched the light grow brighter for a few seconds until it pulsed once, then vanished. *The Legends* shut itself, the action shaking the air around them. A shockwave of energy rippled through the classroom, vibrating the students' ribcages.

"Get down!" Mr. K yelled.

The windows shattered as the shockwave returned. It tore apart the spines of the few students who didn't cower in time. They shrieked in pain before collapsing to the floor. The students rose slowly, and before they could take in what had just happened, the ground began to shake.

"Earthquake, earthquake," said a feminine voice through the intercom. "Take cov—"

The intercom shut off, as did the fluorescent lights above them. The entire school went dark, save for the mild sunlight pouring in through the ruined windows.

After a moment of silence, one of the students yelled, "Everyone, run for your lives!"

"David, Jay. Stay here!" Mr. K barked as the other students bolted out the door in a panic, the faster ones shoving past the slower ones.

"What? Why?" David asked as Jay grabbed her journal and coat.

Mr. K buried his head in his desk cabinets until he found what he was looking for: a brown cloth bag, tied by a thick piece of white string. He opened the bag and from it pulled four separate, foot-long rods of a shiny grey metal, each of them topped with a small cylinder of stone. They were half the size of the average arm in terms of thickness. Jay ran for the door.

Mr. K clutched his amulet and shouted, "*Erca psota!*" As Jay reached the doorframe, she collided with something invisible.

"Ow! What the—?"

"I know how to get out of this, so you *need* to stay with me," the teacher said. "Here, two for you, David, and two for you, Jay. Alright, follow me and *stay close!*" Mr. K ran out of the classroom, and the siblings followed him down the stairs as they slipped the metal objects into their pockets as best they could.

"Mr. K, what's going on?"

David's question was drowned out by the screaming students and falling debris, for the earth's shaking had grown violent. Lights and plaster crashed down on top of students and staff as they scrambled for the nearest exit. A student bolted through them, knocking Jay over. She dropped her journal and coat just as a large piece of the ceiling landed next to her. David helped her up.

"Leave it!" he said.

In the darkness, Mr. K led the siblings to the nearest green 'EXIT' sign. They struggled to stay on their feet and constantly stumbled, but they made it to the emergency exit.

They burst through the door, and the cool but overwhelming November air washed over them. They had reached one of the school's parking lots. It was about halfway filled, and there were other staff members racing towards their vehicles. The clouds above them swirled and darkened in color as they moved closer to ground level, and thunder boomed through the storm of wind and debris. David's foot touched the dark cement of the parking lot, but he immediately retracted it. The earth split, and a large crack ran through the lot.

"We need to get to my car! It's the dirty brown one across the lot," Mr. K yelled over the roaring of the wind.

Mr. K was halfway across the parking lot before he realized that David and Jay weren't following. They were still standing on the sidewalk in front of the door. More cracks in the ground emerged, and they widened. Different chunks of the earth shifted up and down. The emerging slopes were so steep that they sent the vehicles sliding into each other. The sounds of the crashing metal, splitting earth, and roaring winds created a near-deafening cacophony.

"Come on!" Mr. K yelled, barely audible over the noise.

Before David or Jay could move, two teachers and a student burst from the door behind them, pushing them out of the way. The ground finally gave, and it split violently into two slanted halves, sending whatever was in the parking lot crashing into the center. Everyone on the lot fell and tumbled into the gathering point that was center. The cars slid to join them.

"Mr. K!" David screamed as he fell. While in midair, Mr. K grabbed his amulet with his left hand, then threw his other arm outwards. A rope made of a white, shining energy protruded from his palm, and it latched onto the curb. As though using a grappling hook, Mr. K zoomed back up and thumped onto the sidewalk. David helped him stand.

"Woah, what was that? Are you okay?" David asked, trying not to think too hard about what their teacher had just done.

Mr. K nodded. "Just a tad exhausted." He stared into the pit. "Well, there goes my car."

44

"And those people…" David murmured.

"Those will not be the only deaths on this cursed day, I am sure." Mr. K paused. The air was still. "It stopped."

"Good, because I have questions," Jay said. "What is all this? What's going on?"

"That can be answered later. We need to go on foot now, so we must hurry. Follow me!" Mr. K ran off to the right, with David and Jay close behind him.

"Where are we going?" Jay asked.

"This is not the time or place to explain."

The siblings' response was muted by the distractions of their surroundings. The roads, like the parking lot earlier, were torn apart. Vehicles were strewn about in different positions and sides, most not even on their wheels. Fallen trees and lampposts blocked the path, although the road was impossible to drive on anyway. The clumps of death, metal, and machinery were already creating obstacles.

Fires danced about. The air was thick and acrid with the smell of oil, and the smoke only made it worse. There was a horrifying blend of crying, screaming, and sirens wailing. They watched a man on the other side of the street disentangle himself from the begging hand of a woman trapped under a beam. He stumbled off, deaf to her weakening pleas. Another man saw her and called for help before trying to lift the beam, but, within a few seconds, her voice died off and her eyes glazed over. The man sat there in her pool of blood and started to cry. Her corpse joined the many others, all of them torn or mangled.

David felt his stomach go heavy and his throat tighten. "This is horrible…." He gasped. Realization struck. "Mr. K, we need to head home!"

"You cannot," he replied flatly.

"I need to see if our parents are okay!" He slowed to a stop. "You can't make us go with you."

"David, you do not understand the scale of this situation."

"I don't understand. What do you mean? This earthquake destroying the city is easy to understand!" David yelled.

"This is bigger than you think. Whoever will meet you in Elektia will give you the answers you need, but right now, we need to go."

"Elektia?" Jay said.

"Bigger? What could be bigger than this?" David asked.

Jay stared off. "I saw—no, I *felt* what happened in the classroom. There's more to this, and I need answers. Family can wait, so I'll go wherever we need to go."

David scowled at her. "Family can *always* wait for this version of you, Jay."

"If you follow me, you'll also help save your family and everyone else. I can promise you that," Mr. K said.

"What? No, I need to find my parents *now*!"

The sound of a distant explosion boomed.

David took a shaky breath. "What the—?"

There was a second detonation, followed by another from the opposite direction. They increased in frequency, until all they could hear were the explosions. They vibrated the very air

46

around them. The group slowly turned, searching for any sign of its source.

Mr. K grimaced. "David, we need to—huh?"

A silver orb of light floated in midair between all three of them. It was as small as penny. In the same second that it appeared, the orb exploded with a flash of light. Each of them rocketed backward in different directions, skidding across the mangled asphalt and smashing right through already-dilapidated walls.

Jay wheezed for air and then groaned as she rose to her feet. Pieces of timber and stone fell off her. Her chest ached in pain.

Another explosion sounded nearby, and a man in business attire launched into the wall of the ruined convenience store next to her. Blood pooled around him. His face was torn off, and an arm and a chunk of his torso were missing. His fleshy interior and a few of his bones were visible.

Jay tilted her head as she stared at the corpse. "How did I…?"

"Jay!" Mr. K ran towards the girl from the other side of the block. He saw the body, and his eyes widened. "That's… Oh my goodness." He gulped and forced himself to look away. "Do you see your brother anywhere?"

Jay scoffed. "Do we even need him?"

"Jay! Mr. K!" yelled a distant voice.

"That's him. Come on!" Mr. K ran across the street and through an alleyway. Jay, after hesitating, followed.

They crossed the same street they'd first come from and

passed more broken, shredded bodies. Most of them were missing limbs. A block away, David was standing in the middle of the road, his head towards the sky.

"Watch over me," he said, still staring at the clouds.

"Hey! David!" Mr. K called.

"Huh?" David let out a breath. "Oh my God, you guys are safe! Did you hear those voices, too?"

Mr. K raised an eyebrow. "Voices? That doesn't matter right now. Look, all of this will only get worse, so you two need to follow me *now*."

David looked down for a second, then faced Mr. K and nodded. "Alright, as long it doesn't take too long."

"Good. Let's go."

As Mr. K ran off with Jay behind him, David took another look at the sky. "If my gut feeling is right, this is for you, Other Mom and Other Dad."

"David, come on!" the teacher yelled.

The boy caught up with them. As the three of them continued running, the ground rumbled again. Seconds later, the ground in front of them ripped open, and something emerged from the crack. A moving pile of earth forced itself through. It was a ten-foot-tall, humanoid amalgamation of dirt and concrete with limbs the size of tree trunks. It was missing a head.

As it crawled up from the earth, the three of them backed away. The siblings couldn't help but stare at it with their mouths agape. The creature swung one of its gigantic limbs.

"Go! Run into there!" Mr. K yelled.

The creature missed them and smashed the trunk of a car, completely denting it, as the siblings and Mr. K sprinted into a nearby alley. It was a tight space, and the creature was unable to fit inside of it.

"What was *that*?!" David asked as they continued to run.

"Not… now," Mr. K replied, catching his breath.

They reached another street, ripped apart and covered with corpses like all the others. An orange-red light flashed a few meters in front of them, halting them. The light morphed into flames, and the flames took the shape of a slender, seven-foot figure. Its eyes, the only facial features, were two black, oval stones.

"The rods! Press and throw!" Mr. K said as he stomped the ground with his right foot, which somehow made the fire creature stumble back.

David took out one of the metal rods from his pocket. He studied it for a moment and looked back up at the approaching creature. He pressed the stone button down and chucked it underhand like a grenade. It rolled towards the living flames and emitted a quick flash of light. The fire creature was gone as though it had never been there.

"Are we close?" asked David, panting.

"Yep, here we are." Across their street was a line of skinny apartments. It was a three-story building made of bricks. Half of the complex was in ruins.

"Oh, God. Behind us!" David yelled. They turned and met monsters similar to the one that had come out of the ground earlier. They varied slightly in appearance, with one even having pieces of rebar sticking out of it. They moved towards them at a snail's pace, shaking the ground with each step.

"Stay behind me," Mr. K said. With his amulet in one hand, he flicked the other, and in it appeared a small, glowing orb of white light. He squeezed it, popping it like a bubble, and splashed the resulting liquid onto the closest monster. The liquid melted a chunk of it like a corrosive acid, and it collapsed into several large pieces. The other two monsters tripped over the remains, barely missing Mr. K as they fell.

"Come on!" Mr. K said, dashing up the steps to one of the white apartment doors.

"Your apartment?" David questioned.

"Yes." The teacher fumbled with his keys. His hands were shaking. "Here." He unlocked it and stumbled inside.

It was a frigid space that smelled like old socks and stale food. The carpet was stained, and pizza boxes were strewn everywhere. There was only a table and a sofa chair, and the connected kitchen was completely barren aside from the fridge and additional pizza boxes.

David shut and locked the door as the two earth monsters got back on their feet. "Mr. K!" The teacher had dropped to the floor.

"There is a brown box under my bed. Go get it!" Mr. K said, pointing in the general location.

David went after it, his head too busy with the thoughts of what was happening to pay attention to the mess of dirty clothes or the fact that the bed was the only piece of furniture in the bedroom. He retrieved the small brown box and darted back.

"Here." David handed Mr. K the box.

Mr. K opened its lid and revealed a shiny, black, baseball-sized rock. He set it down in the middle of the living room just as the entire apartment shook.

David glanced at the window. "Those things are here!"

"We're dead," Jay said, her voice flat.

"No, you are not… Not yet." Mr. K stretched out his arm, the palm of his hand facing the rock. *"To This Place: Fort Dijenuk, Light Elektia!"* A short bolt of white energy fired from his hand and struck the rock, which exploded into a swirling, grey light. It was a translucent vortex that hovered a few inches in the air and was half the size of a car, but with the thinness of paper. It pulsated, giving off various amounts of light.

With their jaws dropped, the Dijenuks took a few steps back, but then stepped right forward again as something slammed against the wall. The apartment shook again, and bits of plaster fell from the ceiling.

"Pray to the Elementians that you land close enough. There is too much interference for it to be accurate."

David's face had gone pale, and his mouth was still open. Jay, however, went poker-faced. Despite the continuous slamming against the wall, the two weren't moving an inch.

"Go through it. Now! You will be safe," the teacher said. A large section of the front wall fell, sending in a rush of cold air. A giant hand reached inside.

Jay's neutral expression broke as she made a small gasp and

hopped away. She pressed the stone button on her rod and threw it at the grabbing hand. After a flash of light, the arm froze in place, then fell off the torso of its owner.

"Go!" Mr. K repeated. "The portal's going to disappear at any second!"

The siblings stared at the distorted images created by the translucency of the shrinking, spinning vortex. David edged closer.

A second and third arm reached through the missing wall. The hands were almost at their feet. Without any further hesitation, David leaped into the vortex and disappeared through it. Jay stuck a hand inside. It was warm. Another voice, the same one from earlier, whispered in her head.

"*Seek me...*" A series of images flashed in her mind's eye sequentially, each only lasting for a split second: *The Legends*, an arch made of stone, and a scroll of parchment.

"Good luck, Jay. Go, save our worlds!"

"What?"

Mr. K leaped forward and shoved the girl through.

Jay's body tightened as the warm light enveloped her. She immediately closed her eyes as she spun. In the void of darkness that was the back of her eyelids, one more image appeared: a pair of royal-blue eyes.

CHAPTER III:
A WORLD OF DECEIT

DAVID WAS SICK TO HIS STOMACH. He had been spinning for minutes that felt like hours with his eyes shut tight, feeling only the weight of his clothes and the thumping of his heart. *What just happened?* he thought. *Was it something like... magic? Where even am I?*

Cool air rushed over him, as though someone had just opened a window in a moving car, and his body smacked something sturdy. It was painless.

David opened his eyes. He was lying face-down on soft grass. There was the scent of pinecones and the chirps of birds. He stayed there for a few seconds, letting his insides settle down before standing up. Jay was sprawled on the ground next to him, facedown, just like he was. They were in a circular patch of grass and small, white flowers, surrounded by a wall of pine trees.

"Jay?"

The girl groaned.

"Are you okay?" he asked.

She rolled onto her back and tilted her head, eyes narrowed. "The sun..." she said.

"Huh?" David looked up at the clear sky. It took him a few seconds of squinting to notice that the sun was small and blue.

He gasped. "But… how? God, this is crazy. Is this all some kinda trick?"

Jay stood and brushed off her clothes. "Let us—or *me*, rather—think this through logically and calmly. Assuming I'm not currently in a dream or hallucinatory state, we entered through what seems to have been a wormhole, after chaos and destruction rained upon our city following the opening of *The Legends*, the book Mr. K brought in."

"Um, right… Is that supposed to make sense?"

"Of course not. Wormholes that can transport matter across light-years is possible in theory, but for it to happen just like that in someone's apartment…"

"Plus, you know, all the other stuff we saw." David gasped again. "Wait… Where even are we? There's no way back!"

"A way back? So, you're just going to ignore why we're here and everything Mr. K said?"

David scowled at her. "And *you're* going ignore the fact that our parents could be dead?! You saw those creatures and all those dead people and the destruction and…" He ran his hands through his hair. "Damn it, I knew we shouldn't have done that. We need to find a way back."

"We came here for answers, and we won't get any standing around here, nor will we find a way back. Come on, *andiamo*."

"I guess you have a point." David looked around. "Let's go that way and hope we're lucky."

"If you were this doubtful, you shouldn't have come," Jay said as they walked. The air around them was pleasantly cool and crisp.

"I... I don't know. There was this... feeling, I guess? Like, this is what we had to do. Mr. K said this is how we'll save everyone, whatever that actually means. There were also these... voices. One of them mentioned Mom and Dad. Like, our biological mom and dad."

Twigs snapped beneath their feet, and the pine leaves rustled in the soft wind. Each leaf's tip wasn't green, but instead a glistening iridescence. The forest itself was dense, the trees so frequent and close together that walking in a straight line was impossible.

"I meant to ask earlier, but, after everything that happened and those monsters and crap, are you okay?" David asked.

"My state of being is none of your business." She glared at him. "Quit making me repeat that."

David rolled his eyes. "Right."

After nearly ten minutes of silent walking, they found their way out of the forest. They were on top of a hill, looking down upon an open, grassy valley decorated with specks of short, thin trees and the occasional boulder. The setting sun cast an orange glow upon it.

"It's dusk," Jay said, "but it was early morning when we entered the supposed wormhole. Although, I swear it was considerably earlier than sunset when we arrived here just minutes ago..."

"So... what does that mean?"

"A wormhole, or an Einstein-Rosen bridge, is a tunnel

through space-time. We have been taken to a different space, clearly, but it is very possible that the time is different, too."

"What?! Like, how different?"

"The only way to be certain is to ask. We need to find civilization. Do you see any?"

There were more clumps of forest in the distance, broken apart by the rolling plains. To their left, also in the distance, were mountains. Rather than being white from any snow, these mountains were completely brown, and their peaks were obscured by a veil of clouds. To the siblings, it looked like they were in the middle of nowhere.

"Wait, I think I see something." David pointed to the forest across the valley. Under the approaching night, they could barely make out a pillar of smoke and the faintest signs of buildings and lights. "There's gotta be people there! Come on." David sprinted down the hill, and Jay followed.

They only ran a few meters before stopping in their tracks. David swallowed. "What the…?"

The blue sun was moving back up at a speed too fast to be normal, sucking away the sunset's glow. Seconds later, it froze in place.

"I think this is more than a wormhole, Jay," David said, his mouth agape.

Their hearts made a single, powerful pound against their ribcages, causing them to grunt and fall to their hands and knees. Their insides vibrated, just like back in the classroom when *The Legends* was opened, and their muscles became weak. It was like

56

a poison sapping them of their strength. Eventually, the feeling faded.

The siblings let out a relieved breath. Their heads ached. David rose to his feet first.

"Oh my God…"

The sun was blinking across the sky, bouncing from one point to another instantaneously. At first, every blink happened once a second. As the siblings stood and watched, it sped up until it was happening multiple times a second, and then too fast to count. With each occurrence, the temperature and brightness shifted at an overwhelming speed. After nearly a minute of the phenomenon, the sun stayed in place near the horizon. There, it flashed a blinding light, washing them with a brief, uncomfortable warmth.

David hissed in pain and blinked. His eyes stung. He looked to his sister. "Are you okay?"

Jay rubbed her eyes. "We need to find someone who knows what's going on as soon as possible. Even I cannot begin to theorize as to what *that* was, if it was real."

They let their eyes return to normal. "Alright," David said, "let's keep going."

The siblings continued at a jog. The sky was pale, and stars were emerging. Dusk's chill encroached on their bodies, and Jay stopped to rest against a tree on the top of a hill. Its leaves were thin and half a foot long, and the bark was white.

"I can't… keep running…" Jay panted.

David stayed next to her and nodded. He was also catching

his breath.

"Hey!" said a voice.

They turned to the source. A figure approached them from the bottom of the hill. They could only see his outline.

David took out the remaining metal rod from his pocket. "Who are you?" he asked.

The man continued to walk towards them. As he neared, the siblings raised their eyebrows. He wore silver chainmail mixed with leather pieces, including leather boots, a thick belt, and beige pants. A sheathed sword hung from his belt, and, most curiously of all, a staff was harnessed on his back. It was wooden, with a silver orb the size of a tennis ball attached to the top.

After noticing the sword, David pressed the button and tossed the rod. The man caught it and held it right in front of his face as it flashed. He blinked a few times afterwards.

The light, although brief, revealed his features. He was well-built and about as tall as David with a slightly darker complexion, though not nearly as young, for he appeared to be somewhere in his late twenties. He had dark brown hair tied in a messy bun, with various strands hanging down his face, and a short, scruffy beard. His irises were grey.

The man lowered his thick, angled eyebrows. "Huh." He stared at their clothes and faces. "Which one is the Dijenuk?" His voice was low and smooth.

"Um..." David glanced at Jay. She had her arms crossed, staring at the man with her usual intensity. "You know us?"

"Not exactly, no. I just know the family name. Everyone does. Are you the Dijenuk?"

"We're both Dijenuks, actually," David answered.

The man paused. His eyes moved between the two of them a few times, and then they narrowed. "Excuse me?"

"We're brother and sister."

"Really? Well, that is new."

"So, um, what's going on?" David asked.

"Too many things, and I am afraid it is up to me to explain it all to you. But first, let us get someplace safe." He spoke with a jumpy, exasperated tone, as though he were bored.

"Safe? Is it dangerous out here?" David asked.

"Potentially, yes," the armored man answered. He began to walk down the hill and toward the forest.

"Don't waste our time," Jay said as they followed. "You need to answer our questions."

"Yeah, like, what's your name?"

Jay glared at her brother. "That's not what I meant, David."

"My name is Elfekot," he answered.

"Elfekot…?" Jay said.

"Just Elfekot. I am the captain of the guards at Fort Dijenuk."

"Fort… Dijenuk? Is it named after us?" David asked.

"Yes, centuries ago. You can thank your ancestors' nepotism for that," he mumbled.

David's eyes grew. "Don't tell me…. Is our family from here?"

"Aye. I am going to assume that you were not told much,"

Elfekot said.

"I guess not," David replied.

"Where are we, exactly?" Jay asked. "Someone mentioned the name 'Elektia' earlier."

"Aye, we are in Elektia."

"Is that a province or county, or perhaps some country we've never heard of?" Jay asked.

"Province? No. Elektia is a planet."

David stopped moving for a second. His face went pale again. "P-planet? No way."

"David's right. There is no way," Jay said.

Elfekot sighed. "I am not going to fight to convince you. You will know what you need to know soon enough, and you will believe it."

"Right…" Jay said.

The captain huffed. "So… what are your names?"

"David."

"…Jay."

"David and Jay… What interesting names your parents chose."

"Oh my God… Our parents are from here, huh? Like, our biological parents?" David realized.

"Aye. Well, your father was, although your mother resided in Fort Dijenuk for quite some time as well."

"And you knew them?" David asked.

"I did. I trained under them, in fact, and, er, I am sorry for your loss."

"I've noticed your sword. Is that what Renold and Sarah trained you with?" Jay asked.

"Er, no. I learned to use the blade from someone else. Your parents helped me to improve my abilities as a mage."

"Wait, mage? Like... a wizard?" David questioned.

Elfekot scrunched up his face as though offended. "What? Wizard? Tch, no. Mages are entirely different from wizards. I heard the wizards are dying off, anyway."

"Oh, here we go," Jay muttered. "Your claim, at least to us, is that magic exists, isn't it?"

"Woah. I didn't think you were gonna use the m-word first, sis," David said.

"I've been trying to avoid using it for some time now, but recent events have been so preposterous and currently unexplainable that I am forced to." She huffed. "It is rather troubling."

"Yes, this is a world of magic," Elfekot said, "whether you like it or not."

Jay crossed her arms. "Uh-huh."

"Jay's, like, a woman of science. I don't think she'll believe anything if it's not in a textbook first," David said.

"So, *you* do? You believe we're on a planet inhabited by magical people?" Jay asked.

"I dunno. Everything's so weird. Like, *really* weird. How can it not be something like magic?"

"Everything in the universe can be explained with science and logic, eventually. But let us say, Elfekot, that you're telling the truth. What kind of 'magic' do you speak of in regards to mages, and what is our role in this? Why were we brought here?"

"Mages have the ability to cast the Elements, among other things, and—"

"Elements? As in, the periodic table?" She gave him a dirty look. "Ah yes, the power of casting lithium and oxygen, oh so mighty," Jay mocked.

"Lithi-what? I mean the Elements, such as Fire, Water, Wind, Ice—"

"*Ice?* Oh, you really are joking, then. Ice is also water, just *frozen.*" Her voice rose. "Do you honestly take me for a fool, you cosplaying, idiotic son of a—"

"Jay, can you stop?" David hissed.

"No."

"While I am in no way familiar with Terra, I understand that you two come from a very different place," Elfekot said.

"Terra?" David said.

"Your planet, as we call it here. Just be patient and let me explain what I am forced to. We are almost there now."

They had neared the forest. Most of it was made up of thick pine trees just like the previous one, only it was much denser, to the point that there was no way to walk through without cutting them down. They walked around the perimeter of the forest for a minute through a much thinner stretch of trees. They met a dirt path and an iron gate the width of a garage door. It was manned by two guards in similar armor to Elfekot.

"Is this the Dijenuk boy, captain?"

"Aye. Well, the *two* Dijenuk kids, apparently."

"Really? Well, better two than one. The prophecy seems to be true, at least."

"Uh-huh."

The guards put their legs together and bowed at their waists. "Welcome, Master Dijenuks," said the guard on the right.

"Open the gate!" the left guard called.

The gate slowly slid upwards, allowing them passage and a clearer view into whatever awaited on the other side.

"I think we really did go back in time, sis," David said.

It was like no town David and Jay had ever seen. The men wore neutral tunics and trousers with flat, leather shoes, and the women either wore the same thing as the men or long, wool dresses or aprons, also of plain, neutral colors. All of their clothing, however, featured a tight turtleneck.

The siblings glanced behind them at the guards by the entrance. They differed from the civilians in that they wore armor, like Elfekot, which was usually leather caps and chainmail tunics.

All of them, though, wore a metal band around their wrists and carried staves on their backs, and they all had long hair. The men wore it in braids or buns, while the women wore it loose.

The siblings turned their attention from the people to the buildings. They were blocky, rectangular cottages made of wood and stone. The roofs were flat and thatched. There were also wells, piles of hay and logs, and dirt paths that led to other sections.

Unlike the green of the plains outside, the ground here was a light shade of brown. It was naked of any blades of grass, save for the tufts around the remainders of the trees.

"Say something to them. Make sure things stay calm," Elfekot said to a nearby guard, pointing his head at the unnerved civilians.

A portion of the couple dozen of them were moving about from place to place, almost running, while others were in small groups discussing something. They were loud and panicked, and there was even crying.

"Er, is that not your responsibility? You are the captain, sir."

"It is, but I do *not* want to deal with it right now." He looked to the siblings. "Follow me, and stay close."

The siblings caught the attention of the citizens once they took a few more steps inside.   The citizens murmured to themselves with their eyes glued to the two of them.

Elfekot gave each person who tried to approach a glare as he led the siblings through a narrow path in the forest to another section of Fort Dijenuk. He stopped at a two-story building similar in construction to the others. The first story was made of cobblestone walls, while the second used pine planks. It had two windows on the upper floor, but brown curtains on the inside blocked them.

They entered the building, each step creaking the floorboards. It reeked of wood smoke and was lit by bracketed torches. There were also a couple of trunks against the wall next to them. On the other side were dummies made of straw with targets painted on them, and next to those was a staircase leading up.

"This is one of the barracks here in Fort Dijenuk. It is the smaller one, so it does not see much use," Elfekot said.

David walked up to the wall on the side, where a rack of longswords hung. Next to it was a rack of staves. "Woah, a sword. Can I have one?"

"Er, not now, no."

"Focus. Get to explaining, Elfekot," Jay said.

Elfekot glanced around, as though looking for an escape. He took a long breath. "Well, to start, you are here to find and accomplish something, and it is my job to train and guide you for that purpose."

"Train? Train us to do what?" David asked.

"To use your magical abilities so you can save Elektia, of course."

Jay made a low grunt. "Okay…" she whispered. "I am *not* about to be dragged into this interplanetary plot that has nothing to do with me. I just need to know why everything back home happened as it did, and then we can return."

"Return? You make it sound easy. I am sure you can take a leisurely stroll to Terra, all the way across the universe. Would you like some rations for the trip?" Elfekot responded.

Jay slumped against the wall.

"I am afraid you have little choice in the matter, anyway," Elfekot continued. "The fate of your home and the fate of Elektia are tied together."

David perked up. "What do you mean?"

"Long ago, long before your parents and theirs, someone wrote a book full of secrets and wisdom. It is called *The Legends*. For unknown reasons, the book was cursed. If it were to be opened, destruction and death would be unleashed in the vicinity, and Elektia would lose almost all of its magic."

"So that's what we saw," David mumbled. "But... why would he open it?"

Elfekot's face lit up. "You saw it being opened? Do you know who did it?"

"Yeah, our teacher," David answered. "Mr. K. Do you know him?"

Elfekot frowned. "I do. He was sent by our government years ago to watch over you two. Well, David. No one knew about Jay. He was also supposed to keep the book safe. Damn him."

"So, he's from this place..." David leaned against the wall like Jay. "Well, then why *exactly* are we here? What do we need to do?"

"You need to undo the curse and restore our magic. It is a task that requires the powerful Dijenuk family; hence, the two of you."

"What's so special about us?"

"You can use nearly every kind of magic that is possible for a mage. Although, that power is nearly useless unless someone trains you. So, that is why I have to teach you to fight—"

"Fight?" Jay interrupted. She stood up straight. The fingers on her left hand twitched. "We're here to fight and undo a curse that has *nothing* do with us? Look, I have an entire life ahead of me back on Earth, and I am not about to throw it away for some fairy tale, *assuming* what you're spieling about is even real."

Elfekot snorted. "You will not see your planet for a long time."

"What?" David said. "What about my family? When are we coming back to Earth? I have to know if they're safe!"

Elfekot closed his eyes and took a deep breath. "The annihilation that *The Legends* rained down is also part of the curse. So, if the curse is completely undone and our magic is restored, then the destruction tearing apart your home will stop."

David's face went ashen and his mouth hung open.

"Do you understand now?" Elfekot said. "If you try to go back and ignore this, you will have no home to go back to."

The siblings were silent. David looked down as Jay glared at Elfekot.

"To be frank, Elfekot, I still do not believe any of this," Jay said.

"Can you at least be a little more open-minded about it, sis?" David asked.

"David, you believed in Santa Claus until you were fourteen," she said back, raising her voice. "How could you—?"

"Enough!" Elfekot shouted.

The siblings were silent again.

"You will believe everything soon enough, because you have to. Each second you spend bickering is another second in which someone could die." Elfekot grabbed two staves from the rack on the wall. "And, if you want some proof…" He handed them to David and Jay. They were identical in appearance to Elfekot's. "Then you will create it yourselves."

"What are these?" David asked. "Do they, like, shoot magic?"

"A staff is required for magic. So, in a way, yes, but it also comes from within you." Elfekot nodded towards the straw dummies. "Who would like to go first?" he asked without a trace of enthusiasm.

"Me!" David said.

"Alright. Stand here," Elfekot said, pointing to a spot on the floor a few meters away from the row of targets. "All of us magicals have energies inside of us. That energy is drawn and magnified by a strong focus, and sometimes even your emotions. It can be cast and manipulated by your will. It relies not only on your inner and outer strength and how you move yourself, but also your thoughts. So, summon upon those energies, focusing your thought and will onto destroying that straw—"

Before Elfekot could finish, a jet of light shot out of the tip of David's staff and struck the dummy. It exploded. Straw flew into the air and slowly settled to the ground.

"That is called energy magic," Elfekot explained. "It is a simple, raw form of magic that is unaffected by the curse, thankfully. Anyway, Jay, it is your turn."

David stepped away, his eyes wide and his jaw dropped. Jay took David's spot and raised her staff. "This is ridiculous," she grumbled.

"Remember what I said to David. Focus your will and thought."

Jay closed her eyes, breathing deeply. Her arm tensed, and nothing happened. She tensed it again, this time with a soft grunt, but to no avail.

"Come on, you can do it, sis!" David said.

Her grip tightened. "Just shut up, okay?" At this, she successfully fired a bolt of energy, like David, destroying the third straw dummy. It was quite the odd feeling when a surge of warmth ran through Jay's arm, met the staff, and created the obvious magic that had just taken place.

Jay looked down at her staff. Her expression, or lack thereof, was unchanged. "Huh. So, what are we to do exactly? Shooting exploding blasts of light is good and all, but why is it important?"

David gasped. "So you *do* believe, Jay!"

"I believe that whatever it is we're doing is in some way real, yes," she muttered. "But magic defies everything we know about science and the universe, so it cannot exist. There *has* to be a sounder explanation, but sure, I will settle for labeling this as 'magic' for now."

"Whatever you say, sis."

Elfekot sighed, his eyelids low. "Well, to answer your question, the steps to undo the curse will likely be met with hostile forces. If you cannot properly defend yourselves, then you will die before accomplishing anything."

David's eyes widened. "Die?!"

69

"Tch. What, did you expect this to be easy?"

"Well, no, but… I didn't think about dying as a possibility."

Elfekot crossed his arms and leaned against one leg. "Hm. You really are clueless, huh?" He shook his head. "There is much more to explain, but I am not going to waste my time with it if you two are just going to cower out of this.… I need to get a couple things. Stay here; think it over." He exited.

David leaned against the wall again and sank to the floor. "This is real," he said quietly, staring into nothing.

Jay set her staff down and paced around the room. "It doesn't have to be. I can find a way to get back and ignore all of this. We are not obligated to fix or undo anything. After all, it's—"

"None of your business, right?" David finished. He looked at his sister. "I know you pretend that the only thing you care about is yourself and what you can show off to the world, but sometimes you gotta think bigger than that, sis."

"Ah, yes, of all people, *I* have to think bigger."

"What I mean is… What's the point of doing anything if the world's destroyed? You can't show your essays to anyone if those people are dead."

Jay stopped pacing. "Elfekot said only our 'home' is affected, not the entire world."

"Should that really make a difference, Jay? Are you really gonna be so stubborn that you'd let thousands of people or more die?" he said, his voice raised. After several seconds of silence, David sighed. "Sorry. I just think we should see what's going on here. Personally, I… I couldn't forgive myself if something happened to Mom and Dad that could've been prevented."

Jay turned to face David. "You're assuming that they're alive? You saw just how hard the city was hit. Carl and Rebecca could have easily been among the many casualties."

David bowed his head. "Ugh… I didn't wanna consider it." He slammed the wall. "Damn it! We can't lose our family again." His eyes glistened. "We can't…"

Jay crossed her arms and faced away from him. "Well… considering the fact that they both commute to southern Portland for work, they could just as easily have been outside the range of the destruction, now that I think about it, if our 'home' only pertains to one city. We don't know quite how far it all reached, so… quit your crying."

David sniffled. "Thanks. You're right." He sighed and got back to his feet. "Either way, I can't ignore the chance that they're in danger. If Elfekot is right and there's an opportunity to do something about it, I'm gonna take it… What about you?"

Jay stared off, deep in thought.

"Come on," David said, "I need my sister for this… even if you don't need me."

Jay shook her head. "I can't ignore the fact that I would be leaving behind everything I worked for just based off of someone's word."

"I get that, yeah… But don't you get the same feeling I do?"

"What feeling?"

"Things have been weird our whole lives. You know that. From my weird eye color to how we can sometimes sense each other, there have been these things that no one has been able to explain. We both have always been physically different from our classmates. Even though you hated it and barely gave any effort, you crushed almost everyone in every gym class you ever had, and I naturally did well at every single sport I tried. There have been these voices, too, and that one time in middle school where you, um…"

With her arms still crossed, Jay gripped the fabric of her shirt, her knuckles tightening against her skin. "I know."

David gasped. "Oh yeah! There's also this." He pulled out the crumpled note he'd found on his door. "I told Dad about it earlier." He handed it to Jay.

"That's… curious," she said, after reading it and handing it back.

"I wish I knew who wrote it, but that, along with everything else I just said, kinda confirms what Elfekot told us. Right?"

Jay shook her head again. "Even still…"

"You'd leave everything you worked for. It's understandable." He paused. "Hm… Could you write well about anything?"

"Basically, yes. I practically perfected the craft. Why do you ask?"

David shrugged. "No one said that you had to stop writing if you stayed here. Plus, there's probably a lot to learn, too."

"I…" For a brief moment, her eyes sparkled. "I didn't think about that."

Elfekot entered carrying two leather bags. One was small,

like a knapsack, and the other was thin, and five feet long or so. He set them down by the door. "Ugh. It is complete chaos out there. The loss of the ability to cast Elements hit harder than I thought. Without Fire, we cannot cook our food. Without Wind, we cannot operate most of our machinery. Without Light, we cannot heal our wounds. Game is now much harder to hunt, and the Earth mages will have a hard time cultivating their crops."

"It's that bad?" David asked.

"It is." He paused. Both siblings were looking down at the floor. "Have you two made up your minds about the situation?"

"I did," David said. "I'm gonna do what I can to save our home. I dunno about Jay, though."

Elfekot turned to her. "Well?"

Jay brushed her hair out of her eyes. "I'll do it."

"Good," Elfekot said. "The entirety of Elektia is relying on the two of you kids, and, to be honest... that is rather depressing."

CHAPTER IV:
HIS GAME

"SO... WHAT DO WE HAVE TO DO, EXACTLY?" David asked, leaning against the wall again.

Elfekot groaned impatiently. "We have to locate every Elemental Crystal and return them to the Grand Shrine. You see, when *The Legends* was opened, the Crystals were teleported back to their respective Chambers. It is up to us—rather, you two—to enter these Chambers, retrieve the Crystals, and bring them back to the Shrine. That is how the curse is undone... apparently."

"Quite a few proper nouns there," Jay mumbled.

"Okay, but why *us*?" David asked. "What does being a Dijenuk have to do with it?"

"There are two reasons. First, those of the Dijenuk Family are special in that they can cast every single Element, except Dark. Normally, a mage can only cast one, something determined by their bloodline. Second, well... a Dijenuk just has to be involved. I do not make these rules, so do not bother asking."

"Who does, then?" Jay asked, glaring at the captain. "And why are you our guide? You don't exactly seem thrilled to be here."

"You ask too many questions, sis," David said.

Jay rolled her eyes. "How dare I."

"*Anyway*," Elfekot said through gritted teeth, "let us move on. There will be time for questions later. Rather, I will have the patience for questions later… probably. I have something for the both of you." He walked towards the leather bags by the door.

"Oh, I was wondering what those were," David said.

From the smaller bag, Elfekot drew a book. It was bound in scratched, dark-brown leather. He handed it to Jay. "It was your father's."

Spells for Mages: Basics and Beyond was the title stitched onto the cover. Its yellow pages were thick and rough, and its text was large and blocky, as though it were written for someone who was just learning to read.

"Aside from the energy magic I just taught you," Elfekot continued, "mages can also cast spells. Most choose not to learn them, but you seem like the type to be interested."

"Huh," Jay said as she flipped through the pages.

"If you want to cast spells, you will need this." Elfekot extracted another object from the bag: an amulet. It was a circular piece of glass with something glowing within it, giving off a white hue. It was tied to a thin, cloth string. "Staves are needed for almost all of our magic, but spells work differently. Although a staff technically works, an amulet is what is typically used for that kind of magic. Go ahead and try one."

Jay hung the amulet around her neck. She stared at the pages.

"All spells have incantations," Elfekot continued. "By

touching your amulet and speaking the incantation, you cast the spell. Of course, you also need to focus. Try the easiest spell there: the light spell, not to be confused with the Light Element."

After glancing at the page, Jay set the book down and placed her right hand on the glass amulet. She cleared her throat. "*Musnomi levis.*"

Nothing happened.

"Try again," Elfekot said. "Keep your body relaxed, and let your energies flow through you."

"*Musnomi levis!*"

There was a brief warmth from the amulet, and a tiny orb of light appeared in front of her. It gave off a pale blue hue.

"That is about all I know regarding spells. I reckon there is more to read about in that thing," Elfekot said.

"Not bad, sis," David said.

Jay shrugged. "It is a rather simple process. Although, everything is simple for *me*."

Elfekot grabbed the second, longer bag. "For you, David..." From it, he pulled an elegant staff made of red wood. "I unfortunately do not have your mother's or father's staff. I know they were very powerful. However, I *do* have one of your mother's used staves from before she married your father. She gave it to me as a gift after completing a certain level of training. I do not know how much use it has left, but I reckon it should last you a worthwhile amount of time." He handed it to David.

There was a leather grip on it, lined with a light-blue trim. Above the grip was a section of grey metal instead of wood. It was topped with a shining crystal, also light blue. The crystal was small, but beautiful and intricate, like a blue flame frozen in time. Etched in the staff was a name.

"'Sarah Griggs,'" David read aloud, his eyes watering.

"Your mother was initially raised on Terra, like you lot, which explains her strange name. She was an ice mage, hence the blue accents."

David breathed as though he were about to say something, but he only got one word out. "Mom…"

Jay rolled her eyes.

Wiping his tears with his sleeve, he admired the staff from different angles before finally setting it down.

"Hold on," muttered Elfekot. He dug through a nearby trunk, his body hiding its contents from view. "This should work, although I believe it is the only one left in here." He tossed David what looked like a large leather belt. "It goes around your chest. It should hold your new staff for you. Here." With the help of Elfekot, the boy secured the leather strap diagonally around his torso.

"Heh. Looks kinda weird with my clothes, but thanks," David said. He looked down at the staff again. "Do you…" He swallowed. "Do you know what happened to them?"

"To Renold and Sarah? I do, and I have just realized that you probably do not." Elfekot sighed as he looked at David, then crossed his arms. "The nation we live in is called Light Elektia. It takes up half of the planet. A border runs down the middle from north to south, and on the other side is our enemy: Dark

Elektia."

Jay scoffed. "That's rather silly. That's not their real name, is it?"

"Just shush, Jay," David said.

"That nation," Elfekot continued, "is ruled by the Landor Family. They are similar to the Dijenuks, for they too can cast every Element, only they can use Dark and not Light. The current King Landor, as soon as he was crowned, went on a rampage." He looked down, his face pensive. "The Dijenuk Family was already low in numbers. He... he slaughtered every single one of them. Not a soldier or some other git, but... him alone."

David gripped his staff.

"Two Dijenuks were left," Elfekot said. "Your father, Renold, and his brother, Bertya. Renold married here and fled to Terra, following Bertya. But, somehow, Landor found them anyway. We received the news here shortly after."

David exhaled. "Wow, I... I didn't know that. I mean, I get why. Whenever we asked about it, we were told our biological parents were murdered by some random, psycho killer. Damn..."

"Well, if you're done with that tidbit, Elfekot," Jay said, "I've been wondering. What is—?"

There was a knock on the door. Elfekot opened it. "Yes?"

"Captain, we have an issue." The speaker was a guard, like Elfekot, also in chainmail. "There is a, um, mob of people in the square. We are afraid they may get violent, sir."

Elfekot groaned. "Alright. Lead the way." He looked to the siblings. "Again, stay here, and do *not* leave. This should not take too long." He exited.

"Tch. I was about to ask him something," Jay said.

David scoffed. "When aren't you asking something?" He stared at the blades on the wall rack. After about a minute, he began tapping his foot. The commotion outside was growing in volume. "Hmm… Do you think we should check out what's going on?" he asked.

Jay, who was reading the spellbook, said, "Elfekot told us to stay in here."

"Come on, this is a world of magic! Aren't you curious? You always are, and you hate following directions, too. Plus, Elfekot can just find us with magic or something." David headed to the door.

Jay, after a moment of hesitation, sighed, picked up the staff Elfekot had given her, and followed.

They stepped outside and found groups of people huddled around guards. Their words were hastened and muddled as they kept talking over each other. A few of them eyed the siblings, but they ignored their stares. They took a peek down the paths and into the other areas of Fort Dijenuk. They spotted empty market stands and a yelling man in an apron down one path, and back the way they'd come from down another.

"Let's split up and look around. I'll go right. See you!"

Jay scoffed. After watching David run off, she took the left path.

The people here were even louder and more rattled. A couple dozen or so of them had formed a full mob and were screaming at the lone guard in front of them. It wasn't Elfekot, but someone else. As Jay tried making out what they were saying, something in the corner of her vision caught her attention, and she looked directly at it. There was a figure standing on a rooftop dressed unlike anyone else.

They wore an ankle-length tailcoat, waistcoat, and pants, all of it black, as well as leather boots. It was not of a modern, formal style, nor even that of the nineteenth century that Jay had once read about. The clothing was thicker, like that of a military coat, only longer and flashier. They also wore an attached hood, matching in shade. There was a leather strap across the person's torso, which held a dagger. The leather belt contained a long scabbard with a longsword and several pouches and pockets. There was also a band of silver metal around their right upper arm, and a leather bracer and glove on their left arm and hand, which contrasted the naked right one. The figure was directly facing Jay.

She blinked, and the figure was gone. She tried to look around for them, but it was getting increasingly difficult to see, for the mob and their foot traffic were growing in size. Jay turned around to head back to the barracks, but a running civilian forced his way past her and shoved her to the ground. She looked up, and the yelling was gone.

There was not a trace of sound. She couldn't see anyone, so she turned around again, and the hooded figure was right in front of her. She jumped back.

"Hello, Jay."

The voice was young. There was something unnatural about it to Jay, but she couldn't tell what it was exactly. She guessed that it belonged to a man. Now that he was closer, Jay noticed that he was about her height, and his face was unnaturally hidden, as though his hood were magically creating a shadow directly over the face. Only the bottom section of his face was visible, and his attire lacked buttons or zippers.

She gripped her staff. "How do you know my name?"

"I want to talk to you about something. This world, Elektia, is full of deceit. There are people who lie, people who spit out ignorance. There are people who try to hide the truth in order to keep others under them. There are people not to trust." His voice was quick and intense, yet carefully enunciated. Each variation of dynamic, pitch, or pause was deliberate.

"Are you one of those people?" She took a few steps back.

"Perhaps. There's going to be much to take in, Jay. You just got here, no?"

"What do you want?"

"Nothing more than to tell you what to prepare for. You've already begun to figure it out. Doubting the existence of the 'Elements,' doubting the name of the 'Dark,' doubting their lies…" The hooded figure stepped towards her.

Jay thrust her staff forward. Nothing happened. The man

didn't even flinch.

"I'm running out of time here. Trust in your intellect. It's the only way you can put the pieces together and conquer this world of deceit."

"What?" Jay blinked. The man was gone, and the rowdy mages had returned.

"Jay!" yelled a familiar voice.

Jay turned to find Elfekot stomping towards her.

"I told you not to wander off!" He ushered her back to the barracks. "Where is your brother?" he asked as he opened the door.

"He took the other direction."

Elfekot mumbled a curse to himself as she slammed the door shut behind him. Jay leaned against a wall.

"World of deceit…"

─<o>─

Dozens of mages were crowded around Elfekot and two other guards. This was the square that the guard with the leather cap had mentioned. It was a mostly empty zone with a four-foot-tall wooden platform in the middle. On the edges, against the trees, were a couple of narrow cottages, piles of logs, and a well. David watched from behind one of these log piles.

"Calm down!" Elfekot yelled from atop the platform. "Everyone here needs to…" He trailed off. Something in the sky caught everyone's attention.

Five puffs of black smoke zoomed above them like meteors.

They took a nosedive and descended right towards them. The guards, including Elfekot, leapt out of the way. The five puffs of smoke landed on the platform. The smoke dissipated, revealing five people dressed in black.

Four of them, two males and two females, wore loose fabrics intertwined with chainmail pieces over their torsos, relatively tight pants, and pointed shoes, similar to winklepickers. The one in the middle wore robes with a metal chestplate, gauntlets, and boots. His face was adorned with several scars, including a long one over his cheek. He had black, greying hair, tied into a single braid. He stared at the civilians below him.

"Leave! You are not welcome here!" yelled one of the Fort Dijenuk guards. They surrounded the intruders from below the platform as other guards ran to join them.

Are these people from that other place? Dark Elektia? David thought.

"Do not attempt to attack us. We can easily dispatch you all," said the scarred man. His voice was deep and throaty. "We do not wish to start unnecessary violence, for we know what it means to cross the Council. I merely want to give you all a few words." He grinned. The guards stepped back slightly. "*The Legends* has been opened. We are prepared. You are not. I would tell you all to give up the Dijenuks in exchange for immediately undoing the curse, and yes, we have those means, but I know you will not. No. You brutes will not negotiate. You will protect 'em, even if it means causing a crisis across your entire nation— even if it means blood. You want to do this the hard way. Or, we could seek 'em out right now and save you the trouble. We know you are hiding the Dijenuks. Do not lie. Are you keeping 'em in one of your ugly cottages? Or perhaps they are around here, watching?" The man looked into each of the guards' eyes.

David gasped. *No, is this… King Landor? Is he here to kill us? How does he even know we're on Elektia already?* He gripped his staff tighter.

"Maybe slaughtering you one by one will do it? It seemed that worked last time." He twirled his staff and aimed it at one of the guards. The young Dijenuk stopped looking.

Bang! David flinched. It sounded like a gunshot. A chorus of shrieks followed it.

"Lower that sword or you will be next!" the man snarled.

David peeked over the pile of logs he was using as cover. He could see blood and guards carrying what looked like a body.

The robed man continued aiming his staff. "No one wants to tell me?"

Noticing his joy after just potentially committing murder, heat surged through David's blood. *Because of him, my sister and I lost our family. Was he also this cheery when he killed them?*

"David, no!"

Before he could stop himself, David emerged from hiding, his shaky arm pointing his staff, which was slowly feeling more like a pointy stick to annoy people with rather than a magical tool, at the man. The man's lips curled into a smile.

"You must be one of the Dijenuk kids. I can tell by the

clothing. Where is the other one? Hiding back there as well?"

The guards murmured amongst themselves.

"The other one?"

"Wait, *two* Dijenuks?"

"But..."

David clenched his teeth and tensed his arm. His breathing quickened as he continued to point the staff and stare at the man with his intense gaze and furrowed brows. A bead of sweat ran down the side of his face. "You'll... You'll pay for their deaths, Landor!"

The man chuckled. "You foolish boy. I am not His Majesty. I am Istra, his top commander."

"W-What?"

The man, Istra, chuckled again and shook his head. "To be fair, His Majesty told me what to say. I think I did a fair job of setting the mood for this... game, as he put it." He tilted his head. "Do you even know how to use that thing, boy?"

David tensed his arm, his mind focusing on creating a blast of energy, but nothing happened.

"His Majesty will be pleased to know that your death will come even easier than he predicted. Perhaps I should—"

Crack! Istra stumbled forwards. Elfekot stepped out of the circle of guards. He drew his blade: a double-edged longsword with a grip wrapped in dark-brown leather. Unlike all the other swords David had seen so far in Elektia, the metal of Elfekot's blade was grey, and it glistened with a blue iridescence under the sunlight.

Before Elfekot could do anything with it, the area turned into a battlefield. David retreated back to his cover as jets of white light flew over his head. It sounded like a series of silenced guns firing.

"Fine! We shall do this the hard way, then," said Istra's voice.

Shortly thereafter, David heard a strange noise, like someone had just shaken a large piece of cloth. He looked over, and there was a puff of smoke where Istra and the other soldiers used to be.

One of the guards was lying against a well, nursing a wound in his leg. Two were unconscious. Elfekot got up from the ground and walked towards David as he was standing.

"Did I not tell you to stay in the barracks? Is obeying orders a foreign concept to you?" Elfekot was panting as he massaged his side.

David looked down at his shoes. "I... I thought it was him."

Elfekot scoffed. "Even if it were, there is no way you can even put up a fight in your current state. He is a Dark mage, a king, and has been training since he was a *child*, while *you* just learned how to blast things. Barely. I reckon that commander was only marginally less dangerous."

"Yeah... you got a point. I just felt this, like, need, you know? This desire to face him. King Landor or not, that guy was our enemy."

"Spoken like a true Dijenuk. Come on, back to the barracks."

"You know, those kinds of reckless actions are exactly what I expect from you, David," Jay said after Elfekot summarized what had happened.

"What do you mean?" David said. He was sitting on the floor against the wall. "*You're* the one who's gotten in fights before."

"You're predictable. Well, everyone is, but especially you. You let your emotions control you."

"He killed our parents!"

"Am I supposed to care?"

"Let us move *on*, please," Elfekot said, his voice raised. He took a deep breath. "The commander said something interesting. He said that they were prepared for this."

Jay entered her usual thinking position with one arm crossed and the other raised, her hand next to her face. "Huh. That, combined with how quickly they got here, means they knew about the Opening before it happened."

"What? How?" David asked.

"They must have been directly involved in the Opening somehow."

"That does make sense," Elfekot said, his hands on his hips. "That commander was talking about hunting down the two of you. It looks like King Landor wants to finish the job."

"And he had *The Legends* opened to bring us to Elektia... to *him*," Jay added.

"Wait, so does that mean that Mr. K works for Dark

Elektia?" David wondered.

"No," Elfekot said. "Mr. K, or Sir K, as we call him, is on our side. And I doubt he was something like a traitor, because then Landor would have known where you were on Terra and hunted you down that way."

"But he was the one who opened *The Legends*," David said.

"That is the part I do not understand." Elfekot frowned.

Jay shook her head. "It wasn't out of his volition. He was possessed."

David looked at her. "Huh?"

"He wasn't behaving like himself. He was stiff and lifeless."

"Heh, kinda like you, Jay," David said.

"Right before he opened *The Legends*," Jay continued, "he temporarily snapped out of it. It was clear that he didn't want to, but something or someone else was taking control. Once the deed was done, the normal Mr. K returned. When it was happening, I wasn't considering something like possession...." She frowned. "But now I know something like that may be possible."

Elfekot snapped his fingers. "You are right. I know what happened. He must have been controlled by a mage using the Spirit Element."

"Spirit? That's the most stupid-sounding 'Element' so far," Jay muttered.

"We didn't see anyone like a mage," David said. "But I agree with Jay. There was definitely something going on with him."

"Thus, King Landor had Mr. K controlled, somehow, so *The*

Legends could be opened as a means to bring us to Elektia," Jay summarized.

"So, what, we fell into his trap or something? And doesn't the curse affect his people, too?" David slammed the wall. "Damn it! So, he did all of that just for a shot at killing us?!"

"It seems so…" Elfekot said.

"What this means for us is that our enemy has the advantage," Jay said.

"It also means that we have even less time than we thought," Elfekot added. "If Landor removed the Elemental Crystals from our possession, then it is very possible that he wants them for himself. You see, the Dark possess a Grand Shrine of their own, but, while our Shrine provides every Elektian with their Element, their Shrine only provides it to the Dark Elektians. He seeks to completely crush us."

David seethed. "We have to stop him. Right, Jay?"

Jay hesitated. "Right."

Elfekot opened the door and peeked outside. "It is getting late. The attack that Landor sent made some people stay inside and hide, so it should be calmer. Come on. You two need to rest. I will be teaching you more tomorrow."

Elfekot escorted the siblings out the barracks. Fort Dijenuk was now silent, except for a small group of men standing around a small fire, discussing something softly. As soon as they saw David and Jay, they stopped and walked towards them.

"Is one of these the Dijenuk, Elfekot?" the man in the front asked. Like everyone else they'd encountered in Elektia, he was tall, although not as tall as David. He was muscular, with a round face, flat nose, and long, red hair tied into three braids that ran down his back.

Elfekot hesitated, then nodded slowly. "Aye. The other one is a Dijenuk, too."

The man looked astonished. "Really? Tch. And none of us knew. And now you are leading 'em around. *You* are already suspicious enough, and now——"

"*Enough*, Nolten. You know I have no choice. Do not tell me you doubt the prophecy now."

"You do, at least. And yet here you are, following it."

"What's so wrong with that?" David interjected.

The man named Nolten scowled. "You have no idea who this man truly is, eh? He is not just the captain of the Fort's guard, oh no."

"Er, what is he, then?" David asked.

"Nolten," Elfekot warned.

Nolten stepped closer to Elfekot, staring him down. "Ever since he began his training here, he was treated like something special. Like he was above us. How do you think he became a captain this young? Sure, he is decent with a sword and staff, but it is more than that. He has this secret——"

Elfekot groaned in annoyance. "This again…"

"This *secret*," he repeated, "that he will not tell anyone. But his Dijenuk trainers knew about it. That is right, your parents." He shook his head. "It is why he leads you now. But that is not the worst of it, no. His parents were of different Elements! One of Fire, one of Lightning."

Jay stood behind them silently, arms crossed. David blinked at him. "Is that supposed to matter?"

"Huh? Did you not hear me, boy? His parents were of different Elements, and they *married*!" The men behind Nolten muttered in disapproving tones.

David shrugged. "Yeah. I heard you. And?"

"These kids are clueless," said one of the other men.

"It creates a mutation," Elfekot answered. "The child of two mages who differ in their Element ends up not being able to use any of them. That is why I can only use Energy magic." He said this matter-of-factly, without any resentment or somberness.

"But that's not his fault, is it?" David countered. "I don't think it really matters. And if he has secrets, then that is his own business. He doesn't owe everyone an explanation just 'cause you demand it."

"You are defending him? Urgh, all because you are a precious little Dijenuk." Nolten approached David instead.

Elfekot put a hand on the man's chest, stopping him. "Nolten, they are just kids."

"Kids?" David said. "We're not even *that* much younger than you, when you think about—"

"Do you know that for sure, Dijenuk? Who the hell knows what he even *is*?" Nolten drew his staff. "As for *you*, kid, you better—"

"Nolten!"

David drew his own staff. "I better what?"

91

"David, please. Both of you, put those away!"

"Enough," Jay snapped. Her arms now at her side, she forced herself between the three of them and looked right at Nolten. "I get it. You're scared. You're angry. The world is falling apart and there's much at stake, more than just our livelihoods. There seems to be nothing you can do about it. And you're not alone. Your fate has fallen into the hands of two Dijenuks you've never met and, worst of all, a man whom you resent. I'd be angry, too, having my life in someone else's hands like that. But there's more to it. You're also stupid."

Nolten took a step forward. "Excuse me? Who do you think you are?"

"Rather than accept the fact that you can't match Elfekot in your abilities, you've decided either to manufacture, add to, or just plain follow a story that fits your agenda of insecurity."

Nolten scoffed. "What do you even know?"

"I haven't been here long, I realize that. I cannot make any accurate assumptions regarding Elfekot's skills and efficacy. Yet, there has to be a reason for his position, one beyond puerile prophecy and whatever else you accuse him of. So put down your staff, put down your insecurity, and focus on survival. David and I have much to learn about this world, and we have a long path ahead of us. I urge you to—instead of attacking people like us, instead of fighting, instead of lashing out in your anger— look to each other instead. I am not much for believing in the power of the masses. In fact, the voice of the public tends to be nothing but useless blather. I recognize, however, that there is little choice."

A crowd of nearly a dozen other civilians began gathering around them.

"Now, more than ever, you need each other," Jay continued. "None of us know how to survive like this. So figure it out. Normally, I would advise against this, but help one another, for that is the only way to help yourself. At least for right now. *Just for now.* And let us do the job we never asked to be a part of."

When Jay finished, the civilians of the crowd were murmuring to each other, nodding and wearing smiles of determination, a direct counter to their earlier expressions of hopelessness.

Nolten opened his mouth to say something back, but Elfekot spoke first. "Come on, you two. Let us continue."

They entered the square, the area that Istra and the soldiers had attacked earlier. Behind the platform was another passage leading deeper into the forest. They walked through the winding path, following the bits of stone in the ground. They spoke of nothing for a couple of minutes. Upon an uphill climb a considerable distance away from anyone else, David broke the silence.

"So… you're not super popular here, huh, Elfekot?"

"Some resent me for my parentage, yes, but many respect me for my work here protecting the Fort. That is all I wish to say on the matter."

After another minute, they reached a tall, iron gate, similar to the one at the Fort entrance, except this one bore a familiar crest in the center.

"That's what I saw on *The Legends*," David said, identifying the same golden letter 'D,' surrounded by seven small circles of different colours.

Elfekot nodded. "It is the Dijenuks' crest. It symbolizes all the Elements—except Dark, of course—with Light being in the center, as that is the Dijenuks' specialty. Beyond this gate is the Dijenuk House. The Head Dijenuks, the leaders, would live here. They would organize meetings, make decisions, all of that. It has not been lived in, or even stepped in, since your parents left for Terra. Only Dijenuks are usually allowed in, after all. But now, because of tradition—my favorite—the both of you will live here."

"Where did the other Dijenuks live?" David asked.

"Back in the day, when the Dijenuks were stronger, long before you and me, a large portion of them would live in the Dijenuk Manor. I do not know where it is. No one does. Perhaps your mother and father did. The stories say it was enchanted to be hidden from plain sight. It is here in Elektia, I imagine. There is no reason for it to be anywhere else. Your parents were foolish to move to Terra, in my opinion."

Jay tried to look through the bars of the gate and see the Dijenuk House. "How do we get in? I don't even see anything."

"It seems like this place is enchanted to keep it hidden from view as well. Entering it is simple, though. The gate opens when a Dijenuk is near." Elfekot frowned. "You are right next to it, Jay. I do not know why it is not opening."

David stepped closer to the gate, and the crest shined a golden light. There was the sound of wood snapping, followed by a loud *creak* as the gates folded back on their own.

"Ah, of course. They had that partner rule back then...." Elfekot mumbled.

David's hand moved to his staff. "Um... should the front door be wide open like that?"

CHAPTER V:
THE DIJENUK HOUSE

THE TRIO SAID NOTHING as they carefully stepped towards the new building with Elfekot in the lead. They drew their staves, and Elfekot drew his sword.

The Dijenuk House was three floors tall with a mansard-style roof, made primarily of cobblestone but trimmed by a darker wood similar to walnut. In comparison to the rest of Fort Dijenuk, the walls were smooth and flat. There were logs across the building acting as pillars, bracing the walls. The windows were small, and the sills bore flowers with gold petals. Despite its relative height, it wasn't at all wide. The House sat in a small clearing, surrounded by a thick wall of trees, like everything else in the town. Centered stone steps allowed for a wraparound porch decorated with nothing but cobwebs. Its fencing appeared sturdy. An elegant plaque rested above the double doors and read, "The Dijenuk House, built year 698."

Up the stone steps and through the door, they entered an empty hallway. The floor was made of a light wood, similar to birch, and was well-polished despite its abandoned state, while the walls were made of a smooth cobblestone. As for the interior, it was bare. There was hardly any furniture, no paintings, no carpet, nor anything else. To their right and left were barren rooms, although the latter had a large shelf and a singular table. At the end of the hallway, they found a staircase leading up.

Finally, someone broke the silence. "You think someone's in here?" David asked.

"Hm… *Musnomi levis*," Jay chanted.

A golf-ball sized orb appeared in the room, giving off a faint light. It hovered in the very center.

"Stay down here. I am going up," Elfekot muttered as he tip-toed across the floorboards.

The siblings followed him anyway. He noticed, but he didn't say anything. The steps were creaky, each sound echoing throughout the house, amplified in the silence. After what felt like hours, they reached the top and held their breaths as the door in front of them slowly opened without a touch. Holding his blade even tighter, Elfekot went through.

"*Musnomi levis.*"

Elfekot jumped and spun around, but then realized it was Jay who had uttered the spell and created another magical light above their heads. It revealed a rectangular room, with one door on each side. Continuing on, Elfekot scanned each direction until he made it to the center.

"I believe it is safe," he said.

Jay let out a breath. "Good, because I have some questions, Elfekot. To start, why did the gate open the way it did? And why is this place so barren?"

Elfekot took a few steps back. "I do not know everything, okay? And I have never stepped foot in here before, anyway."

The two glared at each other for a few moments.

"But I do know about the gate, yes. Security is part of my job in Fort Dijenuk, after all. Originally, it was only to open in the presence of a Dijenuk. However, when the Dijenuks began to dwindle, they agreed to be out in groups of two at minimum for safety. The gate's enchantment was changed to help enforce that. It opened because of the presence of two Dijenuks. Does that explain it?"

Jay narrowed her eyes. "What about this house?"

Elfekot shrugged. "I reckon it was abandoned when your parents left for Terra."

"Right…" With that, Jay began her walk around the second floor, studying every nook and cranny.

"So… you knew our parents, yeah? What were they like?" David asked as he stared at the name etched in his staff.

Elfekot returned his sword to its sheath. "Your father, Renold, was the oldest amongst his many siblings. He was what you expect from any Dijenuk: strong, courageous, and dangerously prideful. His parents died at a young age, too. They were assassinated just like all the others, so he took charge early on as he best he could. He met one of the Terra-born mages here in Fort Dijenuk. That was Sarah, your mother. She was strong and brave, too, but much calmer and more collected. She was also rather kind and gentle, but fairly strict when needed."

As Elfekot spoke, Jay continued lighting up the floor with her spells. Each one was less effective than the last.

"Both of them, as adults, helped train the child recruits. That is how I met them. Eventually…" Elfekot leaned against the wall and sighed. "With most of his siblings ending up dead, he chose to run away to Terra with the woman he was in love with. Right before they left, they unioned, and your mother became pregnant with you. That is how we knew of at least one more Dijenuk and why Jay was unknown to us."

David took a deep breath, his expression solemn. "Do you think they could have lived, had they stayed and fought?"

"If I had to be honest? Unlikely. The Dijenuks were too prideful to just sit in this house and hide. So yes, they fought, but more than they needed to. The Landors threatened innocents, after all. Eventually, Renold had to swallow that pride, but it may have been too late." He looked at the boy. "I am sorry."

David shrugged, his smile weak. "I didn't know them, so, thank you for the story."

"Are you done with the flavor text, Elfekot?" Jay interrupted. "Take a look at this. This house, unsurprisingly, has secrets."

"What is it?" David asked.

She gestured for them to follow. "This place is quite dusty, which is to be expected. However, the levels of dust are not consistent. There are visible lines and lower concentrations of dust where furniture should be. Yes, all the furniture could have been moved out. I imagine it's easier with magic. But why? It seems an even unlikelier reason when you consider what *you* said, Elfekot. The Dijenuks ran. It obviously wasn't stolen, either. So then I thought back to the house itself. It appeared out of thin air once the gate was opened. Such magic could be applied to the interior. Therefore, I conclude that there's some kind of enchantment hiding things from us, and we must find a way to lift it."

David and Elfekot looked at each other for a few seconds, eyebrows raised. "That is a possibility, yes—" Elfekot admitted.

"No. It's a certainty, considering the fact that it was *I* who said it."

David shook his head. "Alright, Jay, we'll give your theory a shot. Let's look around properly."

Elfekot nodded. "Right. Jay, you stay here. I will go downstairs. David, investigate the courtyard."

"Hey, wait," David said. "Have we forgotten that there's a third floor? It seemed like there was one from outside, anyway."

"Then, Jay, try to find a way up if you can," Elfekot said.

"It's likely hidden by that same enchantment..." she replied.

Back downstairs and out the front doors, David was surprised to face the night's darkness. The sun must have been lower than he thought. The air was cool and refreshing.

"Oh my God..."

The sky was unlike anything he had ever seen. Not only were the stars plentiful and vibrant, but he could even see what was possibly a different planet when he squinted hard enough. It was only a miniscule orange dot, but it was enough to excite him. Seeing this much in a place like Portland or its surrounding cities was impossible. There was something missing, however. David, with his head craned, spun around to search for it. The clouds shifted and revealed two moons. They were similar in appearance to Earth's—Terra's— moon, although smaller. One was twice the size of the other.

"Woah... Well, I guess it isn't too surprising. This ain't Earth, after all." He frowned, then exhaled.

Using the light from inside the house as well as that of the moons to guide him, David made his way around the courtyard. Most of the ground was dirt, and there were weeds sticking out from the foundation. In the back, there was a cobblestone well. Otherwise, there was nothing else.

David peered down but couldn't see anything past a foot. "For a house built for this super-important family, there sure is a lotta *nothing*." As his fingers tapped on the stone, he took another look around. *Wait...*

Attached to the back wall of the house was a triangular pillar of white stone about three feet tall. Etched into one of its sides was a familiar symbol: The letter D in the center of a circle of dots. David touched it with two fingers and retracted his hand when the symbol briefly glowed.

Did that do it?

There was a loud thud from the upper portion of the house.

David bolted back inside. "Jay!" he yelled as he entered.

A golden carpet now ran down the hallway, and the entire house was lit by candles that hung on the walls. Ignoring everything else, David reached the second floor. The rectangular room at the top was now carpeted with a golden rug. Jay stood underneath the open doorway in the back. She was leaning on the frame, her face contorted in discomfort.

"Are you alright?" he asked, rushing towards her.

She swatted his approaching hand away. "I bumped my foot into a table that suddenly appeared from nothing. I presume that you did something to trigger the change, yes?"

"Oh, yeah! There was this weird button in the back."

"Did one of you do it?" Elfekot called. Heavy footsteps creaked from the stairs. "There is suddenly a whole bloody miniature library, all kinds of chairs, paintings, and a few tables, even. It's much less dim, too," he said as he reached the second floor.

"Oh, I didn't even notice most of that," David said.

Jay jabbed a thumb at the room behind her. "More interesting than that is what I just found here. It's a letter."

"From whom?" David asked, his excitement obvious.

"I didn't read it yet. Come on."

The back room was cramped, consisting of a shabby little desk and a sketchy-looking ladder going to a cellar door. They approached the desk and found two pieces of paper. One was the size of a page, apparently torn from somewhere, and the second was a smaller note. They were of the same parchment material as Jay's spellbook. The handwriting was small and scrawny, but readable. The three of them huddled together to read the longer one as David held it up.

Dear Jay and David Dijenuk,

If you are reading this, it means that The Legends has been opened and you are in Elektia. I assume that there are people in Fort Dijenuk explaining all of this to you properly, along with what you need to do. I cannot, for I have to hurry with this.

You should be looking for the Wind Chamber first, so you will need to acquire the keys to it: The Three Scrolls of Gales. Unfortunately, one is possessed by the Kingdom of Landor, but I do know of a tip to help you find another. The Scrolls were once held by a woman by the name of Fayenth Erbezen. She lived in a town called Hegortant, not too far from Fort Dijenuk. Long ago, she was killed by Kingdom of Landor forces, and one of the Scrolls was taken from her. The other two were kept hidden by her family, and at least one is said to be in Hegortant. Start looking there.

"Kingdom of Landor…" Jay muttered.

"Hegortant, eh? I have been there quite often. It is the largest city in Elektia. We need to head there soon," Elfekot said.

"What does it mean by the keys being these scrolls?" David asked.

"All the Elemental Chambers, I believe, are locked in some way and require keys. The ones for the Wind Chamber are the Scrolls of Gales. It is one of those things that Elektians already know about it, but only vaguely," Elfekot answered.

"Huh." David took another look at the letter. "Who do you think wrote this?"

"I am sorry to say that I do not know. It was likely a now-dead Dijenuk."

Jay made a skeptical frown. "Whoever it was knew *both* our names, even though no one in Elektia is supposed to. They also managed to get inside here and decided to keep their identity anonymous. *And*, they also wrote the note that was on David's bedroom door this morning."

"Wait, really?"

"Compare the handwriting. They're the same."

David looked between the note in his pocket and the letter. She was right. "So… what does that mean?" he said.

"It means someone knows the game, and they're playing us." She picked up the smaller note, then clutched her amulet and chanted the written incantation. *"Levis ehté saugh!"*

The whole house filled with a more natural light, one that didn't come from any visible source. It was a great deal brighter than both the candles and the earlier lights Jay had created, which were now gone.

"Hm… Maybe it was our parents who wrote this," David wondered aloud. He gasped. "Maybe they're still alive!"

Jay scoffed. Elfekot shook his head. "We all wish they were, but alas, someone did find their bodies." David looked down. Elfekot cleared his throat. "Anyway, we should take a look upstairs."

The siblings nodded, and they followed Elfekot up the ladder. Through the cellar door, they emerged in a square room, similar-looking to the previous. The wood that made up the floor and walls was a dark brown, and there were two doors on each side instead of one. There was another door opposite, and it was made of metal. The ceiling was lower and the dust in the air was thicker, making for a more cramped environment. The smell was musty, like rotting wood.

"Huh. Your family sure did know how to live in luxury," Elfekot drawled. He took a peek into each door on the sides. "These are all bedrooms."

"The two rooms downstairs are bedrooms as well, although they are larger," Jay said.

"What about this one?" David approached the metal door and turned the circular handle. He heaved as he slowly pulled it open. "Ugh... Let's just leave it open from now on."

The trio entered it and discovered a two-story room connected by a staircase. The top floor, where they were standing, was a wooden platform with a railing that circled the perimeter. It allowed them to look down onto the bottom floor of the room, which was also part of the house's second story.

"This will be useful," Elfekot said.

On the top floor's stone walls, a variety of staves hung vertically on racks, although more than half of the racks were empty. Some were made of metal, and some were made of different-colored woods, and some were topped with glass orbs, while others had crystals.

"Staves can be difficult to obtain. The Light Council issues them," Elfekot continued.

David peeked over the railing. "Woah!" He then took the staircase down.

The bottom floor contained wooden trunks, a couple tables,

and armor stands. There were also a few weapon racks, and they held swords and spears. Like the staff racks, half of the stands were empty. The items ranged from lighter leather armor to heavier plate armor. One of the stands held only a golden cloak.

"This is awesome," David said. He ran his hand across the golden cloak. "I wonder if my dad wore this."

Jay examined the two tables that sat against the back wall. There were empty scrolls of parchment, jars of ink, and quills, as well something that resembled one of the grey, metal rods that they were given, only it lacked a button. Jay removed the rod from her pocket and placed it on the table next to it.

Elfekot eyed the swords. "Your family had quite the collection. It is not surprising, though. Hm." He opened the trunk at his feet and dug through it. "Ah, here. I assume you are tired of carrying that around." He tossed Jay the same staff harness that David had.

"Can we use this stuff?" David asked.

"It is all yours, so yes, but I would not advise it just yet. You have more to learn first. Carrying a sword right now would only hinder you."

"Can we learn more right now?" David asked.

"Tomorrow. You have had a long day and have much to think about. Take any of the bedrooms. It is your rightful home, after all."

David raised a finger. "Hold on a minute. What about food? What are we going to eat while we're here?"

Elfekot thought about it for a few seconds. "I do not know

106

too much about Terran food, but I cannot imagine it being much different from the food of Elektians. However, we do have a food problem now due to *The Legends'* curse." David and Jay glanced at each other. Elfekot continued. "We farm, like I think you Terran folk do, but we do it with the help of magic. We have some in storage, of course, but not enough to last the fort even a sub-sector."

"Sub-sector?" questioned the siblings.

"Eight units, usually."

"Units?"

Elfekot frowned. "A period of night and day."

"So, a day," Jay said.

"No, a night *and* day," Elfekot corrected.

"But it's called a day—"

"What are we going to eat and drink?!" David repeated.

"What we have now. We need to find that Wind Crystal and the rest of them soon or we are going to die. Either of starvation and thirst, or anarchy," Elfekot said as they walked back to the ladder. "For right now, sleep. I will be downstairs. Just pick somewhere."

The siblings looked at each other.

"I guess we should take the bigger bedrooms, yeah?" David said.

"Yes."

They descended the ladder and glanced at the bedroom doors.

"Right," David said.

"Left," Jay said at the same time.

They nodded and entered their newly-claimed bedrooms.

"Well, this isn't so bad..." David said upon opening the door.

Both of them found the same thing: a decently-sized room with a bed about queen-size, a blanket, a couple pillows, and a dresser, as well as an octagonal window. None of the bedding was made of familiar materials. The room was bigger than their bedrooms on Earth, so there was there plenty of remaining space, but they couldn't think of what else to put in a bedroom in a place like Elektia.

"Goodnight, Jay."

Jay hesitated. "Night."

After shutting the door, David slumped into the bed, cringing at the creaks the wood frame made. It was surprisingly comfortable. He stared at the ceiling with his hands behind his head. "This is crazy... Is this real life?" He turned over to his side, yawning. "Or is this fantasy? Heh." The boy stared out the window. "I miss you, Mom and Dad. I hope you're safe." He closed his eyes tight, refusing to think about it further. "I'm going to save Elektia and I'm going to save them. Me and Jay both. We're gonna save everyone."

As soon as Jay shut her door, she searched the room through and through. She turned over every drawer, felt around the walls and floor, peeked under her bed, and shook around the pillows and blanket. "You're hiding more, house, I know it," she said aloud, wagging her index finger. Yawning, she finally lay down. It wasn't too long before her body shivered.

"Are you still cold? Here, I'll warm you up. Haha, just come here, let me cuddle you."

Jay sat up, startled. She took a sharp breath, then slammed the bed with her fist. She stared at the bruises on her knuckles.

"Leave," she whispered, then flopped back down. "Just leave."

⤙o⤚

Despite having the fate of the entire planet now in their hands, the siblings slept well under the exhaustion of it all. The light of dawn came fast…

BANG!

"Crap!" David rolled out of bed and grabbed his staff, which was lying on the floor. He yanked his door open and found Elfekot in the center of the hallway with a slight smile. "Was that you?!"

Elfekot nodded.

"That wasn't necessary," he groaned, rubbing his eyes.

Elfekot shrugged. "I was curious to see if the house was damaged by magic or not. Waking you was a bonus. Plus, it is good to see that you are quick to act. Er, your sister, however—"

"Is already awake," Jay finished as she exited the bedroom. She raised her spellbook. "I've been studying."

109

"Wonderful. Now, I have decided," said Elfekot with a clap. "We are going to Hegortant today. Rather, we are going there soon. There, according to the letter, we will find the Scrolls of Gales that we need to enter the Wind Chamber. So, the more I think about it, the more I realize the less time we have to waste—"

"Do you know what I realize the more I think about it? How depressingly deplorable this situation is," Jay interrupted. "I need a change of clothes, I need a shower, and I need some answers, too, but don't forget about our food conversation last night." David nodded. His eyes were still droopy.

"You also promised more training," David said, yawning.

"How are we supposed to save anyone if we can't even defend ourselves properly?" Jay added.

Elfekot crossed his arms as he continuously tapped one of his feet. "Fine. But we *will* be going to Hegortant later, and I promise you I will address some of those issues. Get your things. Meet me outside," Elfekot ordered.

Jay raised an eyebrow. "Some?" But Elfekot was already gone.

"We just gotta do what he says. He knows what's best. *And* he actually lives here," David said.

With their staves equipped on their backs, the siblings hurried downstairs. The first floor, like Elfekot had said, had now been adorned with proper furniture, carpeting, and decorations. A golden carpet ran down the central hallway, matching the square, golden rugs in each side room. There were four paintings on the wall, each depicting a man and woman in either shining armor or elegant robes. They posed with a royal dignity. The room on the right from the entrance had turned into a lavish sitting room.

"Well, this is kinda fancy," David said as he scanned the room.

There were three white sofas with golden trim and two armchairs of the same design. In the center was a wooden table the color of birch. There was also a doorway in the back.

David moved to the door and opened it, revealing a simple kitchen. It had a fireplace, a pile of firewood next to it, and a short, empty table. Pots and pans hung on the walls around it.

"Neat."

Jay looked at the room to the left. "This could prove quite useful."

The room had gained additional bookshelves, as well as a large, circular table and a couple of smaller ones.

After taking nearly a minute to look around, the siblings stepped outside and met Elfekot on the front porch.

"Here. This is from the well in the back." He handed the siblings a sizeable tankard of water each. They glanced at each other with raised brows before taking cautious sips.

"Oh, God, ugh!" David said as he barely managed to swallow it.

"Farewell, filtered water..." Jay said, grimacing as she forced the liquid down.

"I do not understand you two. It is the same water as on

Terra, yes?"

"Technically…" David said.

"In a way, no," Jay said. "Seeing as this is a different planet, mineral contents could differ greatly. That, of course, changes the taste."

"But it is still water, yes?" Elfekot questioned.

Jay stared at murky substance in her tankard. "Yes."

"Then finish it and let us be off, unless you want to let the mighty Dijenuks be defeated by some water."

They walked to the start of the downhill path past the gate.

"Hold on," Elfekot said. He picked up rusty chains and a hefty metal lock that he had left on the ground.

"What are you doing?" David asked. Elfekot began fumbling with the gate as he closed it behind them.

"If I can correctly recall what your parents told me, the magical seal is gone now. Any bloke could walk in if they wanted to, so I added a proper lock."

David tilted his head. "Gone?"

"The partner rule was never meant to be enforced regularly. I am certain there is to some way to re-enable its security, but I do not know how."

David exhaled. "I'm guessing a lot of family secrets died with them, huh?"

"Likely." Elfekot tossed him a small, yet heavy, iron key. "That should probably stay with one of you."

"David can keep it. I do hope that you become more truthful with us as time goes on, Elfekot," said Jay with clear bitterness and crossed arms.

Elfekot shook his head as he began to walk onwards. "I have neither desire nor reason to lie to you. Now come on."

The siblings followed, with Jay keeping her distance. The orange glow of dawn had peeked over the treetops, warmly illuminating the path before them. Their footsteps and the ruffling of clothes were all that was audible in the morning's stillness.

"Is she always like this?" Elfekot muttered to David. He glanced back to make sure that Jay was outside of earshot.

"Nowadays, yeah. I've gotten kinda familiar with it myself. But she used to be different. Then, one day, after over a month of being silent, she just kinda… changed. No clue why." His quiet explanation carried a solemn touch.

Upon reaching the bottom of the hill, they entered the melancholy atmosphere of Fort Dijenuk once again. Its citizens meandered about the square, barely adhering to their tasks. They had trouble carrying out even the most mundane of chores, like moving firewood or taking water from the well. Some, akin to yesterday, retreated to discussing the matter in groups, sticking to hushed tones. It took only seconds from the trio stepping in to break the gloom and raise the noise as they let out merry cheers.

David looked to his companions. "Should we say something?"

Jay crossed her arms. "Didn't I say enough last night?"

"Just ignore them for now," Elfekot said.

After passing a couple of guards, the captain led them

through a new path in the forest and into an area they hadn't yet seen. It was a clearing the size of a soccer field, adorned with training dummies, tall poles of wood, and four rocks with targets painted on them on the far side.

"Ooh. This looks like a training area, alright," David said. He pointed to a cart of hay in the corner. "What's that for?"

"Breaking falls, if need be." Elfekot brought them to the sparsest section of the field. Eight training dummies occupied one of the edges, while another section was taken up by the wooden poles that were as tall as the trees, leaving an empty square between them. "Take out your staves. We will be using these rocks here as targets." He indicated the grey boulders. They were separated equally and were about half the size of a person in height.

David and Jay each took a different target and stood roughly ten meters away.

"One important thing to note about this kind of magic is that physical movement makes a large difference." Elfekot drew his staff, twirled it a couple of times, and then thrust it forward. A white bolt of energy, wider than the siblings had seen previously, struck the center of a boulder. Bits of rock exploded off of it. "Compare that to this." He held up his staff, and, a second later, fired a much smaller projectile. It hit the target without any impact. "I exaggerated it a tad, but you get the idea."

"That's pretty cool," David said. He moved his staff like Elfekot did, but to no effect. "Oh."

Elfekot scowled. "I did not tell you try anything just yet.

Listen first."

"Oh, sorry."

"Start with what I taught you yesterday: Simple blasts of energy. If those are not consistent, then... well, good luck."

The siblings raised their staves. Elfekot watched them with arms crossed as he leaned on one leg. Nearly ten seconds later, a bolt of energy fired from David's staff and missed the boulder by a couple of inches.

He rubbed his arm. "That warm feeling that goes through you is pretty weird. I did it, though."

After about half a minute, Jay drew for breath as she let her arm fall. "Ugh. It hurts to hold it for so long.

"You gotta keep trying, sis."

"Obviously." She frowned. "Am I missing something?"

"Well, you have to make sure to focus," David said.

Jay glared. "Wow, you solved everything. Amazing."

"If I had to guess, you are thinking too hard about this," Elfekot said. "You are a mage, and a Dijenuk, especially. Magic flows through you, and so using that magic should come rather naturally, provided you keep in mind what you want to happen."

Jay raised her staff again. Her arm was shakier than last time. After a few moments, she fired an energy blast. It hit one of the trees.

Elfekot moved to rest against the farthest boulder. "Now, keep trying; keep practicing. Do it over and over. Practice makes permanent."

The siblings continued with the basic blasts of energy. The

time between blasts gradually decreased from multiple seconds to just under one, although David retained a higher rate and neither of them landed a shot right on target.

David lowered his staff and exhaled. "That really tires you out, like you said." He raised it again. "You know, Elfekot…" His next blast struck the edge of the target. "I've been wondering. Where does this magic come from?"

"I've been wondering the same thing," Jay added as she took a break.

"Hm. It is a fair question." Elfekot cleared his throat. "Magic comes from two sources. The first source is the well of magical energy that is naturally inside every magical."

"Oh, so *that's* what that warm feeling is," David said.

"The more you use this energy," Elfekot continued, "the more you strain yourself. You can become exhausted, sore, or even lose some blood. Rest is the only real way to alleviate this and restore that energy, and experience helps your body be more efficient with its magical uses."

David fired another energy blast and bent over, panting. "Yeah, there's definitely some strain already." He looked at his staff. "So, these staves are the second source, I'm guessing."

"Aye. The staff is even more limited than the body, though. Every time you use magic, the special material inside the staves burns down, sort of like a candle wick. Do not ask me about the material. Staff-making is a secretive trade. I just know that you cannot replace it once it runs out, so be mindful of any staff you are carrying."

Jay closed one eye as she did her best to keep her raised staff still. The resulting projectile landed only inches from the bullseye. "Is that really all there is to it, Elfekot?" she asked.

"Er, what do you mean?"

She turned to face Elfekot. "This is magic we're talking about, supposedly. You're telling me that all we get from using it is some fatigue? It would make sense if that source within us was more limited, but according to you, it just 'exists.' It's always there. But it can't just 'exist.' You can't get something from nothing. There has to be more to it."

David leaned on his staff. "Come on, sis. Stop trying to apply that kinda stuff to magic. It just works differently."

"That is all there is to it, Jay," Elfekot added.

"Uh-huh."

"Ooh, I have another question, Elfekot," David said as he practiced twirling his staff.

Elfekot sighed. "Go ahead."

"What are all the Elements, exactly?"

"Oh, right. Sometimes I forget how little you know. The Elements, in the order we traditionally list them and the order we must restore them, are Wind, Fire, Water, Spirit, Lightning—or Storm, as it is sometimes called—Earth, Ice, Light, and Dark."

Jay lowered her staff and shook her head. "It's so, *so* stupid-sounding," she muttered.

A few more minutes passed, and the siblings rested on their staffs, out of breath.

"Alright, that is enough."

David and Jay looked at Elfekot. "Don't we have more to learn, though?" David said.

Elfekot looked up at the sun. It was still rising. "You will have to learn as we go. Right now, we need to make haste." His sigh was his longest yet. "We have a world to save."

CHAPTER VI:
THE EPICENTER OF SIN

"CITIZENS OF FORT DIJENUK, I, Elfekot, like I have been told by all of you, am joining the quest to restore the Elements," Elfekot said. His disappointment wasn't well hidden.

The captain was speaking to an anxious group of over a couple dozen civilians below. He and the siblings were standing on the wooden platform in the square.

"I have two more Restorers with me," Elfekot continued. "The others, if they exist, will be found in due time as the prophecy and the Elementians guide us." His tone was dubious and insincere. "The rumors are true. These two kids are Dijenuks."

The crowd's murmuring grew in excitement.

"Really? Two Dijenuks?"

"I thought there was just one!"

"What is with their clothes? And their hair?"

"They are brother and sister. David and Jay," Elfekot said.

David smiled and waved. Jay wore visible impatience and crossed her arms, this time adding a tapping finger.

"They are indeed from Terra, so they have much to learn. We will be starting with Wind, as the prophecy indicates. Our journey begins with a trek to Hegortant. As some of you may have heard from Jay, this burden rests with us. Cooperate and survive. Tough times are ahead of us, yes, but we *will* restore the Elements, and we *will* save Elektia."

The crowd briefly cheered before vomiting questions at the trio. "What about the Dark?"

"Do you know who the others are?"

"I am a Restorer, too! Take me with you!"

"What is in Hegortant?"

Elfekot ushered the Dijenuks through the mob.

"Captain!" called a voice.

He sighed. "What is it, Rikod?"

The man, apparently named Rikod, approached the trio. He wore armor similar to Elfekot's. His long, triple-braided hair was grey and his body was well-built despite his visible age. His face wore numerous scars. "I came to say goodbye. It is not easy having my finest man leave the fort like this." His voice was low and fruity.

"I will be back, Rikod. My home, and theirs, is still here. We are only going to Hegortant. Save your sentiments for when I die."

Rikod chuckled and shrugged. "You never know what can happen out there. I wish you three the best of luck."

"It is fortunate that you came to me, actually. You will be in charge in my absence. I am sorry for not mentioning it sooner. Now, if you will excuse us—" Elfekot tried steering the siblings away, but Rikod moved to block their path.

"Now hold on, Elfekot. I bear a gift." He looked to the

siblings. "Which one of you is the eldest?"

David raised his hand. "Me, sir."

"Sir?" Rikod laughed heartily. "The boy has manners. No, Master Dijenuk, such a title is not necessary. I have for you my personal blade. It would be an honor for you to wield it in battle." He removed the sword with its scabbard from his belt and bowed down, offering to blade to David.

"Woah, really?" The boy immediately, although carefully, took the blade.

Elfekot sighed. "David, give it back."

Rikod scoffed. "What for? It is mine to give away."

"He does not know how to use one, Rikod."

"What? How could he not?"

"They don't really teach you that kind of stuff on Earth. I mean, Terra," David answered.

Rikod frowned, taken aback. "If they do not use blades or magic, what do you Terran folk use?"

"Guns, usually. Sometimes knives. But even that kind of stuff isn't something everyone learns to use."

"Guns?" Rikod leaned closer, as though curious.

"Just give the sword back, David."

The boy sighed and followed directions. "Alright. Sorry, Rikod."

"In time, Master Dijenuk, you will learn. Perhaps when you return, eh?"

"Maybe. We must go, Rikod," Elfekot said.

"One last thing, captain. Nolten told me about your recent,

ah, disagreement. He said the young Dijenuk here threatened him."

"Nolten is a lying git. You know that."

"Yes, yes, I know. It is just that... well, Nolten has been running his mouth even more than he usually does now."

"I do not care."

"What he is saying about you—"

"It does not bother me."

"It could reach the Council—"

"The Council can go piss off, okay? Come on, you two." Elfekot marched on. David and Jay looked at each other for a second, confused, before moving to follow.

"So..." David said. "How far away is Hegortant?"

"On foot, a few hours."

David threw his head up. "Ugh... Well, I guess that's not too bad."

"I am going to assume that you Terrans have faster means of transportation?"

"Yep. But don't you guys have horses or something?"

"I have never heard of that word, so... no. Our normal form of transportation has been lost due to the curse. If we restore Wind, we get it back," Elfekot explained.

"You mean *when* we restore Wind," David corrected.

"You underestimate the challenge ahead of us. You understand that all our lives are at high risk, yes?"

The trio had exited Fort Dijenuk and entered a long, narrow pathway that cut through the thick forest. Attempting to go off the path and through the trees appeared impossible. The siblings assumed them to be similar to the pine trees of Terra, although their trunks had more girth.

David's stomach growled. "Maybe this won't be as much fun as I thought…"

Elfekot snickered. "Was it supposed to be?"

"Oh my God, finally," David said.

The group had just emerged from the forest. Before them stretched vast rolling hills of long grass, dotted with the occasional tree, bush, or boulder. The path continued off towards a distant city. They could see its surrounding walls of stone standing tall.

"That's, uh, Hegortant, yeah?" David asked.

Elfekot stretched his arms to the side, blocking the siblings from continuing past him. "Hold it. I heard something." They all idled, listening intently. "Someone could be following us. Let us quicken our pace."

"Why would anyone be following us?" David asked as they resumed their walk.

"I do not know, but we should remain vigilant."

"Could they be an enemy?" David added.

"Not necessarily," Elfekot muttered.

Jay scowled. "Please elaborate."

"It is not just the Dark we must watch out for. They are not a hostile force, but I imagine the Light Council will want to intervene," he answered.

"What is this Council?" Jay asked.

"The Light Council consists of eight men, each a mage of a different Element. They rule over Light Elektia and, as a group, establish all our laws. They have never been keen over Dijenuks in recent history, and they can be irrational at times. However, they genuinely care for our nation and do what is best for it."

"How are these eight men selected?"

"If a Councilman is to leave their position for any reason, the remaining Councilmen vote for a replacement, choosing a male from the same family bloodline as the one that just left. This means there are eight families that rule together in Light Elektia."

"That's stupid," Jay replied.

David elbowed his sister lightly. "Jay!"

"What?"

"You can't just insult a different culture like that."

"It is fine, David. Let her be. You are both from a vastly different place."

David stared at the city ahead. "Does the Council live in Hegortant?"

"No. They live in a place called Light's Source. We will have to go there eventually. That is where the Grand Shrine is located."

The boy groaned. "All these names…"

"The Grand Shrine is what holds the Elemental Crystals and disperses magic throughout Elektia. Obviously, it is quite important, which is why it is secured at Light's Source. Do not falter, David. There will be much more explaining to do as we continue."

"I know…"

"Then continue explaining," Jay said. "It is better to elaborate on everything now than later. Why are you coming with us, Elfekot? You and the others kept mentioning a prophecy."

"Well, we can't do this alone—"

"I didn't ask you, David—"

"Not by my choosing," Elfekot interjected. He sighed. "There is this document treasured by us Light Elektians. It is a prophecy called *The Restorers of the Elements*, or *The Restorers Prophecy* for short. It was crafted centuries ago. As such, fragments have been lost to time. It predicts that *The Legends* will be opened someday and a specific group of people will undo the resulting curse. You two are some of those specific people. I am as well. It also tells us the order in which we must restore the Elements. It is a load of rubbish, frankly. Most Elektians disagree, so here I am. I will admit, it is how I located you two. It said I would find you outside Fort Dijenuk right after the Opening, which was marked by all that nonsense from Elepta, our sun."

"Missing fragments? Tch, of course…" Jay said.

"Woah, that's wicked cool," David said. "This has all been predicted? How? Does that mean we're gonna win? Are there more of us? Who?"

"I do not know whom, nor do I know the outcome, nor do I know the means. There are supposed to be five of us, if I remember correctly, but take prophecies lightly," Elfekot grumbled. "Any more questions? I do not guarantee I will have the patience to answer them later."

Jay took up the offer. "Sure. This so-called Dark Elektia… Is their true name the Kingdom of Landor?"

"Huh?"

"The letter in the Dijenuk House referred to them as the Kingdom of Landor. Why do you call them by a different name?"

"Does it matter? They are called Dark Elektia. Why do you assume the letter is not lying?" Elfekot asked.

"We don't even know who wrote it," David added.

"It clearly matters," Jay said, "because you're so defensive about it, and names are important. And I am not assuming the letter is truthful just yet, but it hasn't lied to us so far. I cannot say the same about you, Elfekot."

"If you want to remain sane, you need to stop scrutinizing every little thing. Question time is over. I have lost my patience," Elfekot said.

"Good going, sis," David said. Jay rolled her eyes.

"Why me…?" Elfekot muttered.

A couple of minutes passed as they walked in silence.

"Elfekot?" David said.

"Huh?"

"Do we have a plan?" David asked. "I mean, what do we do

once we reach Hegortant?"

"I thought I said no questions."

"Oh, right. Sorry."

Elfekot sighed. "There is someone I know who might be able to answer some questions for us. That is where we will start."

David nodded. "Gotcha."

Elfekot eyed him. "Gotcha?"

"Uh, like, 'got you.' It means, 'I understood' or, like, 'I get what you're saying.'"

He made a hollow laugh in response. "Terran speech…"

"Hey, wait a minute," David said. "How can we even understand you? This a different planet, but you're all speaking the same language that some of us do back on Earth."

"Or, perhaps, some of you on *Terra* are speaking the same language *we* are," Elfekot replied.

"Are you implying that our language, the English language, originated here on Elektia, and not on Terra?" Jay asked.

"Aye. Well, it is believed that our ancestors traveled more frequently between here and Terra, and so our influence and that of the Terrans gave birth to our current language."

"Hm. They are at least very similar," Jay said. "There are differences, although that can be attributed more to culture and dialect, as opposed to the language itself. For example, I noticed that Elektians don't use contractions, and their written scripts don't capitalize the beginnings of sentences, for the most part."

"Right. Er… Do not ask me about anything relating to that ever again."

Jay scowled at him. "Why?"

"Just… trust on me that," Elfekot said as he avoided eye contact with her.

"Huh, I just realized all of you Elektians are technically aliens," David said.

Elfekot raised an eyebrow.

David caught the confusion. "It means, like, a creature from a different planet. But we're all human, anyway, yeah? It's kinda weird."

"Yes, we are all human. Some of us come from different places, and some of us are nonmagicals."

"I'm assuming nonmagicals are those without the ability to cast any kind of magic. Magical potential is something you're born with. Something so reliant on genetics is bound to have a myriad of mutations and exceptions. Fascinating," Jay said.

Elfekot nodded. Jay furrowed her brows, deep in thought.

The captain stopped moving. "Down here. Quick!" Elfekot said. The three went down a small slope and hid behind a large, brown rock formation.

"What's going—?"

"Sh!"

The air was silent and still for a while. Eventually, the sound of marching could be heard in the distance. The trio peeked over their cover. From behind a distant hill, a group of soldiers emerged. The couple dozen of them were all dressed in pristine white, gold-trimmed armor that glistened in the sunlight. Their marching was tight and unified. Two of them carried large banners bearing a crest: The Dijenuk "D" with an eye in the center, encompassed by a flaming circle, like a sun. They were led by a man in white robes. The trio only studied the group for a second before hiding again.

"The Light Council?" David guessed.

"Aye. Well, not the Council themselves, but a messenger and some soldiers. They probably want a word with you two."

"You make it sound bad," David said.

"They are just… difficult to deal with. Like I said, they are not an enemy. But for now, I advise we avoid them. We are in a hurry, and they would most certainly slow us down."

"How did you know they were there?" Jay asked.

"I have good ears, I suppose. And I expected the Council would try to intervene in some way. At least we were not being followed."

"Why are there so many of them?" David wondered. "They don't need that many dudes if they just wanna talk."

The captain shrugged. "Their military is independent from that of Fort Dijenuk. They like to make certain that we know whose is bigger. Of course, it is theirs. We are simply guards, not a full-fledged military. And yet, they feel the need to parade their troops wherever they go," he explained with annoyance. "Anyway, for right now, let us hide here and stay quiet. Let them pass."

The siblings nodded. They remained sitting against the rock, listening for the soldiers' steps and the clinking of armor. As they waited, Jay pulled out her spellbook from her back pocket.

She flipped to the exact page she needed, despite the lack of any kind of marking. Elfekot watched her read, mesmerized at the speed with which Jay's eyes scanned the pages.

The Elektian soldiers neared. David tensed against the boulder. Jay closed her spellbook and focused on listening. Elfekot remained collected. Their footsteps came from atop the slope above them. They passed without a word. David let out a held breath, the action audible. Elfekot glared at him. The marching became faint.

"Well, that was kinda scary," commented David, his tense posture finally easing.

Jay shrugged. "At the very least, I was able to finish reading the spellbook."

Elfekot looked at the girl with clear skepticism. "You still have to keep reading and memorizing if you want to practice spells effectively."

Jay scoffed. "No, I already have it memorized. This was just a selection of the spells out there. I will now need to find another."

Elfekot raised an eyebrow. "Really?"

"Yeah!" said David. "Over the summer, Jay memorized what she needed from her Calculus textbook by just reading it *once*. She also memorized every term we needed for Mythology before the year even began. Oh, and there was this one time where—"

"Enough, David," Jay interrupted.

"So, you memorize everything?"

"No. I simply remember exactly what I need to. The ability to recall everything—also known as photographic memory—doesn't exist," she answered matter-of-factly.

Elfekot shook his head. "You two are constantly throwing words at me I fail to understand." He stood. "We should be good to continue now."

"So, who exactly are we looking for in Hegortant?" David asked as the group resumed their trek.

"An… old friend of mine."

"Can we trust this 'friend?'" Jay questioned.

"We have to."

A large chunk of time passed as the three Restorers treaded onwards without a word. The siblings' heads buzzed with more questions, but Elfekot was visibly irritated by something. Gradually, the dirt path widened as it turned into one of paved stone. A river could be spotted now that they were closer. Its calm waters cut through Hegortant perpendicular to their path. It had come to the siblings' attention that they hadn't spotted a single animal yet, although they had heard the cries of birds.

Eventually, the city of Hegortant loomed over them. Its walls of light-grey stone forced the siblings to crane their necks to see the top. Two guards stood in front of a large metal gate, wearing chainmail and leather similar to Elfekot's, although in much nicer condition. They each carried a pike and a staff.

"Halt!" one commanded. "The city is in a state of emergency. Passage is strictly banned without the Council's permission."

"These are the Dijenuks. We need to go through."

The gatekeepers looked at each other. "Dijenuks?"

"Two of them?"

The one who had spoken first cleared his throat. "My apologies, Dijenuks." Both of them put their legs together and bowed at their waists. "And to you as well, Restorer. You three may pass. Open the gate!" he ordered. The gate slowly and noisily lifted upwards. "Welcome to Hegortant, Mister and…"

Jay rolled her eyes. "Miss."

"*Miss* Dijenuk," he finished.

"Woah," David said. "This is…"

"Utterly disappointing," Jay finished.

Before them lay a wide street, bustling with people of varying skin colors, heights, and braid styles. They wore clothes similar to those in Fort Dijenuk, including the tight turtlenecks and metal bracelets. Smaller streets and alleys branched out along the sides, forming city blocks. The buildings themselves were quite unlike the ones found in Fort Dijenuk. Instead of cozy cabins or rustic houses, tall rectangular prisms of flat, pale-grey stone made up most of the structures. The mundane architecture was marginally improved by the inclusion of the most basic of square window designs.

David took a few steps forward. "They all look the same."

The only way to tell the difference between the buildings from a distance was by their exact dimensions. Sometimes, the grey boxes were broken up by narrowing sections on the higher stories.

"At least... this city has the tallest buildings in Light Elektia," Elfekot said.

"I guess. It's nothing like what's on Earth, though. I dunno. For a magical world, I was expecting something grander..."

The building heights varied greatly, as some constructions towered over others. If you were lucky enough, a sign near the front door could help you identify the building's purpose.

"...or more alive."

The streets themselves were not just filled with its citizens, but also unorganized clumps of boxes, crates, barrels, and similar containers, most of these against the walls. A fountain stood in the center, although it was completely dry. Behind it was erected a statue of a robed male figure. It was composed of white marble, offering contrast against the overwhelming grey. Any other details were lost in the overall shoddy quality of the statue. The dull colors of the Elektians' clothing, the building materials, and the suddenly overcast sky were only amplified by the depressed state of the civilians. As a whole, the city as they entered it seemed robbed of its saturation. It created a feeling that matched the common shade: grey and dull.

David shrugged. "I guess it's not *that* bad."

"It's bad," Jay interjected. "*Andiamo.*" She began to walk speedily ahead.

"Hey, wait!" called Elfekot. "You do not even know where we are going."

The girl didn't stop. "We are to see an old lover of yours, yes? A bartender is my guess. So to a tavern or bar we must go."

"Huh? How did you—?"

"You are easy to read, Elfekot. Nothing escapes someone of my intellect. In addition, bartenders tend to be quite knowledgeable, especially in this kind of environment."

David sighed. "There she goes again…"

Elfekot walked in front of her, finally stopping her. "You still do not know where to go exactly."

"Then stop wasting time and lead the way already."

"You just gotta have a little patience, sis," David said as the siblings began to follow Elfekot down the street. His attention was caught by the statue. "Who is this supposed to be?" The boy's eyes strained as he struggled to read the faded text on the silver plaque. "*Clyhvus Karanos*. I think."

"Founder of the city and some war hero," Elfekot clarified.

"Huh."

The siblings continued following the captain down the main street as he led them through another street and down some steps. This smaller street appeared to be somewhat livelier. The buildings here were shorter, but their windows were larger, making their purposes clearer. Numerous shops and services occupied most of this area. Only a few them, however, were bustling with business. A woman carried a large heap of clothing from one, and a family took with them as many cuts of meat as they could carry from another. A couple of guards chased them, one of them yelling:

"Hey! You are exceeding your income. Wait until more is issued!"

At the center, where it was quieter, a sign gave way to their destination: Goblin-Ear Tavern.

Jay read the sign. She groaned as her skull ached and her stomach twisted. She didn't quite know why.

"Relax. Goblins were banned from human settlements decades ago," Elfekot said. "Anyway, this is the place."

David opened the door for the other two as the Restorers entered. A pleasant warmness overtook them. Their eyes took a second to adjust to the warmth of the lights, a stark contrast to the grey, bleak outside. Tables and chairs took up most of the floor space, and a bar stood in the back. Nearly everything here was made of wood. The place was busy but not overcrowded. There were plenty of average-looking villagers, but a handful of them stood out, with their nasty face scars, robes, or the rare eyepatch. They spoke with either hushed and hastened tones or long, lamented cries.

"Do they not like us, or…?" David said.

Nearly every single one of the patrons swiveled their heads and watched the Dijenuk siblings as they walked farther inside. The noise level dropped as they murmured to themselves. Words like "Dijenuk" and "Restorers" were audible.

"They are just unsure about everything. We all are. Stay quiet, though," Elfekot warned. He approached the bar with the siblings following closely.

A woman stood on the other side of it. A long scar across her cheek and alert eyes contrasted her pleasant, genuine smile. Her long, wavy black hair, curvy figure, and confident demeanor made her quite the attractive person. "Elfekot!" she greeted. "It has been a while!"

"It, uh, it has. How have you been?"

"Apart from the world ending, not too bad. So, what can I getcha? The usual?"

"Get to the point, Elfekot," Jay interjected.

The woman snorted. "Ah, and who are these two?"

Elfekot's voice dropped. "David and Jay."

"You two sure have some funny lookin' clothes. Well, it is an honor to meet you. I get what is goin' on now. So, ya here for information, huh? And here I was thinkin' you missed me," she teased.

Elfekot's face grew ever so slightly redder. "Sorry, Denisse, I just, um… Do you know anything about the Erbezen family?"

The woman, Denisse, leaned on the counter, eyes squinting as she thought. "Hm… a Wind family, yeah? They lived right here in Hegortant for many years. Always quiet, those Erbezens, but most people liked 'em. Do you need somethin' from one of 'em?"

"The Scrolls of Gale," David blurted.

Jay slapped her brother on the arm.

"Relax, relax. I know which secrets need to be kept and which do not," Denisse said. "But if yer lookin' for the Scrolls, yer in bad luck. They left in the middle of the night. All of 'em. Fled the city before they closed it down to who-knows-where."

"Dang," David said. "They took the Scrolls of Gales with them, I bet."

"I reckon their home would be worth searching, just in case. Do you know where it is?" Elfekot asked.

Denisse smiled. "I sure do. Do you need me to show you the way?"

Elfekot scratched his head. "You could just tell us, if that is okay—"

"Ohh, so you cannot be around *me* anymore, is that it?" Her serious expression was quickly broken as a laugh escaped her.

"You can go with us," David said. "Be nice, Elfekot."

"Yea, listen to the kid. I will be out shortly—"

"But what about your job?" Elfekot said.

Denisse waved a hand. "It is fine. The boss likes me too much to give me the boot. I will meet you outside in a bit." She smiled at them again before retreating through a door.

David opened his mouth to speak.

"Do *not* say a word," Elfekot said. He took a deep breath. "And do not ask. Let us just… get this over with. Come on."

"Wait, while we're here, shouldn't we eat something? You said we would when we got here," David pleaded.

Elfekot tapped on the counter impatiently. He opened his mouth to answer, but Jay did instead. "No. We have to find those Scrolls as soon as possible," she pressured quietly as she glanced around to make sure no one was eavesdropping.

"Food is important, Jay. I'm still—"

"*Cintria sih famso.*"

David groaned in pain and doubled over, clutching his stomach. "What the hell?!"

137

"Oh. That didn't work. It was supposed to temporarily rid you of your hunger. Oh well."

"Ugh… Can we please eat something, Elfekot? We can't fight if we're hungry."

"Fine. Hey, Denisse!"

Denisse poked her head out from the door. "Yea? I was just about to leave."

"The kids need something to eat. Could you…?"

"No problem! I will be back." Denisse closed the door.

"Don't we have to pay?" David asked.

"Most of us do, yes, provided the Council sent the spare income. Sometimes they close the eateries and hold back on what money they distribute. Regardless, those of the Dijenuk Family get most things for free," Elfekot explained.

David frowned. "Oh, that's… really weird. I wanna pay if I can."

"Good luck with that."

The three of them waited in silence as they avoided the patrons' gazes. After a few minutes, Denisse returned carrying two metal plates.

She set the plates down in front of them. "Here you are."

"What the…? Is this food?" David said.

Both of their plates were covered with tiny cubes, less than an inch in width. There were three different colors of them, off-white, light brown, and deep purple, all mixed together.

"Er, what is wrong with it?" Denisse asked.

"It's all… *squares*."

"Cubes," Jay corrected.

"Uh…" David took the provided utensil, which was a pointy piece of metal with a handle, like a fork with only one tine, and ate the light brown cube. Jay ate the off-white one. They were both flavorless, although the entire plate gave a strong aroma, as though one were face-first in a field of flowers.

"This is… a starch, like potato," Jay said.

"Is this… chicken?"

"Huh? Ch-Chicken? No, we call it 'borokri,'" Denisse clarified.

"Um, right." David then tried the purple cube. It was zesty, and almost spicy. "Oh, this is… radish, I think."

"We call it the western root. I am assuming that 'radish' is something ya eat on Terra?" Denisse asked.

"Yeah." David stared at the plate, as did Jay.

Elfekot groaned in exasperation. "Just hurry up and eat it."

As the siblings forced down the meal, David eyed the metal bracelet around Denisse's wrist as she rested her hands on the countertop. It was just like the ones every other Elektian wore.

"What's that?" he asked.

"Ya mean the labor signifier?"

"Is that what it's called? Everyone I've seen in Elektia wears one."

She showed the siblings the symbol engraved into the metal. It depicted the single-tined utensil they used, with a plate next to it. "It designates me as 'food service.'"

"And mine," said Elfekot, "designates me as either a guard

or soldier." He showed them a crude symbol of a sword.

"So they, like, show what job you have?"

"Aye," said Elfekot.

David swallowed another cube of bland meat. "That's kinda weird. Do you have to wear that?"

"We do," Elfekot answered. "Every Light Elektian, usually after fifteen or so years of living, is assigned a general section of the work force that they will be a part of."

"Wait, you don't have a choice?" David asked.

"*Sometimes* there is, but only between a couple. It depends on what the Council thinks we need."

"Doesn't that kinda suck?"

Elfekot shrugged. "It does not matter to me."

"I assume that you don't get to change it, yes?" Jay asked.

"Aye," said Elfekot. "Rarely does the Council grant such changes."

Jay scoffed. "That's absurd."

"The Council knows what is best for us," Denisse said with a shrug.

Jay finished her plate. "Right."

"Let us go now," Elfekot said, standing up.

"Then I will see you outside. I need to this clean this up 'ere," Denisse said.

The three of them left the tavern and waited outside the door. Denisse later emerged from an alley next to the tavern, now carrying a staff on her back. It was similar to Elfekot's, but with a few cracks in the shaft.

"Ready, boys?" she said. "Follow me. It is not too far."

The siblings, as per Elfekot's earlier instruction, were quiet. Elfekot was wordless too as Denisse led the group through the noisy streets. Heads perked up at seeing the two strangely-dressed kids walking with the Fort Dijenuk captain. To some, their identities were obvious, while for others, it took a few seconds to confirm with their equally miserable companions. Regardless, it didn't take much for the people of Hegortant to learn that the Restorers were now in their vicinity.

Denisse finally broke the group's silence. "So one of the prophesized saviors really is you, Elfekot. A *Restorer*. Look at you out 'ere tryin' to save the world. You have grown," she said.

"I am just doing what I have to."

Maneuvering through Hegortant's many streets, alleys, and roads served to show the siblings that all the buildings really were the same pale-grey boxes. The roads also lacked signs and directions, so there were no addresses. The houses grew smaller, shabbier, and more cramped together as they reached their destination.

"I believe this is it," Denisse announced, standing in front of a wooden door. It looked the same as any other building. Apart from the Restorers and Denisse, the street was desolate.

David tried the door. "Locked. Maybe we could bust it open?"

"Property damage. Yes, perfect," Jay said. "Move, David." She hovered her hand over the doorknob. "*Aperta eht wesya*." From the door sounded an audible *click*.

David tried the door again. It opened, revealing a dark interior. "Oh, wow." He looked back at the others. "Uh, I guess I'll go in first." He stepped inside. Jay, Elfekot, and Denisse followed. "Hey, Jay, could you—?"

"*Levis ehté saugh,*" the girl chanted. The entirety of the house lit up with a pale blue light that came from nowhere.

"Thanks," David said.

The interior was even more depressing than the exterior. Papers were scattered. Chairs were flipped. Cubic food remained half-eaten. The closed curtains let in little natural light. The floorboards creaked under every step, and the air was thick with dust. Most personal belongings, like clothes, books, and heirlooms, were missing.

"They left in a hurry," Jay inferred.

"Well, yeah. They feared for their lives," David said.

Jay grimaced at how much the floorboards creaked. She crouched down to investigate. "A Scroll of Gales could very well still be in the premises. If they knew what it was for, they would have left it for us. Search thoroughly."

The group split up and searched the house. Most of the drawers and cabinets were already opened, however. The messy state and inconsistent lighting only added to the challenge. Denisse searched the kitchen, a cramped side room with cupboards, pots and pans on the wall, and a fireplace. Elfekot peered around the pieces of furniture, like the table in the center and the singular, empty armor stand. David looked in the bedroom while Jay examined the walls.

The bedroom contained a large bed with white sheets, two dressers on both sides, and a broken chair in the corner. He turned over the sheets and ransacked both dressers, but found nothing.

"It might not be here after all," Elfekot said, looking through some of the papers on the table. He crumpled them up.

"Are these important?" Jay asked.

"No."

"Hm." She stepped towards him. "I would like to see them for myself."

"Just focus on finding the scroll."

"But you said it might not be here."

"It still *could* be." He crossed his arms. "You are wasting time."

Jay narrowed her eyes at him. "Why can't you just give it to me?"

"Because it is not important."

A muscle in her cheek twitched, as did her fingers. "...Curious." Jay clasped her amulet and opened her mouth to speak.

"I think I found it!" said David from the bedroom. He reentered the main room, carrying a polished, wooden box.

"Where was it?" Elfekot asked, his eyes still on Jay.

"Under one of the beds. I like to hide things there myself." The boy opened the rectangular lid, revealing a green-tinted scroll inside of it. The parchment was tied closed by a white string. It was less than a foot long and barely thicker than a finger. He picked it up. "Wicked. So this is a Scroll of Gales, yeah?"

Elfekot nodded.

Jay crossed her arms. "And this is supposed to be a key for the Wind Chamber?"

"I am not quite sure how it works," Elfekot admitted. "But I am certain we will figure it out if we get there."

"*When* we get there," David corrected. "Thanks for your help, Denisse."

"No problem, sweetie."

"Reckon we should move on out of here, yes?" Elfekot said.

David nodded. Jay hesitated for a few seconds as she glared at Elfekot. She then snapped her fingers, and the light disappeared.

"So, what now? How do we find the other two?" David wondered aloud as they stepped outside.

"Ugh…" Jay's hand moved to her head. It ached as a single word whispered inside her brain, the voice unrecognizable.

"*Danger.*"

From the rooftops, small green creatures leapt down to surround them. They wore rags for clothes, worse than that of the civilians, and carried spears and shortswords. Their ears were pointed just like their weapons. They all snarled at the Restorers as they approached.

The Restorers drew their own weapons. Denisse stepped away from the trio and calmly walked right through the group of growling creatures. She stood behind them wearing a triumphant grin.

"What?" David said. "What is this? What are they?"

Jay gripped her staff tighter. "Goblins."

Chapter VII:
The Lesser

"Let us keep this nice and simple, darlings. Give me the scroll," Denisse said. The goblins inched closer. "You do not want to end up impaled so early in your journey, do you?"

The Restorers had backed up against the wall. David held the box close to him. "What do you even want it for?"

"It is none of your business, honey."

"Denisse, please. Do not do this. The fate of Elektia resides within us and that scroll," Elfekot said.

Jay ran through a list of spells inside her head, but she couldn't help but be distracted by the pointed weapons and sharp, yellow teeth.

"What do we do?" David asked Elfekot.

The captain said nothing.

Denisse exhaled. "I do not have time for this." She snapped her fingers. The goblins charged.

"*Téléneh nostro!*"

An instant later, darkness surrounded the Restorers.

"Huh? Where are we?" asked David.

"Inside the house. I teleported us away," answered Jay. "Barely."

"Where did they go? Find them!" commanded Denisse from

outside.

"Follow me. Out the window!" Elfekot said.

"I hear them. They are inside the house!" Denisse shouted.

"I can't see anything!" David said.

Elfekot groaned. "Here!" There was a small *bang,* followed by the shattering of glass and the tearing of fabric. A large curtain had ripped, revealing the freshly broken window behind it. Elfekot climbed through it with ease, and David followed suit.

"Jay! Come on!" David urged.

"There's still glass. It's sharp, David."

"We don't have time!"

A spear-equipped goblin charged at Elfekot. The captain used his staff to sweep his legs, knocking him over. He then fired a blast of energy into his back. "We have to go. Now!"

David grabbed his sister's arms and pulled her through.

"Ow! Be careful."

"Run!" Elfekot barked.

The trio darted down the street, not daring to look behind them.

"Where are the guards?!" Elfekot said.

From a rooftop, a goblin slung a rock at the fleeing trio. The rock smacked Jay in the head, knocking her out cold. David stopped in his tracks. "Jay!"

Elfekot stopped with him. He raised his staff over his head, but another rock was slung. He grunted in pain as his staff was knocked out of his hand. The goblins had caught up to them. Elfekot readied his sword. One of the creatures had snuck up on the captain. He swung at his legs with a club, knocking him down. Before Elfekot could do anything, the goblin clubbed his stomach. David pointed his staff at the creature, but nothing happened. With a swift strike to the head, Elfekot was knocked out.

David was surrounded. He finally managed to fire an energy blast, but it barely caused one to stumble back. The dozen or so creatures snarled an incomprehensible language.

A slung rock struck the side of his head and sent him to his knees. The box tumbled out of his hand. A swinging club was the last thing David saw before his consciousness left him.

A bright, clear sky and its blue sun loomed above. David could feel rope bindings on his hands behind him. Whatever he was on constantly shook and bounced. He craned his neck. He was in a wagon, occupied by himself and his two companions. Elfekot had awoken, too, but Jay was still out. The goblins appeared to be pulling the wagon, but he could barely see the top of their heads. David nudged his sister with his foot.

"Jay!" he muttered.

"Huh…?" She stirred. "What…?" Her eyes opened. "What the…? Ow, my head…"

"Are you okay?" David asked.

Jay realized their situation and struggled against the rope. Someone banged the wagon, and a snarl followed.

David turned to face Elfekot. "Did we lose?"

"Just stay quiet for now," he replied.

David exhaled and laid his head back down. *There has to be some way out of this*, he thought. "Where are you taking us?"

No one answered.

The Restorers and their goblin capturers said nothing more as the wagon made its way. David watched the trees slowly move past him. The trek grew even bumpier.

"Jay," he whispered.

"What?" she responded flatly.

"You did a teleport spell earlier, yeah? Can you do it again?"

"No."

"What? Why not?"

"Shh!" said Elfekot.

"That's not how spells work, David."

"What do you mean, that's not how they work? Can't you just do it again?" His voice grew louder, along with Jay's.

"I said quiet!" repeated Elfekot.

"No. David, shut up. I can't do it again."

"Well, at least explain it to me."

"David—"

"Shut up, you two!"

"Jay—"

"Be quiet!" shouted a different voice, one that was much coarser and much less human.

Just then, the wagon stopped. Five goblins climbed onto it and forced the Restorers onto their feet. Their four-fingered hands were cold and rough. They growled their own language as they shoved the trio off the shabby wagon. The Restorers looked around and found themselves in a forest much different than that of Fort Dijenuk. The trees were thin, crooked, and discolored, as though they had been sapped of nearly all their life. The blue of the sky was a touch greyer. Large, unlit torches planted in the ground outlined the path forward.

"This way, boys," said a familiar voice. Denisse emerged from behind the wagon to face them. She was carrying the box that held a Scroll of Gales.

"You! You'll pay for this!" David said, held back only by the pointed weapons.

"Ooh, ya got quite the spirit, kid. And barely even a unit in Elektia, eh?"

"Move it," growled a voice behind them as he prodded with his spear.

The trio did as told, letting themselves be escorted by the large group of armed goblins. Denisse walked with them.

"Where are you taking us?" David asked again.

"Their home," Denisse answered.

"Why?" David questioned. "You took our scroll already."

Denisse shrugged. "I am not their boss. I am merely the snare. Whatever else they want from you is no business of mine."

"Denisse, have you no awareness of the stakes here?" Elfekot snapped. "If the Dijenuks die, we all die."

The woman scoffed. "Because it has to be them, huh?"

The group arrived at the goblins' encampment. Akin to Fort

Dijenuk, multiple clearings of the forest made space for its dwellers. Unlike Fort Dijenuk, the buildings were composed of bundled sticks and grass, shoddily held together by rope. Campfires dotted the site. Most of them were out, but the ones that were lit were being used to roast a kind of animal. Naturally, goblins occupied the space, and the couple dozen of them that they could see were focused on their own business until the three Restorers came into view. Red and orange beady eyes stared the trio down. Within seconds, a chorus of sneers, snarls, and growls rose into the otherwise dead air. Their short stature did little to hinder their intimidating, borderline frightening demeanor.

In the center, a slightly taller, more yellowed goblin in robes was waiting for them. Unlike the others, this goblin carried a staff. It smiled. "You have done well, Denisse," it said with its raspy voice. The ushers behind the Restorers shoved them to the ground in front of the robed goblin. "*These* are those Dijenuks that you humans always speak of?" it questioned.

"Thank you. Yes, these are the two Dijenuks. I am expectin' my payment now," Denisse said politely as she handed the goblin the boxed scroll.

"You will find a small bag in my quarters. But I warn you, Denisse. Never return again," the robed goblin warned.

Denisse smiled. "Of course not." She took a few steps to leave but stopped to stare at the prisoners she had brought, the three of them on their knees. Elfekot stared back.

"You can stop this."

"Oh, yes, I *can*, but I will not."

"They will kill us, Denisse. You have to understand that." He scowled. "Can you at least tell me why?"

She considered him for a moment, then shrugged. "I just want to get paid."

"Denisse—"

"You are just one man, Elfekot. I have learned to move on." With that, Denisse walked away.

David looked at the robed goblin in front of him. "What do you want from us?" he asked.

"Silence, manfilth!" it spat. It then pointed its staff at David's head. "It is taking me and my kind a great amount of effort not to kill you on the spot. I advise you, do not test our patience," it said. "Stay put." The robed goblin left, leaving a group of guards to watch over them.

"Are these goblins, Elfekot?" David whispered.

The captain nodded. "Aye. They are ferocious, barely civilized creatures. Nuisances, frankly. Few of them speak our tongue. I did not expect them interfering, nor did I expect Denisse's cooperation with them." He sighed. "And now I fear what they might do."

"What do they even want with the scroll?" Jay wondered. "Only one of them, the leader, can use magic." She furrowed her brows in thought. "There has to be some other value to the scroll. Unless…"

"Quiet over there!" shouted a goblin. He jabbed his spear at Jay, the sharpened rock inches from her face. Her expression remained neutral.

"A key weakness to goblins: they cannot hear very well," Elfekot muttered once the guard stepped away.

A few of the goblins began searching through a large sack that had been brought to the camp along with the Restorers. From it, they pulled out Elfekot's sword, Jay's spellbook, and their staves.

"Hey!" David shouted, struggling against his bindings. "Put that down! That's my mom's!"

The goblin that had taken David's staff walked up to the boy. It angrily stared him down for a seconds before smacking him across the face with the staff's metal section. It growled a few words of its own language before returning the staff to the bag, along with everything else. Another goblin took the bag and threw the entire thing into a nearby fire.

"No. No!" David screamed. He watched in horror as the flames engulfed the sack. "Elfekot, we have to do something!"

"Calm yourself, David," Jay said. "We need a plan."

"I am trying," said the captain. "Powerless as these goblins are, they can be overwhelming in numbers, especially against mages as untrained as you two."

"Well, it was *your* idea to give us less training and go to Hegortant right away," David said.

"Aye. We all make mistakes. Hm…" Elfekot studied his surroundings. "Perhaps if we—"

"That is enough!" a goblin growled. It shouted something incomprehensible to the trio at its fellow guards. The guards forced the Restorers back onto their feet and pulled them different directions, with two goblins on each of them.

"Hey!" David shouted. "Jay! Elfekot!"

"We said *quiet*, manfilth!" A goblin punched the boy in the stomach.

Elfekot did nothing but shake his head as he was taken away. Jay maintained her composure. David did all he could to fight against his escorts, but it was not enough. The Dijenuk was shoved through a leather flap that functioned as a door into a small interior. He was left alone.

There were no windows, but enough light came through the many tiny openings in the wall and around the makeshift door for David to see his surroundings. It was barren. There was no proper flooring, so David was lying on the dirt. It was soft and loose. Now that the fire was farther away, he could faintly smell meat instead of just burning wood. His stomach and right cheek ached from where he had been hit.

"*David,*" said a low, feminine voice.

"Huh? Jay?"

"*David,*" the voice repeated.

"*Wait, are you in my head, Jay?*"

"*Yes.*"

"*How?*"

"*Do you recall how we can sometimes sense each other's thoughts and feelings? I inferred that I could also directly communicate with you telepathically. It turns out, yes, I can.*"

"*Okay, but how?*"

"*I had to focus, primarily. We are both in a stressful*

154

situation, and you're scared for your life. It is under emotional distress that we tend to sense each other. So I sensed you, and from there I focused on sending over words. It is quite simple, really," Jay's voice explained.

"Woah, that's pretty cool. So, what now?"

"For once, I lack the answer. Do you see anything that could help?"

"I don't think so. It's empty in here."

"Likewise here. Hm. I have an idea."

"You do? That was quick. What is it? ... Jay? Hello?" There was no answer. *"Jay!"*

David rolled around, searching about once more. A few of the sticks and pieces of wood that composed the crude construction jutted out. David scanned the wall and found the sharpest stick end within reach. The boy then used a combination of the wall and his sheer strength to stand himself up. He had no idea as to the strength of his bindings, but all he could do was try as he used the sharp piece of wood to cut the thin rope.

"Come on. Ow!"

He pricked himself a few times. Eventually, the bindings released themselves. David shook them off and stretched his hands and fingers. Before David could do anything else, footsteps approached. The boy dropped back to the floor, hiding both his hands and the cut rope underneath him. A figure was thrown through the leather flap into the tiny interior with him.

"Ugh…"

"Jay? What happened?"

The girl rolled around to lie on her back. "It is quite clear that they need us alive for right now. As such, I convinced them that if I was not physically close to you, I would die, seeing as we're Dijenuk siblings. You know, magical connections and all that rubbish."

"How did you manage that?"

"They are not very intelligent creatures compared to us and especially me. That can be assumed through their technology and infrastructure. Although I do admit that splitting us up was a surprisingly smart move. Relatively speaking, of course. Regardless, their knowledge of magic is even more limited. There was little difficulty in the lie," she explained. "Now, we must find a way to free ourselves."

"Already done," David said as he stood up. He showed Jay his hands.

"Oh."

"See these pointy bits here? I used them to cut the rope."

"Ah. Well, I must confess, that is quite crafty of you," Jay said. "Now, would you mind helping me?"

"Oh yeah, right. Um…" David broke the sharp piece off the wall. "Sit up." He violently poked at the rope.

"Be careful."

"I know, I know. It just takes a few jabs like that. And… there!"

Jay stood as she stretched her hands. "Excellent. As for what to do next…" She carefully peeked through the leather flap. "I believe it would be wise to first acquire our staves back."

"But," David swallowed, "they burned them."

Jay shook her head. "Do you really believe that these magical tools are flammable? We live in a world where a decent chunk of the population can cast fire magic. That includes us. I would be surprised if such things could catch on fire. When we were being split up, I looked back one more time. Our staves seemed to be intact." She peeked through the makeshift door. "And they are still there."

David perked up. "Really?"

"Yes. As I told you, these creatures are not the most intelligent. Now, I have very little confidence in our combat abilities. We would have to sneak past and grab them. Only then would we have a chance. After that, we get the scroll back."

"What about Elfekot?"

"We will find him *after* we reacquire the scroll."

"Or we get him *first*. He's way stronger than us, Jay. Plus, he's our friend."

Jay scoffed. "That's not the word I would use."

"Oh, right, because you don't trust anyone. Because the great Jay Dijenuk can't afford to have any friends," David mocked.

"If you want to find Elfekot so badly, then go for it. *I* will go find the scroll."

"You wanna split up? Isn't that what gets people killed in movies?"

"This isn't a movie, David."

"It sure feels like it, though…" David searched around, as

though looking for hidden cameras. "What do we do, then?"

"We know from Elfekot that they cannot hear very well. Our stealth attempt could work if there is a distraction..." Jay pondered, her right arm crossed and the other's elbow resting vertically on top of it. "I will use a spell to create a distraction. We run and grab our belongings. From there, I will find the scroll, and you will free Elfekot," she said.

"Well, how we do even know where the scroll is? Or Elfekot?"

"I saw where they took him. He is in a shack similar to ours. Look for a leather drying rack opposite of here. It is to the left of it."

"Gotcha."

"As for the scroll, I must simply seek the nicest-looking dwelling. That is where the leader lives. It, or *he*, took the scroll. I am not quite sure as to how gender works with non-human alien creatures. It is likely to be similar, but how is one certain?" she wondered aloud.

"This plan still feels sketchy. We still have to sprint a decent ways. The distraction probably won't even work on all of 'em," David said.

Jay nodded. "Fair point. Hm. I got it. But first..." She pulled back the leather flap ever so slightly. She turned her palm outwards and stared directly at the collection of items sitting in the embers. "*Téléneh hrâa!*" she whispered as she held her amulet.

In an instant, three staves and a longsword appeared within

their confined chamber. The staves emitted smoke, clearly unharmed by the flames, but the sword was now glowing red from the heat.

"I got it," Jay said. "*Gelisté!*"

The objects burst into flames.

"Uh, *gelisté!*"

The flames were extinguished, and the red glow on the sword was gone.

"Yikes." David bent down and hovered his hand over his staff. "Are they all safe to touch?"

"They are now."

David tentatively picked up their staves. He handed over Jay's. "Sorry about your spellbook."

"I no longer need it, anyway."

"I guess I gotta take this to him, yeah?" he said as he stared at Elfekot's own plain staff and sword. The boy placed the other staff in his leather chest strap and then picked up the blade. "Jeez, this is heavier than I thought it was. How does Elfekot carry this around all day?" He did his best to fit the sword into his belt. "This is, uh, dangerous."

"Are you ready? I'm about to speak the incantation."

"I'm ready enough. What are you gonna do, exactly?"

"I'm going to create fake battle sounds."

"Woah."

"Such a spell, from what I read, appears to be quite difficult, and I already feel myself worn out a little. Give me a few seconds to concentrate." Jay closed her eyes and put a hand on her amulet. "*Krihté tiweh auxi!*"

A golf-ball-sized sphere of silver energy appeared in front of Jay, but only for an instant, as it immediately exploded, sending the girl into the wall.

"Jay!" David ran to her.

She gasped. "That... was a backfire," she grunted.

"Can you stand?"

Jay attempted, but fell back down and kneeled. "I just... urgh, need a few seconds."

David took a peek outside. "Are you good now?"

Jay let out a breath. "Yes. I'll try the spell again."

"What? You can't! You'll just hurt yourself again."

"It is none of your–"

"It *is* my concern, sis." David peeked through the leather flap again and pointed his staff through it. He aimed it at the flimsy watchtower in the distance. It was a wooden platform held up on stilts with a ladder. "I have my own idea. Ready?"

"Yes."

After a few moments of concentrating, David fired. The magical projectile struck one of the stilts, collapsing the entire structure. It was followed by footsteps and a chorus of yelling.

David scanned the immediate area. "And... go!"

The siblings sprinted towards their destination. The goblins had all taken to arms and charged at the source of the noise that emerged from the opposite side of the camp. Their path was clear. Within seconds, David reached the shack that Jay had described. He leaped inside.

"David?"

"Hey!" As expected, Elfekot was lying on the dirt with his hands tied behind his back.

"Was all that noise you?"

"Yeah. I knocked something down. Jay's free, too, and she's going to get the scroll back."

"Really? How?"

"We can talk about it later. Can you sit up?"

"…Is that my sword?"

"Er, yeah. I'll give it back! Just… hold on." With Elfekot's own weapon, David easily cut through his bindings. "Wow, this thing is sharp. Oh, here's your staff, too."

"Thank you. I admit, I am impressed. I had almost lost hope."

"Already? Come on, Elfekot. If we have no hope in our own selves, what *do* we have?"

"Bitter reality."

David took a careful look outside. "Do you think Jay's okay?"

≺○≻

While David had gone to rescue Elfekot, Jay was searching for where the leading goblin resided. She spotted a building larger than the others, with actual windows and much more solid wooden walls. The girl bolted towards that one, not daring to check if she had been spotted. She opened the door and shut it behind herself as quickly as she could. Jay exhaled in relief before taking in her surroundings.

Unlike the place where she had been briefly taken prisoner, this interior was furnished, albeit barely. There was a table, a few chairs, a rough-looking bed and its bedside table, and even rugs, all of them primitive in their build quality. By the bedside table, a woman was fiddling with the lock of a small chest.

"Denisse?"

"Huh?!"

Jay pointed her staff and tensed her arm as she concentrated. Denisse acted first and fired a bolt of energy at Jay's legs. Jay let out a shriek of pain as she fell to the ground. Denisse sprinted for Jay's staff, but Jay leaped forward and swung her fist across the woman's face. As Denisse stumbled back, Jay did her best to ignore the feeling of satisfaction that came from the strike.

The both of them pointed their staves at each other, eyes locked. Denisse's lips curled into a devilish smile. "Be careful with how you point that thing. Someone could get badly hurt."

Jay narrowed her eyes. *I have to at least pretend like I know what I'm doing, or she'll just run right past me*, she thought. "What are you still doing here?"

"I am merely trying to *borrow* some gold from Tintla, the robed fellow. He gave me less than promised, the prick. He—"

"We can help each other out, then," Jay said quickly. She readjusted the grip on her staff. "We don't have to do this."

"Oh? In a rush, Miss Dijenuk?"

"I need you to distract the goblins. In exchange, I will open the chest for you."

Denisse took a moment to consider. "Deal."

Jay cautiously approached the woman as she kept her staff pointed at her. Once close enough, Jay took Denisse's staff and tossed it to the other side of the interior. She hovered her hand over the lock of the chest. Not wanting to put her staff away, she channeled its energy for the spell instead of her amulet like usual.

"*Aperta eht wesya.*"

The box clicked. Denisse opened and closed it so fast that Jay couldn't see its contents. "Thank you, sweetie." She headed towards the door. "You know, honey, you did not 'let me go' like you thought you did. Yer hardly threatenin'. But yer lucky I like you." She took her staff and exited.

As soon as she left, Jay snatched the small, polished box from atop the table. She opened it. The Scroll of Gales sat inside, and she let out a breath. The box could barely fit in one hand, so Jay put it back where she found it and stuffed the scroll down a jean pocket.

It's a good thing these are boys' jeans.

She peeked out the window. The goblins had returned to their positions. Judging from their behavior, Jay guessed that they hadn't realized that their prisoners had escaped. Something knocked on the back window. She turned to find David's face on the other side.

"Did I scare you?" asked David's muffled voice.

"I have the scroll," Jay informed him as she walked closer.

"And I have Elfekot. Mission accomplished!"

Someone shushed. Jay assumed it was Elfekot. "We need to depart, but there are too many goblins if I try the door."

"Can you open the window?" David asked.

Jay searched for a latch and tried pushing the glass, but to no avail. "No."

"Darn. Hm… What if you break the glass at the same time I make a distraction? Then no one can hear it, yeah?"

"It depends. What kind of distraction?"

"You'll see. Elfekot, can you break the glass, actually? Okay, Jay. Take a few steps either direction. Here we go." David aimed his staff at a distant tree trunk and fired. *Bang!* At the same time, Elfekot blew the window open. "Hurry!" the boy said.

Again, with the help of her brother, Jay crawled through the broken window, doing her best not to cut herself on the fragments. From the back of the small building, they were concealed from most of the camp, seeing as they were on the edge of the settlement. Jay couldn't help but feel a sense of relief upon seeing David and Elfekot next to her. Her muscles even eased a bit.

"Good job. Genuinely," she said.

Elfekot shook his head. "This was too close. Even now, the goblins must know that something is up. Let us run and gain distance. We can figure out directions later."

David nodded. "You have the scroll, yeah?"

"I do. It's in my pocket."

"A'ight. Let's dip."

"Hold on." Jay's brain pounded against her skull. She leaned against a tree. "My head… it hurts. Ugh. I think I'm dizzy, too."

"What's wrong?" David asked.

"That is an effect of overexerting yourself with magic," Elfekot clarified.

"I barely used any."

"I know. Come on. We cannot waste time. At any moment, they could—"

Numerous growls and screeches pierced the air. The Restorers jerked their heads to look behind them. About a dozen goblins were charging towards the trio.

"Crap!" David yelled.

"Run. Now!" Elfekot said. He fired a single blast behind him, hoping it landed as the Restorers bolted through the woods.

The Restorers dared not glance behind them as they sprinted, hoping the difference in leg length could give them enough distance. They did their best to dodge branches and avoid tripping over roots and small boulders. Twigs crunched underneath them. Their swift strides contrasted the pitter-patter of the goblins' feet. The goblins kept hurling both furious snarls and slung rocks as the Restorers panted. Jay's breathing was the most strained of all. As they ran, David made sure that she wasn't falling behind.

"You got this!" he told her.

Her legs were killing her, but it at least distracted her from the pain in her head. *I either keep pushing it, or I die,* she thought.

A projectile rock struck Elfekot in the back of the leg. He fell to the ground. "Just keep going! I can take care of myself."

"I'm not leaving without you!" David said.

"David!" Jay pulled at her brother's arm to get him to continue. "Let's go, you idiot. It pains me to admit it, but I need you alive."

Elfekot slammed his staff into the ground. The goblins were knocked back by an invisible force, but they continued their charge. The gap between them was closing. Elfekot was blasting down as many as he could. Jay kept pulling.

"Jay, stop!"

As Jay struggled, her feet tripped over a rock. She fell right down, taking David with her. The siblings tumbled down a steep hill, through bushes, over rocks, and between the trees. They landed in a shallow river at the bottom.

"Ugh..." Their bodies ached where the ground and shrubbery had bruised them as they fell. Something in the sky caught David's attention. "Oh, crap."

Tendrils of darkness swirled through the air above the forest. They spun around the siblings a few times, circling like vultures. They then flew straight down, landing in the body of water meters away from the Dijenuks. The dark clouds dissipated, revealing well over a dozen human soldiers dressed in blacks, browns, and navy blues. They each held a staff.

In front of them all was a man in unique attire. He wasn't the man from yesterday named Istra, but his dark robes with the combined metal chestplate were similar. An amulet similar to

Jay's hung around his neck, and he wore a single, small black jewel as an earring on his left ear.

He was tall and slim, with wavy black hair and large, almond-shaped eyes. The sharp, angular features of his face added to the intensity with which he stared the siblings down. His irises were so dark that they resembled black coffee.

"This is the end, Dijenuks," said the man. His smooth, baritone voice was calm and unwavering. His thick, straight eyebrows lowered. "What are your names?"

David took a step forward, obscuring his sister. "Why do you wanna know?"

"It is... tradition, one could say. It serves as a reminder."

"Reminder of what?"

"Why do you want to know?" the man replied.

Tradition... she thought. "Who are you?"

"I believe you have heard of me. I am King Landor."

CHAPTER VIII:
A RUSH TO LIFE

EVERYTHING STOOD STILL as the Dijenuk siblings and King Landor stared each other down. His soldiers remained behind him, ready to attack at any second. The goblins had finally caught up with them. They positioned themselves around the stream, not daring to interfere with whatever Landor had planned.

"You're... you're *him?*" David said. His heart pounded against his chest, and his fist clenched. "You killed them!"

Landor leaned on his staff and smiled. The smile did not reach his eyes. "I daresay, I am impressed, Dijenuks. You managed to escape. Although, considering the intelligence of these brute creatures, it is not so surprising. It is a bit concerning that I managed to arrive just in time. These savages could not even hold you for mere fractions. I will deal with them after I deal with you two." His smile faded. "Raise your staves, Dijenuks. It is time."

David entered a readied stance. "Time for what?"

"To die, obviously. But I will make it as fair as I can. We shall have a proper fight. Just the three of us. It has been oh-so-long since I have had the thrill of a decent battle. Your parents did pretty well, all things considered."

David raised his staff. His teeth gritted. "You are acting way too confident for a guy who brought a bunch of back-up."

"You never know what could happen when you are dealing with goblins. Before we begin… I believe I asked a question earlier."

"What?"

"What are your names?"

"David," he replied after a moment of hesitation.

"Jay."

"David and Jay… Huh." The king looked around the area a little more. "Say, where are your fellow companions? Have the Restorers already lost?"

At this, David searched around. "Elfekot!" he called.

"Up here, manfilth!" yelled a goblin.

To David's left, atop the hill from which the siblings had fallen, Elfekot was ensnared in a net hanging from a tree branch. His eyes were closed.

"Elfekot!" David called again. The captain remained still. The boy spun around slowly, taking in the number of hostiles that had surrounded him and his sister. The goblins kept snarling. The soldiers had become stoic and silent. His attention turned back to Landor. "We already figured this out, Landor. You set up this entire thing with *The Legends* and the curse just so you could have a shot at us. That seems pretty pathetic and desperate to me."

King Landor scoffed. "You lack any idea as to what is really going on, Dijenuk. You see, I was magically banished from

Terra a long time ago," he said with a bitter tone. "And there are… other circumstances." He sneered. "The real pathetic and desperate ones were your parents, who decided to run away, unable to swallow the pride of losing here on Elektia in full display."

An angry heat ran through David's blood. "If you wanna fight, let's fight!"

Without any further hesitation, David fired a bolt of white energy from his staff. Landor quickly raised his own. A translucent shield of the same energy appeared in front of him. The projectile collided with the shield. An alien-like ring emanated from the impact. Landor lowered his staff, bringing down the shield. The corners of his mouth lifted ever so slightly.

David pulled back his arm, ready to fire again, but Landor acted faster. With a twirl of his staff, the king fired back. The projectile hit the boy in his leg, and he toppled over. "Ugh…" His right shin throbbed with immense pain.

Jay, who had her own staff pointed at Landor the entire time, finally managed to fire a blast of energy. He moved his torso and dodged it.

King Landor slammed his staff into the ground. Coils of dark energy rose from the bottom of it. They slowly swirled around Landor. He thrust both his arms forward, and the coils followed suit. The energy wrapped itself around Jay like snakes. The girl watched in horror as she was lifted into the air. She then shut her eyes tight, waiting for the end to come. Her body temperature dropped as her skin chilled. Her heart rate slowed. But nothing

170

else happened.

Jay opened her eyes. Landor had been slowly twirling his staff. His eyes were large, and his mouth was agape. David, still on the ground, tried to land a hit, but Landor evaded it, even while he was concentrating on Jay. The king closed his mouth to grit his teeth. Jay's mind flipped through all the spells she had read through. The cold was worsening.

As Jay shivered, a memory echoed in her headspace. It was one of comfort and a pretty girl with black hair and a glowing smile.

Jay clenched her left fist. The smell of pinecones touched the air. Her body suddenly became warmer. She tried moving her left hand to her amulet, but the grip that Landor's magic had on her was too strong. The warmth in her body turned into a familiar kind of buzz.

"*Cintria excata!*"

Jay's eyes flashed green as a burst of light of the same color erupted from her body. Every single man, woman, and goblin in the vicinity rocketed backwards several meters. The water in the stream erupted, and the trees bent. Landor skidded across the river and through his own soldiers. His staff flew out of his hands, the dark bindings around Jay dissipated, and she fell back down.

She grabbed David by his arm and pointed a finger gun to the side of her head. "*Téléneh!*"

A red light flowed through her veins, glowing from underneath her skin. The lights met at her pointing fingertips and erupted through her skull, creating a brilliant flash of red.

The siblings vanished, and reappeared elsewhere in the forest. Jay's entire body ached, and the dizzy feeling from earlier had returned. Her legs finally gave out, and she toppled forwards, landing on her hands and knees. A burning sensation ran up her chest, and she coughed, blood spewing onto the dirt.

"Jay!" David pulled the girl by the arm and led her behind a tree and into a large bush. "I saw 'em. We gotta hide for now. Are you alright?"

The girl's face wore discomfort as the shrubbery brushed her skin. She closed her eyes and let the dizziness pass. "I didn't have the amulet for that spell…" Her voice was strained. "But I had to take your idiotic self with me."

"Aw… uh, thanks?" David replied. "How did you manage that, though? And what was that crazy green spell?"

Jay shook her head. "Later. For now, just listen for them."

Less than a minute later, several people and goblins yelled, and footsteps scattered. The sounds neared. Their bodies tensed as they watched both goblins and Landor's soldiers run past them.

"We have to go back for Elfekot," David whispered.

"No. We must return to either Hegortant or Fort Dijenuk and acquire assistance. Attempting rescue on our own is futile."

"This again… We need him, sis."

"We just need the… Wait, the scroll is gone."

"You lost it?!"

"I must have dropped it when we fell."

"How? It was in your pocket."

"It was loose in there, and it was a rough fall."

"For as smart as you are, you can be real dumb sometimes. Come on, we *have* to go back now."

Jay exhaled. "Fine." She stood. "Judging from where the sounds came from, Elfekot and the scroll should be back that way. *Andiamo.*"

Keeping themselves low, the siblings traversed back to where they'd come from. They frequently stopped and listened as they repeatedly glanced behind them. They cringed upon each step on a twig. After a couple of minutes, the Dijenuks reached the shallow river. The area was devoid of both goblins and people, except for one.

"Elfekot!" David called out. The captain was still in his net, hanging from a tree branch. The boy ran towards him.

"David, no, wait!" Jay hissed.

"Just as predicted. They are here!" screamed a voice. "Someone get His Majesty!"

"David, you idiot!" Elfekot said.

Numerous soldiers and a few goblins sprinted down from atop the slope. The siblings watched in dismay as they were surrounded once more.

"We lost," Jay said.

David gritted his teeth and held out his staff. "Not without a fight."

Just then, before the soldiers could gain much ground, a spear flew through the air and above their heads. It sliced through the rope on Elfekot's net. He fell down and rolled, breaking his fall. A split-second later, a projectile of energy landed in the middle of the soldiers. The projectile exploded, sending them all flying. David, Jay, and Elfekot turned to the source.

A girl about David and Jay's age dropped down from a tree branch a few meters to their right. She was almost as tall as Jay, with a darker skin tone, blazing red hair nearly down to her waist, and orange-red eyes. Her beige, turtleneck cloth shirt was short-sleeved, revealing her arm muscles, and her light-brown pants were rolled up. A red piece of cloth was tied around her waist, with a portion of it hanging down her front. As she slowly rose from her landing, they could see her triumphant smile. She ran to Elfekot.

"Who are you?" he asked as he picked up his sword from the ground. David and Jay had neared.

The girl effortlessly climbed up the tree and retrieved her spear from the trunk she had stuck it in. "I am Angela, the fourth Restorer of the Elements," she announced. "We need to run. Now."

"Huh?" exclaimed the trio, now regrouped.

Jay was relieved to find the scroll at the base of a tree, essentially hidden from view. She stuffed it back into her pocket. The soldiers had just gotten back up, still groaning and aching.

"Yes, let's run," she said.

The four of them dashed away, with the girl named Angela taking the lead. The water splashed at every footstep. Chunks of wood cracked and flew off its trunk as magical projectiles whizzed just past them. They followed Angela downhill.

"You did a magic thingy and knocked them all down. Can you do it again?" asked David as they ran.

Angela shook her head. "Probably not. That alone took a lot out of me."

It wasn't long until clouds of darkness zoomed over their heads. Just like before, the missiles of dark energy landed in front of them. From it, King Landor and his soldiers emerged. The Restorers and Angela turned to run a different direction, but a platoon of goblins blocked their path. They were trapped again.

"It is as I said. It is time for you to die," said Landor with gritted teeth.

"Jay—"

"I *can't*, David." Jay lowered her staff, recognizing the pointlessness of it all. She looked at the goblins before her. "You all are just slaves to him."

The goblins snarled.

Jay shook her head. "If I am to read the situation correctly, then Landor hired you all, yes? And your leader, in turn, hired Denisse. She got a reward, but what about the rest of you? Will you all be similarly rewarded? What has Landor promised you?"

No one answered, at least not in a language Jay could understand.

"Exactly. Do you not see what is going on here?" she continued. "You are all being manipulated. Why? What has driven you to work for Landor? It is fear. Fear of the 'almighty king of darkness.' Pathetic. If he were so fearsome and so powerful, he wouldn't need you to do his dirty work. Or perhaps it is because you share a common enemy. So you work for humans to harm humans. Does that really benefit you?"

"That is *enough*, girl!" Landor snarled. He thrust his staff forward and sent coils of dark energy. Jay caught the coils with her left arm and let them wrap around it. A chill went up that arm.

"My sister and I ain't even from this planet," David said. "We have no hate towards you guys, and you attack us, anyway. It's what you were bred to do, huh? Hate and attack humans." As he spoke, he turned around to look each goblin in the eye. "But there's more to life than that."

"Attack!" Landor shouted.

His soldiers fired a volley of energy blasts, but Angela and Elfekot each raised a barrier, blocking the shots. The goblins took a step forward.

"Stop!" David made no movements, despite their advancement. "You're better than this. Quit living for mindless violence."

"And start to live for *yourselves*," Jay added. "Evolve."

The goblins looked at themselves, muttering something.

David faced Landor. "And take down those that manipulate you and rob you of your freedom. Landor can be fought, and even defeated. You can be free from the hatred…" He looked back to the goblins. "So do something about it and fight!"

All at once, the goblins charged forward. They ran through

the group of the four in the center and took their aggression to Landor's forces. The king raised his staff. Before he could do anything, several rocks pelted him to the ground. The goblins had completely overwhelmed the magical soldiers. The Restorers and Angela nodded at each other and quietly sprinted away.

Their trek continued to take them downhill. Not a single word was said as they scurried forth. Over time, the sounds of battle faded away. Constant glances backwards and above confirmed that they had finally lost Landor. The thin, lifeless state of the trees allowed for easy navigation through the dying woods.

The sun still shined over them when they at last found themselves at the edge of the forest. Grassy plains, shining like emeralds, sprawled out before them. There was a thin, misty veil over it now. They could identify another forest near the horizon as Fort Dijenuk. Nearer were large stone walls and the grey city within it.

"Hegortant!" David said. "We were this close the whole time?"

"I did not even know that there was a goblin settlement anywhere near a human one," Elfekot admitted. "I shall make sure that the Hegortant guards know." He turned to face Angela. "Are you really the fourth Restorer?"

The girl smiled and nodded. "I indeed am. Once I had discovered that you three had set out to Hegortant, I followed. Unfortunately, they would not let me in the city, so I set up camp a decent distance away and waited for you. Eventually, I found you! But instead of seeing you exit Hegortant, I saw you all tied up in a wagon at the edge of these very woods. I followed once more. When I finally saw the perfect opportunity to strike and rescue you all, I took it!" Angela's words were quick. It wasn't as though she were hurried, but as if she were overwhelmingly excited.

"And you know you're the fourth Restorer?" David questioned.

"I do. Have you not read the prophecy?"

David frowned. "We haven't, actually…"

"We can confirm whether or not you belong to the prophecy later," Elfekot said. "For now, we need to get the scroll and ourselves someplace safe. Once we reach Hegortant, we can discuss and debrief to our heart's content. Understood?"

"Yes," said David and Angela. Jay remained silent. She was leaning against a tree, catching her breath.

The group set out once more, exiting the colorless woods and making their way across the virid field.

"Do you guys hear that?" asked David.

They had barely taken a few steps when faint rustling could be heard in the distance. Within seconds, the rustling was joined by footsteps. The group stopped in their tracks and turned to look behind them. The noises grew louder. The footsteps were not of one thing but of many. The source of the noise came into view. A stampede of small creatures with skin ranging from green to yellow to orange raged towards them.

David squinted. "Goblins?"

Elfekot drew his staff. "Worse, David. Razas. Run. Now!"

"Again…" said a drained, exasperated Jay.

Once more, the group sprinted for their lives. David again made sure that his sister didn't fall behind. The stampede neared. The siblings glanced behind them. The creatures were most certainly not goblins. These were even smaller and completely uncivilized. They charged at the group on four legs. Their eyes were tiny, black dots, but their mouths, surrounded by thick lips, were large. Instead of defined heads, torsos, and necks, they had one singular body mass with four legs beneath them. There were too many of them to count.

"What are they?!" David asked.

"Razas," Elfekot repeated. "If you let a single one near you, it will tear you apart with its teeth alone. We must have gotten too close to one of their nests."

He held his staff out, letting an orb of white energy charge at the tip. A few seconds later, he fired it behind him. The energy exploded, sending razas flying. The horde barely slowed. Elfekot switched his staff to his other hand instead. He charged another orb of energy, but this time he did it in his palm. He crushed the orb and yelled an incantation.

"*Despré kris!*"

The air around them warped and bended. David, Angela, and Jay felt a significant portion of their exhaustion lift. A low warmth channeled through their veins. Angela, now reinvigorated, fired another exploding orb at the razas behind them, although it was smaller than the one previous.

"Losing them is impossible!" Angela yelled. "They are catching up!"

"Then we keep running!" Elfekot said.

Just seconds later, the creatures were now a mere fifty or so meters behind their scrambling feet. The difference only grew smaller. One of the razas leaped. In that single bound, it crossed the land between and descended upon the group. Elfekot spun. With a single swing of his blade, he sliced the midair raza in half. A second one jumped. Elfekot split that one in half, too. The third one that leaped was shot down by Angela. David joined in, firing down another leaping raza.

Despite their ability to take the creatures down in the air, the razas continued to close the distance. The frequency at which the razas launched themselves rapidly increased.

"When I count to three, stop running!" Elfekot ordered as he cleaved another raza.

"Huh?" David and Jay said.

"Just do it. One… two…" A larger group of razas leaped towards them all at once. "Three!" Elfekot slammed his staff into the ground. A pale-blue, translucent dome manifested itself around the four of them. The leaping razas slammed into it.

"Wicked," David said in awe.

The siblings watched one of the razas in horror as it opened its jaws. The entirety of its cavernous mouth cavity was lined with razor-sharp teeth. Its thick, long tongue slid out through its lips. The stiff muscle was also nearly completely covered in teeth. The repulsing tongue spun and tried to penetrate the dome like a drill.

"Angela, do you know the signal?" asked Elfekot, his voice labored.

The girl nodded. She raised her staff into the air. *"Distan."*

A dark-orange projectile fired into the atmosphere. It exploded in the sky like a firework. Despite the time of day, it managed to cast a red glow all across the plains.

"Hegortant should be sending help now," Elfekot said as the razas continued to assault the protective dome.

"Can you hold it until then?" David asked.

The captain shook his head. "Likely not. Soon we will need to run again."

"Just running from these things is hopeless," Angela lamented. "We are surrounded! We will be torn to shreds in seconds."

"Do we have anything better?" Elfekot questioned, his tone low.

"There has to be something we can do… right?" David said.

The razas continued to slam themselves against the bubble and attempt to break it with their weaponized tongues. They were relentless. As the pressure increased, Elfekot appeared visibly strained. He gritted his teeth. The dome gradually grew smaller, giving the four less and less room.

"I got it," Jay said. She stood straighter and placed her left hand on her amulet. "On the count of three, release the dome and run. I have a couple of spells in mind."

"Are you sure, sis? Don't strain yourself," David said.

"Ready, everyone?" Jay asked.

They nodded.

"One… two…" Jay raised her right hand slightly. "Three!"

Elfekot lifted his staff. The dome vanished. The razas leaped.

"*Téléneh nostro!*"

The four of them briefly flashed a red color as they vanished. They immediately reappeared a few meters away. The razas collided with themselves. The creatures scrambled to get back up. Without hesitation, they continued their charge.

"*Klebé eht siin!*"

The razas suddenly stopped, as though they had run into a wall, but there was nothing there. They clawed and bit at the invisible barrier, unable to get any closer.

Jay's head pounded again. "I said run!"

The group, which had taken a few seconds to see what Jay had done, sprinted off at once. With Elfekot leading, they moved as fast as they could to the road in the distance.

"How long is that gonna last?" David asked.

"Long enough, I hope."

"Very comforting."

The sound of snarls and scurrying feet neared once again. Despite the pains and aches in their legs, despite the burning in their lungs, they kept running. They had finally reached the road. Hegortant drew closer, as did the razas.

David took a quick glance to his six o'clock. The feral creatures were nearly in leaping range. "Guys…!"

"We know, David!" Elfekot said. He drew his staff and turned to aim. He lowered it. It was futile. The captain switched to his sword just in time as the razas bounded towards them.

"We're dead, we're dead, we're dead!" David repeated.

"Not yet!" Angela said as she panted.

David took a peek behind him once more. A raza was flying directly towards his face. He drew his staff. But nothing happened. His body was near its limits. The boy closed his eyes. He heard the shriek of a raza, and he opened his eyes.

An arrow had struck the monster. David faced his front. Over a dozen men in chainmail armor stood upon the hill in front of him. Half of them carried bows and arrows. They readied another volley.

"Duck!" one of them yelled.

They released their arrows and took down another chunk of the horde. Two of them, carrying staves, stepped forth past the running Restorers. Together they created a large magical shield, like Elfekot had done, blocking the road. The group collapsed.

"We're saved..." David wheezed. Despite being involved in athletics for years, he had reached immense exhaustion.

"That was... horrendous," Angela said. "Although... exciting!"

Jay clutched at her sides, blood dripping down her nose. "This is why we can't trust anyone."

The remaining guards helped the Restorers stand back up. "You are the Restorers, yes?"

"Unfortunately," Elfekot said.

"It is an honor to be of service to you all, the Dijenuk especially."

"Thank you," David responded. "That was brutal. You really saved our butts. Oh, and she's a Dijenuk, too. She's my sis."

The guards looked at each other with raised brows. "Two?"

The Restorers turned around and watched for a few seconds as the razas were driven back. While many were slain, others finally turned around and scuttled away.

"It has been a while since razas came this close to Hegortant. These are truly interesting times," a guard said.

"'Interesting' is one way to put it…" Elfekot replied. He looked to his blade and grimaced at the guts covering it.

"Shall we escort you back inside the city?" asked a guard politely.

David let out a breath of relief. "Yes, please."

≺o≻

"This is ridiculous," Jay spat.

The group had been taken to a tavern. It was not the Goblin-Ear Inn from before, but a somewhat-shabbier establishment titled *Hegortant's Choice*. The colors were less warm and the woods were of an inferior quality. The bartender was a miserable-looking old man. The place also seemed to serve as a general store, although its shelves were nearly empty. The four of them sat around a circular table. Upon the table were four freshly-emptied plates. Their meager meals—cubes of plain poultry and cold, light-green plants resembling vegetables—

were just enough to satisfy their demanding stomachs. Aside from them, the tavern was barren of patrons.

"What is?" David asked.

"We get tricked and betrayed by a bartender whom Elfekot claimed we *had* to trust, we get captured by goblins, we are forced to fight and escape King Landor himself, and we nearly get mauled by a horde of ferocious monsters. All for what? *One* scroll? Yes, all that was for *one* key out of the *three* we need to enter *one* of the chambers. And I am here throwing my life away, throwing away *everything* I worked for, all because someone cursed a book for reasons unexplained. And that is not the only thing without answers, oh, no. I could question a hundred different things right now and all I would get is vague responses and lies!" The irises of her eyes flared green as she slammed the table. The wood underneath her palm split.

"There it is again! The green!" David pointed out.

"Huh? Green?"

"Yeah, it happened earlier."

"Please elaborate."

"Back in those woods, when we were fighting Landor, or trying to, you did a spell. And your eyes, like, *glowed* when you did it."

Jay leaned back in her chair as she recalled the event. Elfekot and Angela, intrigued, leaned forward. "The spell I casted was an enemy repel. A projectile would knock the target back and inflict a decent amount of pain. But what happened was clearly more."

"Yeah, it was like an explosion! It was nuts. I'm impressed, sis. And hey, it looks like you *can* get angry."

"I'm not."

"Whatever it is," Elfekot said, "I am afraid I do not know what you speak of."

"Neither do I," Angela admitted.

"Of course," Jay muttered.

David turned in his chair to face the girl. "So you're really one of us? 'Cause it's kinda suspicious."

"I indeed am. What is so suspicious?"

"I mean, you kinda just came out of nowhere."

"I promise you, there is nothing to be wary of. I know a great deal about the prophecy and I know, like Elfekot, that I belong to this quest. It is a common story here in Elektia, Dijenuk. Many already know of the heroes who must save our people."

David shrugged. "I guess that makes sense. Well, it is nice to meet you, Angela…?"

"Angela Fryner," she finished.

"I'm David. And uh, she's Jay."

"It is an honor to meet you, Master Dijenuk."

"Master?"

"The eldest Dijenuk is traditionally referred to by that title," Elfekot explained.

"Oh. Weird," David said.

"I am Elfekot. Although I trust you already knew that."

David looked at the two of them. "Wait…"

"I am also from Fort Dijenuk," Angela clarified.

"Oh. Well, that's convenient. And if I had to guess… you're a fire mage?"

"Yes!" Angela answered. Her proud smile then faded. "Well, I was. The curse took our lives from us, Master Dijenuk."

"Just 'David' is fine."

"Are you sure? I have never met a Dijenuk before—well, most people have not—and I do not wish to be disrespectful." Her voice lowered. "And… Jay, was it? She really is a Dijenuk, too?"

"Yup," David said.

"Huh. A pleasant surprise, I suppose. Her hair is rather short, I have noticed, as is yours."

"As much as I would love to have the additional company," Elfekot began sarcastically, "we cannot simply take your word as to whether or not you belong with us. You need proof."

"Speak for yourself, Elfekot," David said. "And don't you know the prophecy yourself?"

"Yes. Somewhat. But, like I said before, it is fragmented. There are also copies, some more… paraphrased than others. The true, complete original is gone. No one knows the entire thing."

"But I know something else," said Angela. She pulled from a pocket a rolled piece of parchment. It was torn; the text was faded and barely readable. Elfekot took it and read it aloud.

"'A young, female fire mage residing in Fort Dijenuk with orange-red eyes and red hair.'" He looked back to Angela, wearing skepticism. "You could have faked this."

"It is not faked. The piece will line up exactly with the tear in the original document. You may go to Light's Authority and see for yourself. I am sure they would let you," Angela argued.

Elfekot sighed. "If that is true…"

"It *is*."

"Guys, I'm confused," David said.

"We have one large fragment of the original prophecy secured in the capitol building," Elfekot explained. "However, no one is allowed to see it, nor its copy. Most commoners like myself only know about the first three: You, me, and Jay. The piece Angela presents is the description of another Restorer: herself."

"Oh," David realized.

Elfekot dropped his voice. "You *kept* this?!"

"Er, yes."

"For how long?"

Angela bit her lip. "A while."

"And no one knew about it?"

"It was in my family's possession!"

Elfekot tapped his fingers on the table. "Assuming that piece lines up with the larger fragment," he said after a few seconds, "then you are indeed the fourth Restorer, Angela."

She smiled. "Of course."

"Are there more? More Restorers, I mean," David asked.

"No," Angela answered right away.

"*Maybe*," Elfekot corrected. "No one really knows for sure. We may find another piece. Or maybe not."

"Regardless," said Angela, "we must swiftly find the other Scrolls."

David looked to the green scroll on the table. "Unless Landor found them first. Hm. Does anyone have any ideas?"

"I do," Jay said. She had been sitting with her arms crossed in silence for a while. "I know where another one is."

CHAPTER IX:
THE VISIONARY

"LET ME CLARIFY. I lack an exact location. But I imagine it will be rather easy to find."

"Just explain it," David groaned.

Jay stood. "Goblins are banned from human settlements like Hegortant. That is clear. But even so, they managed to both infiltrate this walled city *and* leave it without apparent intervention from the guards. I know they are small, but they were carrying a *wagon,* for goodness' sake." She paced around the table as she spoke. "Add that to Angela's narrative. She was keeping an eye on the city gates to watch for our leave, but we suddenly manifested over by the woods. Peculiar, yes? This leads to the question: How could the goblins have snuck in and out like that?"

Elfekot and Angela remained silent.

"Teleportation?" David guessed.

"No. Only the leader is capable of magic. Even so, teleportation magic, at least in large distances, seems to be outside of the realm of possibility for Elektian magic-users."

"That is true…" Elfekot said.

"So then… how did they do it?" David asked.

"Think back to the statue in the city center. It was of Clyhvus

Karanos, a war hero. He founded this city in the midst of war. Like the Romans and many others, he employed tunnels for the sake of warfare. That is what's underneath Hegortant and what the goblins used to infiltrate the city: tunnels."

"Tunnels?" the other Restorers repeated.

"Yes. Judging from your surprise, Elfekot and Angela, these seem to be a secret, yes? If so, how would the goblins know about them? To answer, it is clear they lived here once amongst the human Elektians. But if they knew about it for so long, then they obviously would have infiltrated many times before then, and the tunnels surely would have been discovered as a result. Ergo, Denisse knew. She led their operation here. And who better to possess the knowledge of secret tunnels than someone like her?"

David, Elfekot, and Angela looked at each other. "Say these tunnels exist. How do you know the scroll is there?" Angela asked. "And how would they not have been found yet, anyway?"

"Simple. When we were searching the Erbezen residence for one of the Scrolls, I noticed that the floorboards felt... odd. Upon further inspection with the restricted lighting, I discovered that there must have been something underneath the house. However, David found the scroll, so I thought nothing of it then. According to the hint given to us in the Dijenuk House, *one* is possessed by Landor. Another could very well still have been in the Erbezens' possession. It only makes sense to stash one in the secret tunnels underneath your house. As for their secretive nature, I believe that the guards *do* know about it, but choose to keep it a secret. That seems to be a common theme here in Elektia, yes? If goblins were to infiltrate Hegortant frequently via tunnels, their existence would likely be made public then, hence why we 'common folk' know nothing of it."

The other Restorers glanced at each other once more, stunned. "That is, uh… quite the theory, Jay," Elfekot said.

"If you don't believe me, I have something else to mention." She picked up the scroll. An image flashed inside her head: dark tunnels and explosions, followed by a green scroll exactly like the one in her hands. "Whenever I touch this, something flashes in my head. Like… a feeling. A vision, maybe? It's almost as though it tells me where to go, but only vaguely. I just *know* that I'm right. Well, I'm always right."

Elfekot leaned back in his chair. "Huh…"

"So, there are tunnels underneath Hegortant and the second scroll is probably there, yeah?" David summarized.

"It is a *guarantee*, David."

Elfekot stood. "Then we shall see for ourselves." He turned to the lone bartender. "We are sorry about the table." The man simply shrugged, his glum expression unchanged.

Jay stuffed the scroll back inside her pocket. "*Andiamo.*"

"I am unfamiliar with that word," Angela said as she also stood.

"It means 'let's go,'" David translated.

The Restorers exited the decrepit tavern. The street they entered was nearly vacant. A few citizens meandered about, but most were hiding indoors. The news about the goblins and razas had spread fast throughout the city. It had become eerily quiet.

"Wait, wait, shouldn't we be getting new clothes?" David wondered aloud. "I'm kinda tired of sticking out in my American teenager stuff."

"Later, David. You two will be fine. Our priority is finding and securing the three Scrolls of Gales. We need to stay ahead of Landor."

David sighed. "I guess so. What are we even gonna do about the third scroll, anyway?"

"We… will get to it," Elfekot said.

"Great answer. You don't even know, huh, Jay?"

"We literally got here yesterday," Jay snapped. "Even *I* have my limitations."

"At least you admit it," David responded.

"Speaking of lackluster answers," Jay said, "I hope you haven't forgotten about what I said earlier, Elfekot."

"You mean your rant? Look, kid, we are all on the same side. It would be much easier if you were to trust me. I am not lying to you. I just lack the correct answer sometimes. Is that so wrong from a simple captain?"

Jay paused. "We shall see."

"Trust ain't exactly her thing, Elfekot," David loud-whispered.

"What *is* your thing, Jay Dijenuk?" Angela asked.

"Superiority," she answered flatly.

The Restorers returned to the street from which Denisse worked. Elfekot stared at the bar as they passed it.

"So… do you wanna talk about what happened with you and Denisse?" David asked.

"No."

"Oh. Okay. I guess that's fair."

Following the route that Denisse had taken them on earlier, the Restorers found their way back to the abandoned Erbezen residence. The door remained unlocked.

The interior was just like they had left it, including the smashed window. Lighting was limited and the rooms retained their mustiness. Jay crouched down and pressed her hand against the wood floor.

"*Musnomi levis.*"

From underneath the floor, beams of small light shone through the gaps between the planks. The other Restorers bent down to inspect it for themselves. Like Jay had said, there was a chamber underneath the floorboards. The magical light illuminated the rock walls and large crates. Most of it remained dark. The group stood. Angela drew her staff and aimed it downwards.

"Wait, wait!" said David. "This is someone's property. We already broke a window."

"The Erbezens are gone, Master Dijenuk. I doubt they would mind," Angela said.

"And the property was never theirs to begin with," Elfekot added.

"I guess…" the boy responded.

Angela tensed her arm as she concentrated. The others took

194

a few steps back. A singular orb of white energy charged at the tip. After a few moments, the shot was released. The wooden planks exploded as chunks flew violently into the air. Once the dust cleared, the Restorers peeked down the freshly-made hole in the floor. David put a foot forward into the dimly lit abyss.

"Hold on, Master Dijenuk," Angela warned. "Do we even know how deep it is?"

David shrugged. "Only one way to find out." Without further hesitation, the Dijenuk dropped through the opening. He landed on the top of a crate only a few meters down.

"I mean, there are multiple ways to find out, but sure, take the riskiest," Jay muttered.

The group watched as David stepped down off the box and descended into the darkness. "A light, please?" the boy asked.

Jay reached into the opening. "*Musnomi levis.*"

A second small orb of light appeared out of thin air next to David. With it, they could see the ground and how far down they had to climb. The drop went about twenty feet.

"Come on, guys," David said. "Jay was right. There *are* tunnels down here."

"Of course I was."

Angela went next, followed by Elfekot, then finally Jay. They took the same path as David and climbed down the stack of large crates.

"Jeez, they could have at least put a ladder here or something," David said as he helped his companions down.

"The Erbezens are wind mages, David. They lack a need for

ladders," Elfekot explained.

Jay raised her arm, palm facing the darkness. *"Levis ehté saugh."*

The shroud lifted, revealing a cramped tunnel stretching for many meters before reaching darkness again. There were openings in the rock walls, signaling other directions. Unevenly spaced wooden beams seemed to hold the entire thing up. Unlit torches dotted the earthen walls.

David groaned. "This is gonna take forever." He turned to investigate the multitude of crates behind them. "What if the scroll's in one of these?"

"It isn't," Jay said.

"How do you know?"

Jay reached into her pocket and grasped the scroll within it. The same tunnels flashed in her head and seared themselves into her mind's eye. Another vision joined it: a room with furniture. "I simply know."

"Helpful," David said. He drew his staff.

"If you destroy them, we lose the only way out that we know of," Jay warned.

The boy sighed.

Elfekot walked onwards. "Come on, then. A maze it might be, but standing around will not help us."

The Restorers, with Elfekot in the front, began their tread. The tunnels gradually descended farther and farther down as the claustrophobic walls smoothed out. Sooner than later, they met their first branch in the path.

"So... left or forwards?" David asked.

"Left," Jay instructed, her hand on the scroll.

Without anything else to go on, the Restorers took the left path. The light from Jay's spell continued to show the way for a while. The tunnels began to widen, and cobwebs became more frequent.

"That light spell sure is handy," David said, "but aren't those spells limited?"

"Huh?"

"Earlier, when we were in the wagon, you said you couldn't cast a certain spell again. Although... now that I think about, it was the teleport-y spell, right? Didn't you do it again, anyway?"

"According to the spellbook I read from, spells can only be cast a certain number of times before a sort of 'cooldown.' In a way, it is the same as the other magics. You get tired, so you rest a tad bit, and your inner pool of magical energy is replenished somewhat. However, spells don't exhaust you like that. When you speak an incantation, you call upon the magic of the universe itself. For reasons I don't completely understand yet, it becomes harder to call upon the same power over and over again. As such, you need to give it some time. The more difficult and complex the spell, the stricter the limitation."

"Well, how limited is it?" David asked.

"Something like a light spell I could cast dozens of times, even at my level, but something like the short-distance teleportation is something I can only do every once in a while. How many times I can cast the spell and how long I must wait to call upon those powers again varies depending upon the spellcaster's own power and experience. There is no hard, universal number. So, to answer your other question, David, I *might* have been able to cast that spell again. I didn't even know how much time had passed then. But it was a stupid situation to use the spell in anyway, so that is also why I ignored your stupid suggestion," Jay explained.

"Ah. Wait, didn't you get tired from one of your spells back in the forest? You even coughed up blood, sis."

"And I mentioned I couldn't use my amulet for that spell, as I had to hold on to you and cast the spell with my other hand. Something about the secondary source allows us to call upon the universe's magic relatively easily. My desperation in the moment and… something else allowed me to bypass that limitation. There was a price, though; hence, my physical degradation."

"By 'something else,' do you mean that green glow you had?"

"I didn't see it myself, but yes, I believe so."

"Huh. That all sounds kinda complicated."

Jay scoffed. "For someone of your intellect, sure. I am certain the same applies to other Elektians. Most of you seem too dimwitted even to try it, as spellcasting appears to be a rarity. Denisse couldn't even perform a lock-picking spell. *Levis ehté saugh.*" The darkness they had been nearing was pushed back again.

"But the only reason *you* know about spells is because

Elfekot gave you the book," David countered.

"And if he didn't, then I would have found out sooner or later anyway, *if* we'd managed to survive."

"Are you saying we only lived 'cause of your spells?"

"No, but that was one of the factors. Quit assuming these absolutes. It makes you seem even more simple-minded than you actually are."

"Just, *please...* stop talking," Elfekot begged. "Save your sibling bickering for another time."

"Sorry," said David.

"So, if what Jay explained to us is correct, then surely at least one of these paths must lead outside the city. But right now, it feels like we are going nowhere," Angela said. "It is only going deeper."

"Maybe we went the wrong way," David said.

Jay grabbed the scroll in her pocket. The group stopped. "No... we must have passed it."

"Passed it? Did we pass something?" asked David.

Elfekot shrugged.

"Ugh. If you're supposed to be our guide, you're doing a pretty crappy job, sis. Here, give me the scroll thing."

"Excuse me?"

"You touch the scroll and it, like, tells you where to go, right?"

"Not exactly—"

"Just let me try it."

Jay hesitated for a few seconds before handing David the

object. The boy held it with both hands, eyes closed as though he were concentrating.

"I don't get it," he finally said. "It doesn't tell me anything."

"It's more of a vague hint in the back of your head. I doubt it can actually communicate," Jay clarified.

David passed the scroll around to Elfekot and Angela. They both shook their heads. Angela handed it back to Jay. As soon as she touched it, she felt a weak pull, as though someone were trying to lead her in a general direction.

"Whatever it's showing me, it's getting weaker. We need to hasten."

"So it just works with you, then? Why?" David asked.

"I lack the answer, which is quite aggravating."

Elfekot groaned. "So many pointless questions. Let us go back, then, and see if we really missed something." The captain turned around and paced back the way they'd come. The others followed.

"If you are wrong, Jay Dijenuk, and King Landor finds the other scroll—" Angela started.

"I'm *not*. Keep in mind that—"

Jay's words were interrupted by a shrill scream from deep within the tunnels. They echoed. The reverberations allowed them to determine that the high-pitched sounds were nowhere near human.

The Restorers stopped. Jay's body tensed, and David drew his staff.

"What was that?" he asked.

The ground shook. Bits of the earth fell from the ceiling.

"You said these tunnels were kept secret to prevent things like goblin attacks. What if there is another reason?" Angela wondered aloud as the earth shook again.

Jay looked to the captain. "Elfekot?"

His face appeared grim. "We must keep moving."

Their pace quickened, and the Restorers resumed their trek. Closer to where the path had split first, a large piece of cloth hung over a section of the wall. David approached it, and he placed a hand on the cloth.

"This is it," he said. David grabbed an edge and lifted it, revealing an opening to another branch in the tunnels. "Let's go."

"We missed *this*?" asked Angela in disbelief as she walked through first.

"That is why the two of you need to shut up sometimes. In a mission this sacred, we can afford no distractions," Elfekot scolded.

The new branch was much narrower than the previous. The walls were smoother, and the elevation rose ever so slightly. Before long, the group found something finally different than the tunnels previous: a room carved into the earth.

Roughly circular, the room held a few pieces of furniture, including a table, two chairs, and shelves. The shelves contained an unorganized mixture of books and scrolls. The furniture itself was all short, so as to accommodate the low ceiling.

"This is it." David ran up to the shelves, where he spotted

the only green-tinted scroll in the collection. He removed the scroll from its socket. It was seemingly identical to the one in Jay's possession. "That makes two."

Meanwhile, Jay flipped through the pages of the various tomes. "Huh." She then opened one of the mundane-looking scrolls. As she unrolled the parchment, she discovered it to be blank. "Interesting." She went through more of the texts. "These scrolls are all void of anything, and the books appear to be diary entries and observations."

"Of what?" David pressed.

"War, by the looks of it."

"We need to go. Now," Elfekot said.

"Why?" Jay questioned. "There's so much here, aside from the empty scrolls."

"You heard the same noise I did, yes? Then you know we need to get out of here."

Jay sighed as she returned the small book in her hand back to the shelf. "*Andiamo.*"

The Restorers exited the small chamber. As they made their way through the cloth flap and back to the main tunnel they'd come from, the sound of an explosion echoed from the distance. It was accompanied by a slight shake.

Elfekot drew his weapons as he peered down the dark corridor. "That was different," he muttered.

The Restorers stared into the shroud for a few seconds. There was nothing. Just as they were about to turn away, something zoomed out of the darkness. A man in dark robes tackled David.

He wrestled the Scroll of Gales out of his hand. Angela struck the man with the blunt end of her spear. She pressed her staff against his chest and fired. There was a flash of white light from the blast, followed by an audible *crack* as the man collapsed, unconscious. David retrieved the scroll. The group stood around the fallen man.

"He is of Dark Elektia," Elfekot said.

"That name…" Jay murmured.

Angela twirled her staff. "There must be more of them."

"Which means we need to get out of here," Elfekot said.

The group sprinted for the exit. Darkness suddenly surrounded them. Jay's magical lights had vanished. Before they could reach the main tunnel, numerous bolts of energy volleyed towards them. Elfekot raised his staff. He barely managed to intercept them in time with his magical shield.

"They are blocking our exit," said Elfekot through gritted teeth.

"Then we find another way out. We know there are other exits somewhere. Come on," David said.

Despite their inability to see, the Restorers dashed through. The only light came from whenever a bolt of energy met the rock wall, almost like sparks. Fortunately, the darkness did little to aid their attackers, as their attacks missed. A few projectiles managed to whizz by their heads. Elfekot and Angela occasionally fired back as the group ran.

"How did they find us?" Jay asked.

"They must have already known, those tricky bastards,"

Elfekot replied. "Or…"

Just then, the ceiling over their heads exploded. Sunlight and earth poured in, and soldiers from above leaped inside. Angela acted first. She screamed as she waved her staff horizontally. Three soldiers directly in front of her were violently knocked down by an invisible shockwave. Elfekot blocked a couple of projectiles as he sheathed his sword. The captain thrust his free hand forward. A much larger hand, about the size of a person and made out of a white energy, appeared before them. It mirrored Elfekot's own hand as he waved it to the side. The magical hand slammed two of the soldiers into the rock wall.

David ducked under a projectile, the energy buzzing as it went past his head. His lowered elevation allowed him to a fire a projectile of his own into the attacker's leg. *Crack*. The soldier doubled over. David swung his staff and smacked him in the head, sending spit flying out. He finished it with a blast to his skull.

Meanwhile, Jay had come face-to-face with another soldier. He fired a blast of energy. She moved her head, barely dodging the attack. The girl raised her palm forward and, with her other hand, grasped at the amulet.

"To Darkness!"

The soldier hovered in the air. His face wore fear as he screamed. After a second, the man rocketed backwards into the darkness of the tunnels. Jay let herself collapse against the wall. Her companions had taken down the rest of Landor's soldiers.

Their rest was only brief, however, as the sound of footsteps approached. Elfekot stood firm, ready to block against anything. Angela stood with him. David and Jay turned. The sound of footsteps emerged from the other direction as well.

David swallowed. "Guys…"

Jay retrieved the Scroll of Gales from her pocket. She undid the white string and pulled the parchment open. A sudden of rush of air blasted upwards. The Restorers felt their clothes and hair ruffle in the intense winds as they were lifted. They landed facedown on a grassy surface.

Elfekot rolled over. "What the hell?" He sat up. "We are outside the city walls."

David stood. "I guess we went kinda far." He helped his sister up. "What was that?"

"It was the scroll. I opened it," she explained as she glanced over the parchment. The text was in a language she couldn't even recognize.

"How did you know it would do that?" Angela asked.

Jay tied the scroll back up. "Lucky guess." In truth, she'd applied what she had learned from when she used to play Dungeons & Dragons, in which scrolls could also be spells.

Elfekot looked up the city wall. "Hey!" he called. "We need help!"

A guard equipped with a bow and arrow looked down. "We saw those bastards. Fret not. Help is on its way," she assured him.

"Thank you," Elfekot replied. The guard nodded and moved out of sight. Elfekot shook his head. "First goblins, then those gits… Those tunnels will have to be sealed." He looked to the hole in the ground. "They must have both blown up the ground and the normal entrances to get to us."

"But for that, they would need a detailed map of the place," Jay said.

The captain nodded. "Right. Well, for now, I reckon we—"

"Watch out!" called David.

Bang.

The boy shoved Elfekot out of the way as a cloud of darkness flew towards them. At the same time, a jet of white energy struck Jay in the back of her arm, causing her to drop the scroll. The moving cloud passed right by David. Tendrils of the dark energy seeped into David's skin, and his whole body went numb. He too dropped the scroll. The cloud dissipated, and Commander Istra slid on his feet across the grass. Both Scrolls were in his hand.

The numbness left, and David took a deep breath. He looked up at the grinning Istra. "What the—?"

Elfekot and Angela both launched a blast of energy, but the commander returned to his cloudy form. He blasted into the sky and flew off, effectively dodging the attacks. The Restorers watched helplessly as Istra zoomed away. A few arrows fired by the guards atop the wall tried to bring the man down, but he was already too far.

"No. No! Come on, we gotta get them back!" David ran off. The others joined him, albeit reluctantly.

"David, wait!" Elfekot called.

"We *can't* wait."

"This again…" Jay muttered. Once again, the Restorers sprinted across the plains.

"David, there is no use!" yelled Elfekot.

"We need to at least try!" David yelled back.

"You are wasting your time. We need to go back and make a *plan*!" Despite his efforts, the group wasn't slowing down.

The Restorers, to the best of their ability, dashed through the long grass and occasional bush. They could feel their bodies already begging them to stop. They forced themselves to keep going.

"We are not going to catch up just running like this!" Angela said as the dark cloud that was Istra sped away above them.

Eventually, he disappeared from view beyond the horizon, and the Restorers stopped their chase.

David bent down and panted, resting his hands on his knees. "Damn it! He's too fast with that flying thing."

"It is a Dark mage's favorite trick," Elfekot grumbled.

David looked to his sister. "Your teleport spell can't take us that far, huh?"

She shook her head. Her hands were on her hips as she stared at the ground. "I doubt I could even perform it again anytime soon."

"Once he crosses that Barrier, there is nothing we can do," Elfekot said, his face crestfallen.

"What's that?" David asked.

"The border between the two nations," answered Angela.

She looked defeated. "Any Light Elektian that crosses it dies within seconds."

"What?! Wait, then how do Landor and his soldiers get here?"

"The effect on them is much less severe. Their power is weakened, but they can live for hours, I believe."

"So... we're screwed? We lost?"

Angela swallowed. "Yes, Master Dijenuk... We lost."

Elfekot shrugged. "To me, that is no surprise."

"This isn't funny, Elfekot!" David snapped. He took a breath. "Sorry."

Jay snapped her fingers. "No, there is a way. We just have to get to the Barrier before Istra does."

Elfekot shook his head. "We cannot get there in time. Like you said, the teleport spells only do so much. The Barrier, and Istra, are a substantial distance away."

"What about her green power thingy?" David said. "That seemed to really beef up that one spell against Landor. I bet it could help, somehow."

Jay's jaw clenched. "I would rather not. Regardless, I have no idea as to how to activate it."

David frowned. "Yeah... Can you at least try, though?"

Jay sighed. "Yes, I will try." She closed her eyes and retreated into her headspace.

The Restorers watched her as she concentrated. Her expression remained the same—empty and without emotion—as they did so.

Slow seconds passed as Jay delved into the void of her soul. A vision eventually appeared within her mind's eye: A run-down apartment complex, and then sudden darkness. Her heart began to race without any influence that she could identify. It pumped a pleasant heat through her veins.

"I have a hold of something," she said, her eyes still closed. "But I am unsure if I can cast the teleport spell again."

"We need to try," Angela said.

"What if I cast it?" David offered.

Jay was silent for a second, stunned. "What?"

"Well, that magic energy that we've been feeling is something that moves, right? It moves from my arm to the staff."

"You're suggesting I transfer my energy to you."

"Yeah."

"You know how I feel about physical contact, David."

"Is this really the time for that, sis?"

Jay huffed. "Fine. Grab my right wrist…. Alright, the incantation is '*téléneh nostro.*' Do *not* mess it up or lose your grip."

"Got it."

"On my go, we all run as fast we can. On my second go, David casts the spell. Make sure your staff is in your hand."

The Restorers nodded.

"Ready? … Go!"

The four of them sprinted across the plains once more. As Jay focused, another vision popped inside her head. It was the strange, hooded man who had spoken to her on the first day that she'd arrived on Elektia. He faced her for a couple of seconds before making a single clapping motion. Jay did the same thing at the same time, as though someone else were controlling her arms.

"Go!"

"*Téléneh nostro!*" David chanted just as Jay clapped her hands.

The fatigue they were already carrying multiplied. A burning sensation shot through Jay's body. Their legs gave out, and they collapsed onto the ground....

⤙o⤚

David rolled around to his back, groaning. "Ugh... Did we do it?"

"Oh, finally," said Angela.

David sat up. "Huh?"

Their surroundings were entirely different. Shrubs and bushes dotted the dry landscape. A forest of short, twisting trees occupied the top of the hill next to them. In the distance behind David was the eerie Barrier.

"Whoa..." he said, standing.

The Barrier was a veil of shimmering, golden light that gradually lost its saturation and opacity as it reached into the sky. Left, right, or up, there was no end in sight.

"How long were we out?" Jay asked, sitting up. Her eyes were closed as she tried to manage a throbbing headache.

David frowned. "We were unconscious?"

"Yes. It has been nearly half an hour," Elfekot answered, resting against a tree at the top of the hill.

"Really?" David said. "It felt like no time at all."

"I only noticed because of the sun's slight change in position," Jay said as she stood. She looked at the Barrier. "Has Istra crossed it yet?"

"No, but he is close. Come up here," Elfekot said.

The other three followed him up the steep incline and through the forest. A short trip later, they met the edge of a cliff. It looked over a swath of grassy, rolling hills and a river that snaked into the horizon.

"I can't see Hegortant anywhere. We're really that far, huh?" David said.

"Aye," Elfekot replied. He pointed to the clouds. "More importantly…"

Using the clouds as cover, the dark puff of smoke that was Commander Istra was heading towards them.

"Do you think he can see us?" David asked.

"Likely. He is going to try to fly past us," Angela guessed. She raised her staff. "We have to strike him down now."

"Are you sure?" Jay questioned. "He is rather far."

"With the four of us, we are bound to hit him good."

Jay shook her head and took a few steps closer to Angela. "That won't work. You will just miss. We need to save our energy and come up with something else. I don't even think that kind of magic—"

"How do you know?"

"Your accuracy, while impressive, isn't perfect. I strongly advise against useless volleys. Plus, I recently noticed that your magic won't work in this situation, anyway."

"Again, I ask you, how do you know? You have only been here two days. You should not be telling us what to do."

Jay was taken aback. "Are you questioning me again?"

"Mm hmm."

"I take it you have yet to realize exactly who I am."

Angela raised an eyebrow. "You are a Restorer, just like me."

Jay took another step closer, her hand tightening into a fist. "No. I'm Jay Dijenuk. I have yet to meet anyone smarter than me, or even close, and I doubt I ever will. You Light Elektians, David included, are so ignorant to the world around you that it no longer surprises me how you fail to see the lies spoon-fed to you, as though you all have the mental capacity of mush-brained children." She sneered, and her voice dropped, becoming more intense. "I imagine it would take me little effort to manipulate this reason-devoid excuse of a civilization to my own liking."

Angela clenched her teeth. "You are a—"

"Ignore her, Angela," Elfekot said to her. "*I* will be making the decisions here, children, and no one else. And my decision is to attack now."

Jay scoffed and rolled her eyes. "I wish you hopeless imbeciles the best of luck," she said, then walked away.

"Sis, wait!" David called.

"Leave her alone, David."

"But—"

"Focus on the task at hand. Follow my orders, not hers," said Elfekot. He raised his staff with Angela. David followed suit, and all three aimed at Istra. "Ready?" the captain asked.

The other two nodded.

"Fire!"

Volleys of white energy fired sporadically from the three staves, whizzing through the sky. The dark cloud that was Istra weaved around the few energy blasts that came close to him. Most missed by several meters.

"It's not working," David said.

"We will be more accurate once he nears," Angela assured him.

Half a minute passed, and David paused his volleys. He straightened his posture and held his breath, focusing on Istra. He fired a single shot. It struck the smoke and passed right through it.

"It doesn't hurt him," David realized, disappointment in his voice. "Jay was right. Of course."

Angela and Elfekot lowered their staves. The girl sighed. "Then what do we do?"

"We..." Elfekot frowned. "I do not know, actually."

"We gotta do *something*," David said. "If he crosses that Barrier, we lose. We need to stop him here and now."

"Then we keep firing," Angela said. "It has to work eventually."

"Are you sure? Like Jay said, we'll just waste our energy—

"

"What other options do we have?" Angela said, her voice raised. "I apologize, Master Dijenuk."

"Don't worry about it." He looked back at Istra. "He's about to fly right past us."

Angela fired one more blast of energy. It whizzed through him.

David shook his head. "No... No, this can't be it," he said as they watched Istra zoom over their heads. He took a shaky breath. "We lost.... Right, Elfekot? Like you said we would?"

"I..." Elfekot was speechless.

Angela huffed, then let out a scream as she thrust her staff to the side. The resulting blast of energy blew up the nearest tree, sending chunks of bark into the air.

They stood in silence, listening to the low hum of the wind.

David shook his head again. "No, this is *not* over." He looked up. "Jay! She's super smart. Like, *really* smart. She knows what to do. If she walked off like that, and if I'm right about that look in her eyes, then she must have a plan."

"She's made that quite clear," muttered Angela. "Where is she?"

"I dunno."

Elfekot approached the boy with narrowed eyes. "Are you sure?"

David frowned in thought. "Oh, right! I forgot! Me and Jay... we sorta have this weird thing where we can sense each other's locations and even feelings sometimes."

"Really?" Angela said.

"Yeah. I don't really know how. We've been doing it for as long as I can remember, and we've never known why. No one's had a proper answer."

"I think it should be obvious to you now. It is because you are Dijenuks. It has been known that that family has strong connections like that within itself," Elfekot explained.

"So, you know how it works?" David asked.

"No. I suggest just... trying. Try to put yourself in her head, literally. Reach out to her magical presence. Focus."

David shut his eyes and let out a breath. After a few seconds, he opened them again. "This isn't working. I've never really tried to do it on purpose before. It just kinda happens randomly."

"You only tried for a few chroshards, Master Dijenuk," Angela said.

"Chroshards?"

"Seconds, but slower," Elfekot translated. "One hundred chroshards make one fraction. Sixty of those makes one hour."

"Oh. Weird. Um, well, we can just go look for her, then," David suggested.

"No. Jay made the choice to run off. And she could be anywhere. I say we accept the end of the world and move on..." said Elfekot.

David's hearing faded away as other feelings crept in. His heart beat faster, and there was a sense of determination. As he continued to linger in her head, he found something else, or, rather, the lack of something. It was a void, absent of anything, yet present all the same. Despite its emptiness, it was overwhelming, and, to David, frightening. The darkness etched into his soul, and he felt something he wished never to feel again: complete indifference to everything. The more David focused, the more he knew just how much it was a part of his sister. It was not a force within Jay. It was Jay herself. David then realized it was the first time he had done this since the night of the party.

As kept digging through her head, he discovered one more thing. Buried deep within the void of her soul was something hot. It pulsated, yet it was hidden in the darkness. It was an intense, burning hatred.

Before he could leave the space of her mind, an image flashed in his head. "The Barrier. She's at the Barrier! …We could have guessed that, actually."

"Did she try to catch Istra on her own there?" Angela asked.

"I dunno. It doesn't matter. But she has a plan. Probably."

CHAPTER X:
AN ERROR IN THE SYSTEM

THE LUMINESCENT, TRANSLUCENT WALL that was the Barrier rippled in front of her. Now closer, its colors swirled between gold and dark purple. Jay moved her left hand near it. It was warm. Around her lay a barren land, spotted with dead trees and the occasional collapsed, dilapidated building, sitting right on the Barrier. There was little to no life here, from what Jay could see. The sky was greyer. Dead grass crunched underneath her feet.

"Jay!"

Jay frowned. It was David's voice. "I saw Istra pass through. I was right, then; your 'plan' failed."

"Yeah. That's why we found you," David said. "You have something in mind, yeah?"

"I do."

"Ha! See, I knew it, you guys."

Jay turned to face him. "You 'knew,' yet you went along with Elfekot and Angela's idiocy."

"Well, I, um—"

"Don't bother with an excuse. The reason is clear: You have no spine, David."

David clenched his jaw as he scowled. "At least I feel

something, Jay!"

"Tch. I would feel sorry for you if I possessed even a minutia of care for your insignificant existence," she said as she continued to stare at him with her neutral, almost bored, expression, her eyes displaying her usual intensity. *Do I even completely mean what I say? ...No, it doesn't matter. But, if it doesn't matter, why do I want him to feel so hurt?*

As David and Jay went back and forth, Elfekot and Angela glanced at each other with irritated expressions.

David took a step back, muscles still tense. "You care about something, at least."

"You lack any idea as to how I feel. Just because you peeked inside my head doesn't mean you can preach to whatever you think is going on within me."

"What? How do you—?"

"*Nothing* escapes me. Remember that."

"Are you done?" Elfekot asked, his arms crossed. "The longer you bicker, the more time Istra has to get away, and the more I feel like jumping off that cliff over there. So, what do you have in mind?"

Jay turned back to face the Barrier. "We have but one option," she said, stepping forward. "We follow; we pass through."

"What? We will die doing so. Have I not made that clear?" Elfekot argued.

"*That* was her whole plan...?" Angela mumbled.

"Go and try it yourself, if you wish," the captain added.

Jay took a couple more steps.

David grabbed her by the arm. "He was joking!"

She shook his hand off. "I know. And don't touch me."

Elfekot made a long sigh. "Fine. We will go through it. But we will go right back once you feel your life slowly draining, your body weakening," he said.

The four of them stood side-by-side, equidistant from the glowing Barrier.

"This is ridiculous," the captain muttered. "Okay, on one. Three, two, one!"

They all sprinted forward, crossing the few feet between them and the Barrier. David felt all warmth drain from his body as he immediately collapsed. He grew a pounding headache. His field of vision narrowed, and all his muscles felt weak and frail. It was as though he were drowning. The boy managed to crawl back through, and once he did, he gasped for air. All warmth came back, and his vision returned to normal. With the help of Angela, he got back up.

Elfekot shook his head at him, slightly panting, his eyelids low. "See?"

"Yeah, I do now," David responded, trying to get his breath back. He looked to his left. "Jay?!"

Jay was still on the other side of the Barrier in a neutral stance. She turned to face them.

"This does not make any sense. Jay, do you feel worse at all?" Elfekot asked.

Jay shook her head. "Not right now. Though, at the initial

219

crossing, I felt colder, but that was brief."

David gasped. "What if... what if you're actually a Landor?!"

Elfekot scoffed. "A Landor? No, that is impossible. She could not have survived on this side for so long if that were the case."

"Then... how...?"

"Some sort of exception. A special exception," Angela said, her arms crossed. "A Dijenuk, your visions, those green-colored powers, and now this."

"But, why?" David asked.

"I also wish to know," Jay said.

"Powers like that can only be explained by one thing: gifts from the gods," Angela said.

With her arms crossed as well, Jay clutched at the fabric of her shirt. "If that's true, then they can take these powers back."

"What? Why?" David questioned.

"You dare reject the Elementians' blessings, Jay Dijenuk?" said Angela, taken aback.

"Let us discuss this later, please," Elfekot interjected, "unless you *want* to let Istra get away over a discussion as dull as that." He looked to the Barrier. "How we move forward here is clear: Jay needs to go through the Barrier alone."

"What?" said both Angela and Jay.

"No, this is preposterous. I lack the strength," Jay said, stepping back through.

"It is our only choice," Angela mimicked.

"I am afraid it is," Elfekot said.

"I'm sorry," David said.

The girl looked out and took a deep breath. "Then I will see what I can do."

David took a step toward his sister. "Please be careful. If you can't do it, run. Don't push yourself like you always do. We can figure something else out if we have to."

Jay remained silent for a few seconds. "We shall see.... Thank you, David."

"We will wait for you here," Elfekot said. "I am unsure as to how long we must remain here, though."

Jay nodded. "Here I go."

Jay's swift pace took her once more through the Barrier. A cold shiver ran down her spine, and her heart stopped momentarily. She kept going, unaware that the other Restorers watched until she disapeared from view.

The world on the other side was initially quite distinct. Everything was greyer, as though the world was sapped of most of its color. There were also scorch marks on the ground, and the overcast had grown more dramatic, along with the intensity of the dilapidation. Otherwise, everything was the same.

Can I even find him? she thought.

Her eyes moved to identify the highest vantage point in her vicinity. She climbed the hill, vision glued to the sky. Ahead of her were rolling hills and clumps of lifeless trees. At the horizon, a miniscule puff of black smoke zoomed farther away from view. Suddenly, the black smoke that was Istra flew straight into an area Jay couldn't quite make out. The girl exhaled for a few long seconds before beginning her trek.

It only took a few minutes before Jay groaned. *I will never make it in time at this rate... Unless...*

She closed her eyes, keeping the area ahead implanted in her mind's eye. She clapped her hands. Nothing. She tried again a couple more times, until a shockwave of energy vibrated her own ribcage and rippled the air around her. She paced for a few more seconds, then rolled her shoulders and began sprinting ahead. Once again, she closed her eyes and envisioned getting farther ahead. Like last time, an image of the hooded man invaded her headspace. With a clap, her fatigue once again stacked as her body briefly burned on the inside. This time, the girl noticed the brief scent of pine. She allowed herself a few seconds to rest on the stiff grass.

She exhaled. "I did it. Well, of course I did."

"I see you're getting the hang of what I taught you," said a voice.

Jay scrambled to her feet, drew her staff, and spun around. "Who said that?" she asked.

A figure dressed in black leapt down from a nearby tree. "Hello again, Jay."

She pointed her staff at him. "You. What are you doing here, and what do you want from me this time?"

The hooded figure, the one who had briefly appeared back in Fort Dijenuk, wasn't at all fazed by the staff. "Relax. I am here to help you take back the Scrolls of Gales."

"Is that so? How can I trust you?"

"You can't," he said, "not really, but it would help to know that *I* am the one who let you teleport like that."

"What? I never asked for your help."

"And yet, where would you be without it? Where would you be without what has been given to you?"

"I…" Her mouth hung open, as if she were dumbstruck. Her eyes stared past the man.

"Regardless, you have no choice at the moment but to accept my aid. Below this cliff is a Kingdom outpost. There are dozens of Landorian soldiers stationed here. You have no chance of getting through or past them alone."

"But I can with you?"

He made a low chuckle. "I can go by myself, if need be. But I would like you to join me. You desperately need the practice if you want to help save Elektia."

Her staff was still pointed at him. "I… I suppose that is fair."

"I'm glad you can come to reason. That's a rarity here in Elektia."

"You're not going to take the Scrolls and run, are you?"

"No. They are of no use outside of opening the Wind Chamber. Now, follow me." He led Jay to the edge of the cliff. Below them was a small fort. A palisade wall surrounded a group of buildings and tents. Guards walked about. "Let us make our way." They began their descent down the cliff using a moderate slope about a quarter of a kilometer away. The landscape remained lifeless and grey.

"How did you find me, anyway?" Jay asked as they trekked, making sure not to be spotted. "And how do you know about all of this? My name included."

"Let's just say that I always keep my eye on you."

"So, you've been following us?"

"Not exactly. It's complicated. Any details further than that are secret for now."

Jay rolled her eyes. "Of course they are." She took a good look at the hooded figure next to her. "Who even are you, anyway?"

"Just a man looking to fix what's wrong with the world."

"That's awfully nice of you."

"Tch. Don't misunderstand. I'm not doing this out of kindness. I seek to establish a legacy for myself."

Jay nodded. "I get that. You didn't quite answer my question, though. Who are you exactly?"

"If you're seeking to acquire my name, know that I'll never give it to you."

"Yet you want me to trust you?"

"I never asked for that."

"What do I even call you, then?"

"I've gone by a handful of names, none of them my own. Hooded man, the Shadow, the Knife in the Dark… the Objectivist," he listed.

"Huh. So there are others who know of you. Do you have a preference?"

He shook his head.

"I'll call you… the Objectivist."

The Objectivist nodded. "Here. Take this."

He reached into his boot and pulled out a knife. The dagger was composed of a brown, almost gold, metal alloy. Jay assumed it was something she couldn't find on Terra. The oval hilt lacked a guard, and the handle was intricately wrapped in a comfortable hide like a braid.

"I'm not going to stab somebody."

"It is just in case, and you might have to someday. Perhaps more than once. Here's the sheath for it, too. Anyway, we are approaching. Make sure to keep your voice low."

"Right." She took the dagger with its sheath and carefully tucked them in her pocket. "Do we have a plan?"

"Do *I* have a plan, you mean? Yes. I always do. Just stay close, be as silent as possible, and do as I say."

Jay opened her mouth to object. Realizing she lacked a plan of her own, she said, "Fine."

A couple of minutes later, they reached their destination as the fort's wall came upon them. They could hear voices from within.

Jay studied the wall, attempting to look for a way through or around. "What now?"

The Objectivist drew a dagger. He stuck the tip of it into the wall and began cutting a rectangle in it. The knife didn't go all the way through, as he was essentially perforating it.

"That should be good enough," he muttered. He then waved his hand over the doorway-sized perforation. *"Slinta!"* The nearby air momentarily warped and bent. The cut portion of the wall was sent flying inwards as the Objectivist thrust his other hand forward. It didn't make a single sound.

"A silencing spell?"

He nodded. "Shh." The duo stepped through, immediately taking cover behind the nearby wall of a small building. "*Kanba tempus!*" The removed piece of the wall floated in the air and zoomed back into its place. Afterwards, the Objectivist seemingly stared into nothing for a few seconds, apparently concentrating.

"What are you doing?"

"There aren't that many of them," he determined with a slightly louder voice.

"How do you know?"

"All magicals who practice magic regularly radiate a specific kind of presence. And the more you practice magic, the better you can feel this presence. Active use of magic, on the other hand, is rather easy to feel. I can't detect anything very specific. Just general presences."

"Huh..."

"There's a potent one not too far away."

"It must be the commander, then."

"Istra? Perhaps, but it could also be Zecatsu."

"Zecatsu?"

"King Landor. Now, stay quiet and close."

As they moved from wall to wall, the voices became louder and clearer. Sections of the encampment were completely empty. They had gone past the group of buildings and were now approaching a courtyard. There were all kinds of barrels and crates that a number of men took as seats. Those men sat in a circle, deep in discussion.

"If you ask me, none of this is even worth it."

"No? We got the three Scrolls pretty quickly. I would say we are going to win this."

"Maybe. But to sacrifice almost all of our magic just to get at the Dijenuk, even if it is temporary?"

"It is not just about the Dijenuk. I hear the long-term plan is conquest of Light Elektia."

"Blimey…"

"Did ya hear the rumor, though? There are apparently *two* of those Dijenuk kids."

"Really?"

"Really. The king told his advisors just a few units ago."

"Does it even matter, though? They are from Terra. I doubt they stand much of a chance. What difference does one more Dijenuk make?"

"Good point."

The conversation moved on to food and the upcoming lack thereof. The Objectivist drew two small knives from his belt.

"W-wait! Are you going to kill them?" Jay whispered.

"Yes."

"They're people. You can't just—"

"You are essentially at *war*, Jay. Death is unavoidable." He put the knives back. "But fine. I will do my best to avoid killing for right now. However, you'd best soon learn to live with it."

"Alright. I count four. What do we—?"

The Objectivist left his cover and sprinted directly towards the group. "*Slinta!*"

The resulting skirmish was completely soundless. The men moved their mouths as if to shout. Their eyes grew and their bodies tensed, as they were unsure what was going on.

Jay watched the Objectivist take advantage of this confusion and blast two of the men away, the bursts of white light firing directly from his palms. He then engaged the closest, and his strikes were fast and precise. He gave his victim no time to counter, let alone breathe.

This is… incredible, Jay thought.

One of them fired a blast of energy at the hooded figure. He shifted his upper body backwards. The blast whizzed by just in front of him. He shifted forwards, bringing his left arm with him. He collided his fist with the man's jaw. His head flew up, spit flying into the air. And he collapsed.

The other two men were back up, staves drawn. The Objectivist watched the three of them for a second, head at a slight tilt. His body flashed a red light. And he was gone, effectively dodging the incoming volley of magic.

With the same red effect, he reappeared behind the farthest attacker. He kicked his foot down into the man's leg, forcing him to his knees. The Objectivist then placed his left palm not even an inch away from that man's stunned face. Something in Jay's mind told her to look away. She didn't. The blast of energy erupted the side of his skull. Its red innards ejected into the air, and continued to spill onto the ground where the corpse collapsed.

Jay couldn't help but stare at the mess of brains and flesh. To her surprise, there was no sense of horror or disgust within her. She turned her attention back to the Objectivist. In the few seconds that she had spent staring at something else, one soldier was left standing. The other was on the ground, every one of his limbs bent in the wrong direction.

The Objectivist waved his hand forward. A black-blue light flashed between him and the soldier, and his sword and staff pulled themselves away from his sweaty grip and into the air.

The Landorian put his now-empty hands into the air. He was shaking. The Objectivist took a step forward, then spun around. Before Jay could tell what was going on, his foot struck the man's temple. He crumpled into the wall behind him.

The Objectivist burst forward. His momentum sent his fist into the soldier's skull. He struck again. Then again. His strikes continued, spilling his face onto the stone wall.

As the Objectivist pummeled him, his first of the encounter was starting to get back up. Unsure as to whether the Objectivist would notice or not, Jay removed herself from cover and raised her staff. Her steps were gradually getting louder, and the other noises of the fight were increasing in volume as well.

Bang! The energy blast landed right in the man's side, causing him to double over. He turned his attention to Jay as he knelt.

"Why, you—!"

He was interrupted by his own scream as the Objectivist materialized right in front of him, his leg already in the air. Something emitted a sharp *crack* just before the soldier fell to the ground.

Jay glared at the Objectivist. "You said you wouldn't kill."

"And yet, I did. What're you going to do about it?"

"I…" *Why is it so hard to come up with a reply?* "Just forget it. It doesn't matter."

"You're right. It doesn't."

Jay turned away from the mess of guts and blood. "I was told you needed a secondary source like a staff or amulet to perform magic. And I didn't know Elektians even practiced martial arts. I assumed magic would be enough."

"I've transcended the need for a magical focus or a direct secondary source. More or less. And while magic is quite powerful, it has its weaknesses. For one, like I mentioned, it can be sensed, especially in excess use. Secondly, melee combat can sometimes be more effective up close, especially in a world now devoid of magical variety such as this. Thirdly, the need of a secondary source can be a burden at times. That last point only partially applies to me. That is why magicals practice melee combat, although it is usually in weapons training. I simply prefer using my fists sometimes."

"If you're so good, then why don't you help more often? Shouldn't someone like you be a Restorer? None of us can fight like you can, and we're supposed to be the most powerful, apparently. Tch, and we were even captured by goblins earlier."

The Objectivist gave an empty laugh. "Like I said, I have my own interests outside your quest. I am not a Restorer, and I have no desire to join you, anyway. The Restorers are *destined* to be the most powerful. You'll struggle for a while longer. Regardless, it is not my place to defy the prophecy."

Jay scoffed. "So, you believe in that?"

"Not entirely. I know the actions that must be taken, and the path you all must tread for the endgame to succeed. In that knowledge, the Restorers' prophecy has *some* merit." He clenched his left fist. "Some things are inevitable."

Jay looked down and quietly echoed, "Inevitable… Well, it is fortunate that I learned a few things back on Terra to defend myself without you."

"Did you, now?"

"Yes. I took Muay Thai and Taekwondo classes back on Terra." *Why did I tell him that?*

"Meaning, you can fight?"

"Not quite. I just know moves. Practical, real-life combat is much different."

"Then how do you explain your knuckles?"

Jay frowned, rubbing her bruised and scarred hands. "Tch. What is this? I have to keep reminding myself that I don't have to tell you any of these things. You're still a stranger."

"Am I?"

"Don't try to act so mysteriously. I hardly know anyone in Elektia, so yes, you're a stranger." She shook her head. *Yet…*

why does he feel so familiar? Why is he so easy to talk to?

"Well, let us keep going. We've already wasted too much time. Follow me. Keep your voice low."

"You already know of the Scrolls' location?"

"No. I just sense that presence from earlier. Barely. His recent expenditure of magical energy still lingers."

The two of them moved past the four unconscious bodies towards a large, organized group of tents.

"They're all likely empty. This place is hardly occupied," stated the Objectivist. Remaining low, they maneuvered through the rows of tents. At the end, they met a single building.

It differed from the others in the fort in that its walls were composed of wooden planks instead of stone. Its roof was slanted instead of flat. There were windows, too, but they were all covered by rags. A single door stood in the middle. The Objectivist hovered his hands over said door.

"*Revelé.*"

The entire front wall vanished, revealing the cramped interior. Numerous soldiers either stood or sat around a long table, its surface bare except for a small wooden chest and a large piece of parchment. Landor was nowhere to be seen. The soldiers were in a frantic discussion, many talking at once. None of them noticed the missing wall, which popped back into existence after a few seconds. The Objectivist then grabbed Jay and pulled her a few meters away from the wall.

"I'm going to break it to you: Most of these men will have to die. I cannot incapacitate that large a group without taking too long and potentially raising the alarm. I'm not *that* good, I have to admit."

Jay took a few moments before nodding. "I understand." *Death is inevitable… right?*

"Istra isn't there, which is unexpected. I thought I felt his presence…"

"I saw him fly in here, though. Hm. That presence must have been the Scrolls, then," Jay said.

"That is likely it. They emit a magical aura, too. However, this means we don't know where he is. Landor and his lackeys have different ways of getting around, which is dangerous. Hm…" He stood in contemplation for a short while before snapping his fingers. "Okay, I have the plan. I will need you to break the door down for me."

"And then?"

"I will take it from there."

"What if I can't blast it down? Keep in mind that I didn't properly know how to do any of this until this morning."

The Objectivist shook his head and scoffed. "They really didn't train you, huh? It's fine. I'll just do it myself." He drew two small knives from his belt, one in each hand, and stepped towards the door.

"No, wait. Let me at least make an attempt—"

"No. Stay back. I have a feeling you will be doing that often, anyway."

"What?"

"It was an insult. Was that not clear? All you will do is

lightly dent the wood and ruin the plan." He paused. "I suppose the real practice for you here was learning how to stay out of situations you clearly can't handle without someone else."

Jay fought it as hard as she could, but her face turned red. She clenched her fist and raised her staff. The scent of pinecones manifested. The girl's eyes flared green as a projectile of energy fired out of her staff and past the Objectivist. The door exploded into pieces, allowing the Objectivist to act immediately.

He threw the knives, both of them landing directly in someone's heart. They let out a final gasp before collapsing. The Objectivist then dashed inside.

As he engaged the room's occupants, Jay's legs brought her closer to the action. Her eyes refused to look at anything else.

The Objectivist's attacks were mesmerizing. He used an elbow to stun his opponent, then went in with his left arm. His dagger plunged into the man's throat. Blood spilled. Jay's heart jumped. And the Objectivist wasted no time moving to his next victim.

He struck with precision, then finished him off with a brutal stab. The others—finally realizing the danger of the situation—drew their staves. They each fired.

The Objectivist put little effort into dodging the volley. He either took a step or weaved his body. Yet, there was intent, as though it were a dance. Each projectile whizzed by him. Most of them struck the wall, creating miniature explosions as bits of wood flew into the air.

One of them went somewhere else: towards Jay. She gasped.

The glowing white ball flew over her shoulder, creating a buzz as it narrowly missed her ear. Jay—now out of her trance—then noticed that she was standing in the doorway. She moved to the wall for cover and continued to watch the unfolding carnage.

There were a couple more bloodied corpses on the ground, as well as a staff split in two. The others were scrambling for their melee weapons. The Objectivist threw out his right arm, palm facing the center of the room.

The white orb that followed hovered in the air. The Objectivist tensed his hand. The orb pulsated. He then closed it, and the orb burst. A shockwave emerged. Every Landorian in the room toppled over as the chairs split apart. The sound of snapping wood was overpowered by the high-pitched ringing. Jay's body tightened as she covered her ears.

With the Landorians on the floor, the Objectivist easily plunged his dagger down into one of them. Jay heard the blade slice through his throat's flesh as he choked for air.

A different soldier, dazed from the energy shockwave, tried getting to his feet. The Objectivist grabbed him by his hair.

A voice inside Jay wanted her to yell, to tell him to stop. A different voice, however, fought against it.

The Objectivist slit the soldier's throat. Blood poured from the wound, spilling onto his black clothing and the floor. He took gasping breaths through his severed windpipe as his gargling blood continued to squirt out, until he finally collapsed.

Why is this so easy to watch? Jay thought. *This isn't an action movie. This is real, and it's horrible. And yet...*

One soldier screamed, and then charged at the murderer with a longsword. The Objectivist dodged and parried the swordsman. The metal blades clanked and scratched against each other. At the same time, he avoided blasts of energy from two others. Their attacks were like gunshots.

Another approached him from behind. A knife was in his hand. He raised it in the air.

Bang.

Jay fired a blast into the would-be attacker. He collapsed. As he tried to get back up, she dashed towards him and jumped. In the air, she spun, bringing her leg up with her. The kick missed, and Jay toppled over. She looked up. The tip of the soldier's blade gleamed above her.

A bolt of energy struck the man on his side. He was knocked down, his knife falling with him. Jay kicked it away and pointed her staff at the man's face. She continuously glanced between him and the Objectivist.

As she kept her staff aimed, the Objectivist successfully disarmed the swordsman and stabbed him in the heart. He quickly turned around, bringing his right arm out. He aimed it at someone, then tensed the muscle. From a small, wooden mechanism built into the sleeve underneath his forearm, a long, thin knife fired. It impaled the soldier, once again in the heart. He fell to the ground, groaning.

One more was left standing. His eyes were widened as he clutched his staff and spear. The Objectivist tilted his head for a moment. The soldier fired a blast of energy. It struck the wall.

A red light flashed. The Objectivist reappeared behind him. He kicked him in the back of the leg, then grabbed his head. Once again, Jay held her breath in anticipation.

The Objectivist smashed his face into the table. The wood was crushed, creating several loud snaps. Large splinters drove into his skin. He lifted the mangled head up, letting his blood drip down. He tossed him to the ground.

The soldier grabbed the edge of the table to support himself. The Objectivist noticed the outstretched limb. He swung his arm down. There was a snap, and then a scream.

The soldier collapsed against the wall, then slid to the ground.

"Just do it," he groaned.

The Objectivist jumped and brought his leg out, using the same move that Jay had attempted earlier. His foot landed, and the soldier was knocked right out.

He looked to Jay and gave a nod. "Finish him."

Jay swallowed. "Right."

Jay crouched over the man below her, closing the distance between her staff and his face.

"Please… do not do this," he panted.

"Jay… please don't do this."

The voice of a familiar female rang through her head. She held her staff tighter as her brain tried resisting the incoming memories. Jay let out a shuddering breath.

Jay dropped the staff and let out a vicious scream of rage. She punched the pleading man, and then punched with her other fist. Then the other. She kept going, alternating between fists as she relentlessly hit him with all that she had, until finally it was only her left doing all the damage. Each blow was enunciated with a grunt of anger and the sound of flesh striking flesh. In the blood that pooled around the man's leaking head, Jay noticed the reflection of green light. Her senses returned to her, and she stopped. She made a small, shuddering gasp as she stood, taking in all her surroundings.

Corpses littered the once-busy room in bent, crumpled positions. Crimson was splattered all across the walls, floor, and furniture. She didn't know so much blood could leak from a person. They were like crushed watermelons. Some of the bodies still had their eyes open, broadcasting their last emotions before their lives had left them: fear.

Jay looked down at the face of the man she had just beaten. Even without the blood that covered it, his face was unrecognizable. His jaw was broken off its hinges, and the skin of his face was torn open. Jay knew he would live, but he would never be the same. Her eyes moved to her fists. They were shaking and covered in red, and there were similar stains on her sleeves and shirt. Her body was quivering. There was no feeling of guilt or abhorrence in her, but instead a deep, horrifying trickle of satisfaction.

She tried opening her mouth to say something, but couldn't. The Objectivist, who had been staring at her this entire time, made a small, hollow laugh.

"This isn't funny!" Jay snapped.

"I thought you had a distaste for violence… and bursts of anger."

"I…" She tried to avoid staring at all the blood, but her eyes betrayed her. "I don't know," she said softly.

"Put aside your unnecessary feelings. We have accomplished our primary objective." He nodded his head towards the toppled chest.

"Right." Jay undid the latch and opened the box. As expected, the three Scrolls of Gales laid safely inside. "This is it," she said, closing the chest. "I suppose I have to say thank you."

"No, do not thank me. I have my own reasons for being here. Remember that." The Objectivist began to retrieve his knives from the bodies. "Istra is still a mystery, however. Unless…" He trailed off as he yanked a throwing knife from a torso.

"Unless… what?"

He shook his head. "Nevermind. You say you're smart, so I'm certain you will figure it out yourself."

Jay moved to the doorway, taking in the cool, fresh air. "Always so irritatingly enigmatic," she muttered. "Why do we need to find Istra, anyway? Do you plan on killing him?"

"Come here, Jay."

"And what was that about insulting me out of nowhere, by the way? Is that supposed to make me stronger, too?" she said as she approached him.

"*Clono eht onis.*" The blood on Jay's hands and clothes slowly vanished into nothing. "I have a new spell for you."

"Oh, so you know what spells *I* know?"

"I'm merely making an assumption. The incantation is *'kawa eht nalfa.'* Use it on this one here." He indicated the man he had knocked out with his kick. Blood poured from where the splinters remained in his face. "It's an awakening spell. I'm going to interrogate him."

"About what?"

"Their king. I would like to locate him for my own reasons. Istra might be there, too."

Jay raised her arm and took hold of her amulet, her palm facing the slumped mage. "I *did* know that one, by the way. *Kawa eht nalfa!*"

The man awoke with a cough. He groaned. "What..."

Bang! The Objectivist fired a blast straight into his left shin. There was an audible *snap* as the victim screamed.

"My query for you is simple: Where is your king?" he asked.

"Screw you," he spat.

"Hm." The Objectivist stomped on his injured leg. His second scream was louder than the first. "Your name is Lihmus, yes?"

"How did you—?"

"I will stop hurting you, Lihmus, if you answer the question. I merely have business with your king. I will not be killing him, nor will he know of your treachery. You will be saving yourself. Where is the wrong in that?"

Lihmus wiped the blood off his mouth. "I am a servant of King Landor. My life has no other purpose."

The Objectivist pressed his boot into his shin, causing the man to scream again. "A life with no purpose other than to serve someone else is a wasteful one. An immoral one, even." He relieved the pressure. "Answer the question, or I will resort to a certain spell. You know what I speak of."

Lihmus's expression changed in an instant. His eyes bulged, and his body began to shake. "No, no, I... King Landor is at a different fortification, down south along the Barrier. He is waiting to hear that we took the Scrolls."

Jay turned to the hooded man. "Istra isn't here, so he must be going to Landor right now to tell him."

Lihmus coughed again and shook his head. "You underestimate their speed and efficiency. His Majesty is most certainly on his way here." He looked at Jay. "You are one of the Dijenuks. I can see it in your clothes. But... how are you here in the Kingdom?"

The Objectivist turned away from him. "You can run your mouth as to what happened here; it matters to me not. We must go, Jay."

"Wait!" called Lihmus. He laughed. "I know who you are."

The Objectivist took a calm step forward. "I doubt it."

"You are the Black Hood. The legend himself! The—"

The Objectivist spun. Lihmus was promptly knocked unconscious by a foot to the temple. "The camp should be alerted by now. We need to go back to your fellow Restorers. Follow me. Stay close!" With that, he bolted outside. "Come on!"

"I'm trying!" The girl struggled to catch up.

"We need to return to Hegortant. The Restorers are waiting for you there."

"What?" She paused to catch her breath as she ran. "How do you know that?"

The Objectivist whispered something.

"Did you say something?"

He covered his face with a hand. "Hold on to my arm and hang tight. Do *not* let go, no matter what happens. Understood?"

"Yes."

"Now close your eyes."

"Why—?"

"Just do it!" There was yelling nearby. A bell had just rung.

Jay did as told. Suddenly, her entire body felt a deep cold and she could no longer feel the ground beneath her. Worse than that, it was as though every single molecule in her body was ripped apart. It was painless, but the sudden nausea made up for it. Instinct forced her to open her eyes. The ground was hundreds of feet away and grew farther by the second. The terrain blurred as it raced by. She wanted to scream but couldn't. There wasn't a mouth to make noise with.

As she passed through the Barrier, she felt a marginal increase in warmth. Within minutes, Hegortant became visible in the horizon. From the sky, the city's tall buildings and towering walls were almost breathtaking. It only somewhat distracted from the otherwise-ill experience. Without any of Jay's input, she began to descend. The flat roof of a building zoomed scarily close. Only a few meters away, her body returned to normal as it tumbled across the stone. She groaned and rolled to her back. The Objectivist stood over her. He was spinning in her view, along with the rest of the world.

"What… in the hell… was that?"

He offered a hand. The girl took it. "Dark Flight," he answered as he pulled her up. "You've seen it before. It is a popular form of transportation within those who can cast the Dark sub-type."

"Hold on… You're a Landor, aren't you?"

The Objectivist said nothing. The two of them stared each other down as gentle wind ran through them.

"Answer me."

"I don't know."

"Huh?" Jay ran her hand through her hair and then threw her arm down. "Gah, you're irritating! Just like everyone else, you avoid my questions. Why? Why can't I get a straight answer? What 'actions' must be taken, like you said? Why am I the way I am, more special than just being a Dijenuk? You have the answers, don't you?"

"I understand why you're upset. I really do. If I could tell you everything, I would, but…"

"But what?"

"It's not up to me. As I mentioned, there are certain steps everyone must follow. I have the burden of knowing a handful of them."

"So, what, is this some kind of game we're stuck in?"

The Objectivist looked down. "Yes." His voice dropped, and his overwhelming arrogance and confidence was replaced by a grim, somber tone. "And we're the chess pieces."

They were silent again.

The Objectivist turned around. "Goodbye for now, Jay. Your fellow Restorers should be somewhere nearby, fighting an Arcane Abomination as we speak. We will meet again."

"A what? Hey, wait!"

He sprinted away and leaped off the roof.

"Hey!" The girl looked down to the alley below. He was nowhere to be seen. She searched around. "And now I'm stuck up here. Wonderful."

She hissed, for the wind elevated the pain on her hands. She stared at her left knuckles. It wasn't the first time they had been torn open and bloody. She recalled the first instance, just before her senior year had begun…

—<o>—

The air was cool and still. Few sounds at this hour disturbed it. Jay breathed in this late summer air, white rope in hand, and prepared to get to work. She sat down in one of the chairs of the backyard, three more all positioned around a small glass table. The deck went out a few more feet before meeting a jungle of unkempt grass. Most of it was squashed by a pool in the right corner. Its water was the only clean thing in the cramped yard.

Jay put the rope down on the table and moved to the large tree in the left corner. A grey, dirt-stained punching bag hung

244

from one of the branches.

She began, as always, by practicing a few kicks, her feet striking nothing but midnight's air. Straight kick, roundhouse kick, tornado kick, and various others. She then tried one in which she spun around and kicked behind her. On each attempt, she lost her balance, and on the fourth try, she fell. Jay looked up from the ground. In the darkness, she spotted something stuck under the deck: a playing card. Her eyes moved to the table.

There, she saw the day when she and Stacie had been playing a card game, something Jay had never done before. Stacie had been surprised by that fact and had insisted they try every type of card game. That spring day had been windy, and it hadn't taken long for their game of Speed to blow away. They'd laughed it off.

Jay moved to pick up the white rope from the table. She began to wrap it between her fingers and around her hands and forearms.

"Do you know what I love about our friendship, Jay?"

Jay squeezed her fists and exhaled. "No…" She gazed at the punching bag.

"We never, no matter what, abandon each other."

Her eyes tickled, like she was about to cry. She slapped herself. "No."

She removed the unfinished wrap and threw the rope down. Her fingers twitched, and she stomped towards the punching bag. She struck it with her naked fist and paused, taking in the scratch and the sound of the swinging chains.

"No matter the hardship, I'll be there for you. I promise you that."

Jay hit the bag. "Promise?" She hit it again. "No..." She swung twice more. "No!" Each word was enunciated with a strike. "You—promised—Stacie! You—promised! You—were—supposed—to—be..." She paused. "Get out of my head!"

She unleashed a flurry of strikes, her breathing amplifying as her speed increased. As she let out a scream, she moved past the punching bag and went at the trunk of the tree, her punches relentless. Seconds passed, and the pain finally caught up to her.

Jay fell to her knees, groaning in agony and clutching her shaking left hand. "Get out... of my head," she said, panting. Sitting down, she rested against the tree, listening to the croak of the chains. "Feel nothing... be everything. Feel nothing; be everything, damn it."

She stared at her bloody hand. Despite the immense pain, she felt satisfied.

"No one will control me ever again... and I will neither bend nor bow down for *anyone*."

CHAPTER XI:
INFILTRATOR

"WELL... THAT WAS UNEXPECTED," David said.

The Restorers, who had been waiting by the Barrier, suddenly found themselves in Hegortant after an explosion of green light. Angela had her hand against a wall, supporting herself, and Elfekot had fallen into a kneeling position.

"We're in Hegortant, yeah?"

The road was missing chunks of cobblestone, revealing the dirt beneath, with a layer of ankle-deep fog over it. Instead of stone, the buildings were built of rotting wood, held together by rope too skinny to be safe. Their windows, if they had any, were mostly either cracked or smashed open. It was all quiet. A few men and women were shuffling about, all wearing dirty rags for clothing. More than half of them noticed David and stared at him for a few seconds, then continued to hobble onward.

Elfekot nodded. "This is what most of Hegortant is like. Most of Elektia, actually."

Angela finally looked up. "I was unaware."

"Few outsiders are."

"So, do you not get to leave the fort much?" David asked.

"No, unfortunately. We are not usually allowed to just visit other places without a good reason. My parents do, sometimes, since fire mages are moved around by the Council more."

"How come?"

"I do not know how it works for you all on Terra, but here, the only way we can stay warm and cook our food is with the magic of fire mages. We are in high demand, I guess you could say."

"So, since you guys don't have fire magic…"

Angela frowned. "It is not great for anyone, Master Dijenuk. The Elektians really are relying on us. However, we must not forget to reach out to the Elementians in prayer."

"Or maybe they should have stopped Landor in the first place…" Elfekot mumbled.

"Do not lose your faith, Elfekot. It is in these times that we must confide in both each other and the Elementians."

"So, from what I understand, these Elementians are gods?" David asked.

"Oh, I suppose you do not know about them either, as a Terran," Angela said. "Yes, they are our gods. They created us, our magic, and our home, and they protect us."

"Huh. I bet Jay would have a few words to say about that. One for each Element, I'm guessing, yeah?"

"Mm hm. They visit us through our dreams, and it is said that the Light Elementian often makes contact with the Dijenuks. Is that true?"

"Um, I'm not sure. I don't remember any dreams like that, at least, and I don't think Jay's had that happen either. Do they ever visit in person?"

"They have in the past, but those are very rare and very special events. The last time it happened was a horrific war between Light Elektia and Dark Elektia. A powerful mage of each Element on the Light Elektian side was visited by the respective Elementian, and they were given a blessing to turn the tides of battle." Angela's eyes sparkled as she explained.

"So, the Elementians are on our side?"

"All but the Dark Elementian, yes. I hope to one day receive a blessing from the Fire Elementian himself, and I think it could very well happen." She smiled and made a little hop. "This is exciting, isn't it?"

"Ah, yes, global starvation and mass panic is quite exciting indeed," Elfekot said.

"You know what I mean, Elfekot."

"I do not. Anyway, we should get going to the city center. Jay is smart, so perhaps she will also think to meet us there."

"Do you think Jay got us here?" David asked as they began walking.

"I believe so, considering the green light," Elfekot answered.

Angela shook her head. "She really is something..."

"We're *all* something," David replied. "I mean, we're the Restorers, after all."

Elfekot sighed. "Unfortunately."

"You wish to be back, yes?" Angela said.

"To my old life, yes. I was trained to be in charge of a fort, not children."

David and Angela both looked at each other. David rolled

his eyes, and Angela frowned.

"So... I dunno how long my sis is gonna take, so, like, what do we do in the meantime?"

"Finally get you some proper clothes, I reckon," Elfekot answered.

"Sweet."

"I could also do with new attire. Are you paying, Elfekot?" Angela asked.

"I did not bring any tehk with me, so no. David gets whatever he desires free, at the very least."

"Tehk?"

"Our currency."

"Oh, so, like dollars. I expected gold coins or something."

"I believe coins were actually used centuries ago, but we use linen notes now," Angela explained.

The three of them came upon the river that cut through Hegortant. It was well over a hundred meters in width, and its banks had been turned into patches of farmland on both sides that stretched down the entire city. Long, thin plants rose from the soil, like blades of grass the height of a person, with purple coloring at the tips.

"Is this a farm?" David asked.

"Aye. I reckon it is one of the few surviving on Elektia."

"Why's that?"

"Without water mages, irrigation is difficult. Rivers like Stohgent here make it easier."

"Dang. So you need magic for that, too?"

"Not just that…"

They watched a group of eight men and women in dirt-stained clothing arguing with each other over what to do with the crops. Next to them were empty collection baskets. One of them pulled out a plant, only to find a tiny, unripe vegetable, similar to a potato, but a deep purple.

A nearby guard yelled, "Just figure something out!"

The farmers responded in a chorus of desperate arguing. It didn't last long, for they finally noticed the three Restorers watching them.

"Are these…?"

"Is he…?"

"Come on," Elfekot muttered, leading the other two across the simple stone bridge, one of the many in Hegortant.

"I wish I could help them," David said once they were out of earshot.

"Restore the Earth Element, along with the others, and you will."

"And they will all call us heroes," Angela added.

The streets continued to narrow as they walked, the sun still beaming over their heads. The cobble road took them uphill and back towards the wide area that was the city center. There were fewer civilians than in the morning, but more guards.

"There is a standard attire dispensary down that street, opposite the direction of where we went to see, er, Denisse," Elfekot said. "I will stay and wait for your sister, assuming she can make her way back just like we did. You may go with him if you wish, Angela."

"I shall. Follow me, Master Dijenuk."

"Er, isn't this your first time in Hegortant?" David said.

David and Angela went down the street to the left from the gate and closer to the wall. As they walked, they scanned their surroundings for any indication of a clothing shop, but found none. There were no signs for anything.

The buildings on this street were shorter, but much wider, and their windows lacked curtains. Through them, anyone could see the guards mingling inside and the ladders that led to the top of the wall. The two of them took a set of steps down and around a corner. They found a dead end and a crowd of a dozen or so civilians, and two guards blocking the entrance to a building.

Angela went on her tiptoes. "I believe this is an attire dispensary, but... I think it is closed. Hm..." She began pushing her way to the front of the crowd.

"Hey, wait! What are you doing?" David said, following her.

She reached the two guards. "We need to enter."

"Huh? We apologize, Miss, but all the dispensaries in Light Elektia are closed for the time being. It was a very recent order, but you surely understand, with what is going on and all."

"Closed? Well, you see, this is the Dijenuk, and—"

The guards gasped. "The Dijenuk? Really?"

At this, the crowd's chatter dropped to low, excited murmurs.

The guards looked at David. "Is this true?"

"Um, yeah, but—"

"Welcome to Elektia, Master Dijenuk." The two guards put their legs together and bowed at the waist. The crowd around them followed suit. "Go ahead," one of them said, opening the door.

David and Angela stepped into the musty interior. There were six stands, three on the left and three on the right, and a counter in the back, all made of a brown-grey wood identical to the floorboards. The stands on the left held the same everyday clothing that they'd seen on the civilians, and the right stands held long, white robes with differently colored trims and oversized sleeves.

A young man emerged from the room behind the counter. His brown hair was tied in a messy braid, and his large eyes drooped. "Er, are you supposed to be in here?"

"Yes. The guards let us in," Angela said. "This is the Dijenuk, you see."

"Oh!" The young man put his legs together and bowed. "Welcome, Master Dijenuk. I assume you seek to replace your Terran attire, yes?"

"Um, yeah." David leaned towards Angela. "Don't call me *the* Dijenuk. It's kinda weird."

"Are you looking for anything in particular?" the clerk asked.

"Not really. I guess whatever is the most normal."

"Well, just pick something from the stands on your left. The robes on the right there are *strictly* for formal events."

"Gotcha."

David took a better look at the clothing. One of the sets was a brown shirt with a turtleneck collar, as well as brown pants and shoes with buckles. Another set had an off-white shirt, also with a turtleneck collar, and brown boots instead. The third was the same as the first, but with off-white pants.

David looked to the clerk. "Is this everything?"

"Of course not. We have different sizes in storage."

"No, I mean, is this every design and color?"

The clerk blinked. "Design...? Er, yes. Is something wrong?"

"Uh, no."

"Oh! We also have cloaks, if you desire them. I almost forgot."

"In what colors?"

"Brown."

David nodded as he pursed his lips. "Gotcha."

Something in the backroom shattered. The clerk froze. "Uh..."

An older man burst through the door and shoved the clerk to the ground. He fired two blasts of energy at David and Angela, knocking them down as well. The man rummaged through something behind the container, took a leather sack, and bolted away.

"Hey!" Angela drew her staff and ran to follow. David joined her. The clerk remained grounded.

They entered the back room, a space filled with open crates and piles of unfolded clothing. Without a second thought,

Angela jumped through the broken window.

"Hey, wait up!" David said. "Be careful!" He followed, but made sure to watch for the glass edges.

They dropped down to a wide street, perpendicular to the one they'd come from, but a story lower. The thief had parted a clear path through the civilians, and the two Restorers chased him down. He approached a sharp turn. Angela took out her spear and threw it.

"Angela!"

The spear stabbed a barrel just a couple meters in front of him, causing the thief to stop in his tracks.

"Halt!" Angela shouted.

As the thief began to move around the spear, Angela fired a blast of energy. It exploded the ground next to him, making him stumble and fall backwards. They caught up to him as Angela approached with a pointed staff.

"Hey, what was that about?" David asked her.

"He stole something, Master Dijenuk. Can you not see?"

"Yeah, but—"

"This man is a thief," Angela said to the two guards running towards them. "He stole some tehk from a nearby dispensary."

They hesitated before sheathing their weapons. "Is that so?"

She turned to the gathered civilians. "Yes, and it was I, Angela Fryner, and one of the Restorers of the Elements, who caught him," she said with a raised voice.

"Right. Er, thank you." One of the guards forced the thief up and bound his hands with a piece of rope. "Just be careful, alright? With everything going on, we have been seeing criminals like him pop up everywhere."

"Wait, what about the money?" David asked.

"Huh? What about it?" the guard replied.

"Isn't it the store owner's? Er, dispensary owner's?"

The guards' eyes grew. "Oh! You must be the Dijenuk! Bless the Elementians. I knew you would come to save us!"

"Not this again…" David muttered as the two guards and the prying civilians bowed with their legs together.

"To clarify, all tehk is the property of the Light Council. It need not be returned anywhere unless stolen directly from a civilian."

"Oh. Uh, gotcha."

"May the Elementians bless your journey, Master Dijenuk," said the other guard before they both left with the thief in tow.

Angela exhaled through her nose. "They only acknowledged *you*… Master Dijenuk," she said with a low voice. Her excited expression was gone.

David frowned. "Yeah. I'm sorry, Angela. You were the one who caught him. But you don't have to be upset. It's not that big a deal, and I don't even like the attention anyway," he said with a soft laugh.

"Right." She took her spear back and sheathed her weapons. "Shall we return and fetch the clothing you need?"

"Sure."

They turned around and began making their way back. The Elektians were still chatting amongst themselves.

"Woah, what's with the fog?" David said. It had been gradually rising since they arrived on Elektia, and now it nearly reached their knees, prompting the Dijenuk to notice.

"This is quite normal," Angela replied. "Although, it is a little thicker than usual, now that I think about it. Do you not have fog on Terra?"

"We do, it's just… not this shallow and thick. I can hardly see my own feet."

Angela stopped in her tracks. The other Elektians went silent.

"What's wrong?" David asked.

"Do you not feel that?"

"Feel what?"

Angela pulled out her staff. Her face was scrunched in concentration.

David closed his eyes and concentrated on his senses. His surroundings gave off a faint hum. The source of the hum shifted around them as it grew in intensity.

"What is that?"

"It is the feeling all magical energy gives off. But, to feel it so easily…" Angela looked down. "Whatever it is, it is moving through the fog."

"You can tell?" David took a deep breath and closed his eyes again. Whatever was giving off the hum was moving along the ground like a snake. It was getting farther away.

David clutched his chest as he doubled over. His entire rib cage vibrated for a moment. A split second later, a gust of wind washed over them, throwing about their clothes and hair and knocking over any lighter objects. The fog thinned out.

The Dijenuk helped some of the fallen civilians back up as Angela looked around.

"Is this Landor's doing?" she wondered aloud.

A chorus of screams emerged from elsewhere in the city. Not long after, nearly a dozen civilians ran past them.

"There is a monster!" a man yelled.

"Where?" David asked the mob.

"City center," Angela muttered. "There is a strong presence there." She held both her staff and spear. "Stay back, Master Dijenuk. He is mine!"

"Angela, no!" Drawing his staff, David ran after her.

They pushed through more fleeing civilians and reached the location. Over a dozen guards were already unconscious. Only Elfekot was standing as something else occupied the very center.

The monster was a nine-foot-tall humanoid, although about a quarter of that height was empty space, for it floated in the air using a pillar of spinning wind beneath its brown-rock torso and head. Its left arm and hand were made of water, while its right was made of a shiny, silver metal. Its head, which was engulfed in flames, lacked ears and a nose, and it had a large, gaping mouth and two holes for eyes.

It was spewing small balls of fire from its mouth at Elfekot, who blocked each projectile with his sword. The blue-grey blade deflected the magic back, but all of it missed.

"Elfekot!" David shouted.

Elfekot glanced over at David, allowing the monster to burst forward and swing at him with its left arm. As it moved through the air, the water froze, and the now-solid arm struck the captain in the head and knocked him right down. It turned to face the other two.

David took a step back. "What is that?!"

"I have no idea." The corners of Angela's mouth lifted. "But that only makes it more fun." She charged forward as she sent a barrage of energy blasts.

Tiny bits of rock flew off where it was struck, but the monster had no reaction. It swung its left arm and cast a large chunk of ice. Angela jumped to the side to dodge it, then lunged forward with her spear. It barely penetrated. Angela removed it, ready to strike again, but the creature turned its icy arm back into liquid and sliced at her.

The water passed through her torso, causing Angela to shudder and gasp as she fell to her knees.

"Angela!" David called.

He finally managed to fire a bolt of energy. It chipped off a corner of its torso. The monster floated up a few inches higher and hurled more balls of fire. David sprinted to his left, circling the monster as its flames landed just behind his heel.

Elfekot, now on his feet, sheathed his sword and brought out his right arm, creating a large, mirroring fist of white energy in front of him. With it, he grabbed the creature, preventing it from turning and using its arms. David and Angela both pointed their staffs at it.

"Give it all you have," Elfekot said through gritted teeth. "I cannot hold it for much longer."

They both fired large projectiles of energy. Just before either landed, the creature dissolved into a silver light, which immediately disappeared into the fog. The projectiles collided with each other, exploding into a small shockwave that blew their hair back.

"Where did it go?" Angela asked.

David looked to the captain. "Elfekot, what is this?"

He was silent as he watched the fog.

"Behind you!" Angela shouted.

The creature rose from the fog right behind David and struck him with its icy arm. David was forced to the ground. He touched his head where he had been hit and peered at his hand. It was bloody. David looked back up to the creature. It was raising both its arms.

"Angela, beam, now!" Elfekot yelled.

The two of them thrust their staffs forward, each creating a solid beam of white energy. It pushed the monster back, gradually etching at its rocky torso. After several seconds, they dropped the beam and let out a breath.

David scrambled back to his feet and joined the others. "Where are the guards?!" he said.

"Some already tried," Elfekot said, glancing at the bodies. "I doubt more will come."

Angela rolled her neck. "Fine by me."

She pointed her staff at the creature, but it turned into a silver light and disappeared into the fog again.

"Stay close to me," Elfekot said as the trio scanned their surroundings, watching for movement.

The silver light appeared again with a flash, and the creature came with it, its arms raised above its head. Elfekot slammed his staff into the ground, creating a shockwave that knocked the monstrosity back several meters. David and Angela each fired a projectile, but it created a blast of wind under itself, knocking the trio onto their backs and propelling the monster into the air.

Above the buildings, the monster raised its metal arm. Electricity coursed through it. A clap of thunder boomed, and it swung its arm down. A bolt of lightning fell on the trio. It collided with a magical shield raised just in time by Elfekot. The zap continued to pressure the barrier, causing it to decrease in size and opacity until it was barely visible.

Elfekot groaned and flopped back to the ground. David and Angela stood back up. The creature was now dive-bombing them, arms outstretched. Flames spun within its mouth cavity.

David shut his left eye and aimed his staff. A ball of white energy charged at the tip of it. His arm went up from the recoil as the projectile fired. The ball of energy landed right in its mouth, flipping it backwards as it sank to the ground. It landed with a hefty thud.

Angela rested her foot on the creature and charged an orb of energy, point-blank. In the few seconds that the attack readied, a golden light appeared in the creature's right eye socket. She leaned forward to inspect it.

"Is that—?"

The light flashed, and Angela screamed. She stumbled back, dropping her staff as she moved her hands to her eyes. The monster then lifted itself upright and raised its right arm again. It crackled with electricity.

"Angela!" David yelled, raising his staff. He held his breath, tensing his arm to fire. Nothing happened.

The monster swung its arm. It landed on the back of her neck. Lightning coursed through her, contorting and tensing her body before she dropped to the ground, limp.

David took a couple quick breaths and tried to fire again. Another golden light appeared in its eye socket. Before he realized what it was doing, the light flashed. David blinked. It had no effect. He fired a blast of energy, making another small indentation in its torso.

It threw both its arms up. A blast of wind knocked David over and sent him skidding across the ground. It turned its attention to Elfekot, who had just returned to his feet. The monster thrust its electric arm forward. Elfekot crossed both his arms in an X shape, creating a magical shield in front of himself. The fist collided with the shield. Sparks flew out from the point of contact.

David stood. "How do we destroy this thing?!"

"I do… not know," said Elfekot, straining under the pressure of the creature's fist. "Do something!" he barked.

David fired a blast of energy. It did nothing more than chip off a piece of rock. The monster began spewing flame from its mouth, adding to the pressure on Elfekot's shrinking shield.

"Uh…" David's arm was shaking. He fired another blast. It missed.

Elfekot's knees buckled. His teeth were clenched.

"I can't fight like you!" David said.

"Try! You're a Dijenuk. It's in you!"

"Try…" David took a deep breath.

Elfekot's shield grew small enough so that some of the flame was spilling over its edge. David switched his staff to his left hand. Elfekot fell to one knee.

David leaned back and swung his right fist forward. A larger one made of white energy manifested before him, mimicking his movement like it had with Elfekot earlier. The magical fist struck the creature, and it flew into a wall.

"Keep him back!" Elfekot said, desperate for air.

David swung again. The wall behind it cracked under the force. "We need the guards' help!" he said, attacking it once more. "We need Jay!"

"We do *not*," said Angela, back on her feet.

As the creature was stunned from David's attacks, Angela charged with her spear. She lunged forward, penetrating the creature's icy left shoulder. With a yell, she forced her spear all the way through, shattering the ice and turning its entire arm into pieces, then jumped back,

She exhaled. "See?"

David nodded. "Yeah." He reeled back for another magical punch, but a sharp pain battered the inside of his skull.

"Ugh…" He stumbled as he put his hand to his head. A drop of blood fell from his nose.

"Stay with us, Master Dijenuk," Angela said.

"I'm all good," he said, nodding. "Uh… what's it doing?"

The creature was looking directly at the ground, arm down and limp.

David took a step forward. "Did we do it?"

It looked back up and immediately created a flash of blinding light. Elfekot and Angela both yelped in pain as they were stunned. David raised his staff.

The monster turned towards Elfekot, who was closest. It thrust its arm forward, creating a blast of wind that sent Elfekot flying across the square and right through a building's wall.

David gasped, and his eyes widened. The monster floated towards him. His body refused to move. Flames spun inside its mouth. It reeled its head back and then leaned forward, spewing the fire.

Angela leaped in front of him. She bodyblocked the blast. Its attack was persistent, like a flamethrower, but Angela stood her ground. The monstrosity inched forward as it continued spewing its flames.

She looked back to David, a smile on her face. "I can handle this."

"Look out!"

Water flowed from the monster's empty shoulder socket, forming a new arm. It thrust the watery arm forward and into Angela. It stabbed her, as though a solid blade. The monster pulled the arm out, and Angela fell to her knees, her body and breath shaky.

David could only watch as the monster swatted her away, sending her to the other side of the square. It raised its arms, and David raised with them, a pillar of wind supporting him. He rose nearly two stories high.

"Guys?!"

The monster threw his arms down and to the side, and the wind carrying David rocketed him the same direction. He crashed into the ground, creating a loud *crack* where the stone broke under him.

David groaned as he stood. His body screamed in pain where he had landed. He looked back to the creature. A black orb had formed in its left eye socket. His muscles tensed as he braced for impact.

A bolt of dark energy fired from the same eye. It pierced through David's chest. All the warmth in his body left him as he fell to knees and dropped his staff. A numbing sensation and an overwhelming cold ran through him. Another black orb appeared in its eye.

The sensation was gone, but he was left feeling weaker, as though his muscles took more effort to move.

"I… can't let it end like this," David said as he rose to his feet once more.

The creature fired the dark projectile. David brought his arms in, crossing them like an 'X.' He created a shield and blocked the attack just in time.

"Dark magic," he whispered as the creature hovered higher into the air. "Landor's magic."

The creature curled its fingers and slowly brought its arms up. The flames that engulfed its head grew in size as the electricity in its metal arm went haywire. The fog lifted from the ground and absorbed into the monster. The magical hum that it emitted multiplied, shaking David's entire core.

"Oh, God."

A silver sphere of energy manifested in front of it, and it ballooned in size with each passing second.

David created the shield again and shut his eyes. With the sphere now half the size of its creator, the monster thrust his arms forward. A solid beam emitted from the sphere and collided with David' shield. It slowly shrank as the beam continued. The monster would not let up.

The shield broke, and the beam went through. It persisted for several seconds more until the silver energy was gone. David opened his eyes. The only new thing he felt was a warmth emanating from his staff. A faint buzz came from it. He adjusted his grip. The metal section was glowing.

"David, the staff!" Elfekot said.

David looked back up at the creature. It was readying the same attack.

"It's over!" he shouted.

With the force of a cannon, his redwood staff discharged an explosion of grey energy. That alone made David's ears ring as the large projectile sent the creature up into the atmosphere. Not even two seconds later, it exploded with a brilliant flash of light, illuminating the canopy of clouds, and it was gone.

"It is destroyed! He did it!" a masculine voice shouted.

At last, nearly two dozen of Hegortant's guards stormed the square, joined by an equal amount of civilians.

Elfekot and Angela approached David. "They were here the whole time?" David said.

"Not a surprise," Elfekot muttered.

The previously hidden audience started cheering. A few more emerged from their rooftop and window hiding places. "He did it! The Dijenuk defeated the monster!"

"It is the Restorers of the Elements. They saved us!"

"Praise the Elementians!"

"The boy is a hero!"

David smiled, brushing the hair out of his face. "Hero..." he echoed softly. He felt a hand on his shoulder.

"Good job, kid," Elfekot said.

"Thanks," he said weakly. "That was too close. And again, dude, you're hardly older than me."

"I have to admit, that was incredible, Master Dijenuk," Angela said.

"Thank you. I... I..." David fell to his knees. He was hit with a wave of exhaustion.

"David?"

"Ugh, my head..."

"Is that Jay?"

"Sis?" David tried to scan for her, but his vision darkened

and he collapsed, the cries of the crowd still joyful and vibrant.

CHAPTER XII:
SOMETHING TO HIDE

"ARE YOU SURE YOU ARE ALRIGHT?" Angela asked.

David nodded. "It's like Elfekot said. I just overexerted myself."

"I have never seen anyone faint because of it, though."

"Remember that he is new to using magic," Elfekot said as he stepped inside the Dijenuk House's sitting room.

David was sitting on a sofa with Angela next to him. It was nowhere near as comfortable as he was used to, but it sufficed. The orange light of the setting sun flooded the room.

"And he is also a Dijenuk," he continued. "Such immense, natural power being used through an unexperienced body is a larger toll than most Elektians are accustomed to."

"Yeah. I didn't know I was capable of all that." David frowned. "Hey, I have a question. Well, a few. Elfekot, you were thrown through a wall, and I was slammed into the ground from the sky, and yet we were okay, more or less. Angela even took on the monster's flames like it was nothing. Are we, like, superhuman?"

"I know only a few things about the Terrans, and one of them is that they are much frailer than we are, physically speaking," Elfekot said. "To put it in your perspective, Elektians are more resilient to physical damage. Magic, too. We also possess better reflexes, endurance, and strength, but to a lesser extent than our sturdiness."

"So, we're just 'better?'"

"Not necessarily, although most would say so. From my understanding, the Terrans have reached a much more advanced level of society."

"We, er, they have, yeah. So, they're smarter?"

"In a way, yes."

"As for me, I can withstand flames so easily because it is my innate ability as the fire mage of the Restorers," said Angela with a proud smile.

"Every mage is resistant to their own Element, Angela. Do not lie to the boy."

"Jay and I can cast every Element though, right? Except Dark. So, what are *we* resistant to?"

"Light, as that is the Dijenuks' 'specialty,' if you will."

David nodded. "Huh. Well, it's good to know that we can be thrown through buildings and still survive."

Jay entered carrying a book and wearing disappointment. "There is nothing I could find regarding those symbols."

"I thought you could solve anything," David mocked.

"I *will* solve it." Her green eyes sparkled with confidence and thrill. "I simply need more information. Or any information at all, really. If I had to guess, it is likely an ancient language, as opposed to some secret code."

"They might not be important at all," Angela said with a

shrug.

"It is what we found on the Scrolls, the keys to entering the Wind Chamber. I reckon it is quite important," Elfekot countered.

"It could help us find the Chamber itself, too," David added. "I mean, no one knows where it is, right?"

"I will, soon enough," Jay said.

"Hey, wait," David said as his sister turned to leave. "Did you find anything on that creature?"

"Oh, that. It is called an Arcane Abomination, and, judging by the scarcity of information, it is quite rare. Why it appeared there in Hegortant and what it has to do with the fog, I am not yet certain. I have a theory, though."

"Well, what's your theory?"

Jay paused. "It is my own," she replied, and then left.

As David, Elfekot, and Angela discussed the potential location of the Wind Chamber, Jay returned to the room across the hall. One of the Scrolls of Gales and numerous books lay open across the small table where she had been reading. On the floor next to the table sat the wooden box, open with the other two Scrolls of Gales inside.

She began to put all the tomes back in the shelf, making sure to keep it organized. As she replaced the last one, a book labeled *A Basic History of Light Elektia*, a numbing sensation ran through her entire body. Her head ached slightly. For a moment, all her senses vanished. An image of Terra flashed in her head, followed by another image: blue eyes. Jay's senses returned to her.

"It can't be…" she said quietly to herself. The girl stared out the window and sighed. "I just want clothes and a shower right now." Her attention returned to the bookshelf. "Hm…"

"What I want to know is how you blocked the monster's attack like that," Angela wondered with awe.

David nodded towards the redwood staff resting against a wall. "I think it was because of that."

Angela moved to pick it up. "This staff?"

He nodded. "I think it absorbed its magic or something. It was kinda cool."

Angela looked to Elfekot. "Is that possible?"

The captain crossed his arms and stared at the staff in Angela's hands. "For the tenth time, I do not know everything. But… that metal bit has something to do with it. I have never known a staff to have something like that. I could not tell you what it really is, though."

"It is called greymetal," Jay answered as she reentered. "Quite the creative name, really. Greymetal has magic-absorbing properties. The energy can also be violently released if used correctly. Such a metal was used in the rods Mr. K gave the both of us. You've never seen it before because it is extremely rare. I lack an idea as to how Sarah—and Mr. K—managed to acquire such an alloy," she explained. "Basically, you were lucky, David."

David shrugged. "I like to think of it as… Mom's blessing, or something."

Jay rolled her eyes and crossed her arms. "I'll just call it dumb luck." With that, she exited the room once more.

David adjusted in his seat, feeling numerous aches across his body. He groaned. "So... now we just gotta find the Wind Chamber, yeah?"

"I wish it were the Fire Chamber instead," Angela grumbled.

"You know that there is an order, Angela," Elfekot said. "But yes, we must find it. And we need to continue to train the two of you. Angela and I should work to improve ourselves as well. We all have much to learn."

"Jay and I especially. Although, I feel like she knows so much already. But that's my sister for you." He stared off into nothing. "It's crazy.... In a couple of days, everything's changed. I often wonder if I'm dreaming. But I'm not. This is real, and, honestly, it's pretty dang cool."

King Landor had been sitting on his throne for hours. No servant, commander, or advisor dared to disturb him. The castle was quiet, as most of its occupants had fallen asleep. The next morning wasn't far away.

The Black Hood... he thought.

It was what Lihmus, one of the two survivors of that room, had told him. Landor had flown to the encampment, only to find numerous corpses and a missing box. He had demanded the soldier tell him had happened.

"It was him, Your Majesty. The man of legend," Lihmus

answered with a shaky voice. "The Black Hood. He killed the rest of us but spared me." He coughed violently.

Landor frowned. "I am unfamiliar with this figure you speak of."

"I recommend you read about him, Your Majesty. I am certain it was him."

The king shook his head before slamming the table. "You were all supposed to guard the Scrolls. We were supposed to assemble an infiltration team here. And you let this… Black Hood get away with it all!" he screamed.

Lihmus sighed. "I am truly sorry to have failed you, Your Majesty. Kill me if you must. I accept it."

Landor considered the option for a few seconds. His shoulders eased as his voice calmed. "No. That is unnecessary. You will be demoted, though."

There was a groan from the other side of the room. Landor stepped around the table to see the source. "You are alive as well, Tihmyen."

"I… am, Your Majesty." His broken, swollen face was drenched in his own blood.

"Did this supposed Black Hood spare you, too?" the king asked.

He shook his head. "Someone else," he muttered, still lying on the floor.

"Someone else?"

"A girl, I think," answered Lihmus as he attempted to stand.

"And you mention this now?"

"I apologize, Your Majesty. It is taking some effort to remember." He coughed again. "But yes, there was someone else with him. She—or he, maybe—was young. Odd clothes and odd hair. It was short. Green eyes, too. I thought it could be one of the Dijenuks, but... that is impossible, right, Your Majesty?"

Landor stared away. "Yes... yes, that is impossible," he murmured.

A group of soldiers, untouched by the Objectivist, rushed inside. Their determination was washed away by the death before them. "Your Majesty—"

"Clean this up!" the king barked.

He returned to his castle and made it clear to everyone that he was to not be bothered. Although, that had already been made explicit when he slammed the large, bronze double doors open to enter his throne room. This room was long and grand, with two lines of pillars running down it. A balcony hung above the main entrance. Between the pillars, a long, red carpet with black trim ran down the center of the room. At the end stood the throne itself. It was composed of a deep black metal with a scarlet seat. Numerous jewels of darkened tones inlaid into the metal gave the throne a sinister sparkle. It was sizeable enough for any man to sit in it comfortably.

Upon this throne sat Zecatsu Landor. He had been leaning back with his hands on his legs, unmoving. A small book sat at his feet, opened to a section labeled, "The Black Hood."

The king stared at the book for several seconds, tapping his feet. He then kicked it away, sending it sliding across the smooth floor.

"Fantasy garbage," he muttered.

Taking a long breath, Landor thought back again to what Lihmus had told him. *Jay was here, in the Kingdom of Landor,* he thought. *Was it really her? That would be impossible. No Light Elektian can cross the Barrier. And yet... who else other than her? And then there is...*

Landor's eyes widened, and he stood straight up. "No…" He swallowed, then made a deep, hollow laugh. "Renold Dijenuk, what did you do? What kind of monster did you create?" he said softly.

He slammed his throne. "No, focus! I have grown disorganized and scattered. I must simply continue what we already set forth. I must not rush. We are to intercept them when the time is right." He laughed a little. "Yes… Yes, everything will be fine. The Crystals and the Dijenuks are not lost at all."

One of the doors burst open as a messenger sprinted through it. "Your Majesty—"

"I said I was not to be disturbed!" he shouted. "Leave at once!"

"It is an emergency! Well, it could be—"

"*Could* be?"

"The rebellion, Your Majesty. They are gathering in the city square with another protest—"

"Do you know how many little *rebellions* this kingdom gets? It happens to every king, to every one of my ancestors. And do you know what happens? *Nothing.* And they will continue to do nothing but shout. *Leave!*" he spat.

"Your Majesty, please—"

"*Kanba tempus!*"

The messenger flew back into the hallway. The doors shut themselves in front of him. Landor exhaled and sank back into his throne.

"You should really listen to your messengers, Zecatsu," said a voice. A hooded figure clad in black leapt down from the balcony. "They tend to carry valuable information."

Landor snatched his staff from the floor. "Guards!" he shouted. "Who are you? How did you get in here?"

"He was right. You must be wary of these rebels," the figure, the Objectivist, said. "Even the most powerful of defenses can be overcome by sheer numbers."

"Guards!" he shouted again. "Where are they?"

"They are not coming," the Objectivist answered.

"If the Light Council put you up to this—"

"I only work for myself, Zecatsu." The Objectivist outstretched his left arm toward the book on the floor. He snapped two of his fingers inwards, and the book flew towards him.

"How did you—?"

"Interesting read."

"No… *You* are the Black Hood they speak of?"

The figure said nothing.

"Are those preposterous stories true?"

"Of course not," he said, tossing the book to the side. "How could anyone live for centuries like that? It is pure fiction."

"No... No, I remember you! You were there that night. You are the one who banished me from Terra!" He pointed his staff. "I swear, if you are behind this pathetic rebellion—"

"Calm yourself, Zecatsu. I performed no such banishment. Quit scattering and losing your focus."

Landor gritted his teeth. He fired a singular orb of dark energy. The Objectivist caught it in his left hand. It hovered between his gloved palm and fingers momentarily before he crushed it without effort.

"Calm yourself," he repeated. "I am not here to fight you nor threaten you. I seek to set things right for my own self-interests. In that pursuit, I have gathered some... information. I am confident it will aid you in your pathetic little hunt. Yes, I am here to offer you my assistance."

It was a quiet night. David Dijenuk's victory over the Abomination and the acquisition of the keys to enter the Wind Chamber were now known across Light Elektia. Some slept better as a result. Others still worried. As the Restorers prepared and Landor schemed, the world was at a standstill. For now. But not all was still.

Within Fort Dijenuk's wall of trees and within its separated, gated house, Jay Dijenuk remained awake. She had turned her dresser into a desk and stolen a chair from downstairs. Numerous papers and books cluttered the wooden surface.

This is it here, she thought. "'The power of mages,'" she read aloud softly, "'is vast and powerful, but is limited just like that of any other magical. It is bound by restrictions. These restrictions are determined at birth and therefore by heritage. Magic, after all, is partially sourced in the body.' So…" She leaned back in her chair and twirled her quill.

Just like a nonmagical cannot be given magical abilities, she thought, *a magical cannot be given additional ones without directly modifying their genetics, something currently not possible. Logically, that has to work backwards, too. Therefore, you cannot give nor take a magical's innate abilities unless it is temporary.*

She made a hollow, unsmiling laugh. "Elektia isn't ready for Jay Dijenuk."

Her eyes moved to faded text at the bottom of the page. The letters read: *QEB ZOVPQXIP PBXI.*

Hm… Ah, it's just the Caesar cipher. Three letters back. In mere seconds, she had decoded it without writing anything down. "'The crystals seal.' Intriguing…"

As she considered the phrase, her gaze drifted to the small journal buried underneath sheets of maps and historical locations. It was the only possession she'd managed to bring over from Terra. Jay took the journal and flipped to the first entry.

It was headed with a date: July 2nd, 1992.

Dear Stacie,

I had to get a new journal today. I filled out the last one—

the one you gave me for my birthday—pretty quickly. I guess that's what happens when your only form of communication is writing to yourself, haha…

I couldn't ask ~~my parents~~ Carl and Rebecca for another, but fortunately I found an empty one that I got some time ago. It's my last one for now, so I guess I'd better pace myself.

Anyway, I wanted to tell you, again, that I'm sorry. I'm sorry for being a bad friend and not telling you how I feel. There's so much I haven't told you, now that I think about it. Like, how happy you've made me, for instance. I never had friends, other than David, until I met you. I thought I was a pity case when you started talking to me in middle school… Well, I still kind of think that. Regardless, you were there for me when I was going through my worst. You were my light that banished the darkness.

Remember two years ago, when I ran from home, once again drowning in self-doubt, and I was gone for hours? You found me crying and—instead of yelling at me or berating me for my actions like everyone else did afterwards—you just held me. In that moment, it was everything I needed. You found me, and not just literally. You found me when you comforted me that day in middle school when we first got to know each other. I really am lucky to have you as my best friend.

Very sappy, I know, but it's the truth. One day, maybe when I start talking again, I'll tear out all these letters I've written and give them to you. Perhaps then I could tell you something else I've been wanting to say.

I hope you're doing alright. One of us should be happy, at least... You seem to be happier with other people, anyway. Maybe I should stay like this, I don't know. I want you to be happy. Wouldn't you be happier without me?

~~*Darling, could it be I have my doubts?*~~

I can't wait to see you again.

Yours, forever and always,

Jay

Jay let out a shaky breath and closed the journal. She stared at the plain, green cover for several seconds as she held it with a tightening grip.

"Pathetic," she said in a low voice. "You really were pathetic, Jay." She shook her head as she set it back down. "Good riddance."

She exited her bedroom and traversed down the stairs. Keeping her steps as quiet as possible, she walked to the bookshelves. Jay moved her hand across the spines, feeling their leather bindings. She stopped at a certain one. Jay took the book and switched it with another. There was a faint *click*, and a section of shelving gently slid across the wall on its own. After taking a moment to listen for footsteps, Jay entered the spiral staircase within.

PART 2:

THE WORLD OF DECEIT

CHAPTER I:
THE PROMISE

THE GIRL WITH SILVER HAIR yawned as she once again watched the four Restorers enter Fort Dijenuk. Each morning for the past few days, they would come down from their gated house and—each morning—a crowd of desperate civilians would gather around them, pestering them with questions.

Each time, she watched from a distance with her royal-blue eyes. The fifteen-year-old wore a long blue coat over otherwise mundane, neutral clothing: a beige, cotton shirt, brown pants, and brown boots. Her straight hair went down to her shoulders.

This morning, the crowd was smaller. Some of them were finally learning that their spokesperson, the captain, ignored most of their questions.

As he deflected their dribble, the girl returned to her task. She picked up a wooden bucket and peered down into the stone well next to her. Normally, a water mage could lift up the well's contents, but that luxury, like many others, was gone. Nothing was the same anymore since the Opening.

The girl reached down with the bucket as far as she could. It barely made contact with the water. She leaned even further, straining to lower the bucket more, until she lost her balance and stumbled forward. The bucket splashed into the darkness of the well.

She sighed as she rested her head against the stone. After a moment, she lifted herself up and looked back to the Restorers. The two that came from Terra looked different. The boy, who she knew was David Dijenuk, now wore a white, button-up cloth shirt with a brown cloak, dark-brown pants, and leather shoes, as well leather braces on both of his forearms. The girl wore something similar, only she lacked the arm guards and wore boots and an olive button-up instead. Both sets of clothing were free of both stains and the standard-issue turtleneck collar. She guessed that the two had been granted an exception.

The silver-haired girl took a couple steps closer, her eyes fixed on the two of them. The Terran girl was staring off into the distance, and the boy was answering someone's question. She took a few more steps.

Now, on the outside edge of the crowd, she considered their faces. The girl's green eyes were attention-catching. They were sharp and fierce, but pretty. Her short hair complemented the shape of her face well. She had never seen hair that short on any grown human before, but she thought it fit her attractive features perfectly. David's hairstyle was unusual, too, but it was at least longer. He had a chiseled, handsome face, and yet it was soft and relaxed. That, combined with his inviting, golden-brown eyes, gave her the impression that it was hard to be uncomfortable around him. Her feet continued to take her closer.

"Well, the problem is that we can't find any translation," David said. "It's like a totally different language. So, we're looking for someone or something to help us out with that."

"Alright, David, that's enough," the captain said.

As she studied them, the green-eyed girl turned. Their gazes met. She felt as if the Terran stared into her soul, and her heart jumped. She immediately broke eye contact, hoping that the Terran did the same.

Her heart still racing, the girl scurried away.

She stuck out like a sore thumb.

As soon as Jay turned a little, the silver-haired girl caught her attention. She was staring at her, and Jay stared back. She continued to watch the girl as she turned around and hurried away to a different section of Fort Dijenuk.

Interesting, she thought.

"So, please, just let us do what we need to, and resume your duties," Elfekot said. The crowd was hesitant. "That is an order!" At that, they all dispersed. He sighed. "Even though there are fewer of them, it gets worse each day…"

"Agreed," Angela said.

"Come on, guys. They… Hey, sis, where are you going?" David asked.

"When I return, our problem will be solved," she said as she walked away with her usual brisk pace.

"What?"

Jay's walk turned into a jog as she followed the path that the girl took. She entered a housing section: Eight flats aligned into two rows of four with a fire pit in the center. There were two more paths that led elsewhere.

"Hey," she said to a bony man crouched down by the fire pit. "Have you seen a girl with silver hair recently?"

"Oh, her?" His voice was croaky. "Ah… she went that way, I believe. Hey, are you not one of the Restorers?"

Jay ran off to the left path. She came upon another housing area and another intersection. She asked around if someone had seen the girl she described, but no one knew for certain.

There must be an easier way, she thought, mentally flipping through all the spells she knew. Coming up blank, she huffed in frustration and sat down against a nearby tree. *She's the key to this, I know it.* She hit the ground. "I can do this by myself, damn it."

The Objectivist's words echoed in her head.

"Stay back. I have a feeling you will be doing that often, anyway… I suppose the real practice for you here was learning how stay out of situations you clearly can't handle without someone else."

She shook her head and brushed her hair out of her eyes, and then withdrew the knife he had given her from her boot. She studied the golden-brown alloy of the blade for a few seconds before returning it to its hiding place. Her attention turned to the leaves above her. They waved softly, dispersing their familiar pine scent.

Where could she be? she thought, visualizing her appearance.

Jay closed her eyes. The noises of Fort Dijenuk's busy citizens and rustling leaves in the wind disappeared. The feeling of bark against her back and dirt underneath her vanished. Finally, the scent of the forest was gone. She wanted to open her eyes but couldn't. A single image flashed in her head: a small clearing in a forest with a single stump roughly in the center. The image burned into her mind as her eyes snapped open. All her senses returned to her at once, and she jumped to her feet.

She bee-lined for the destination she saw and took, again, the left path. After going downhill, she entered a completely empty section of the fort. Through a section of trees and shrubbery less dense than the rest of the forest, she found the place. There the girl was, sitting on the stump with her head in her hands. Jay moved closer.

The girl looked up. "Hello? Who's there?" She scanned her surroundings for the source of the footsteps.

"It's okay, it's—"

The girl gasped as she stood. She was a few inches shorter than Jay. "Are you... one of the Restorers?" she asked.

Jay nodded.

"W-What are you doing here?"

"I've been looking for you," Jay said, somewhat out of breath from her trek.

"Y-You have?"

Jay nodded. "What's your name?"

"Oh, um... Clove."

"My name is Jay."

"Are you really a Dijenuk, too?"

"I am." Jay inched closer. "What is this place?"

"It's…" Clove frowned. "It is my hiding place. At least, it was."

"I apologize."

She looked away and shrugged.

This is going to be difficult, Jay thought. *I'll have to be careful with what I say, for once.* "I came here to ask about your language skills."

Clove's eyes widened.

"You see, we believe that the location to the Wind Chamber is locked in the text of its keys: The Scrolls of Gales," Jay continued. "But the language it's written in is completely foreign to me and the other Restorers. I, with *some* help, scoured every book in Fort Dijenuk and Hegortant and found nothing that serves as a translation."

Clove swallowed. "I-I'm sorry. I wish I could help."

Jay narrowed her eyes. "Oh, but you can. A few days ago, when I first entered Fort Dijenuk's excuse of a library, I discovered an abandoned journal. Almost all of it was written in that language. We have found traces of it elsewhere, yes, but the newer pages of this journal lacked any fade whatsoever." She paused. "They were written relatively recently."

Clove let out a shuddering breath as she stared at the ground.

"That journal belongs to you, Clove."

She looked up. "W-What?!"

"It was an easy deduction. The miserable man supervising

288

the library told me it was a girl with silver hair and blue eyes. Seeing as there's almost no one in this forsaken place who even gives the slightest damn about opening a book, you were even easier for him to remember. Your behavior at the moment further validates this." Jay frowned. "How do you know that language?"

"I... I..." She exhaled. "Yes... that was my journal. I must have left it there because of all the chaos that day."

"Ah, the Opening." Jay moved a hand to her chin. "How do you know? About that language, I mean. How did you learn it?"

Clove bit her lip. "I... I... I'm sorry. I really can't say anything about it."

Jay took a step forward. "Why can't you say?"

Clove opened her mouth as though she were about to say something. Her eyes stared off into the distance, and she began to shake. Her lips trembled.

"Is it a difficult question?" Jay asked.

She nodded.

Jay exhaled. "Sitting down might help."

Clove nodded and sat. Jay stood a couple of meters in front of her with her arms crossed.

"While knowing how you learned it would help me, you decoding it for us is good enough."

The girl shut her eyes.

"You are quite the mystery, Clove." Jay paused. "And no mystery shall escape me."

"Can... Can you please leave? I-I can't help you." Moisture

leaked through her eyelids, and her voice was shaky.

Jay rolled her eyes. "We both know you can. Quit denying it."

"You're wrong," she said. She stood, finally looking Jay right in the eyes. "Leave me alone! I have nothing to tell you. I'm just a girl!" She sat back down, her face now overtaken with terror. "I'm so sorry, I'm so sorry! That was mean of me. I'm sorry…"

Jay frowned. "Who is it you're afraid of?"

"Everyone." Her voice had become barely audible.

"Why?" Jay asked.

"Because… people have this culture and tradition. They hate anything that undermines it. *Anything.*" A tear rolled down Clove's face.

"Culture and tradition…" Jay echoed. "I'm not from here. I'm from Terra."

"That's different. You're a Dijenuk. All you get is praise," Clove said.

"That's not what I mean. I currently know very little of Elektian culture and tradition. Even if I did, I still wouldn't do something so horrible to someone as to pointlessly ridicule them." She paused. "If there's someone on this planet that will not slander you for your background or past, it's me… and my brother, too. He's irritatingly kind." *What am I even doing?*

"Do you promise?" Clove asked, staring into Jay's intense green eyes with her own blue, teary ones.

Jay's left hand curled into a fist. *Don't say it.* She hesitated before saying, "I do."

-‹o›-

"We can't just leave without her," David said.

"But we cannot wait any longer for her. We are in a race against the enemy, and if we lose that race, then we are all in danger," Angela replied.

"While it would help to have her with us, it is better to get to Hegortant as soon as possible," Elfekot said.

The three sat around a table, with a sheet of parchment in the middle that was labeled *The Wind Chamber* in ugly handwriting. It had nothing else written on it.

David tapped on the table with his finger for a few seconds, attempting to stall. "Alright," he said, defeated. "I guess she can meet us there or something."

Elfekot rose from his chair. "Then let us make haste." David and Angela followed him out into the bright yet mild outdoors, the cool morning now gone.

"What if the Council does not know anything either?" Angela wondered.

"I am afraid it is likely," Elfekot replied as they approached Fort Dijenuk. "In that case…"

"Jay, there you are!" David said.

Jay and Clove walked up the hill towards them.

"Where have you been?!" Angela asked.

"Who is this?" Elfekot added.

"Sh," Jay said sharply and snappily, silencing them. "I was

looking for the answer to our problems."

Elfekot looked at Jay with a raised eyebrow. "This girl?"

"Her name is Clove, and she knows how to decode what's on the Scrolls," Jay answered as Clove hid behind her.

"What?" the three Restorers said at once.

"Tch. Listen the first time. She knows how to translate that language."

"You cannot just believe anything a stranger says, Jay," argued Elfekot.

"If I, Jay Dijenuk, believe something, then it is almost always correct."

David rolled his eyes.

"Jay, I am sorry, but if we are not certain, then it would be very unwise to spend precious time going after that uncertainty," Angela said.

"Also, we cannot take her with us, Jay. It is only the Restorers who can take any meaningful part in this quest," Elfekot added.

"Elfekot, was it not you who said that prophecies were 'just rubbish?' Although you regret it, you were also the one who first suggested that we ask others for help. Don't falsify your stance on the subject for the sake of proving me wrong," Jay countered. Elfekot clenched his teeth. "There is also this… feeling I get," Jay continued. "It is similar to what I felt back in the tunnels. Something told me that finding Clove was the right path… Although, I considered the evidence more than anything."

"Visionary," whispered Angela.

"Huh?" David said.

"One of the Restorers is a Visionary," Angela said.

Jay closed her eyes for a few seconds, then gave a nod.

"A Visionary?" asked David.

"Visionaries can sense the future, sense what is needed, have flashbacks to the past, and even predict that future," Angela clarified. "The exact abilities vary from Visionary to Visionary."

Jay nodded again. "And my ability seems to be a vague sense of what I need to do." She looked down. "I have had those kinds of visions for as long as I remember. I had thought of them as merely dreams or hallucinations, but now I know better."

"Woah," David said. "That's cool! But... are these senses always accurate?"

"Always," Angela answered.

"How do you know so much about this, may I ask?" Elfekot said.

Angela's cheeks were touched with red. "I... um, well, let us just say that I have been looking forward to something like all of this for a while. I have done a bit of research."

Elfekot shrugged. "I suppose we have a Visionary on our side, then. Not only is that more power for us, but it also means that you are right, Jay. I apologize." He cleared his throat. "Let us head back inside, then." Elfekot led the group, including Clove, back up the hill and to the Dijenuk House.

"Welcome, Clove," said David as he held the door open for

293

her.

"Huh?" Clove snapped out of her inner thoughts. "Oh, uh, t-thank you."

The group entered the house's study. Jay moved to the bookshelves in the back while the other sat around the larger table, the one with the piece of parchment labeled *The Wind Chamber*. Elfekot and Angela sat facing away from the window, David sat facing away from the hall, and Clove sat opposite him. Jay fetched the three Scrolls of Gales from the top of the shelves and placed them in front of Clove before taking her seat.

Clove opened each scroll and leaned forward.

"So, what does it say?" David asked.

"Um..." She squinted at the text.

"Give her a bit of time," Elfekot said.

"What?" Clove scanned over it again. "This... um, i-it doesn't make any sense."

"This is what happens when those that do not belong to our quest try to take part in it," Angela said, arms crossed. "It has to be just *us*."

"Ignore her," Jay said. "What's the issue?"

"I-I can't understand large chunks of it. All the characters seem familiar, but..." She slumped back in her chair. "I'm sorry. I told you that I couldn't help."

"What part of it *can* you understand?" Angela asked.

"Um... Just sounds, or... pieces of words."

Jay exhaled through her nose and leaned over the table. She flipped the Scrolls around to look over it herself.

Clove's eyes lit up. "W-Wait! I-I see something." She pointed to a section of the text. "This part reads as something now."

Jay looked at her. "It was upside-down?"

She nodded.

"You couldn't recognize it when it was upside-down?" Angela questioned.

"I'm not quite an expert with the language… I'm sorry."

"Just read what you see," Jay said.

"Most of it is still nonsense, but… this part says… 'Beginning.'" She looked to the second scroll. "Um, this one says 'Terra,' and this one… uh… 'End.' No, 'Ends.'"

David's brows knitted. "Terra? So, Earth."

"Beginning, Terra, End's. That means nothing," Angela said.

"If this is a location, then…" Jay's eyes briefly twinkled. "End's Beginning, Terra. That's where the Wind Chamber is."

"What? No, that is impossible," Elfekot said, his face contorted in shock.

"How come?" David asked.

"The Elemental Chambers were all built here on Elektia. Or, at least, they have existed here on Elektia for as long as history can tell," Elfekot clarified.

"And a place called 'End's Beginning' does not exist on Terra, anyway, to my knowledge," Jay added. "And yet, that's the only thing it says."

Angela glared at Clove. "Are you certain?"

"I-I think so."

"It's the only lead we have," Jay said.

The five of them stared at the Scrolls. David placed his elbow on the table and rested his chin on his hand. "What language is that, anyway?"

"It didn't have a name back then, but nowadays it is referred to as Ancient Elektian," Clove answered.

"It does look pretty ancient," David said. "Like, Egyptian hieroglyphics or something."

Jay glanced at each of her fellow Restorers. She rose from her chair. "Our only hint points towards the location being on Terra, so we're moving on, now. I believe there is another important matter at hand. Angela, is Clove the fifth Restorer?"

"Huh? W-Why would I know?"

"Supposedly, portions of the Restorers' Prophecy have been lost, yet one of us is oddly familiar with it. Angela, do you care to comment?"

Angela glared at her. "Like everyone else, I have only read fragments."

Jay crossed one arm and hovered a loose fist over her mouth. "Ah, yes, but you had a fragment of your own, and you could very well have more of them. So, do these fragments speak of a female water mage, hiding her insecurities with her timid nature, too afraid to do anything about it?"

"Jay," David warned as Clove sank in her seat.

"She is a water mage?" Elfekot asked.

"I-I never told you that," Clove stuttered.

"It's obvious, given the color of your irises. Powerful, genetic magical energies can result in genetic mutations. Essentially, Clove's strong potential as a water mage makes her eyes blue. That's why, David, your eyes are golden-brown, since you have strong potential for Light, even for a Dijenuk, and why, Angela, your eyes have an orange-red tint for your strong potential as a fire mage. And of course, it is why Elfekot has grey eyes. He is rather potent in... *energy magic*, or whatever it is you want to label it," Jay explained.

"And *your* eyes?" Angela questioned.

"I believe my green eyes are normal and not the result of any magic-related mutation."

"So... you are weak, then," Angela said, smirking.

"Answer my earlier question, Fryner."

"No. The prophecy said nothing of a water mage."

"Who's the last one, then?"

"I do not know."

"I do not believe you," Jay said. "You knew about yourself. Convenient, isn't it?"

"My family just happened to have that fragment and that fragment only. I do not know if there even is another one," Angela responded.

"Incorrect. Elfekot told David and I earlier that there are five of us in total."

"Then... I do suppose that Elfekot is wrong."

Jay faced Elfekot. "Are you wrong?"

"Prophecies are a waste of time and energy; that is all I can say," he said, his eyes shut.

Jay let out an irritated breath as she sat back down.

"Why even answer this question anyway?" Elfekot continued.

"If we want to stand a fighting chance, we want all five of us, no?" David said.

"You are correct, David. For once," Jay replied. "We are supposed to be the powerful saviors of Elektia, or so it is claimed. Finding the fifth Restorer is crucial to... well, not dying."

Elfekot crossed his arms. "It does not matter. We cannot answer the question anyway. Let us just take her along with us, just in case—"

"No," both Jay and Angela said.

"No?"

"We do not know for sure. It has to be *only* the Restorers of the Elements—" argued Angela.

"She'll slow us down; she hasn't yet proven her strength—" argued Jay.

"Enough!" David yelled. "We're taking her with us. If she wants. The more of us the better." He looked to Clove. "I'm sorry about them, Clove. You're welcome to join us," he said to her.

She gave an attempt at a smile.

"Plus, it's a prophecy, right?" David added. "Wouldn't it make sense if the fifth Restorer came to us like that? It's fate... or something."

Jay rolled her eyes. "It's your own life at risk, you know—"

"I'll do it," Clove said, sitting up straighter.

"Fine," Angela said, looking away.

"I'm David," he said. "That's Elfekot, and that's—"

"Angela Fryner." She narrowed her eyes at Jay. "I do not suppose you know how to get to Terra."

"No. That reminds me... I asked Clove about how we would even get back to Terra—seeing as we *will* be returning home eventually and someone as shockingly literate as her may have the answer—and she said that it wasn't common knowledge. Since that is clearly a lie—"

"She is right. It is not," Elfekot said.

Jay scowled. "You've all lied plenty of times before, but this is just the worst one."

Elfekot tilted his head. "I beg your pardon?"

"I'm no fool, Elfekot. Even David can figure out what is wrong here."

David's head perked up. "Huh? No, yeah. Jay's right. You guys *do* know how to get to Earth. I mean, Terra."

Elfekot and Angela looked at each other. "I am afraid we do not know what it is you are talking about," said Angela.

"Use your brains, you two, however undeveloped they are," Jay said. "How do you think David and I got here in the first place?"

Elfekot and Angela looked at each other again, then shrugged.

"You have got to be joking," said Jay, exasperated.

"We took a portal here," David explained. "Back on Terra, Mr. K had some kind of crystal. He said somethin', broke it, and this… grey spinning thing appeared. We jumped in it and ended up here."

Elfekot leaned forward. "A crystal? Huh. So that is how the Council does it…"

"Huh?" sounded David.

"Elektians do know that transportation between Elektia and Terra is possible, but the exact method is unknown to most of us. It is only the Light Council and those who work close to them who hold that secret."

Jay crossed her arms and scoffed. "Of course…"

"So… how did our parents get here, then?" David asked.

"Likely the same way," Elfekot answered. "The Council probably trusted them with the method for the sake of their escape from Landor."

"Well, since most don't know and the Council insists that it's a secret"—Jay glared at Elfekot—"we will acquire that information through other means: The Secret Keepers."

"No," Elfekot said.

"No?" David repeated. "The Secret Keepers, what are they?"

"They are a hyper-intelligent species and organization. Not only do they know almost everything in the universe, but they are also dangerous. They are called Secret Keepers for a reason. They do not simply give knowledge away," Elfekot warned.

"I doubt their intelligence even comes close to mine," Jay said matter-of-factly.

"You can see for yourself if you ever meet one, but we will *not*. It is much too dangerous," Elfekot said.

"Isn't this entire quest dangerous?" David countered. "We fought King Landor! And won! If we're not supposed to take any risks, how will we ever save Elektia?"

"It was luck, David," Elfekot said. "And I would not exactly say you 'fought' him. I agree, though, risks are necessary, but only if we run out of options. We have not."

"But we are running out of time. You said so yourself," David replied.

"And I think we have run out of options," Jay added.

"Ugh… Then let us call a vote," Elfekot said.

"Let us not," said Jay immediately.

"All in favor of contacting a Secret Keeper in an attempt to seek information, say 'aye.' All against, say 'nay.'"

"Aye," said David and Jay simultaneously.

"Nay," said Elfekot and Angela.

Jay glared at Clove. "Aye," she said softly.

"Then it is decided," Jay said.

"It should be a unanimous vote," said Elfekot quickly.

Jay dropped her voice and glared at the captain. "Why are you so against this?"

"Because it is certain death."

"Is it really?" She scoffed. "It matters not. The rest of us shall find one without you." Jay stood up.

"Urgh… Fine! We will see a Secret Keeper."

"Yes!" cheered David.

Angela shook her head. "You know how to find one, yes?"

Elfekot hesitated, then nodded slowly.

"Brilliant. Let us make haste," Jay said.

"Hold up. Doesn't Clove need her staff? And Jay, too," David pointed out.

"I will go retrieve it," Clove said.

"I can go with you if you want," David said.

Clove gave a weak smile. "Thank you, Dijenuk, but I can do it myself."

Elfekot sighed. "We are doomed."

CHAPTER II:
AT DARK'S END

"WOULD YOU LIKE AN UPDATE, Your Majesty?"

"At once."

King Zecatsu Landor was standing at the end of a long table. It was a small room with a tall ceiling, lit by torches that gave the place a moody brightness. There was a large cathedral window in the back, and the Landor family emblem above it was carved into the dark-grey stone of the castle's walls. It was the letter L surrounded by seven circles, with an eighth circle in the center.

"The Restorers have been moving, but not to anywhere significant. It is mostly to and from Fort Dijenuk and Hegortant. They have even visited Hegortant's library," a man in black robes said.

He was one of the dozen occupants in the room, also standing around the table. Some of them wore black robes, while others wore more intricate waistcoats and cravats, the entire outfit comprised of dark, neutral colors. One man and a woman wore leather and chainmail armor instead, adorned by a black, silk scarf with the length thrown behind the shoulder.

The man continued, saying, "It is likely they are looking for information regarding—"

303

"I do not need your theories. Stick to the report," Zecatsu replied.

"R-Right. I apologize. As for the group themselves, there are still only four of them. It appears as though they have not yet found the fifth."

"Brilliant," Landor said, toneless. "What about the nation itself?"

"We have not spotted any of their soldiers outside of their normal locations and patrols," informed the man in armor as he stared at the various maps on the table. He was muscular, with a thick beard and light-brown hair tied in a bun.

"As for the civilians, they are struggling. Severely. They cannot handle life without the, er, 'Elements,'" added the woman in armor. She was a gangly, freckled woman with dirty blonde hair tied into a braid. "Their food supplies are swiftly dwindling. Starvation is imminent. The farmers and ranchers appear to be quite inept without their normal magic. The chaos is keeping the Council fairly occupied. Even the fishers are clueless. They are foolishly praying to both the Elementians and the Dijenuks."

The king stared out the window into the overcast sky. "Right. As expected."

"But even *I* did not expect for the Light Elektians to suffer this badly. This is our chance, Your Majesty," said the armored man. "Istra was right. We need to—"

"*No*," Landor interjected. "Istra might be effective at his job, but he is a fool, deep down. Full conflict with Light Elektia is suicide at worst, and a mass detriment to our nation at best."

"With all due respect, Your Majesty," said an older, balding man in a waistcoat and cravat, "we cannot keep doing nothing. We, *you*, have spent years formulating this plan. Now that it is finally in motion, you have decided to make only a few interventions. We are wasting time."

"I would have to agree," said a voice.

Istra entered through the wooden door, bowed to Landor, and stepped forward to face him.

"You are late, Istra," King Landor said. "And you are no longer new enough for me to excuse it."

"I am, yes. I apologize, Your Majesty." He cleared his throat. "Anyway"—Istra faced the advisors in the room and clapped—"about these 'interventions,' or rather, the lack of them. You see, *I* succeeded in warning the blokes over at Fort Dijenuk *and* at stealing the Scrolls of Gales from 'em at Hegortant."

"Which you then lost," Landor said to him, irritated.

"On the other hand," Istra said with a louder voice, "King Landor failed to eliminate the Dijenuks after spending so much time and effort on a working relationship with the goblins—which is now lost, by the way—and he failed to keep an infiltrator from taking out the guards and reaching the throne room. You know, that 'Black Hood' fellow."

A muscle in Landor's cheek twitched. "What is your point, Commander Istra?"

Istra turned to face him. "My point, your Majesty, is that you have been a coward. Even when you manage to act, you hesitate.

305

A couple of soldiers told me you spent some time chatting with the Dijenuk siblings. And they got away. You even waited until just half a sector ago to tell us that there were *two* Dijenuks instead of one. Confrontation is not your strong suit... Your Majesty."

"You do not need to just stand there and take his slander, Your Majesty," said the armored woman. "Istra, watch your tongue."

"It is no matter, Viscery. Our king lacks the guts to do something like reprimand me, let alone kill a couple of kids."

Landor's eyes narrowed as he gave him a cool, twitchy smile. He then plunged his fist into his stomach, causing Istra to double over. Landor grabbed his head by both hands and slammed it into the table. The king beat Istra's head into the wooden surface over and over again, until the large splinters that formed pierced the commander's face. He lifted Istra's bloodied head up by his hair, and leaned close to his ear.

"You have no idea what I am capable of, commander," Landor whispered. "You have no idea as to the blood I've spilled to get to where I am now." He let go of the gasping Istra, then pounded a fist onto the table. "I am *not* ordering a full assault!" the king barked. "And we will *not* have this discussion again unless I bring it up! Understood?"

The advisors nodded, all of them either staring at the floor or glancing at each other.

Landor took a deep breath as he aligned his posture and brushed his hair out his face. He looked at Istra, his torn face still on the damaged table, then to his advisors. He rubbed his hand where it had hit the table and bit the inside of his cheek.

Zecatsu turned around. "When the Dijenuks are dead, you may have your war…. Meeting adjourned," he said as he exited.

He stepped into a large, elegant hallway, lit with the same mild torches as the previous room. A red carpet with black trim ran down it. Paintings of previous royal family portraits, all Zecatsu's ancestors, hung across the entire wall. Between these paintings sat grey busts, all of them depicting the kings before Zecatsu.

The man stormed through the hallway and up a lengthy spiral staircase. He passed many exits until he finally reached his desired floor. Through a wooden door, Landor entered another hallway. This one was smaller than the previous one. From there, Landor stepped onto a large balcony.

There, he was near the top of his castle. The city of Dark's End sprawled out before him. Most of its buildings, wooden in composition, were short and wide, although there were some tall and thin ones that peppered the city. Their metal, pyramid hip roofs made them look like spears sticking straight into the sky. None of those buildings, however, even came close to the height or width of the castle.

It was simple in design, with a large, rectangular base, two towers in the front corners, and two taller towers with spires in the back corners. The front, middle section rose up a few stories over the base before tapering slightly into the fifth and tallest tower. It stood at nearly seventy feet tall. The castle walls, including its forty-five-foot-tall curtain wall, were made of a smooth, dark-grey stone, and the spires were made of black clay tiles.

The king gripped the railing of the balcony. He leaned over slightly as he stared into nothing. He could still hear his mother's words.

"To crush Light Elektia and kill every last Dijenuk: that is your goal, Zecatsu. That has been the goal of the Landor family for generations. Your grandfather nearly succeeded, and your father failed. You have to be the one. Fail that, and you fail us."

Landor shook the voice out of his head, then stared out into the distance. Evening was approaching, and magical lights began popping up from Dark's End. It was nothing like what he had seen on Terra, though. That place had seemed to hate the darkness, with how much light they had once the sun went down. Despite the magical lights, darkness persisted like a fog. It loomed over the entire nation, and especially over Dark's End. The sky was always grey, although it was greyer near the Barrier. Zecatsu had a couple of theories as to why, but no certain answer.

Naturally, the city was the largest in the kingdom, but it was confined to the great walls that surrounded it. They had stood for centuries, and there was no desire to expand beyond it.

Not much had changed in the kingdom, neither in his lifetime nor in history. He recalled the day he had taken the throne, and the guilt he'd been fighting to suppress, as well as the stoic, almost disappointed expressions of his people. Since then, his top priority had been hunting the Dijenuks down.

In the years since the death of the eldest Dijenuks and his banishment from Terra, Landor had spent his time scouring Elektia. He had made certain that David and Jay were truly the last Dijenuks. He had also made progress on his private research, although he had stopped working on it long before his plan could be executed.

So far, it hadn't been working quite like he had hoped. One Crystal was nearly in their possession, but Landor knew that all they needed to do was intercept them and turn the tides onto Light Elektia.

Zecatsu's memory drifted to his father's words, shortly after the coronation of his older brother.

"Why cannot I be king? I will do much better than that blubbering fool."

"How dare you?! The eldest son is the king! Have you no consideration for tradition? However good you may or may not be matters not. Be gone with you."

He had abided by those words, for there he stood on the verge of killing the last Dijenuks. *If it is what the people want, if it is what my family wants*, he thought, *then I am happy... right?* With that, Landor stood up straight, feeling the wind run through his hair.

"O my kingdom, why could you not possess a higher ambition? Why is the vicious murder of a distant threat enough to quench your desires? Let me serve you better." He paused. "I can once they are finally rid of," he added softly. *What would become of the "family goal" then? Would the people ask for more? More murder, more barbarism? Am I truly alone in knowing what is best for my kingdom?*

Movement in the courtyard below caught his interest. Peering down, he spotted a cloaked, limping woman engaging in an exchange with a pair of castle guards. Judging from their quick action to aid her in walking, Landor guessed that she was injured. He frowned. *She is none of their business.*

He grew tempted to fly down and intervene, but instead watched the guards guide her inside. The woman rested her hand for a second too long on the wall. Before Landor could think about the suspicious action further, the woman swiftly stabbed both men and ran inside as she snapped her fingers.

The front wall exploded as the courtyard gates flew inwards. A mob of civilians, previously hiding behind the buildings and walls, stormed through, all carrying weapons and staves.

"They were right!" the king gasped.

He drew his staff, and a ball of white energy spun in his left hand. He closed his eyes for a few seconds, concentrating, before throwing it down at the mob below. The ball exploded, erupting the ground and sending dozens into the air. He then began to spin a ball of darkness before someone pulled him back.

"Your Majesty! You must go somewhere safe!" a servant said.

"I can take care of them myself!" he replied just as a force hit the balcony, causing it to shake.

"Your Majesty, I insist!"

"Damn it. Fine! Lead the way."

Back inside the castle, Landor found himself surrounded by his guards. They ushered him through the halls. As they descended the floors, sounds of small explosions, yelling, and clashing metal became more audible. The entire building kept shaking. Dust and debris rained from the ceilings. Through the bodies in front of him, Landor could make out the iron door that was his emergency bunker.

The wall next to them collapsed, and the king slammed his palm onto the floor, creating a protective dome around them. It blocked an incoming volley of energy missiles just in time. With his other hand, Landor summoned a sphere of dark energy and fired it through the dome. It exploded into a cloud of mist. With himself and his protectors hidden from view, Landor took down the dome.

Landor placed his hand on the center of the metal door. After a moment, it swung open. A guard shoved him inside. A few followed him in before the door shut.

The room was small, though comfortable with its lush purple-and black-furniture and soft, grey carpeting. It was brighter than the other rooms. The king stood in the center, ignoring the available seats. He stared at the door.

"I mean, surely this... safe room cannot be protected by a mere lock alone, Father."

"Perhaps it is not the best, but it is what we have."

"Hm... Oh, I know! See, I was reading about enchantments, and—"

"Zecatsu! Not this again. You know what we said when it comes to foreign magics."

"Father, sir, I assure you. This door can be improved—"

"Improved? You seek to change it?"

"Yes."

"Zecatsu, this room and its door was made many years ago by Landors just like us. You cannot just change it."

"I am confused, Father. Why not?"

"It is not just a door. It is a piece of history. Family history."

"And?"

The room shook, snapping Landor out of his recollections.

"The door! It is this door!" someone said.

"Is there a handle?"

"Just try knocking it down!"

Landor smiled, but it quickly faded. *I am useless here.*

"So the rumors are true…"

"Never doubt safety concerns."

He turned around to face his conversing guards. He opened his mouth as if to say something.

"Yes, Your Majesty?"

"Remain wary. The door is not indestructible."

"Yes, Your Majesty," they said.

"It is a good thing the prince lives elsewhere now, huh?" a soldier added.

Zecatsu nodded. "It very much is."

They continued their conversation, muttering about numbers and win/loss probability. The king went back to staring at the metal door, not realizing his feet were guiding him closer. His hand just inches away from the surface, the room violently shook again. There was stillness and silence. The guards stood.

"It is clear!" said a muffled voice from the other side. It was deep and growly.

"That was fast."

"Do we trust the call, Your Majesty?"

The king nodded. "I recognize the voice, but I will make certain." Louder, he called, "State your name!"

"Commander Istra," the voice answered.

The king, using the palm of his hand as he had done earlier, opened the door.

"I am glad to see you safe, my king," said Istra with a bow. His face was now bandaged after the bashing from earlier.

"Right… What are the damages and the losses?"

"Rather bad in certain areas, but we can recover, Your Majesty."

Landor nodded. "And the attackers?"

"The rebellion, as you could have guessed. Some fled, some died, and some are incapacitated. As for the latter, they will be met with execution for their crimes."

"No."

"N-No, Your Majesty? They are traitors to the kingdom, are they not?"

"They shall be interrogated first."

Istra paused. "Of course. Understood, Your Majesty. On another note, there is an important matter you must attend to.

Follow me, please." His tone was remarkably polite.

They began walking. "What is this important matter?" Landor asked.

"A, uh, certain structure of value was damaged, and we need your say on what to do about it."

"What structure?"

"A family one. A statue of an ancestor."

"I see. Just get rid of it, then."

"Your Majesty, I recommend you see it yourself."

"There is no need, Istra."

"It will be quick. After all, should you not be informed before making a decision... Your Majesty?"

Landor stopped walking and paused. "Fair enough. Lead the way."

Corpses of both commoners and castle guards littered the halls. It was the sight of the ruined interiors around him that finally set the anger in. They had struck at the worst possible time, right in the midst of the operation. He could not afford the time to oversee repairs and prosecution.

How could they have known? Was it a coincidence?

The throne room was better than he had expected. The large doors in the front had been knocked off their hinges. Through the opening, he could see the devastated entrance hall. The throne itself was damaged, but repairable. A chunk of it was missing. The pillars were chipped and dented, making the structural integrity of the room rather concerning. The long red carpet was burned and bloodstained from the dozens of corpses he had seen thus far.

Bloodstained.

"Zecatsu! What are you doing here? Did I not tell my men to keep everyone out? Those incompetent fools. Guards!"

"Incompetent? Perhaps you should look at a mirror sometime."

"How dare you speak to your older brother, your king, that way? Guards!"

"Relax. I merely jest, brother."

"What is the meaning of this?"

"Well, I have come bearing a gift…"

He shook the memory out of his head, refusing to continue it.

"I am sorry about the throne, Your Majesty."

"It is no matter. They can be repaired, replaced," he said as he stepped over a corpse.

"Of course…" said Istra.

A man then let out a short scream.

"Huh?"

Landor turned around to find one of the guards' spears plunged through another's chest. Others followed his action. In nearly an instant, more than half of the twenty guards were murdered by their supposed brethren. Landor slowly spun around as the remaining guards pointed their spears and staves at their king. A smile creeped upon Istra's face.

Landor drew his staff. "What is the meaning of this?!"

Istra stood behind the turncoat guards. "It is not personal,

Your Majesty. I took an offer some time ago."

"An offer? Who put you up to this? It was Estlap, was it not?"

"Unimportant."

Landor sneered. "No wonder you were so brazen earlier today."

Istra shrugged. "I knew our time together was coming to an end soon. I am truly sorry, Your Majesty, but this is it. I suppose it is retribution for what happened to your brother." He nodded at the guards.

Before they could act, Landor stomped the floor. An emerging shockwave knocked every other man down. He twirled his staff as he jumped, enabling his dark, cloudy form: Dark Flight. The king flew through the large, open doorway.

"Landor is escaping! Resume the attack!" Istra commanded.

Gradually, the battle within the castle resumed. The clashing sounds and screaming of combat joined it. Landor had barely gained distance when a piece of the ceiling above him was struck with a blast of energy. A large piece of it fell. The chunk of stone collided with Landor and pinned him to the ground.

He groaned. *"T-Téléneh!"*

Landor's body flashed red. He teleported a few meters away from where he had been crushed. As he ran, his entire body screamed for him to stop. He guessed that at least a couple of bones had been broken. He turned his head to look behind him. The group of guards from earlier charged towards him, with Istra in the lead.

"Téléneh aristeh!"

In an instant, Zecatsu teleported to the floor above. He did a quick scan of his surroundings. The room, previously a luxurious dining room, was empty. The walls, ceiling, and floor were full of holes. The long table was split in two, and the chairs were in pieces. He sat on the only functional chair left and took the opportunity to think.

This is outrageous. Istra?! How long has he been deceiving me? Well... it is no matter, at least not right now. Right now, I need to get rid of these traitors. Can I even do it alone? Who can I trust?

Zecatsu stood. He headed for the eastern entrance to the room and pressed his ear against the door. There were footsteps. He held his staff tightly. Warmth and anger coursed through his body. At the tip of the staff, an orb of dark energy charged. He burst through the door and raised his staff. There were two guards mingling with a commoner. Zecatsu fired without hesitation.

The orb exploded in the center of the group. From it, hand-like tendrils of dark energy emerged. They wrapped themselves around their necks like rope and choked them out. Within seconds, they fell unconscious.

As he traveled down the hall, the castle continued to shake. With each vibration, tiny pieces of the ceiling rained down. Upon reaching one of the spiral staircases, Landor went up.

The higher I go, the less opposition I will most likely find.

As he rose, one of the windows caught his attention.

317

Normally, they were stained for minimum light and visibility, but this one was broken, allowing him to see outside properly.

The grey wash of Dark's End was amplified by smoke and dust. The front walls were obliterated, and the courtyard had been torn to shreds. Even the buildings outside the castle walls had seen destruction. Not much time had passed since the attack, so Landor pondered in horror what else the attackers were capable of. He squinted. There was something in the distance. With the limited size of the window, Landor could spot numerous wooden contraptions sitting safely outside the castle grounds, stationed right in the middle of the streets. They were trebuchets.

"What?! How did they—?" The castle shook violently again. With that, Landor continued his sprint up the stairs.

On the top floor, Landor found a group of conversing guards in the hallway. He raised his staff. The guards jumped back.

"Your Majesty, what is going on?"

"Are you alright, Your Majesty?"

"My king, please, calm down."

Landor gritted his teeth. "We have been attacked by rebels and traitors. I ask as to your alliance and what you are doing all the way up here!"

The guards bowed. "Our apologies, Your Majesty. We retreated here to come up with a plan for retaliation."

"Did you say traitors, Your Majesty?"

Landor continued to speak with his staff raised. "Yes. Some of the guards and servants here have turned against me and the kingdom. They have allied with the same rebels who are sieging the castle. I imagine it is me they are after."

"Then we will protect you—"

"Hold it!" Landor yelled. "I cannot trust anyone."

The guards looked at each other, unsure what to say.

Landor finally lowered his staff. "You will lead the way. I will have no one behind me."

"Yes, Your Majesty. Where are we going?"

"Just down. If you speak the truth, there will be others on our side on the upper half of the castle. We need to gather as many forces as possible. Only then can we formulate a proper plan. Lead the way and watch your fire. Anyone could be a turncoat."

The five guards nodded and turned to move. "I believe there are more of us in the secondary armory. We shall head there, Your Majesty."

Through a hallway similar to the previous ones, Zecatsu followed his men to a different set of stairs. Despite the similarity, the interior here maintained one sharp difference from the others: It was intact. Near the top of the castle, the sounds of battle had become faint. It was almost difficult to tell that the place was under a fierce siege.

"Do you know who is behind this madness, Your Majesty?" a guard asked.

"Istra appears to be the leader, at least for the turncoats."

"Istra? That is surprising."

"In retrospect, not quite…"

One floor down, the group reached another hallway. This

one was taller than the last, and there was only one set of doors. They were large and cast of iron. Opposite the double doors was a large window. It was one of the only ones in the castle that was clear. The guards stepped inside the room past the doors. Landor followed. He gripped the handle. Something caught his eye.

Landor turned his head. From outside, a cloud of darkness was flying towards him. He raised his staff, preparing a shield, but something struck him in the back. The shield faltered.

The dark cloud crashed through the window and into Landor. It took him and dragged him across the hallway. The cloud dissipated, and Istra stood over him with a pike aimed at his throat. He thrust it, and Landor screamed. The tip of the pike stabbed through the king's hand. He had raised it to block the attack. Landor moved his other hand to his amulet.

"*Cintria excata!*"

A projectile of green light struck Istra square in the chest. He rocketed backwards, taking his weapon with him. Landor stood. He stared at the bloody wound for a second before noticing the group of guards from earlier dashing towards him, weapons in hand.

"Of course…" he muttered.

Zecatsu reached for his staff. There was nothing. Slight terror creeped up on his face when he saw his staff in the midst of the broken glass, behind the storming turncoats. Without any other option, Zecatsu turned around and went downstairs. As he descended, he took random landings and turns in an effort to lose his pursuers.

Lower in the castle, the noisy ambience of battle returned, although it was quieter than before. In fact, it was gradually dying down. It eventually became nearly quiet, enough that Landor stopped in his tracks. He stood still for a few moments, listening. On the other side of the hallway was another clear window. Landor approached it with slow steps and peeked outside. Apart from the destruction, there was nothing.

A sudden noise cut through the silence. It was that of a wooden machine. Yelling followed it. Landor stood still again, his ear straining for more information. Something crashed through the wall and into Landor. It was not a human this time, but a large ball of lead. It forced Landor through the window and through the ceiling of a room below.

"*Téléneh!*"

Before the ball could crush him into the floor, Landor disappeared and reappeared a few feet away from it. He groaned. His whole body ached, and there was dust and debris all over him. He brushed his messed-up hair out of his face. The yelling had returned.

They must be on their way to me…

Zecatsu did his best to limp away. He then felt a disturbance in the air. There was a significant magical presence nearby. He turned. It came from the lead ball. Before he could contemplate it any further, the metal exploded. The force rocketed the king through the outside wall, and his body smacked the grass below.

The air had become quiet, disturbed only by Landor's groans of agony. He tried getting up, but only made it to his hands and knees. Painful, cold sensations stabbed him in his chest and legs. It was then that he was met with horror. Shards of metal from the lead ball had punctured his body. His clothes had become soaked in his blood. He fell back down to his face.

The king rolled around to lie on his back, which was absent of lead shards. The effort alone was met with excruciating pain. His body then went numb. His stomach twisted as the world spun around him. Before his digestion could betray him, his vision darkened and the world faded away. The king heard one last voice before his consciousness left him.

"Oh, Zecatsu, you fool…"

CHAPTER III:
THE DOOMED STAR

DAVID WAS DISAPPOINTED TO FIND that the land beyond Fort Dijenuk's vicinity was more of the same: rolling hills, grass, and dots of trees and boulders. The mountain that the siblings had spotted when they first arrived had neared.

"How much longer now?" David asked.

"We are about halfway, so… six hours, I reckon," Elfekot replied, adjusting the large, leather bag slung over his shoulders like a backpack.

The captain led the Restorers forth, with David directly behind him. Angela was only a few feet behind them, and Jay was the farthest back at over a dozen meters away. Clove walked along the midpoint between the two. Her eyelids drooped.

Like most, Clove wore her staff on her back using a strap of leather. Its wood was purple, but gave off hues of blue under the light. The focus, the tip of the staff, was a white seashell that opened up like a flower. A soft, light-brown hide was braided around the center of the shaft.

David sighed. "I was afraid it was something like that."

"I thought Dark magic was the mighty Dijenuks' weakness, but it turns out it is actually just walking," Elfekot said, continuing to look onwards.

"I'm not my dad, alright?"

"I am not him either, and yet I do not complain. None of us do, in fact. Just you."

"Like I said, Terrans are just not as used to it. And Jay would be saying something too, but she refuses to do anything that makes her look human. Just..." David's voice softened. "Just remember that we're new to this, alright?"

"Right, and that is why I am in charge."

David paused. "Right," he replied with a low voice.

As the five Restorers continued their trek, the grass became more yellow and wild as it went up to their knees, and the boulders became more frequent.

"Watch the rocks," Elfekot said. "They are harder to see under the grass."

There was the sound of a thud from behind them, and the Restorers turned to see that Jay had tripped over one of these boulders.

"What did I just say?"

Jay quickly got back up, her expression as neutral as ever.

"How does she do that?" Angela asked quietly.

"How does she not listen?" David responded.

"No, I mean, how does she just show *nothing*? She hit a rock with her feet, fell, and got back up, all without a wince or a grunt. It did not phase her."

"Nothing phases her. Not these days," David said. "It's just... Well, I don't really know, either."

"Are Terrans normally like this?" Angela asked.

"Oh, no, definitely not. We're not too different from Elektians, you know."

Angela tilted her head. "Really?"

"Yeah. I mean, we're, er, they're not magical and live in a very different collection of societies, but they feel and act about the same."

"Huh." Angela looked up at the sky, where the sun was beginning to approach the horizon. "I would like to see Terra someday, if you would be willing to take me, Master Dijenuk."

"Yeah, totally! Once this mess is over, of course."

"Pft. You know you cannot, Angela," Elfekot said.

"Well, yes…"

David raised an eyebrow. "You can't travel to Terra?"

"No Elektian can, not without a special exception like what your parents were granted," Angela clarified. "However, I am confident that they would grant similar exceptions to us, the Restorers, being the saviors of Elektia and all."

"Yeah, probably." David looked back at Clove, who was staring off into the distance, similar to Jay. "Are you doing alright?" he asked.

"Huh? Oh, um, I'm fine." She quickened her pace as David slowed.

"Sorry to drag you from home and put you on this journey all of a sudden. Probably not what you expected your day to turn into, huh?"

Clove shrugged, avoiding eye contact. "It is okay, really."

"You sure? I mean, I know you volunteered, but your family

probably worries right?

"Oh, um…" Clove bit her lip.

"She is an orphan," Elfekot said, "and has no family. Not in Fort Dijenuk, anyway."

"Ah. Er, I'm sorry, Clove. Hey, Jay and I are orphans, too," he said.

Clove gave a weak smile, but still refused to look directly at him.

"What about your family, Angela? I've been wondering about that for a while. I know you mentioned your parents before."

"I am actually one of the few non-orphans in Fort Dijenuk. My parents were somewhere in the north when the Opening happened, helping out the ice mages there, since that is their job. I imagine they are still there, as Light Elektia is in a lockdown."

"Are orphans common in Elektia?" David questioned as he moved back to the front with Elfekot.

"No. They are quite rare, actually," Elfekot explained. "Leaving your child behind is quite the severe act. It is an illegal offense, too, regardless of reason. Just about every orphan is sent to Fort Dijenuk to live."

"Why there?"

The captain shrugged. "It is just what the government decided a great deal of time ago. I reckon it is so the nation is easier for the Council to manage, since so much of the infrastructure and economy is based around family units."

"Weird. But I get it."

The Restorers grew silent again as the wind hummed in harmony with the birds. It was the first time the Dijenuk siblings had gotten to see them on Elektia. The creatures flew across the sky in unorganized clumps. Their colors, even within the clumps, varied from reds to blues to greens, although the majority were a pale red. Their only similarity was their shape, for their sizes varied, too. Some were tiny, while others were massive.

A few of the birds flew closer to the ground than the others, allowing the siblings to notice that the tips of each of their feathers were iridescent. It was the same effect that most of the leaves had.

Another hour had passed, and the stars were beginning to peek out of the fading blue of the sky. Both Angela and David asked Elfekot about water. The tankards they carried with them had just gone dry.

"I have—careful there—I have a spare couple of tankards in the bag, but for now, you will have to wait until we set up camp for night," Elfekot said as he moved around another rock hidden in the grass. "I can better assess the situation then."

David sighed. "Yeah, alright…" He frowned. "We're not gonna have enough for the way back, are we?"

"If Jay and Clove are right and we succeed, we should be fine. Remember, we are looking for portal crystals," Elfekot responded.

"Oh, right, we can just take a portal back. Duh."

"We *could* fail, though, so use our lack of supplies as

motivation to *not* make a dumb decision," Elfekot added.

"We will *succeed*, captain," Angela said, nearly tripping over a rock. "We are the chosen ones for a reason."

"A reason, eh? I wonder why they chose four kids, then, two of whom are new to magic, and a captain who is better off doing his real job and not babysitting," Elfekot replied, his voice touched with irritation.

"Hey, Clove, I have a question... Clove?"

"Huh?" said Clove, snapping out of her inner thoughts. She only glanced at David.

"So, without the Water Crystal, is all of Elektia screwed since you can't generate more water? Or is there, like, a backup plan?"

Angela giggled. "That is not quite how it works, Master Dijenuk."

"It's, um..." Clove cleared her throat. "Water magic can't actually create water. The water we do make is very temporary. Um, it's an instance, and, although energy is put into it, mass can't be, uh... nevermind," she said, wrapping her arms around herself.

Jay looked up at her for a second, her eyes narrowed, then looked back to the ground.

"So, it's fake water, basically," David said.

Clove nodded as she yawned.

"We use the wells likes the ones you have probably seen around the Fort, if you even know what those are," Elfekot added. "Water mages can also move water, real water, and so they usually help with that."

"Gotcha. So, we're not completely screwed with that, at least."

"No, but there are plenty more headaches."

Night crept in as Elektia's blue sun vanished below the horizon while its two moons emerged. They had left the stretch of plains with the long, yellow grass and tripping hazards, and returned to the green, rolling hills.

"We should set up camp there in the forest," said Elfekot, pointing to the wooded expanse about a hundred meters away at the bottom of the hill they were on. "We are nearly there, so finishing the journey should be easy tomorrow."

"Why can't we just finish the journey now?" David questioned.

"Because I do not want to bother a Secret Keeper in the dead of night, let alone at all."

David walked in front of the captain and turned to face him. "You say 'I' a lot, Elfekot, but we're supposed to do this as a group. A *team*. All our voices matter, not just yours."

Elfekot scowled. "Do not take it so personally, but none of you are experienced in this kind of thing, you and your sister especially. I have been in charge for several days now, against my will, even, because that is what is best for *us* and therefore the planet. Do you understand?"

David took a step closer. "That doesn't mean you can just make every call. We had to threaten you with going off on our own for you to even 'approve' this journey."

"I have to agree with him here," Angela said, also facing Elfekot. "This is about us, the Restorers of the Elements, not Captain Elfekot and the four others he dragged around."

Elfekot crossed his arms and leaned on one leg. "If you want to be in charge so badly, David, then go for it. But are you confident you would not get us all killed?"

"Well, no, but…" David took a step back. "That's not what I meant!"

"At least for now, you need to just listen to what I have to say. If you hesitate and ask questions each time, we could die." Elfekot walked past him and towards the forest.

"I get that, but we're in no kind of danger in moments like these," David said, following him with the other Restorers. "Jay has a point. Why do you hate questions so much?"

"It is also a matter of efficiency, David. The faster we can get this done, the faster we can return to our normal lives."

"You mean, so you can get back to not caring about anything and being a deadbeat captain? Real noble of you."

Elfekot stood in place for a moment, took a deep breath, and then continued onwards.

The Restorers reached the sparse woods, where above-ground roots creeped over the ground like snakes. The leaves were long and thin, and also possessed the same iridescent glow at the tips. The light brown trunks were short and jagged. Outside of the usual aroma of a forest, there was a faint, metallic smell.

"Let us look around for a relatively flat area. We do not want to be lying on the roots," Elfekot instructed.

The group spread out and searched, making sure to stay within view of each other. There were no animals that they could see. Even their sounds were absent. It was then that the siblings realized that they hadn't seen a single mammal, other than the goblins, since arriving on Elektia.

"I think this will work. Over here!" David called.

The others, minus Jay, jogged over to him. It was a roughly circular area without trees, where only a few roots bled in. The grass here was longer and greener. The clearing was small, but enough to fit a few tents.

Meanwhile, Jay noticed the metallic scent in the air and stopped by a tree. She plucked one of the leaves and gave it a sniff. "Hm."

"It should all fit, I think," David said, scanning the area. "If we put it over here, then—" He tugged his feet. "What the—? I can't move!"

"Neither… can I!" said Angela, struggling to lift her feet.

Elfekot grimaced. "Damn it! It is the grass!"

"What? The grass?" David looked at his shoes. "What the hell?!"

To his horror, the grass was wrapping itself around his legs like vines. One by one, the blades of grass joined the effort, all of them inching up his body. They squeezed tight, creating a tingling sensation in his shins and feet.

Elfekot pulled out his sword and hacked at the roots of the snaking grass. His blade bounced off. "Damn it. These are tougher than I am used to."

Angela grunted. "If I had my fire, this would be no issue," she said as she delivered a blast of energy to the ground. Some of the dirt flew up, but the grass remained unharmed.

David looked to Clove, who was standing paralyzed with fear, then to Jay, who was still staring at the leaf. "Jay! What're you doing? Help us out over here!"

Jay dropped the leaf and faced them. "Interesting. Some of the flora has a sentience, of sorts," she said to herself.

David pulled at the grass, but to no avail. "Jay, do something!"

She took a few steps forward, but remained poker-faced, her hands at her sides.

"Don't be like this, Jay. Not now."

Her eyes moved between each of them. The vines of grass had made it up to their waists.

David looked directly into her eyes. "Jay. Please!"

Jay tilted her head as she continued to observe him. The grass was now halfway up their torsos.

"Sis!"

"Now... ugh, is *not* the time for this kind of attitude, Jay!" Elfekot said.

"I do *not* want to go out dying because some girl decided to hesitate. Do something!" Angela yelled.

"Jay, please," Clove said silently, mouthing the words.

Jay shook her head and placed a hand on her amulet. She brought the palm of her other hand outwards, facing them, with two fingers and a thumb pointed up. The girl closed her eyes and took a deep breath.

"*Téléneh nostro.*"

As soon as the words escaped her lips, something in her chest burned, causing her to double over.

At the same time, the four other Restorers briefly flashed a red light before disappearing and reappearing in front of Jay. They all gasped in relief and shook out their limbs.

David stumbled towards Jay. "Are you alright?"

Jay let out a breath, then realigned her posture.

Angela stomped up to her. "What was that about?!"

She had no reply. Her green eyes were as dead as ever.

David shook his head. "Just leave it. For now." He turned to Elfekot. "We need to find someplace else. Obviously."

After a half hour of trekking through the woods, they found another flat space. It was smaller than the last one, and the grass was different in saturation and length. David placed a foot in there, waited a few seconds, then gave a thumbs-up.

Elfekot set his bag on the ground and removed five rolls of white linen and five sets of wooden stakes, each of which fit in the palm of one's hand.

"Alright, Jay, revert them," he said.

Jay hovered her left hand over the tent equipment as Elfekot took a couple steps back. "*Kanba kris.*"

The air around the objects warped for a moment before they grew in size in an instant. She sniffled. The inside of her nose burned.

"We all know how to pitch a tent, yes?" asked Elfekot.

Clove shook her head while Angela nodded.

"What about you, David? Do you even know what tents are?"

"Of course I do," he answered, picking up one of the rolls. "I did a lot of camping back on Terra. Jay did too, actually. Hey, sis, do you wanna—?"

"No."

"Thought so," David replied as Jay studied their surroundings.

"You do not have to do it for her," Angela muttered to him as he picked up a second tent roll.

He shrugged. "It's whatever. Hey, Clove, I can help with yours, too."

Another half-hour passed, and five white tents were pitched in a roughly circular formation, leaving only inches between them. They were just large enough for one person.

"We have space for a campfire, I think," David said. "We can gather rocks and kindling pretty easily, I bet."

Angela and Elfekot stared at him, eyebrows raised. "We cannot start a fire, Master Dijenuk," Angela said. "We lack the Elements, remember?"

David stared back at them with a similar expression. "You... don't need magic to start a fire."

Angela blinked. "What?"

David sighed. "Oh, boy."

Ten minutes of material gathering—which Jay refused to

participate in—and a tutorial on fire-starting later, a small campfire was brought to life in the center of the tents. David, Elfekot, and Angela sat around it, while Jay stood against a tree with her arms crossed. The shadows cast by the fire created a dance of darkness over her sullen face. Clove was already in her own tent, fast asleep.

"This is amazing, Master Dijenuk," Angela said, wide-eyed.

David gave a soft laugh. "Thanks, but it's really not that impressive. It's common knowledge on Terra."

"Wow. I wonder what else they know that we do not. It is quite thought-provoking, is it not, Elfekot?"

"No, not really." The captain was visibly unimpressed by David's fire, aside from a couple lifts of the eyebrow.

Angela stared at the campfire with delight on her face, her eyes twinkling. She reached forward.

"Hey, wait, what're you—?!"

"Ow!" Angela reeled her hand back. She hissed. "Your fire is not quite working, Master Dijenuk. I am unable to touch it."

"Oh, right. You're normally able to touch fire, yeah?"

She nodded.

"I reckon it has something to do with it being a real fire," Elfekot said. "Or maybe it is because you lost your ability to cast it. Or perhaps both."

The twinkle in Angela's eyes was gone as her expression went glum. "I used to be able to do so much with Fire, Master Dijenuk... I could create beautiful dances, intricate patterns, and breathtaking demonstrations." She slouched. "It was amazing...

I could also obliterate any opponent I wanted by setting their entire existence ablaze."

David swallowed. "Oh, um... that sounds nice."

"Mm hmm. And now I am forced to rely on you. And Jay."

David sighed. "I'm sorry, Angela."

She perked up. "It will be okay. If temporarily losing my abilities means we can be known across all of Light Elektia as heroes, then it will be worth it."

David smiled at her. "Yeah."

They watched the fire for a minute, listening to its crackling and the occasional shift of leaves.

David craned his neck to look back at Jay. "You doing alright, sis? You've been awfully quiet for several hours now."

"And what a wonderful several hours it has been," Elfekot muttered.

Jay faced David, her gaze piercing. "I have been thinking— something foreign to Light Elektians, apparently."

David turned back to the fire. "Uh-huh."

One by one, starting with Elfekot and ending with Jay, the remaining four Restorers went to bed. Their rough mattresses on the hard ground were nothing close to comfortable, but the exhaustion of their day-long journey allowed them to ignore it.

It was also eerily silent. Even the wind was mute. That was, until a large snap cut through the air and startled David Dijenuk. His eyes snapped open. Something snapped again. It sounded like the breaking of wood.

David rose from his sleeping bag and pressed his ear against the wall of the tent. Only the pounding of his heart was audible until another piece of wood snapped. It was closer than the first two.

He scrambled out of his tent, staff in hand, and scuttled to Elfekot's tent. "Hey, Elfekot," he whispered. After hearing no answer, he peeked his head inside. "Elfekot!"

The man stirred and groaned. "What?" he said, his voice muffled by fabric.

"I heard some noises."

"And?"

"It could be trouble."

"It is not."

"How do you know?" said David, his whispers growing more frantic.

Elfekot rolled to his back. His eyelids were low. "I cannot think of any animal or monster in this area who would prey on a group of humans. And even if there was something, we are safe in our tents, and the lingering smoke would probably scare them off."

"What? Is that even true?"

"Just go back to bed, David. Please."

"Can we just check it out?"

"Can you just trust my decision? Stay put."

"What if—?"

"If you wander off, whatever may be out there will find you, and it could kill you."

"You just said—"

"Nothing here *preys* on humans, yes, but if you were to try to find them…"

David sighed. "But—"

"'But' nothing. Noises are normal. Now *sleep*. More importantly, let *me* sleep."

David spent a couple of seconds in thought. "Fine."

David stood in the center of their tents, listening again for sounds. Once more, there was the snapping of wood, this time joined by the scurry of footsteps. He looked to Angela's tent, then shook his head.

"I can do this myself," he whispered. "I'm a Dijenuk, after all."

He took a step forward and froze in his tracks. He swallowed and stared at his staff, then mouthed a curse.

"What if…?" David turned towards Elfekot's tent. *What was that spell again?* he thought. *It's one of Jay's favorites. She practiced it a good bit at the fort.* He chewed the inside of his cheek as he pondered it. His heart continued to pump, his body too high on adrenaline to notice the air's biting chill.

"Oh!" David moved staff his to his left hand and hovered his right palm over the flaps to Elfekot's tent. "*Slinta.*" Nothing happened. "Uh… *slinta*. Is that wrong? *Slinta!*"

Something in the sky above them popped like a firework. David flinched.

"Crap, uh, *slinta!*"

The air around Elfekot's tent bent and warped.

"Test," David mouthed. No sound came out. "Woah. It worked." As he reached for the tent flaps, something in his chest seared with pain. He took a sharp breath through his teeth. "So, that's how Jay feels… Got it."

David stepped into the tent and, with care, moved Elfekot's bag to the side and fetched the longsword underneath it. Before the spell could dissolve, David slinked back out.

He exhaled. "There."

With the sword in his right hand and his staff in the other, David faced the dark abyss of the forest. After taking a deep breath, he walked forward until he was behind the tents. Another noise froze him in his steps.

Scratching sounds and leaves rustling joined the night's symphony. David's eyes strained as he peered into the darkness. The footsteps and scratching noises were approaching. He gripped the handles of his weapons and held his breath. His breathing grew rapid as a bead of sweat slipped down the side of his face.

"Come on, David," he muttered.

He took a few more steps forward until he heard another rustle. A branch directly above his head shook. David pointed his staff.

"Hello…?"

Something leaped from the branch and towards David's face, accompanied by a shrill cry. Without hesitation, David let loose a blast of energy. The creature flew upwards, crashing through the tree branches before falling to the ground.

"A raza...?"

The unmoving creature at his feet was small and almost reptilian, with yellow-green skin, a circular body with four legs, and a gaping mouth with razor-sharp teeth lined along its interior.

"If there's one, then—"

His words were interrupted by more nearby rustling. David turned his attention back to the trees, where one of the branches snapped off. He squinted as he used the faint moonlight to peer into the foliage, but he saw nothing.

As though it manifested from the air itself, a raza leapt towards him, its array of teeth on full display. David blasted that one away as well, sending it crashing into a tree trunk. A third came from his right, which was also sent flying.

Where are they even coming from?! he thought.

Another raza jumped at him. By the time David noticed it, the creature was already halfway through the air. Driven by instinct, he raised an arm in defense.

The raza's teeth latched onto his forearm. They penetrated the leather bracer and sank into his flesh. Yelling in agony, he dropped his staff. David took the hilt and bludgeoned it, forcing the creature off. He then thrust the blade downwards into the raza, slicing into it like butter. Its green blood oozed onto the metal.

Still groaning, he spun around, blade at the ready for more of the monsters. The cold air stung his wound.

"Guys! Wake up!" he screamed as he cut a leaping raza in half. "Razas!"

A raza he'd barely had the chance to register flew into David's chest and knocked him to the ground. The sword clattered away. With David pinned, the monster opened its cavern of a mouth and screeched in his face.

The head of a spear thrust right through the raza, its blood squirting out like the popping of a water balloon. David looked to his right and found Angela at the spear's handle.

She extracted the weapon, spilling the monster's viscous innards all over David. "Leave it to me," she said to the both-horrified-and-relieved David.

As he rose to his feet, Angela used the length of her spear to cleave through a raza before it could even get close. She stabbed through another, then twirled around and threw her spear like a javelin. It pierced through two razas and stuck itself into a tree.

Angela took out her staff. "Come at me!" she yelled.

"They're jumping from the trees. Watch for the branches," said David, picking up the sword and staff.

"I have noticed."

Elfekot joined them. "Damn it. One problem after another," he mumbled.

"Took you long enough," David said.

"I can be a heavy sleeper sometimes."

Angela lowered her staff. "I believe that was all of them."

"How do you know?" David asked.

"Razas hunt in packs. If there were more in that pack, they

would have come out by now," she explained as she retrieved her spear.

Elfekot turned towards David. "Is that my—?"

"Oh! Uh, well, you weren't listening to me, so I kinda had to take it. Just in case. Sorry," he said, handing the weapon back.

Elfekot huffed. "Well, you were right. For that, I apologize."

"It's all good."

"Was it really razas?" Jay asked, emerging from her tent.

"Oh, there are you are," David said. "Yeah, it was."

"*Musnomi levis.*"

Jay's light spell revealed the monsters' corpses and spilled guts.

"Huh. That is interesting," she said.

"What is?" asked David, taking a few steps away from the mess.

"I memorized a map of common raza nests in an area around Fort Dijenuk. There were none here. At least, there weren't supposed to be. The map could easily have been wrong, but still..." Jay entered her thinking stance, with one arm crossed and the other upright, her fist hovering in front of her chin.

"Is everyone alright?!" blurted a voice.

They turned to find Clove standing just outside of her tent. Her body was rigid and her eyes were wide.

"Yeah. We're all good here, Clove," David answered.

She closed her eyes, took several deep breaths, and then nodded.

"Razas nest in riverbeds, yet there are no rivers nearby," Jay said.

David's face crinkled. "Ugh, that smell…" He looked down at his clothes. His shirt was covered in raza guts and blood. "Oh. That explains it." He looked at Jay. "Can you, um…?"

Jay stared at him.

"Please?"

Jay huffed. "Fine." She hovered her hand over his shirt. *"Clono eht onis."*

The horrific stains gradually dissolved into thin air.

"Thanks," he said. "Man, that was real scary, though. It was almost like they just kinda appeared. You noticed that, right?" he asked Angela.

She nodded.

"Appeared from where?" Jay asked.

"The branches. But I didn't actually see them there. It was pretty dark, though."

"Razas do not climb trees," Elfekot said. "They prefer attacking by leaping right from the ground."

"They are not normal razas," Clove said. She walked closer to them.

"Elaborate," Jay responded.

"Look up. See how the branches closer to the treetops are more mangled and broken? I also noticed that there were scratch marks on the bark that indicated a path upwards, and since there are no other animals here, um…" She swallowed as a touch of red lit up her cheeks. "Mm hmm."

"Huh. I didn't notice…" Jay trailed. Her attention turned to the leaves. "This iridescent quality. It's related."

"It is?" said David and Angela.

"Likely. It corresponds with a theory I've been developing."

"Well, what is this theory?" David asked.

"A secret. For now, at least." Jay's lips curled ever-so-slightly, as though she were about to form a smile.

David turned towards their campsite just behind them. "Well… what do we do now?"

"Sleep," Elfekot answered, already trudging towards his tent.

"What if there are more raza packs out there? Shouldn't someone keep watch?" David said.

"If you want to lose sleep over it, be my guest," Elfekot replied before slipping inside.

"Have fun," Jay said before returning to her tent as well. Clove did the same.

"Are you gonna join me?" David asked Angela.

"Maybe." She yawned. "We both really should sleep, though. We cannot save the nation if we are exhausted."

"Yeah." He glanced at the carnage of razas. "You know, you're pretty incredible even without Fire. I dunno why said you have to 'rely' on me."

"Huh?"

"Like, you can do some pretty gnarly things with that spear. And you saved my butt twice now."

Angela giggled. "You speak strangely sometimes, Master Dijenuk, but your words really do mean well nonetheless. You were the one who was on alert, though. We could have died had you not noticed something. So, you saved us, too. This time."

"Thanks."

"You need to give yourself credit… but only sometimes," she said with a smile and a shrug.

"Fair enough. Although, Jay gives herself plenty enough credit, so I think it's balanced between the two of us."

Their soft laughs rang through the silence of the forest and into the night.

CHAPTER IV:
THE INTELLECT COPS

SITTING IN THE VALLEY BEFORE THEM was a mansion. It was a peculiar sight, given its surroundings. There were no roads or other buildings. The trees were few. It was as though someone had taken the mansion from elsewhere and dropped it into the middle of the valley. Given the lengthy forest that surrounded the area, it could be assumed that few had accidentally stumbled upon this place.

"This is the Lonely Basin Mansion," Elfekot said. "The location is not very public, so as to keep its only occupant from being easily found."

Jay scoffed. "Right, because someone who doesn't want to be found decides to live in a mansion that sticks out like a sore thumb."

The building was unlike anything in Fort Dijenuk and especially Hegortant. Its dark woods contrasted the light color of the stone pillars. While the walls and support beams of the three floors were straight, the roof was long and curved. It jutted out on all sides, giving plenty of shade to the grassy landscape below. The top floor bore long windows with intricate, flowery designs in the glass. The entire building was in excellent condition.

The five Restorers studied it from the edge of the valley. The long slope in front of them was steep. A moderate wind was blowing, ruffling their cloaks and hair. The breeze was refreshing, given that the sun beamed directly over them.

"How do you know about it, Elfekot?" David asked.

"Like I mentioned, I was directly trained by your parents for some time. As a result, I happen to know some things. They knew more than the average person. The Dijenuks are a powerful family with connections, after all. At least, they *were*."

"So what exactly *are* these Secret Keeper dudes? Are they human?" David questioned.

"Not quite. No one knows exactly what they are or what their origin is or what they want. All we know is that they have an immense knowledge of the universe and that they tend to be very protective of this knowledge. We need to be careful," Elfekot warned.

"Or, we could beat what we need out of him," Angela offered.

"Go ahead and try, but you will fail. I suggest that only one or two of us speak to him. Any more than that could be perceived as a threat," Elfekot suggested.

"I'll go!" said David immediately.

"And me," said Angela.

"It will be David and Jay," said Elfekot.

Clove nodded. Angela groaned. "Why?"

"She has proven herself to be the scholar type."

Jay nodded. "*Andiamo.*"

"Huh?" said Clove.

"It means 'let's go,'" David replied.

The Restorers continued to stare at the building. "What are we getting cold feet for?" David said. "Come on, Jay." He turned to the others. "Be ready just in case somethin' goes down."

The remaining Restorers watched the Dijenuk siblings as they made their way. The steepness proved to be difficult to traverse, but it was doable. Elfekot's expression gave away his boredom as he stood with his arms crossed. Angela watched the mansion carefully. Although she had a hand on her hip and the other at her side, she otherwise appeared ready to run down there at any moment. Clove, meanwhile, stood farther back than the other two, her arms close to her. She was picking at the skin around her nails in worry.

"This is a pretty cool place, huh?" said David. "What do you think of Clove and Angela? It's pretty neat that we have a whole group to help us out.... Hey, what if—"

"Just be quiet, David, and let me speak first when we get there."

"Jeez, alright."

Within a few minutes, the siblings reached the mansion. The building loomed over them. Its front doors were over triple their height. David knocked on the wooden surface.

"Do you think he can hear us?" David asked. He knocked again.

"Just be patient."

A minute passed. One of the doors creaked open. From the

darkness within, a man stepped out into the light. He was tall, even taller than David. His long grey hair was tied into two braids. Despite the grey, his skin was smooth and wrinkle-free. His irises were black and lifeless. He wore plain brown robes and a puzzled, almost irritated expression.

"Hi," greeted David. "I'm David, and she's—"

"Jay. We are here seeking information on interplanetary travel. It is said that you might be able to help us in that regard."

The man squinted at them. "I cannot help you." It was as though he spoke with two voices at once, with a high, shrill one layered over a deep, gravely one.

"Please, sir," said David. "We need to go back to Terra. The Wind Crystal's there."

"Back...? Ah. I see. You are the Restorers of the Elements. And you must be the Dijenuk, yes?"

"Right. Well, we're both Dijenuks, actually. She's my sis," David corrected.

The man squinted at them again. "Huh. Come inside. Follow me, and do *not* touch anything."

"Thank you," David said as sincerely as he could.

The siblings followed the man inside. The grand hallway they entered was dark. Only the front doors that remained open let in any light. They were forced to follow the sound of the man's footsteps to maneuver around. The clacking of their shoes on the floor indicated a hard surface. The room was nearly odorless. As they walked deeper into the mansion, the air became warmer. There was another creak. It was the sound of a second door opening. A musty scent washed over them.

"Please, sit," invited the man.

"Er... We can't see anything," said David.

"Oh, right. I apologize. I forgot that Elektians need light to see." He snapped his fingers.

A large fireplace came to life. Its orange glow revealed the entirety of the room. Jay nearly made a small gasp. They were in a grand, two-story library. All four walls were lined up to the ceiling with shelves crammed with all manners of books. It was so large, the Dijenuks wondered how one fire could light up the whole thing, for it was nearly the size of their house back on Terra. There were multiple ladders to ascend the shelves and a set of stairs in the corner.

"Wait, you can see in the dark? Ooh. What's that called...? Infravision, right? From D&D?" David said to Jay. She glared at him.

"Please, sit down. Would you like some tea?" the man asked, gesturing towards the furniture.

The floor space was occupied with tables, sofas and chairs, lecterns, and even more shelves. The sofas were made of contrasting white wood with red cushions. There was no sign of dust, and the only indication of aging came from the books.

"Oh, uh—" started David as he sat on one of the couches.

"No," said Jay immediately. She remained standing with her arms crossed. "We are in a hurry. Just give us what we need on portals and we shall be on our way."

"Humans... So many of you are constantly in a rush," the

man said.

"So… you're a Secret Keeper dude, yeah?" David asked.

"I am a Secret Keeper, yes. How did you find me?"

"Unimportant," said Jay. "What do you know about portals?"

"That is rather confidential information, I am afraid."

"Of course," said Jay through gritted teeth. She began to pace around the library, leaving the conversation to David.

"Please, sir. It's super important. The fate of Elektia, and my home, too, is at stake here."

The Secret Keeper leaned back in his chair. "You said the Wind Chamber is on Terra. Is that really true?"

"Yeah. Jay's a Visionary. That, plus what someone else told us, led us to believe that that's where it is."

"Huh. I suppose that is possible."

"It is? How?"

"I will be honest with you, Dijenuk." He leaned forward. "The fate of Elektia matters very little to me."

"Please. People's lives are at stake here. We need to save them." David leaned forward as well. "I need to save Mom and Dad."

"Hm. You are quite earnest, Dijenuk. I see it in your eyes." He paused. "I will give you what you need. The world is rather dull without the Elements, after all."

"Thank you."

"Hey, girl!" the man called. "What are you doing over there?"

Jay turned to face him. She had been walking along the bookshelves. "I am merely browsing. I will not touch anything," she said without any trace of sincerity.

"Hmph. Anyway, yes, portals. Their existence is kept quite secret for good reason. It would be a mess if Elektians could travel anywhere they wanted without direct supervision. In addition, nonmagicals, like those from Terra, die upon going through them. It is dangerous. That is why only the Council and the Secret Keepers know of it. Although it seems like they trusted the secret to a few Dijenuks. I presume one of those was your father. I trust *you* will keep this a secret as well. If this gets to anyone else, there will be... repercussions. Is that understood?"

David nodded eagerly. "Yeah. I promise. I'm good at keeping secrets."

"Good." He cleared his throat. "Portals are created from portal crystals. They are shiny black rocks found naturally in the earth. They are rather uncommon, however. The closest deposit of portal crystals is an abandoned mine due north. Do you have a map?"

"Nope."

The Secret Keeper stood from his chair and scanned one of the tables. He took a large scroll from it. "I will mark it for you." With a quill dipped in ink, he drew a small circle on the parchment. He handed the map to David.

The hand-drawn map depicted the area around them, centered on the Lonely Basin. Fort Dijenuk was on the southern edge of the map. David spotted the black marking. There was a circle on a tiny spot on the drawing of a mountain range. It was labeled *Elepta's Range*.

"Thanks."

"When you have a portal crystal, speak clearly and concisely the complete name of your desired location after saying 'to this place.' Immediately after, strike the crystal with a blast of energy. The crystal will then explode into the portal. Step inside it, and you will be transported to said destination. The bigger the crystal, the longer the portal will last. Be warned, though. It has limitations. The end destination cannot be anywhere inside. The sky must be its ceiling. Additionally, you must keep in mind a clear, visual image of the destination. Without one, there is a decent chance it will falter. It might also falter randomly, anyway. There is… frequent interference," he explained.

David nodded. "Got it. Say the name of the place, keep an image of it in your head, and then shoot the crystal with an energy blast," he summarized.

"Correct. Is that all you need from me?"

"Uh, yeah, I think so. Again, thanks a ton." He stood from his chair. "Come on, Jay. Let's go."

"You lie," Jay said as she faced as the Secret Keeper.

"Sorry?"

"Oh, uh, excuse my sister," David said with a nervous laugh. "She can be kinda—"

"You stated that only the Council and Secret Keepers possess the knowledge of portal crystals…" Jay walked closer, her hands at her sides. "However, you just told us to go to the nearest abandoned mine for a crystal deposit. Those two things contradict each other. See, by using the term 'nearest,' you are implying that there are multiple. Why would the Council need that many portal crystals? It is clear that this planet is isolated. The Council does no diplomacy with anyone else, be it the Kingdom of Landor or, gods forbid, any other civilization across the universe. In addition, you would need several miners to fill these mines. I doubt it would be easy to keep an enticing secret from that many people."

"You are spewing nonsense, girl." The Secret Keeper's face morphed from a neutral expression to one with clenched teeth and furrowed brows as Jay spoke.

"So, to clear this contradiction, either portals are more commonly known than you are implying, and our companions are lying to us, or…" She paused, taking in the Secret Keeper's visible rage. "Portals were *once* commonly known, and you and your fellow Secret Keepers have committed some horrific act of magic to change that, along with your Council conspirators. It would explain their abandoned nature. Either way, you have attempted to deceive me." She gave a hollow, unsmiling laugh. If she still had glasses, she would push them up. "And no one can deceive Jay Dijenuk."

The Secret Keeper took a few steps closer to Jay. "You are quite interesting, Miss Dijenuk. You were born and raised on Terra, like your brother, yes? I have never known a Terran to be so… capable of intelligent thoughts. Nor most Elektians, for that matter. I can see it in your eyes, Dijenuk. They are mostly empty, void of anything, but there is a hint of something. There is this aggressive intelligence and this buried excitement… but there is something else underneath even that. It is anger, is it not? A burning rage. Either someone hurt you, or others simply bother you. Perhaps both. You hide it quite well. Hm, or perhaps that rage is meant to conceal something else?"

Jay's fingers twitched, and she sneered. "So you can read eyes? Curious. And what is your point, Secret Keeper?"

"My point is that your aggression is leading you to throw baseless claims. As I mentioned, you are from Terra. You are on a new planet, Miss Dijenuk, and in a new country. The rules are different here. Quit seeking what you should not, and quit seeing lies where there are only truths."

Jay gritted her teeth. "Of course. My apologies," Jay said flatly. She turned to David. "*Andiamo.*"

"I'm so sorry," David said. "She can be kinda… too much sometimes. Er, thanks again for your help. We'll be, um, going now."

The Secret Keeper said nothing. David caught up with Jay as they walked towards the exit. The library went back to darkness once they left it. The grand hall was lit with torches.

"Jay! What was that all about?!"

Jay scowled. "You still fail to understand."

"Understand what? That you're paranoid that everyone's lying to you?"

"***STOP!***" boomed a distorted voice.

"Huh?" David turned around.

The Secret Keeper was dashing towards them with superhuman speed. His face had been contorted into pure anger. His eyes had become entirely black. David reached for his staff, but the Keeper was now close.

"*Klebé eht siin! To darkness!*"

The Keeper stopped his running mere feet away from the siblings. He had run right into an invisible barrier. Jay's second spell held the Keeper in the air for a few seconds before launching him back into the dark library.

David turned to Jay, visibly impressed at her combination of spells. "Were you—?"

"Yes. Come on. We need to leave before he catches us." Jay sprinted for the front doors. David followed.

"Did you do something?" he asked.

Jay made no response.

The siblings reached the front doors. David tried the handle. "Argh, it's stuck!"

Jay moved her hand close to the door. "*Aperta eht wesya!*" Nothing happened. "What is this?!"

The siblings looked behind them. The barrier was gone, for the Secret Keeper was now racing towards them. He stretched out his hand. "**Return it!**" he commanded as he fired a beam of energy.

"Return what?!" David asked he raised his staff. A magical shield manifested before him. It blocked the beam.

Jay put one hand on her amulet and the other in front of her.

"*Cintria psota!*" A grey-blue projectile fired from her palm. The Secret Keeper dodged it. He dropped the beam.

"One last chance," he said in a normal voice. "**Return the book!**"

David looked to her sister. "Jay?"

Again, Jay said nothing.

The Secret Keeper charged an orb of white energy in his hand. "So be it."

"David, the greysteel."

He launched the projectile. David blocked it with the metal in his staff. The magic was absorbed into the metal. It glowed faintly. David spun his staff and fired it back. The Secret Keeper raised an energy shield.

"*Unestra!*"

Before it could collide with the shield, the ball of energy that David shot back quickly shrank until it disapeared from view.

An instant later, Jay threw her hand into the air. "*Téléneh nostro!*"

The interior of the mansion left them as the siblings reappeared outside just a few feet away from the other Restorers. They were midway from the top of the basin and the mansion.

"Shield. *Now.*"

Elfekot did as told. It was just in time.

There was a large white flash. The mansion exploded. Every window shattered. Chunks of wood and stone flew into the sky. The source of the shockwave, the first floor, gave away, and the upper floors collapsed into themselves. The shockwave hit

Elfekot's shield first. He grimaced as the debris hit it next, but he stood strong. And then there was silence.

Elfekot took a deep breath. As calmly as he could, he asked, "Explain to me... what just happened in there?!"

"We were just leaving, and then he ran after us. He wanted something back, I think. I dunno."

"Did you take something?"

David shook his head. "I mean, he gave me a map that he had marked. That was it. Maybe he changed his mind?"

"No," said Clove.

"No?"

"If the Secret Keeper gave away any kind of his knowledge, then he was very much willing," Elfekot clarified. "You would have to have provoked him in some way to evoke a reaction like that."

"So... why did he chase you, then? And what caused the explosion?" Angela asked.

"Me," answered Jay as she stood. She had been kneeling on the ground, panting. Her nose was dripping with blood.

"Are you alright?" David asked.

"I cast a number of spells in quick succession. Such an effort drained me. The Secret Keeper fired a charged projectile of energy. David used the greysteel in his staff to shoot it back. I took advantage of the situation to shrink the projectile, the instance, and create an explosion of instability."

The other Restorers expressed their collective shock.

"It was you?!" said Angela.

"Instability?" said David.

"Yes. I have been reading about magic theory. Instability describes the state of unsafe, therefore unstable, magical instances with various kinds of causes and various kinds of effects. Some of these are changes in color, like the iridescent leaves we've seen, and some of these are explosive. I knew he was powerful, so our only method of escape was to bring the building down on top of him. I also wanted to test a method of creating magical instability, so I did," Jay explained.

"Wait," said David, "The Secret Keeper said to return the book, and Jay... you were looking at the books."

The girl crossed her arms.

Elfekot stepped closer to her. "Did you steal something from the Secret Keeper?!"

"Halt! Make no movements!" yelled a distant voice.

The Restorers looked to the source. Elfekot muttered a low curse.

Atop the hill stood a group of eight uniformed men and women. They wore white, gold-trimmed armor. The Council's crest, a flaming circle surrounding the letter "D" with an eye in the center, was emblazoned on their chest pieces. They descended the slope.

As they approached, David reached for his staff, but then recognized the clothing. "Aren't they...?"

Elfekot groaned. "Yes, the Light Council. Some of their soldiers, rather."

"Tch," Jay said.

"What do they want with us?" David asked.

"We shall see," said Elfekot.

The man leading them stopped a few meters away from the Restorers. "The Council summons you." His voice was stagnant, yet polite.

Elfekot took a step forward. "May I ask what for?"

"The Council has some words for you Restorers... and some warnings. Please, come with us."

"We are busy," Angela said.

"We are not asking," replied the man, his tone stern.

"Is it far?" David asked.

"Without our normal mode of transport, it is," Elfekot answered.

"Hm." The man looked to the ruins of the mansion. "You have come to see the Secret Keeper. Have you discovered...?"

"Portals? Yeah," David said.

"David, you idiot. Don't tell them," Jay scolded.

"What? Why not?"

The robed man tilted his head in contemplation. "If you know about it already, then would it help if we were to portal over there to save you time?"

"So the Council's soldiers know, too. Hm," Jay said.

"Only some," clarified the man. "I only say all of this because there is no point in hiding it further. The Council will discuss this with you, among other things. I hope they excuse my use of this. It is really only for emergencies, you see." From a pouch on his belt, the man extracted a shiny black rock. "It is somewhat small, so the portal will be open for a very limited amount of time. Please be quick." He dropped it on the ground.

Jay crossed her arms. "We didn't agree to this."

"I am afraid you have no choice," the man responded. He nodded at his comrades. The soldiers surrounded them. "We do not intend any harm. Now, please, follow me." He drew his staff and aimed it at the black crystal. *"To This Place: Light's Source, Light Elektia."*

A bolt of energy struck the rock. It exploded into a swirling, grey vortex of light. The man immediately stepped in. He disapeared. The other soldiers ushered the Restorers forth. Elfekot walked through first, followed by Angela. Jay begrudgingly entered next.

David looked at Clove. She stood frozen in hesitation. He smiled at her. "It'll be okay," he said. Clove nodded, and she followed David through.

Although he had already been through this once before, it was just as disorienting. This time, he opened his eyes. David's surroundings had turned into a void of grey lights. They spun around him as he himself revolved in a different direction. He closed his eyes again. The trip was significantly shorter than last time. After just a few seconds, David felt himself fall forward. He caught his landing with his knees and forearms. Angela offered a hand. David took it. Once the dizziness had faded, David looked up at their new location.

A white, marble castle loomed over them. The entire thing glistened in the sun. Numerous towers shot up into the sky. Its walls were smooth and its edges were round. Although it was relatively small, it carried a large sense of grandeur. However, the Dijenuks were disappointed to see the sharp contrast that was the city around them. It was similar to Hegortant with its sad, grey boxes for buildings and shoddy cobble roads. The only difference was that some of the buildings had wooden, dark brown roofs with overhang. The castle stuck out, perhaps more than any building should.

"Welcome to Light's Source, Dijenuks," the man greeted with a slight bow.

"This is pretty freakin' wicked," David said. He was in awe.

"I've never been here before," Clove muttered.

"Neither have I," added Angela. Her eyebrows were raised. She was impressed, too.

The group of soldiers from earlier escorted them up a few wide steps, past two large pillars sat giant double doors made out of a golden material. Two more guards stood in front of it. As the group neared, they pulled open the doors for them. Their slow movement indicated their heaviness.

Through the doors, the Restorers found a grand, but barren, hall. Like the outside, nearly everything inside was made of white marble. Two lines of chiseled pillars ran down the room, while a gold carpet ran down the middle. It was wide enough for multiple cars to fit length-wise, and tall enough to dwarf the average house. A man stood next to one of the pillars.

"It is good to see that you are still alive," said the man.

David gasped. "Mr. K!"

The old man with smooth skin, long grey hair, and round glasses nodded. His filthy civilian attire from Terra had been replaced with clean, white robes with the Council's crest on the center. "I did not expect to see you here until you located the first Crystal."

"Yes, the Council wants a word," Elfekot said.

The soldiers that were ushering them stopped. One of them stood by the doors while the other entered. "Wait here," he said.

"So, you were a mage from Elektia this whole time, huh?" David asked.

"Yes. The Council wanted someone to keep a close eye on you two, and a few years had gone by since the passing of your parents, so they were getting antsy. I needed to take that darn book somewhere far away, so I volunteered."

"*The Legends*... Do you still have it?" Jay asked.

"Gods, no. For the first time, I was able to leave that cursed thing behind, and so I did."

"What? Why?" Jay's voice was raised, and she scrunched her face, as though offended.

"It is cursed in more ways than one." The man looked down with somber eyes. "I was bound to it for years, worse than my ancestors ever were."

"I am confused," Angela said. "Do you know this man already, Master Dijenuk?"

"Yeah. He was a high school teacher back on Terra," David

363

answered.

Angela tilted her head. "High school...?"

"It's a type of school for kids my age. Er, our age."

"What is a school?"

David blinked. "Huh? Do you really not know what a school is?"

"Light Elektia does not offer any means of public education," Jay answered. "I already looked into it."

"Oh. Well, it's a place where people learn things," David explained. "There are classes on all kinds of subjects. Mostly boring ones, but it's important. The students come to learn things and teachers, well, teach them."

Angela's eyebrows raised and her eyes lit up. "Oh! That sounds amazing!" She put a finger on her chin and looked up. "I wish we had a school, then. It would make it much easier to learn to fight."

"Oh, no, um—"

"Anyway, as exhilarating as *that* conversation is"—Elfekot looked to Mr. K—"do you know what the Council wants from us?"

"I do not, captain. I arrived recently, you see."

David's face lit up, and his heart pumped faster. "Wait... Um, what's home like? Is it...?"

Mr. K sighed. "It is not much better, Master Dijenuk. It has calmed down, but the Elemental Giants continue to terrorize the citizens. Their weaponry does almost nothing against them."

David's eyes were large and his mouth hung open. "Oh." He

swallowed.

"I have a query for you, Sir K," Jay said, crossing her arms.

"Ask away, Miss Dijenuk."

"Do you know why the Council hid portal knowledge from the public?"

"Oh, here we go," David muttered.

Sir K drew a sharp breath. "Ah... I knew it was risky showing you that, but there was no other way of getting you to Elektia." He pushed up his glasses and dropped his voice. "The Council is not a fan of, um, letting the public travel elsewhere, among other things. No Council has been, really." His eyes shifted as he glanced at the soldiers around them. They stood only a few meters away, but they were paying no attention.

"Hm. That matches up with what the Secret Keeper said, at least. However, evidence, namely the abandoned mines, points to this being public knowledge at some point. Can you really swear that many miners to secrecy? I think not. So, how was this knowledge erased?"

The soldiers were now staring at Jay. A bead of sweat glistened on Sir K's face. "Um... you see..." The soldiers' glare moved to Sir K. He cleared his throat. "The miners were, um, sworn to secrecy, but they died in a horrible accident. All of them. So, uh, that knowledge died with them, and now only the Council and some of us Council subordinates know. That is all it is."

Jay opened her mouth to speak, but the soldier from earlier reentered, saying, "The Council has gathered. They will see you now."

"I will, um, be in my study on the second floor, if you need me, Restorers," Sir K said. As the soldiers began to lead the Restorers onwards, he neared Jay. "Year 708," he muttered.

"Hm?"

"F-Farewell." Sir K speed-walked past them into the next room and took a left.

The Restorers entered a room similar to the previous. It was twice as wide, and there were three large, gold-stained windows on the back wall. In front of them was an array of eight sizeable, equidistant marble thrones. In these thrones sat eight white-robed men. A door on the left and one on the right led elsewhere.

All eight men leaned forward slightly upon seeing the Restorers enter. Their robes were nearly, identical aside from the trim of their tall collars, for they were all of different colors.

About halfway into the hall, their escorts stopped them. Angela and Clove bowed. David followed suit. Elfekot sighed but did the same. Jay remained standing. Her arms were crossed.

"Hm… Welcome, Restorers of the Elements," greeted the man in the eighth chair in a low, slow-spoken voice. His collar was gold-trimmed. He was the oldest of the group, with somewhat wrinkled skin and grey hair tied in a high ponytail. "I am Pralicriyus, the Light mage of the Council. The others here are also Councilmen. They—"

"Skip the pleasantries and move on to whatever you need to say," Jay interrupted.

Pralicriyus smiled coolly. "I believe it would be wise to at least get the names of the Restorers. As we have all recently learned, there are *two* Dijenuks, yes?"

"Yeah. Hi. My name's David Dijenuk."

"I am Angela Fryner, the fire mage."

"I am Elfekot, captain of the Fort Dijenuk guard."

"I'm, um, Clove."

"Jay."

"The other Dijenuk. She's my sis," David added.

"Oh, sister, you must mean. David and Jay Dijenuk, hm." Pralicriyus paused. "We have wanted to speak with you all, and with the Dijenuks especially, for a while now. Your recent, ah, activities, so to speak, have given us a good excuse to summon you. The group that brought you here followed you from Fort Dijenuk. Upon seeing where you were going, they reported to us. And here is where we give a few warnings."

"Uh oh," muttered David.

"Now, I understand that you are both new here to Elektia, and so there will be no punishment."

"Be thankful for the generosity," added the man in the second chair. His collar was trimmed with red.

"We are, sirs," David assured.

"Now," Pralicriyus continued, "contact with a Secret Keeper is a serious offense nonetheless. You will not seek one out again. Destruction of property is, of course, an offense, too. While we trust that you only mean to seek what it is you need to restore the Elements, you must understand that there are certain... pieces of knowledge here in Elektia that are not meant to be possessed by any man. We take it upon ourselves to cooperate with the Secret Keepers to ensure such safety. You will adhere to that. Is this all understood?"

Four of the Restorers nodded. Jay didn't.

"Excellent. Please just do the job you were meant to do. Light Elektia needs you to." He clapped his hands. "Now, please tell me why you are seeking portal knowledge."

"How did you know we were?" Jay questioned.

"That is unimportant, Miss Dijenuk," disregarded the man in the fourth chair. His collar was trimmed with orange.

"We were looking for how to use portals because we need to get to Terra. The Wind Chamber's there," David explained.

The Councilmen murmured amongst themselves. Pralicriyus frowned. "Is it now?"

"Yeah. We decoded it from the Scrolls. Plus, Jay's a Visionary. She also sensed it there," David clarified.

The man in the sixth chair looked over to Pralicriyus. His collar was trimmed with brown. "How is that possible?"

"Hm..." Pralicriyus considered David's words for a few moments. "Very well. We will allow you to use portals if you must. Elektia may depend on it. But, please, make sure no other Elektian knows of it."

"Of course," David said. "But, why?"

The Council was visibly taken aback by his question.

"We wish you the best on your journey, Restorers. Now, as a thank-you for your time, would you like a portal to somewhere?" Pralicriyus asked.

"We have very few of these crystals. Be grateful, Restorers," said the man in the second chair.

"Yes, please," Elfekot accepted.

"Awesome. We can go straight to Terra!" said David.

"Terra?" Pralicriyus' expression grew stern. "What for?"

"Well… that's where the Wind Chamber is," David answered.

"There are no Elemental Chambers on Terra. That is simply impossible. To add to it, travel to anywhere outside of Elektia is banned. We very rarely grant exceptions."

"But—"

"Oh, of course," Jay interrupted. Her voice became honeyed and polite. "The Wind Chamber must be somewhere else, then. Our apologies. If it is alright with you, may we return to where we came from? The Lonely Basin, I mean." David and Elfekot looked to her with befuddlement.

"Yes, that is alright. Guards, please, take them back there. And to reiterate, do *not* cross the line. We seldom give out warnings. You are only being treated this way due to your prophetic importance. Now, farewell."

The Restorers nodded.

"Follow me, please," said the same soldier from earlier. The Restorers followed.

Jay felt the back of her shirt underneath her brown cloak. The book was still there. "Tch… Fools."

CHAPTER V:
HOPE IN THE DARKNESS

"JESUS CHRIST, JAY!" said David.

Ugh, here we go, Jay thought. "What?"

The Restorers had been taken back to the Lonely Basin via another portal. The Council soldiers had just left when David stormed towards his sister.

"Oh, you know what. Don't pretend like you did nothing wrong!"

"If you wish to accuse me of something, please spare us the time and be more specific," she said with an air of boredom. Despite David's aggressive approach, she remained in her calm and controlled stance. *I doubt they will understand what I'm trying to do. Do I even bother?*

"You stole a book from the Secret Keeper! *That's* why he attacked us!"

"You did?!" Elfekot said.

"Hmph." Jay reached underneath the back of her shirt and extracted a small, red tome. "Yes. I did."

"Do you realize how dangerous that is?" Elfekot scolded.

"We could have died!" David added.

"And for what? A book?" Angela chimed in.

"Tch. Let me at least explain my thinking before you go and

deem my actions reckless." She held up the book. "*This* is a book that could help unlock something truly powerful. It's about magical energy sources. Judging from the Secret Keeper's reaction, I am certain it is key in my discovery to whatever *truly* provides our magic, seeing as Elfekot only ever gave me part of the answer."

Elfekot groaned. "None of us are lying to you, Jay."

"Perhaps. At least, you may not be *trying* to. From what we have learned of the relationship between the Council and the Secret Keepers, and adding what I accused the now-deceased Keeper of earlier, it is clear that I have to find the truth for myself."

"So... what? All that was for a freakin' book about... magic sources?" David's expression was a mix between confused and angry.

"Yes."

"And you risked our *lives* for that?!"

"Yes."

David clenched his teeth. "Urgh! God, Jay, can't you ever think of someone other than yourself?"

"No." *I already tried that, David,* she thought. *I'll never be that fool again.*

"We came to this place for *one* purpose, Jay: To get what we needed on portals, and that was *it*. None of... whatever it is you're trying to do!" David continued.

"I am trying to find the truth. And with the truth, I gain power," she said.

"Power? What truth, Jay? We're supposed to be in this quest together. We're the Restorers! But right now, it feels like you're scheming to do your own thing," David said, jabbing a finger at her. "And for what, yourself?!"

Jay let out an irritated breath. "I am trying to establish something for myself. Shame on me for pursuing such a right."

"Well, this is *not* the way to do it. You don't doubt your own companions and nearly blow us up! If there is some stupid 'truth' you wanna uncover or whatever, then ask us for help. You don't have to do things behind our back!"

"Help?" She scoffed. "The last thing I want is to be further misguided."

"What're you talking about?"

"You are so much blinder than I thought, David. Do you fail to see the shroud they throw over us? Do you fail to see the lies and the manipulation? The fallacies and the plot holes?"

David lowered his eyebrows, confused. "Huh?"

"Let us start from the beginning, then. For reasons never explained to us, a book was cursed. This curse has been unleashed and now, for more reasons unexplained, *we* have to get the Crystals back. No one else. We arrive on Elektia and we constantly hear about how they all only know about *one* Dijenuk: You. And yet, the letter we found in the Dijenuk House addressed both you and me by our full names." She crossed her right arm and placed her left elbow on top of it, putting her hand in front of her face. "To add to it, we are forced to embark on this quest with seemingly random companions. Who decided it had to be like this? Who decided these seemingly arbitrary keys? Oh, and as for the quest itself? Most of our magic has been taken away by the absence of these Crystals, but such an external source cannot be the primary source of our powers. It goes against everything I have studied so far. Someone or something long ago deliberately chose to severely alter what should be a natural genetic gift. Again, I ask: why? And how?"

"Oh boy. She's monologuing again," David muttered.

"And then there's the contradiction in name. It is not 'Dark Elektia,' but the Kingdom of Landor. That fact was more buried than the others. And don't forget about Denisse and her knowing both the secret tunnels and that we would arrive there. And now, your staff. Both Sarah and Sir K managed to get ahold of this supposedly rare metal. And do you know what both of those people have in common? They have traveled between Elektia and Terra. Why is it kept such a secret?" She put her arms down. "The Council and Secret Keepers are clearly in cahoots to hide something from us, but what exactly? It can't just be interplanetary travel. There is more to it. You saw how the Secret Keeper and the Council dodged my questions, and you saw how nervous Sir K was. From what the Keeper *did* tell us, it is clear that the knowledge of portals was common before. So, what happened?"

"Are we supposed to answer these questions, or…?" Angela said.

"And now I shall present my greatest point: the magical abilities presented to us. Supposedly, the mages of Elektia possess these powers, and I shall use the labels given to us: energy magic, spell magic, and the 'Elements': Wind, Fire, Water, Spirit, Earth, Lightning, Ice, Light, and Dark. All mages can perform the first two, and then one 'Element,' with Dijenuks and Landors being the exceptions. First, these 'Elements' have a few problems in their grouping. 'Ice' and 'Water' are the same thing, to name one."

"That is just how it is," Elfekot said.

"Secondly, and more importantly," Jay continued, raising her voice, "we have seen other magics that don't belong to *any* of these groups. Specifically, in the Dijenuk House. That building has the power to turn invisible and conceal its interior furnishing. It also has a gate that kept away non-Dijenuks. Mages cannot perform such magic. So, who did it?"

Angela shrugged. "Many of your questions have simple answers, Jay Dijenuk. The Elementians could have very well intervened."

"What, so some gods decided to help build a house? If these gods can intervene like that, why did they let *The Legends* be opened?" Jay questioned.

Angela blinked, taken aback. "Do not dare question the Elementians, Dijenuk."

"I could go on and on, but I have rambled long enough. You may be thinking, 'So what?' You may not care about getting these questions answered. But one thing is clear: the truth, about our quest, this planet, and our magic, is being kept from us. We are either given lies or an unacceptable plethora of questions without answers. *That* should be a concern of yours. Instead, you ignorant peons refuse to take in anything I say. And that is why I cannot be bothered to trust a single other person."

The other four Restorers said nothing for a few seconds. David took a few steps back, shaking his head. "You're unbelievable, Jay."

The girl rolled her eyes.

"Sure, maybe we don't know enough, and maybe some of it doesn't make sense yet. But what if there's a reason? What if there's a *good* reason?" David pressed. "The whole world isn't against you, Jay, even if you think it is. The same goes for Terra. It's not all some big conspiracy that the super-smart Jay has to uncover. If you trusted others, maybe you wouldn't be so uptight and paranoid about everything."

Jay scoffed. "What good reason could there be for concealing everything?"

"I dunno, but I have to believe there is, because we have other things to worry about. Plus, you're hiding things, too. Isn't it kinda…" David snapped his fingers in thought. "What's the word, hypocritical of you?"

"Oh, please. I keep my own secrets because I'm forced to play the same game."

"This isn't some competition, Jay!"

"If I treat it like one, it only makes victory clearer."

"And what kinda victory is that? One with only you as the winner?"

Jay's eyes twinkled, like she was excited, yet the rest of her face remained neutral. "Perhaps."

"We're supposed to be a team, sis!" David said, throwing an arm down.

"Then agree with me."

"Why? Just because you said so?"

"Yes."

"You could be wrong!"

"I'm never wrong. While it may sound like unnecessary boasting to you, keep in mind every instance in which my intelligence has been called into question. You will find that—in every instance—I am right."

"*Everyone's* wrong at some point in their lives."

"And I'm not everyone. The day I'm wrong is the day I make the worst mistake of my life."

"Ugh. Yes, you are. You're human just like the rest of us, so stop pretending to be some robot that's above everyone else!"

"Robot?"

"You know what I'm talking about. Ever since the summer, you have been a stuck-up, rude, and a condescending pain to every single person! And despite all that, me, Mom, and Dad still love you. We still try for you! Stacie tried for you!"

For a moment, Jay's body tensed. "Of course you would mention her. Your minuscule brain still stupidly believes that I possess even a minutia of care." *And of course, he's wrong... Right?*

David scoffed. "The old you cared."

"The 'old' me? What relevance does that have?"

"People don't just change like that, Jay."

As Jay spoke, her voice climbed in volume. "What if I didn't change? What if I instead threw something away? What if I instead decided to unchain myself from everything holding me back?"

"It doesn't matter exactly what it is. You're different now, and in the worst way. I'm not gonna let you ruin what we need to do just for your selfish paranoia! You don't think I know what this is all about?"

"Cease, David," she said. *I know exactly what he's about to spew.*

"H-Hey, um—" Clove started.

"Shut it, Clove," Jay snapped. *Did I have to say that?*

"And there it is again! You're so annoyingly rude to everyone! And you became even *more* of a prick when Stacie left. When she left the *both* of us."

A surge of warmth ran through Jay's body. It morphed into a buzz, shaking her core.

"So, yeah," David continued, "the Secret Keeper was right about your anger. You take it all out on everyone just because you—"

"*I said cease!*" Her voice was magnified in volume. It echoed across the basin. The other four stumbled back from the force, as Jay's body flared a brilliant green light along with her eyes. The warmth in her body amplified before dissipating, as did the scent of pine.

"Whoa…" David cleared his throat. "Um, I'm sorry, sis. I

went too far with that." His voice was sincere.

Jay looked down at her body. It was the first time she had seen the green light. *Interesting.*

Elfekot sighed. "Are you done? The three of us are sick of your bickering."

Jay glared at Elfekot. "Like I said, I could go on, but it seems like you all went even further below my rock-bottom expectations and processed none of what I said, so, yes, for now, I am 'done.'"

Angela stepped closer to her. "You still recklessly blew up the building. If you cared so much about knowledge, why did you destroy it at all?" she questioned.

"The books in there, at least the important ones, are fine. They emitted a weak magical hum, so I have no doubts that they are magically protected. I am also quite confident that the Secret Keeper remains alive, despite what I mentioned earlier. They are powerful, after all," Jay answered.

"And if you are wrong?" Angela added.

Jay squinted slightly. It gave Angela her answer.

"You said you found a map. Is that correct, David?" asked Elfekot, desperate to change to subject.

"Yeah." He pulled out the piece of parchment that he'd stuffed into his belt and unrolled it. The other Restorers gathered around it. David indicated where the Secret Keeper had marked.

Elfekot frowned. "Hm…" He traced his finger along the parchment. "I reckon we should be able to make it there before nightfall."

David sighed. "So we're still gonna walk more? We're not gonna go back and get the Scrolls?"

"I had the Council take us here because it is the closest possible location to the mines," Jay explained. "Returning to Fort Dijenuk would be an inefficient use of time."

Elfekot nodded. "We can travel to the Chamber tomorrow."

"Right," Angela replied.

David put the map away and sighed. "Well, I guess we should start walking…"

"You know, Master Dijenuk," Angela said as they began their trek, "we are not used to walking this much either. Our usual mode of transportation has been lost."

"Oh, yeah, Elfekot mentioned something about that," David said. "What exactly did you guys use?"

"Carriages," Angela answered.

"Like… wagons? Why do you need magic for that?"

"How do you think we moved them?"

"Animals? Kinda like a horse, but Elfekot said that's not a thing here," David guessed.

Angela raised an eyebrow. "An animal? No. A wind mage can train to be a carriage driver. They use their magic to steer and accelerate the carriage."

"Ohh. That's kinda cool. So it's sorta like a… land boat or somethin'."

Angela giggled. "I suppose you can call it that, yes. What do you use for transportation on Terra?"

"Cars, mainly. If you need to go far, you can also go in a

plane."

Elfekot and Angela stared at David with visible confusion.

"Oh, um, a car is like this metal box that a bunch of people sit in. And there's a driver, and they use this wheel to steer it, and they press down a pedal to move the car forward. It doesn't run on magic or anything. It uses this liquid called gasoline. They move pretty fast."

Angela shrugged. "It sounds like magic to me."

"Maybe 'cause it's foreign? So… I guess magic really just means something you can't understand or explain, but it works anyway, even if it's normal for others." He paused, stunned by his own words. "Whoa. That was kinda deep."

Jay sighed. "Magic is defined by the kind of energy it uses and how it's measured. The unit is called magical kris. If it can be measured in magical kris, it's magic. Simply put, magic is the use of a specific kind of energy. A car, meanwhile, is powered through chemical combustion. It's objective, David."

"Jeez, I wasn't being serious, Jay." He looked to his sister. "Wait, I just remembered something. Can't you teleport us all the way there? You've done it before."

"She has?" Clove said.

"Yeah. Back when Landor took the Scrolls from us and we were chasin' him, Jay clapped her hands and we all freakin' teleported super far away. It was pretty cool," David summarized.

"You bring that up now?" Angela muttered.

"I doubt I could repeat the action," Jay said. "Something

came to me when I did that. As in, some exterior force."

"Like, a person?"

"I don't know." Jay looked down. "Hm." *They can't know about the Objectivist. I have to prove that I can do it without anyone... Without the Objectivist, and... without her.*

The sun was inching closer to the horizon. The mountains that they had once looked upon from afar now loomed over them. Rocky, barren ground had replaced the grassy plains. The shrubbery was drier, while the air itself wasn't as fresh or crisp. The mountains themselves were nothing like David and Jay had ever seen. They were monstrous brown spikes, lacking the snowy white peaks they were familiar with. A layer of clouds blocked view of the summit. A subtle darkness blanketed the area.

Along the way, they used a variety of spells to keep the group as energized as possible. Fatigue came anyway. Their pace had slowed, especially with the uphill tread growing steeper.

David opened the map. "So, we're close, yeah?"

"I reckon so," Elfekot said, in the lead, like always.

"Man, these mountains are *huge,* though," David remarked. "It sucks that I've never been mountain climbing back on Terra. It probably would have helped, huh?"

"I doubt we have to climb much," said Angela. "The entrance could be quite low."

"Do you know for sure?" David asked.

"No. It is just what I hope," she admitted.

Less than an hour later, the Restorers had reached their first obstacle. The ground rose up dramatically several meters. From what they could see, there was no other way around that was close. David and Elfekot repeatedly checked the map to make sure they were in the right spot.

"How accurate do you even think that map is?" Jay questioned. "You also have to consider its scale. It could still be far."

"No... I see something," said Clove. She was looking off to the right. The other Restorers moved to see what she did.

Downhill, there were broken planks of wood mostly buried in the shrubbery. They were scattered and covered in dirt.

"Huh?" David said. "Some pieces of wood...?"

"It's a sign of civilization. Relatively speaking. The mines may be closer after all." Jay moved down the hill to investigate. The others followed. She exhaled. "Of course..."

Moving closer revealed messy stacks of crates and barrels pushed in a corner. Some of them were broken. There was a larger piece of wood from what appeared to be part of a ladder sitting at the base of the cliff. Dangling from the top of the precipice was a torn segment of rope. It was nowhere close to arm's reach.

David walked up to the cliff. "Dang. Do you think you there's a spell you can use, Jay? Like, one of those teleports?"

"I would rather save the uses if possible."

"Of course," Elfekot muttered. "You already forgot what I

taught you."

"The energy rope," Jay said. "Yes, I know."

"Oh, that!" David said, eyes wide. "I forgot about that. You never taught us how to climb something with it, though."

"Then follow my lead."

Elfekot drew his staff and swirled it around a couple times, like he was cranking something, then thrust it forward. A rope of glowing white energy lashed out from the staff. It latched itself onto the edge of the cliff above them.

"Once it is attached, you retract it."

As though it were a grappling hook, Elfekot zoomed upwards and grabbed the cliff edge, then pulled himself up.

"Whoa," David said. "I remember Mr. K doing that same thing, actually. Here, let me try."

He pulled out his staff and mimicked what Elfekot had done. The energy rope attached itself to the edge.

"Uh, now what?"

"Just pull yourself up, like I did," Elfekot replied.

"Um... okay." Holding as tight as he could to his staff, David let the length of the rope shorten. At first it was slow. He walked with it a couple feet forward. He then lost control. The Dijenuk was forcibly yanked upwards. He was flipped over the cliff edge and out of sight.

"Are you alright, Master Dijenuk?" Angela called.

There was a groan. "Yeah. There's something up here!"

Elfekot looked down at the rest of the Restorers. "Can the rest of you...?"

"Of course *I* can do it," said Angela.

"Um…" Clove swallowed. "I do not know if I am able."

"Good luck, then," Angela replied, immediately performing the trick and lifting herself to the top of the cliff.

Jay retrieved her staff and aimed it at the cliff edge.

"Hold on, Jay," Elfekot said. "Take Clove with you."

"Wha—?" said both Jay and Clove.

"Um, I-I can try to learn it," Clove stuttered.

"What she said," Jay added.

"Just save us all time and take her with you. What is so hard about that?"

"Nothing, but…" Jay lowered her staff and sighed. "Fine." She pointed two fingers at Clove. "*Unes dyelgé.*" She fired a light-grey projectile.

Clove gasped, her eyes wide.

"It's a weight reduction spell. I lack the physical strength to carry you otherwise."

Clove, still in shock, nodded.

Jay looked at her for a second. Her muscles tensed.

Clove approached. "Do I, um… o-or do you…?"

"You hold on to me."

Clove tentatively put one arm around Jay, then grabbed her right arm with the other. Jay's muscles tightened even further.

"If you fall, it's on you," Jay said.

As she readied her staff, she couldn't help but notice that there was some fragrance about her. It was like the ocean, but cleaner and sweeter. She thrust her staff forward, and both of

384

them zoomed upwards. The moment they reached the top, Jay detached herself from Clove, forcing off her tight grip.

"*Kanba.*"

Clove almost fell over as Jay's spell was reversed, her weight returning to her. "Th-thank you."

At the top of the cliff was the gaping mouth of a cave. It held darkness within it. The outer frame of the mouth was wide enough to fit several people. There were a few more crates and barrels joined by various chests sitting outside. They contained equipment like lanterns, rope, and shovels.

"This has gotta be it, right?" David said.

Angela approached the entrance. "Only one way to find out." The group followed her.

David glanced back and found that Jay hadn't moved. She was still standing on the edge of the cliff, looking out. "Come on, sis."

"I am trying to make sure we aren't being followed again."

"Like I said, you're always so paranoid. Come on, we gotta move."

"Hm." Jay stared out for a few more seconds before rejoining the group.

David snagged one of the lanterns from the cluttered chests. It had a grey metal frame with a bent handle. It contained a used candle. "We're probably gonna need these."

Jay looked at the dusty object with disgust. "We have my spells, remember?"

"Yeah, but I thought you said you wanted to use them only

if you had to."

"Light-source spells are hardly an issue. You can't even light it, anyway," Jay said.

"Oh. True." David frowned, disappointed. "I'm gonna take one anyway." He hung the lantern on his belt.

"Whatever." Jay moved to stand at the cave entrance. She put a hand on her amulet. *"Musnomi levis."* A tiny floating orb appeared in front of her. It lit up the entire entrance, revealing its steep descent.

David and Angela stepped forward. They peeked down the slope. The loose, dirt ground and the incline made it almost like a slide. One at time, the Restorers slid down the incline and into the darkness.

"Musnomi levis."

Another magical light lifted the darkness off of their surroundings. The width of the cave had opened up. There were numerous wooden braces along the path, holding up the earthen ceiling. They were completely surrounded by brown, rocky walls and dirt. It was all dry. The path continued to slope downward, although it was less dramatic. They continued through the cave, and Jay created lights as needed. Eventually, the path narrowed.

After a few minutes of careful walking, the Restorers encountered a sudden drop. There was a large hole in front of them. David knelt and squinted.

"I can see the ground… maybe? It doesn't look like that far of a drop."

"I have seen nowhere else to go. We may have no choice but to descend," Elfekot pointed out.

David nodded. Without any hesitation, he dropped right in. There was a *thud*. "I'm alright! It's safe to go down."

"I did not mean like *that*," Elfekot said.

"Well, I'm alive, yeah? So we're good. Just come down."

The other four joined him. Another light-source spell revealed to them a spacious, roughly circular room. They could spot a couple more paths leading in different directions. The room itself was empty of both man-made objects and natural structures.

Suddenly, a bizarre, vaguely human noise cut through the dry, silent air. It was as though someone had taken a mix of various screams and cries, then remixed it to the point that it was hardly recognizable. It was almost like static. The sound echoed in the room. It was impossible to tell where it came from.

David drew his staff. "What was that?! Was that a... monster?"

Elfekot pulled out his sword. "Maybe. Stay cautious, everyone."

Angela rolled her shoulders. "I have been waiting too long for a fight. It is time to show us what you can do, Clove."

"R-Right."

"Just be safe, alright?" said David.

The Restorers moved to the center of the room. They formed a circle. Their weapons were drawn.

"It could be anything," Elfekot warned. "And it could be

anywhere, whatever it is."

The marred mix of screams came back. It was louder this time.

David charged an energy blast. His eyes darted around. "Come on…" he muttered.

Without any build-up, the entire cave shook. Bits of the earth rained from the ceiling. Even the cores of their bodies vibrated. At the same time, the lights that Jay had created went out. They were completely in the dark.

"What? *Musnomi*—" Jay's spell was interrupted by her scream.

"Jay? Are you okay?" David heard no answer. A faint, chilling breeze ran past him. Something about it made his heart sink.

"What is going on?!" said Angela.

David spun around. He couldn't see any of his teammates. Whether they had separated or were still right next to him was impossible to tell with sight alone. David gritted his teeth.

"Come at me, whatever you are! Show yourself!"

He felt the breeze again. It was stronger. He immediately felt his entire torso scream in pain, as though it were on fire. His body struggled to keep the very matter that made him up from being twisted and pulled apart. David collapsed to the ground. It was unbearable. A few seconds later, the feeling was gone as quickly as it had come. However, his body refused to move. He couldn't get back up. There were screams, real screams, only he didn't know which of his companions were screaming.

"No... Come on!" With a short yell, David forced himself on his feet. "Jay! Where are you?"

She groaned. *"M-Musnomi levis!"* Jay's orb of light returned. At the same time, the horrible amalgamation of screams rang.

David scanned his surroundings. Jay was kneeling on the ground, amulet tightly in hand. Angela and Elfekot were standing, bent over with their hands on their knees. Clove was completely on the ground. David helped her up. They were all within the light's radius.

"Is everyone alright?" he asked.

They shook their heads. "This is no normal creature," Elfekot muttered.

David gazed into the darkness. "Has anyone seen the thing?"

"No," said Angela.

"Nothing at all," said Elfekot.

Clove then raised her staff. She tensed her body as though she were about to fire something. Nothing happened. "I... think I saw it! But..."

"It's alright. You'll get it next time," David told her.

"Keep an eye out. It may try to get us from behind," Elfekot warned.

The Restorers reentered their circle formation. Their heads and eyes constantly moved about.

David squinted. "There!"

At the border between the light and the darkness, he could spot movement. It was black and ghost-like, floating around without a solid form. Its wispiness lacked any distinct shape.

"What is that thing?" Angela asked.

"It does not matter! Just attack it!" Elfekot said.

Before any of them could do anything, the creature retreated into the darkness.

"Stay put, all of you. It will probably come back. It seems to be rather aggressive," Elfekot said.

"Or maybe it's really defensive. This could be, like, its home," David guessed.

"Just stay focused," Elfekot replied.

The Restorers continued to stand and watch with their weapons at the ready. It was silent enough that their rapid breaths were clearly audible. Their staffs were slipping in their sweaty palms.

Clove screamed. The creature had returned. It was in front of her, again at the edge of the light. She thrust her staff forward. A tiny bolt of energy fired. It missed. The wispy creature flew off.

"So, that is your power..." Angela muttered.

"Huh?" Clove sounded.

"She is *not* the fifth Restorer, then," Angela said.

"What? Why?" David asked.

"Did you see how weak that blast was? There is no way one of the Restorers could be that weak."

Clove slowly lowered her staff and dipped her head.

"Such an analysis cannot be based off of one example, Angela," Jay said.

"And why not?"

"Because it can easily lead to an inaccurate assumption. Give her an adequate chance first before making yourself look like even more of an idiot," Jay replied.

"That *was* her chance."

Jay looked at her. "Is this really important right now?"

Angela broke formation and took a few steps towards Jay. "Right, because *you* have the right priorities."

Jay faced her. Just as she opened her mouth to say something back, the earth momentarily shook again. The light they stood in blinked out of existence. Darkness swallowed them once more.

"What?" Jay said. "It must be destroying the instance somehow. But…"

The familiar breeze returned. Like before, David's companions screamed in agony around him. It had yet to strike him.

"It doesn't like the light… Wait… Wait!" David reached for his lantern. A chilling gust swept through him. He fell to his knees. "I'm not… staying down!"

With effort, David returned to his feet. He pointed his staff upwards and fired a volley of energy blasts. Small chunks of rock fell on top of him. There was another freezing wind. The boy fell back down and kneeled. He continued, pressing the crystalline tip of his staff against the candle inside the lantern. He did his best to find where the wick was in the dark.

"Come on… Come on…" he muttered.

The candle lit up. Its small, orange flame was enough to give him a great deal of comfort. David stood back up with the lantern in hand. He frantically waved the lantern around as he moved through the room. There was another warped scream.

"Gotcha!"

The Dijenuk barely spotted the creature as it retreated from him. He chased it down, using the lantern to keep it at bay. The boy managed to corner it. It was stuck between the small glow of David's lantern and the cave wall. David took a step forward, forcing the creature into the light. It made a softer scream. As much as he wanted the horrific noise to stop, David continued. The light seemed to burn it. He could see it shrinking gradually.

"*Levis ehté saugh!*" chanted Jay. She was standing at the opposite end of the room by one of the path openings.

The entire chamber lit up. The creature's screams amplified in both noise and level of warping. After a few more seconds, it had enough. It forced itself through the light and zoomed towards Jay. She ducked. The phantom-like creature flew over her head. The force from that alone was enough to knock Jay off-balance. She fell backwards into the opening and into the darkness.

"Jay!" David called.

The girl tumbled down. Finally, following a few seconds of painful rolling, she hit the level ground.

"Ugh…" Her head had taken most of the beating. She felt the ground beneath her. It was unnaturally smooth. "*Musnomi levis.*"

The darkness lifted as Jay moved to stand up. She was in a

small, circular chamber. The floor was composed of a paved stone. There was something large in the center of the room. It was a rocky structure, too smooth and chiseled to be natural. There were numerous etchings of foreign symbols. Jay took a few steps back from it. It was a stone arch.

"Seek me..."

The shrill whisper came from the arch. It was tall and wide enough for anyone to fit through. Its smooth, grey composition had a few chips and cracks. Her eyes moved to the symbols carved into the rock. While it was a language she couldn't understand, she swore she'd seen letters like those elsewhere.

As she examined the structure, a faint outline of a person emerged underneath the arch, as if someone had drawn it with white chalk. It was that of a girl with shoulder-length hair, a slim body, and glasses, standing in a neutral position. It was a younger Jay.

Chapter VI:
The Other World Here

"Jay! Are you alright?" called a voice. It was David's.

"Huh?" She realized that she was now closer to the arch. "Yes, I'm fine," she called back. The figure disappeared.

"Watch your step," said David.

Several other voices neared from behind her. She turned around to find the other Restorers coming down from the chamber above. Their attention immediately turned to the stone arch.

"Oh no," said Elfekot.

"Do you know what this is?" Jay asked.

"A stone arch," Elfekot answered.

"Is that all it is?"

"Well, no. But that is simply what we call it. No one knows who built them, when they were built, or why. We know the arches are ancient and… strange. They are said to transport you to very dangerous realms. It is where the gods live."

David raised an eyebrow. "You mean, those Elementian dudes?"

"Yes. I doubt this stone arch in particular would take you to them, but, somewhere in there, they are there. Supposedly," Elfekot added.

"Does this... place, this realm, have a name?" Jay asked.

"Er, not really. However, where the Elementians live, we call Prime Elementia," answered Elfekot.

"A bit of a silly name, but it is understandable. Hm." Jay faced the arch.

"Do *not* even think about it," Elfekot warned. "To step through any of these stone arches is a severe offense."

"As in, it is illegal, yes?" Jay continued to face the arch.

"Yes."

"Huh."

"Are these things hard to find?" David asked.

"I have not seen one before, so I imagine they are," said Angela.

"It is the same with me. Let us leave. We need to find those portal crystals and stay away from this thing," Elfekot said.

"Wait, but where did the thing go? The weird... creature." David scanned the rest of the room but found nothing else. "Did you get it, Jay?"

"No. It must have disappeared somehow."

"Maybe it went through the arch," David said.

"Maybe..." Jay echoed.

"It matters not. As long it is gone, whatever it was, we are good to proceed. Come on." Elfekot turned to leave first. The others followed suit.

"Just be careful climbing this thing back up," David warned.

Clove glanced behind her. "Jay?" She turned around. Jay was nowhere to be seen.

David also turned. "Oh no. Don't tell me…"

Elfekot sighed. "She went in. Why am I not surprised?"

"But, why would she do that?" David wondered.

"With her, who knows?"

David stepped towards the arch. Angela grabbed him by the shoulder.

"Master Dijenuk, stop!"

"Someone's gotta get her!"

"It is *dangerous*," Elfekot warned.

"Is that supposed to stop me?"

Elfekot sighed again. He stared at David for a few seconds. "Fine. But we still need to find the portal crystals, so we will split up. One of you will go with me through the arch."

The other three Restorers glanced at each other.

"Clove, come with me."

The girl made a small jump. "Me?"

"I can go," David volunteered.

"We *cannot* have both Dijenuks in that realm. The risk is too high," Elfekot said.

David exhaled. "Fine…"

"We will meet back up in that large circular area. Understood?"

They nodded.

"I have no idea what is waiting for us in there…. If we perish—"

"Y'all are gonna be fine," David said. "I mean, we're the Restorers, yeah?"

Despite David's words of confidence, Clove appeared worried. She was biting her lower lip, and her eyebrows were low.

"I will enter first, Clove. We need to hurry before Jay gets too far in."

Clove nodded quickly.

"Good luck," said David.

David and Angela remained to watch. Elfekot stepped under the arch. As soon as he crossed through it, he was gone. Clove looked back at David and Angela. They gave her a nod. The girl took a deep breath and walked forward.

The moment that Clove walked through the stone arch, her surroundings changed in an instant. The cave she had stood in was gone. It was replaced by a small, grassy island. There was a cloudy, brilliant blue sky above her. To her shock, the island was floating. There was no ground beneath it. A blue void had taken its place. Elfekot stood a couple of feet away. The stone arch remained behind her. The only other occupant on the minuscule island was a palm tree. Clove slowly spun in place. She could see similar islands in the distance.

"Where are we?" she asked softly.

"Not Elektia, that is for certain." He groaned. "Where did she go?!"

"Did she end up somewhere else?"

"As far as my understanding of the stone arches goes, I know

they are consistent. She ended up in the same place, alright."
Elfekot knelt down and peeked over the edge. "We might have
to jump."

"W-What?!"

"There is nowhere else to go. It might work. It is clear that
nothing functions the same here."

"A-And if we die?"

"Then we die," he said simply.

Clove gulped. She leaned over the edge. The void appeared
bottomless.

Elfekot took a few steps back. With a running start, he leaped
over the edge of the island and plummeted into the endless blue
below. Clove watched with disbelief. Her heart was racing, and
her stomach was churning. She closed her eyes.

"If I die..." she whispered.

The girl jumped. Her eyes remained closed. Air rushed
through her. After several seconds, she opened her eyes and
looked up. The island was out of sight. She looked down. There
was something new. A layer of clouds had appeared. It was
zooming closer. Clove shut her eyes again. Her body tensed. She
hit something with a noisy *thud* and landed on her hands and
knees. It was painless.

"Huh?!"

Clove had landed on a different island. It was slightly bigger
than the other, with two palm trees instead of one. There was no
stone arch. Elfekot stood next to her. He appeared hopelessly
confused.

"It makes no sense...." the captain muttered. He was staring at the ground, frowning.

Clove scanned the area. "Do you see that?" She pointed to another island in the distance.

Elfekot squinted at it. He could make out a single palm tree and a stone arch. "Is that...?"

"It's where we came from," she realized. "Maybe... maybe we looped around somehow." She put a hand on her chin as if in thought. "If one falls, they quickly loop around and descend from the sky."

"But how? Why?" Elfekot questioned.

Clove shrugged.

"We need to get out of here."

"But..."

"Yes, I know. Jay." He tapped his foot impatiently. "We could fall over and over and still never find her. Ugh... Do you have any ideas?"

She shook her head.

"Then I suppose we try again." Elfekot leaped off once more.

With slightly less hesitation this time, Clove did the same. She once again shut her eyes tight. Even though she had met no harm the last time, she couldn't help but tense up. The fall lasted a few seconds longer. She landed, again without any hint of pain.

This floating island was much larger than the last. It could fit an entire house. The grass here was wilder, and the palm trees were plentiful. The island they'd come from was within view. The one with the stone arch, however, was not.

"Look around. This one is big enough for someone to hide in," said Elfekot. "Although I do not know why Jay would…" he added quietly as he walked away.

Clove meandered around. She made sure to check behind the trunks of the trees and watch for anything hidden in the grass. There was nothing she could see. The girl took a few seconds to stare out into the distance. It was peacefully quiet. The only other noise was that of Elfekot stepping through the foliage. Clove shivered and drew the coat around her closer. It had been temperate until now. The palm leaves to her right shook. She gasped and instantly turned to the source of the sound.

The black, wispy, formless creature from earlier swirled in front her. It was unaffected by the brightness of the realm. Clove stood paralyzed. As the creature swirled in place, it took shape and eventually formed into a feline just barely larger than a lion. It was still composed of its wispy, black energy.

Clove drew her staff and pointed it at the creature. Her arm was shaking. It stood and faced her. If it had eyes, they would be staring at her. The girl tensed her arm. The creature lowered, ready to pounce. She jabbed her staff forward again. Nothing happened. It jumped, and Clove shrieked.

Bang!

The beast exploded, and its energy disintegrated into nothing. Clove turned around to her savior. Elfekot shook his head at her as he returned his staff to the leather slip on his back. She looked down at her feet.

"…I found something," Elfekot said.

Clove looked back up. "Huh?"

He led her to the other side of the island, and asked, "Do you see it?"

"Um…"

Elfekot was pointing at the ground, where there was a shadow, only there was no object that it belonged to.

"It's… an arch," she said. Clove grasped at the air and touched something invisible. "There's something here!" She felt around. "Um, I *think* it's a stone arch."

Elfekot titled his head. "But… we cannot see it." He sighed. "If what I know about these arches is right, then it could take us another layer deeper, which is *not* a good thing."

"But… Jay…"

"I know. She might be through this one." He looked to her. "Ready?"

She nodded.

Clove watched Elfekot disappear through the invisible arch before going through it herself. Like last time, the world around her was replaced by another.

The blue sky and its clouds had turned into a grey void. The only piece of land was the large, black stone disc they stood upon, which was about the size of the island they'd come from. The stone was flat, but many cracks ran through it like veins. In the center, a tiny plant sprouted from one of these cracks.

"Jay!" Elfekot yelled.

On the other side of the disc, Jay stood. Her back was facing toward them. Elfekot and Clove ran towards her. As they approached, they noticed what she was looking at.

It was a shadowy figure, shaped like a human girl. Unlike the monster they'd fought earlier, this one was a darker shade of black and was completely opaque. The figure was slim and wore glasses with its straight, shoulder-length hair. It matched Jay in height, and it lacked any facial features.

"Jay, what is this?" Elfekot asked.

"Why?" said the figure. Its voice was distorted, as though it was speaking radically different pitches at the same time. "Why did they do that?"

Elfekot drew his staff. "Jay, answer me!"

"It's my fault. It's all my fault," the figure continued. "Why couldn't they just be honest with me? Why did they have to pretend?"

"This is ridiculous," Jay muttered.

The figure dropped to her knees. "I'm worthless. They proved to me that I'm worthless. I don't deserve their kindness, real or fake."

"Shut up," Jay said.

It looked up to face her. "But you... *you* are honest. Why couldn't the others be like that? Why couldn't she just—?"

"That's enough. Elfekot, kill it."

"What is this?" he asked.

"I just wanted to be with her..." said the shadow.

"Just do it," Jay snapped.

Elfekot raised his staff and fired a blast of energy. It passed right through the unmoving figure, who continued to stare at Jay.

"You don't have the answer either, do you?" the shadow asked. It looked to the ground. "Of course. No one does. I'll never find the answer." It punched the ground. "What meaning do I have anymore? What purpose? Without her, I'm nothing. No, I've always been nothing." It looked back up at Jay. "Are you even any different?"

Jay's eyes grew, and her mouth hung open slightly. "I…" She clenched her fists. "I've found *my* true meaning. I've found my path *because* I lost her. So, she'll *stay* gone… and so will you."

The shadow sniffed. "Yeah. Everyone wants me gone. I… want it, too. I-I… I just wanna—"

"You're pathetic," Jay said. She put her right hand to her amulet. "How about I do it for you?" Jay formed her left hand into a finger gun, and raised it to the side of her head. "I'll end this."

Clove gasped. "Jay, no!"

Jay took a shaky breath, then shut her eyes. "*Cintria excata!*"

A jet of green light fired from her fingers and passed right through her skull, her hand recoiling like a gun as her head jolted. An instant later, the shadowy figure exploded into nothingness, its fragments scattering into the abyss.

Jay lowered her hand. "Don't bother asking. Let's get out of here," she said, turning around.

Elfekot and Clove stared at her with their jaws dropped. "Er… Can you at least explain to us what you are doing here in the first place?" Elfekot asked.

Jay began walking towards the stone arch they'd come from. "I wish I knew."

"What do you mean?"

"In a way, it was like a trance. I was somewhat aware of what was going on and what I was doing, but it felt as though another force was drawing me in."

The three of them reentered the world with the floating islands.

"It was quite perverse," she continued. "When I snapped out of it, I was in front of that shadow." The girl looked out at the tiny pieces of land in the distance. "This really is a place without rules."

"It is. I have just about given up trying to make sense of it. Anyway, David and Angela are likely waiting for us. We need to…" Elfekot trailed off. "Wait… How are we supposed to return to the first arch we went through? I cannot even see it."

Clove gasped and flinched. Jay and Elfekot turned to see what she was staring at. The floating island from which they'd come was now in sight. It was about a hundred yards away. Before their very eyes, a bridge of clouds manifested itself between them and the other island.

"It—it *flew* at us!" Clove stammered.

"Is this place… listening to us?" Elfekot said.

"Does it have a form of sentience?" added Jay.

Just before their feet touched the magical bridge, something rumbled behind them. The trio turned around. A mass of black clouds in the sky drifted menacingly towards them. There was an ear-splitting *clap*. A bolt of lightning fell. It struck one of the distant islands and exploded it into pieces.

"Run!" Elfekot yelled.

The three Restorers darted across the bridge. The rate of the thunder increased and the island behind them shattered. As they sprinted, the other island wasn't getting any closer. The dim light of a thick overcast covered them. The storm was directly above them. Another bolt of lightning struck. It connected with the lone tree and set it ablaze. The island remained intact.

"Go, go, go!" Elfekot leaped through the stone arch. Jay and Clove followed.

Back inside the cave, they landed in a pile. Jay stood and removed herself as fast as possible. She leaned against the cave wall and panted.

"That… was upsetting," she said.

"And that is why we avoid the arches," said Elfekot with an "'I told you so" attitude.

"Do you hear that?" said Clove.

Elfekot and Jay quieted. Elsewhere in the mines, someone was yelling.

"You think they'll be okay?" David wondered.

"To be honest, I have no idea," Angela admitted. "The stories about what lies through the arches… Usually they are about the Elementians, yes, but sometimes you hear about the people who disappear through them or come back insane."

"Oh…"

"But, um, we must have faith."

"Exactly!"

The two Restorers had just reentered the circular room in which they'd fought the mysterious creature. It took considerable effort to climb back up the slope. David approached one of the openings in the cave wall.

"This is the only way we haven't gone, yeah?"

"Yes."

He peeked inside. "Crap. I can't see anything. I mean, I guess I could try lighting the lantern again."

"What about those spells Jay used? They are not exclusive to her."

"Oh, yeah! Uh… what does she say? Musno-something? Levis?"

"Hm…" Angela took out her staff as she approached the shroud. "*Musnomi levis!*" Nothing happened. She frowned. "*Musnomi levis!*" A tiny orb of light appeared in front of her. It dimly lit the narrow path before them.

"Nice," said David.

With Angela leading, the two walked onward. It was barely wide enough for them to comfortably stride through. The path was straight as it led slightly downwards. Each time they reached the edge of the light, Angela cast another source. Considering the small radius, she had to do it often.

"I have been meaning to ask… How did you light the lantern earlier?"

"Oh, yeah, that. Well, I think it was kinda obvious, even for me, that the black creature thing didn't like the light very much. It kept putting out Jay's, so I thought, 'Maybe it only does it for magical ones.' It was a lucky guess, to be honest. I had to try something, but I had no lighter or match for the lantern. That was when I remembered something. When we were training a couple of days ago, I noticed that the tip of a staff gets very hot very quickly."

"Ah. So that is how you burned yourself," she realized.

"Yeah," he said with a laugh. "I was lucky I only fired a couple of blasts. Anything more than that and I could've hurt myself pretty bad. Anyway, after I remembered that, I fired a bunch of energy blasts in a row. I prayed the staff would get hot enough to light the candle in the lantern, and ta-da! It did."

"Huh. Well done, Master Dijenuk."

"Thanks. I'm honestly kinda impressed with myself. Like, that's the sorta big-brain stuff that only Jay pulls off, ya know?"

Angela chuckled. "I suppose so."

"Oh hey, this is something."

The duo entered the largest chamber in the cave yet. The ceiling was high, and the length stretched out past the edge of what Angela's light could provide. Like the entrance, there were numerous tools and storage containers littered about. There was something glimmering in the darkness.

David pointed at it. "What's that?"

They approached it. "*Musnomi levis.*"

Another light revealed a small, tipped cart and the

continuation of the mine. There were other tunnels leading elsewhere, while the larger tunnel they stood in kept going. David knelt down. Shiny black crystals of varying sizes were scattered across the ground from where the cart had tipped. He picked one up and examined it.

"This has gotta be a portal crystal, right?"

"I have no idea."

"Hm… I think it is. I'm pretty sure this is the same type of thing that Mr. K used to get us to Elektia, so… mission accomplished!"

"Great! Let us go back, then, and wait for the others."

"Shouldn't we take a few more with us?"

"Ah, yes. Good thinking, Master Dijenuk."

They grabbed as many portal crystals as they could safely carry, for a total of ten. Arms full, they made their way back.

"To be honest, apart from all the walking and the weird monster thing, it hasn't been too hard," David shared. "At least Landor hasn't gotten in our way."

"Yet," added Angela. "I imagine he is scheming something."

"Probably."

They reached the circular area again. There was no one else.

David sighed. "Guess we gotta wait. I hope Jay and the others are okay."

"I finally caught up to you," said a voice.

David and Angela spun around. They faced a teenage boy around the same age as the two of them. He had long, dark brown hair tied into a ponytail and fierce purple eyes. He wore a simple cloth shirt, brown pants, and dirty boots, as well as a triumphant smile. If it weren't for his eyes, he would be easily mistaken for an average civilian. He didn't carry a staff or any other weapon.

"Who are you?" David asked slowly. Dropping the portal crystals, he drew his staff as Angela drew her spear.

"My name is Hiatyu," he said. The boy had a silvery, carefully enunciated tone. "I understand the weapons, but please trust me when I say that I mean no harm."

"You followed us, didn't you?" David accused.

"Of course. I have been trying to reach you for a while now, David Dijenuk, but I had to talk to you when you were more or less alone. Fort Dijenuk isn't exactly easy to quietly infiltrate, surprisingly."

"Infiltrate? So you are an enemy," Angela said.

"To some, yes. But my conversation here is with the Dijenuk." He faced him. "I need you to come with me."

"What? Why?"

"It is an important matter. Yes, more important than your quest to restore the… 'Elements,' as you people call them. It'd be unwise to further discuss this in front of anyone else."

"You gotta give us a little more than that, dude."

Hiatyu glared at him. "There are various people in this universe who would like to use you, you specifically, for their own selfish gain. You see, Dijenuk, buried within you is a power unlike any other."

David lowered his staff. "There is?"

"Indeed. The group I represent seeks to cultivate that power.

We want to bring peace to the universe. Surely you seek the same."

"He is lying, Master Dijenuk," Angela warned.

"What if he isn't?"

"I ask you once more, Dijenuk: Come with me."

"I mean…"

Hiatyu jerked his head to the side as though he had heard something. "Do you feel that?" he asked with a low voice.

"Huh?"

"I feel it, too," Angela said.

David focused on his magical instincts. Something far away was giving off a slight hum. As the feeling grew, he could tell that the source was speedily approaching. "Is that…?"

Angela made a small gasp. "What kind of power is this?"

The lights went out. A second later, they came back on. A figure in a long black coat and hood had shoved Hiatyu against the earthen wall. They had their left arm pinned against his neck. The arm held a dagger.

"Who are you?!" Hiatyu choked.

The figure increased his pressure. "You and I are going to have a long chat." The voice was that of a young man.

A small knife appeared in Hiatyu's hand. The mysterious man immediately grabbed his wrist and twisted it. He yelled in pain as the knife dropped.

The man threw a punch across Hiatyu's jaw. He grabbed his collar and engaged Dark Flight. The two of them zoomed through the tunnels leading back outside.

"Hey!" David shouted. He tried running after them, but the hooded man's flight was too fast. "Come back here!"

There was silence. The powerful magical presence was gone.

David was stunned. "Um… okay then…"

"Do you know what just happened there?" Angela asked. She was helplessly confused.

"Nope."

"I… suppose it worked out, then."

"I guess…?

"David! Angela!" called a familiar voice. Elfekot ran in, with Jay and Clove just behind him. "What happened?" the captain asked.

"I honestly have no idea. This guy named… Hiatyu, I think, came in and was like, 'I finally found you!' and wanted me to come with him. Something about a group that wanted to train my hidden power, I dunno. He seemed pretty shady. And then this other dude in black came in. He was wearing a hood, so I couldn't see his face. The guy grabbed Hiatyu and flew away with him. It was pretty weird."

"Oh… I see," Elfekot said. He frowned, unsure as to what to make of David's story.

Jay looked away.

"We can talk more about it later." Elfekot indicated the pile of black rocks at their feet. "I take it those are the portal crystals?"

"Yep," David said. "So, now we can go to the Wind Chamber!"

"Calm down. Before we do anything, I think we need rest," said Elfekot. The others nodded in agreement. "If possible, we can travel to the Chamber tomorrow. For now, let us return to Fort Dijenuk."

"I guess..." David picked up one of the crystals. "So, according to the Secret Keeper dude, there's a special thing you gotta say. It's 'To This Place' and then the place you wanna go to. You can go anywhere, apparently, as long it's outside. And the better you can envision where you wanna go, the lesser the chance it'll mess up," he explained.

"So, it can mess up?" Angela asked.

"I guess so."

"I believe we all can envision Fort Dijenuk pretty clearly, so we should be alright. Since you know what to do, go ahead and try it, David," Elfekot invited as he picked up a portion of the portal crystals. Angela did the same.

"Sweet." David set down the crystal and took a few steps back. He pointed his staff at it and took a deep breath. "Alright... here we go. Oh, one more thing. Apparently, the portal can close quickly, so we all need to go through it as fast as possible."

"Scary," Angela said, "but alright."

"Take us to the Dijenuk House, David," instructed Elfekot.

"Gotcha." He cleared his throat. *"To This Place..."*

"Fort Dijenuk, Light Elektia!" Jay finished.

"Jay, no!" Elfekot shouted.

It was too late. A bolt of energy fired from the girl's staff. The black crystal exploded into a translucent grey vortex. The other Restorers, minus Clove, glared at her.

"Oh well," she said. Before Elfekot could respond, Jay stepped backwards through the vortex and disappeared through it.

The captain muttered a low curse and stepped through it. David went next, followed by Angela. Clove walked through just before the portal shrank away…

It was dusk. The portal had taken them to the area right before the entrance to the Dijenuk House, where a crowd of civilians spoke to them every morning. As the Restorers gathered their bearings, a similar group formed around them. They murmured to themselves.

"What was that?"

"They appeared out of nowhere!"

"Was this the doing of the Elementians? Do we have their blessing?"

"Did you see that swirling light?"

"And now they all know," muttered Elfekot.

"Exactly," said Jay.

Before the civilians could bombard them with questions, the Restorers scurried away. The civilians knew to stay away from the Dijenuk House and its path.

"Oh man, I'm beat," David said as he went through the door. He had only lived in the Dijenuk House for a few days, but he already felt a sense of comfort when stepping inside. His sore legs took him to one of the couches, where he collapsed. "Like, I'm pretty used to being active, but something about magic just kicks it up a notch."

The others joined him in the sitting room. Clove slumped onto another couch, eyes closed, while Angela sat on an armchair. Elfekot remained standing, as did Jay, who leaned against the wall with her arms crossed. Despite her best efforts to suppress it, Jay's eyelids drooped.

"Before we go and pass out, I would like to discuss the Wind Chamber," Elfekot said. "We need to formulate a plan."

"It's simple," said David. "We take a portal there, enter the Wind Chamber, watch out for any monsters or guards or whatever, take them out, nab the Wind Crystal, and take a portal back. Easy peasy."

"Right," said Elfekot slowly.

"Be careful not to underestimate the dangers, Master Dijenuk," Angela warned. "No one has ever been in any of the Chambers before, so no one knows what exactly waits inside. Honestly… it is somewhat exciting."

"Exactly. We need to decide whether or not we should split up, whether or not we should draw a map as we go and who would draw such a map, whether—"

"We can decide all that when we get there. It could be one tiny little room, for all we know. Come on, I just wanna go to bed," David begged.

"As do I…" Angela said.

Elfekot exhaled. "Fine. We will depart for the Chamber after breakfast tomorrow morning. You are all dismissed. And do not sneak out at night to train, David. Yes, I heard it."

"Oh, don't worry, Elfekot. I'm 'boutta pass out," David assured, yawning.

David, Jay, and Angela headed for the stairs. Elfekot grabbed a set of keys from the table and almost headed for the front door, but he noticed that Clove remained on the couch.

"Is something wrong?" he asked. "Clove?"

Her eyes snapped open. "Oh! Um, uh…" She rubbed her eyes. "Do I go home now, or…?"

"You will be staying here. I take it there is no one that requests you stay at home, yes?"

"R-Right."

"Alright. I advise you retrieve the rest of your belongings sometime tomorrow. There are spare bedrooms on the top floor. Take the ladder in the back of the second floor," Elfekot instructed. "Angela and I sleep on that floor as well."

"Okay. Thank you." Clove nervously shuffled away and took the stairs. She followed Elfekot's directions and climbed the ladder up to the third story.

She stared at the doors, unsure which to take.

Guessing at random, Clove approached the farthest door on the left. She knocked. There was no answer. After a few moments, she slowly opened the door. Inside was a bedroom, like she expected. It was small, but nothing she wasn't used to. There was a bed, a bedside table, and a small dresser.

Clove exhaled and slumped onto the bed as she ran her

fingers through her silver hair. She pulled out the necklace that was tucked into her shirt. It was a blue, octagonal gemstone roughly a third the size of her small palm. The gemstone was set into a slightly larger silver disc. There were tiny, white indentations on the eight corners of the gemstone, making it resemble a flower. The gemstone and its disc were attached to a thin, silver chain.

She stared at the necklace for a few seconds before tucking it back into her shirt. "It's too late to go back now…"

CHAPTER VII:
THE PRICE OF THE THRONE

BY FORCE, Landor's eyes snapped open. A forceful jolt had run through his body. A figure in a black coat and hood stood above him.

"You!" Landor said. He groaned. An unbearable pain took over his body.

The Objectivist put one hand over his shadowed face and the other straight out towards Landor. From his palm, a golden glow of light bathed over Landor. He screamed. There was a harsh hiss from the light's contact. His wounds slowly healed as his blood absorbed back through his closing cuts. The Objectivist closed his fist, and the magical light ceased.

Landor gasped for air. "Are you trying to kill me?!"

"Get up," he said.

The king groaned as he moved to sit. While his wounds were gone, his body still ached. He took a second to think. "How did you—?"

"Unimportant," he interjected. "You need to take back your throne."

"Take it back? How long was I unconscious?"

"Just a few seconds. The rebel forces will not wait for you to rest. We need to move."

Landor stood. "I already told you. I do *not* want your aid."

"Tch. You have no choice. After all, I saved your life. This time. You need me here."

"I cannot trust you."

"Then don't." He turned around. "Follow me."

"I need a staff."

"Then we will find one, but our priority is finding Istra. That is his name, yes?"

The king nodded. "How much do you know?"

"Enough. Istra needs to be eliminated, as do his followers. Now, follow." The Objectivist walked a few feet forward and approached one of the outside castle walls. "*Erca eht trizi kolbo,*" he chanted as he swiped two fingers horizontally in the air. A section of the wall collapsed, creating a hole for them to enter.

From the grassy courtyard, Zecatsu Landor and the Objectivist stepped inside a hallway. As they'd expected, it was in shambles. Rubble littered the ground. There were even a few bodies. To their left, a turn and a set of stairs led down to the dungeons. To their right, the hall led to the front area of the castle.

"If we wish to find Istra in this large of a place, we must bring him to us," the Objectivist said.

"And get us both killed?"

"Hm." The Objectivist said nothing more and headed right. The castle had become relatively quiet again, save for the sounds of marching and voices in the distance. "Ah." Buried underneath debris, the Objectivist found a plain staff. "This should do." He tossed it to Zecatsu.

"Where is yours?"

"I make do without one. More or less."

Landor followed the mysterious figure. He walked with an aura of dangerous confidence. Every step and movement was purposeful and goal-driven.

The hallway eventually led to a short section of stairs. Following that, the two found themselves on a balcony looking over the spacious entrance hall. It was similar in design to the throne room with its symmetrical pillars and interior balconies. The biggest difference was its size. Any other details were lost in its destruction, for even the front wall had completely collapsed. In the room itself stood a group of soldiers and armed common folk. They were conversing peacefully. There were ten of them in total.

"If we wish to draw out Istra, we will need to be noisy, but not careless. Albeit contradictory to my usual preference, stealth isn't the right option here," the Objectivist murmured.

"I can think of a couple things," Landor said.

"Leave it to me. Save your energy, and your staff, for any emergency." It was then that the group of rebels and traitors saw them on the balcony. They began shouting and drawing their weapons.

The Objectivist cackled. He took a sharp breath and moved his hand over his face. "Time for some bloodshed!" Although Landor had barely known the man, his words, his sudden psychotic tone, and his laughter all came as a complete surprise to him. He wished to never hear it again.

The Objectivist leapt down to the ground floor and immediately threw his right arm up in the air. A pillar of dark energy burst through the floor and swallowed one of the guards. The magic drained all life from his body as he crumpled to the ground, his skin grey. The Objectivist then dodged an energy blast and flicked out two throwing knives. They pierced a man and woman, each in their hearts.

The group encircled the hooded attacker. The Objectivist stood calmly with his hands at his sides. The nearest one charged with his spear. The Objectivist remained unmoved. He thrust the weapon.

"*Swani nostro!*"

A pale red projectile struck a club-holding woman. In an instant, the hooded figure and the woman switched places. She was stabbed through the torso by the spear. With that, all those carrying a staff had fallen.

The Objectivist wasted no time and elbowed the face of the man next to him. He followed by drawing his dagger and stabbing it through the back of his throat. He turned around. A sword-wielding guard approached him.

Using the small mechanism attached to his right forearm, he fired a small knife. The projectile struck the guard's arm. He dropped his weapon. The Objectivist used the opportunity to shank him multiple times in his chest and neck.

When his bloody corpse fell, the man with the spear came at

the attacker. His teeth were clenched. The Objectivist blocked his strike with a magical bracer of energy. He blocked a second attempt before sending him into the wall with a blast of magic.

Another guard approached the Objectivist. He took a deep breath as he readied his sword. He charged forth.

"*Dre eht hrâa!*"

Just as the guard swung his blade down, his weapon flew out of his hand. The Objectivist spun around and leaped into the air. He kicked his leg out behind him. His boot struck the guard in the chest and knocked him back. Now turned 180 degrees, the Objectivist came face-to-face with another opponent. His battle-axe was already coming down. He simultaneously leaned back to dodge the axe and swung his left arm down, hand open. A blast of energy fired behind him, further knocking back the guard from earlier.

With his right arm, he delivered a fierce uppercut. The man's head snapped back from the force. The Objectivist grabbed his head with both hands and slammed it down onto his knee. With his cranium still in his control, the Objectivist easily fired a blast of energy point-blank. It was enough to send the man down with his skull cracked open.

The remaining three rebels spaced themselves around the man in black. Their feet danced nervously. Out of options, all three charged him at once. With another cackle, the Objectivist hovered his hand over his face and again thrust his arm into the air. Tendrils of dark energy emerged from below the floor. They wrapped themselves around the three men and lifted them into the air. The color in their skin quickly vanished.

Meanwhile, Landor watched the entire thing go down with awe, curiosity, and slight horror. In about half a minute, the Objectivist had taken all ten down with little effort. *Without a staff or any other focus, his Dark magic rivals my own. Just who is this man? Is he even Elektian? Is he even human? More importantly… what does he really want?*

"What is the meaning of this?" Istra had just run inside from the throne room. He brought more guards with him. The Objectivist was still holding three of his men hostage. They were in the air, trapped by Dark magic and slowly bleeding out though their orifices.

Istra drew his sword and staff. Before he could take a step further, Landor flew right into him. He dragged him across the floor and back into the throne room. Istra's weapons skidded away. Landor's Dark Flight form dissipated as he knelt over the traitor.

"I must say, you came close. But getting rid of the king himself is going to take more than your little entourage of turncoats." Zecatsu reached for his knife. It was gone.

Istra took advantage of the moment and punched Landor in the jaw, knocking him off. He kicked him down as he scrambled for his staff. At the same time, the two of them fired a beam of energy. The beams collided. They maintained their beams as they fought to overpower each other.

"Damn it… Objectivist!" Zecatsu called.

"Of course. You could not do this alone, could you?" Istra

mocked.

With his free hand, Landor charged an orb of dark energy behind his back. His struggle to maintain the beam only grew. "You have no right. *I* am the king."

He threw the orb. It struck Istra. Despite him being a dark mage, Istra fell to his knees as his body choked for air. Landor jabbed his staff forward. A rope of white energy emerged and wrapped itself around the commander's neck. Using the staff, Landor pulled Istra all the way down and dragged him closer. He tried to pry the magical rope off of his throat, but to no effect.

"Your tyranny—the tyranny of your entire family—will end!" Istra spat. "You are blind. The people fight back because they have had enough. We have all had enough."

The rope tightened. Istra choked. "The Dijenuks are near extinction," Landor said. "I have been superior to most of my ancestors. You are all too blind to see it."

"Urgh... D-Do you truly think that is all that matters? A-Answer me this, Landor. When not hunting the Dijenuks... how many times have you stepped outside your castle?"

Landor shook his head. "Your treachery ends now." He released the rope. Istra gasped for air. The king pressed the tip of his staff against his chest. Slowly, Istra's life left his body. His skin grew pale and his eyes lost focus. He let out a final breath. Landor lifted his staff away and took a few seconds to confirm his death. He groaned. His body still ached, and his nose was plugged. *How long has it been like that?*

"I must say, it took a considerable amount of effort for you, the King of Darkness, to take down such a mundane threat." The Objectivist stood in the massive doorway.

"And you would have done it instantly?"

"Naturally. But I was a tad preoccupied. Your castle should now be mostly clear of the rebel forces."

"And the trebuchets?"

"Trebuchets? Ah, yes." The Objectivist walked out. Landor followed him through the entrance hall and the massive opening in the front wall. He observed the increased number of bodies on the floor.

In the front courtyard, Landor was surprised to find it peaceful. It was clear that a fierce battle and siege had taken place here, but there was little movement. The attacks had ceased. The trebuchets that Zecatsu had seen earlier remained.

"There is no one to give them orders at the moment. I imagine their operators are confused. Regardless, they must be taken down."

"Ugh." The inside of Landor's nose burned.

The Objectivist once again put his outstretched hand over his face. He was lifted several meters into the air. He threw his right hand up and swung it down. A subtle light pierced through the cloudy canopy. It grew. After a few seconds, a shower of blazing fireballs pierced through the clouds. Nearly an instant later, they struck their targets. Each trebuchet exploded into blazing chunks of wood and metal. Sounds like fireworks rang throughout the entire city.

As he landed gently, the Objectivist exhaled. "It is done." He turned to face Zecatsu. "Istra may have led the operation within your little castle, but I doubt he is behind the rebellion. Your true enemy remains unknown."

"My true enemies are the Dijenuks," Landor said.

"Right. Hm. I would not recommend trying to outright trample the rebels, anyway. Perhaps they raise a point."

"Then why did you fight them?"

"Because I need you alive for right now. Regardless, your priority at the moment seems to be restoring order and resuming your petty operation. After all, killing the Dijenuks is certainly more important than, say, serving your people," the Objectivist said sarcastically.

Landor was taken aback. "Pardon me?"

"You're not disagreeing."

Landor said nothing.

"I bid you farewell, Zecatsu. Until we meet again. Perhaps I will try to kill you next time. Who knows?" he said playfully. Before Landor could respond, the Objectivist entered Dark Flight and zoomed away.

Zecatsu watched for a few seconds as the dark cloud sped off. He clenched his jaw. Nearby footsteps made him snap out of his contemplation. He turned around to see a group of guards approach him.

"We are relieved to see you alive and well, Your Majesty," one of them said as the group bowed.

"We will have a meeting about security and the rebellion later. Right now, we need to gather our forces and take down any stragglers. We also need to assemble a group to intercept the Restorers at moment's notice. Get me intel on their progress. Go," the king commanded as calmly as he could manage. The guards set out at once.

As Landor meandered back inside, he took his time, absorbing his surroundings. Not much time had passed since the start of the attack, but the interior was ravaged. The structural integrity was beyond perilous. There were holes in the floor, walls, and ceiling. The pillars were either greatly damaged or torn down. Most of the floor was covered in debris. Bodies, both dead and unconscious, were upsettingly common. His servants were doing their best to clean it all up. Occasionally, one would cast a spell to make a repair, but there was only so much that could do. The entire castle had become dolefully quiet.

The man groaned as he moved to sit on his throne. His muscles continued to hurt. He closed his eyes and leaned his head back. His body demanded sleep. But there was work to be done. He opened his eyes and examined his body. Dust and blood covered his battle-robes. It was full of tears. Blood dripped from his nose and ears. Taking a deep breath, Landor stood and headed towards his bedroom to clean himself up.

"Your Majesty… what happened here?" said a voice. One of his messengers entered.

King Landor sat back on his throne. "Simply put, there was an attack. By rebels and traitors within our own forces, no less. It has been dealt with, for now. Do you bring news?"

"Oh, um, yes. The Restorers have discovered the existence

of portal crystals. They used them to travel back to Fort Dijenuk from an unknown location. It is our belief that they intend to use the crystals to reach the Wind Chamber. Their attempt to restore Wind is imminent, Your Majesty."

Landor clenched his fists. He took a slow, shaky breath. As he exhaled, his muscles relaxed a little. "Thank you. Is that everything?"

"They have found the fifth Restorer: the water mage."

"Of course…" Landor stood. "Get my strongest men and women. We are intercepting the Restorers." The servants cleaning up the throne room simply stared at their king. "Now!" he barked.

In less than an hour, Landor and a couple of captains prepared an emergency squad. A few maintained minor injuries from the battle and most of them were exhausted, but they did their best to gather those who were in the best condition to fight. Unfortunately, most of Landor's best soldiers had taken the brunt of the siege. The small platoon gathered in courtyard. Its last corpse had just been taken away.

Landor set a large portal crystal in the center. He turned to face his soldiers. "I know the past few hours have been complete turmoil. I know that many of you need both rest and answers. I promise you that rest will come. But right now, our enemy is close to completing their first goal. It is imperative that we stop them here. Yes, we have many more chances if they succeed, but both time and additional Crystals only give them the advantage. Our magic is limited, but there are two Dijenuks to worry about. It would be foolish to allow them unnecessary power. *Today* is the day we stop them, and *today* is the day the Dijenuks die at my hands. Is that understood?"

"Yes, Your Majesty," the soldiers said simultaneously.

"Be quick, be cunning, and be ruthless."

"Wait, Your Majesty," said a captain.

"Make it quick."

"You know where the Wind Chamber is?"

Landor said nothing and turned to the portal crystal. He raised his staff. *"To This Place: End's Beginning, Terra!"*

"Time is of the essence, David," Jay scolded through the door.

"Yeah, yeah, I know." The boy scrambled to retrieve his shoes under his bed and buckle them on. He grabbed his staff and bolted downstairs. The others were standing in the entrance hall waiting. "Sorry. I kinda fell back asleep. So, we're all good to go now, yeah?"

"I believe so. Are you sure you should be taking that staff with you?" Elfekot nodded at the red staff that David had been using since he first arrived in Elektia.

"Is there something wrong with it?" he asked as he fetched the box containing the Scrolls of Gales from the other room.

"I do not know how much your mother used it, but I imagine that it is close to burning out."

"Burning out…?"

428

"When the wick in the staff runs out and it basically becomes a long, useless stick."

"You should get a different staff. Better safe than sorry," added Angela.

"But it was my mom's. I can't just throw it away."

Jay rolled her eyes.

Elfekot turned for the door. "Do whatever you want, then. But be warned."

The Restorers followed the captain outside. From a leather bag he'd hung on his belt, Elfekot extracted a portal crystal. He set it down in the middle of the yard. "I have two more crystals. One is for returning to Elektia, and the other is for an emergency. There is a chance we may be separated, either by choice or by force. I do not think any of us want to leave someone behind, but if it comes down to it..." He paused. "Just be careful, is what I am trying to say." He drew his staff.

"Ooh, can I do it?" David volunteered. "Jay stole my thunder the last time."

"Er, by all means."

David closed one eye as he aimed his staff at the black crystal. *"To This Place: End's Beginning, Terra!"*

Chapter VIII:
Chamber of Lies

JUST LIKE THE PREVIOUS INSTANCES, the crystal exploded into a grey vortex. Knowing they had no time to waste, the Restorers entered through it. This time, the trip was much longer. David clutched the box tightly. He feared what would happen if he dropped it. As he spun, David forced his eyes open. His digestion was begging for him to stop. Nearly a minute passed. Finally, the void vanished in an instant. He hit the ground.

"So... this is Terra," said Angela.

David stood and took in his surroundings. The portal had taken them to a temperate desert. The light-brown dirt and shrubs stretched for miles. There was no civilization in sight, only large rock formations in the distance. Although the sun was bright, the temperature was moderate. It was pleasant. The only noises were distant birds.

"Yeah, I have no idea where we are," David admitted. "But we're on Terra, alright." He pointed to the sun directly above them. It was a blinding yellow instead of blue. Elfekot, Angela, and Clove noticed the difference with a touch of awe, but quickly had to look away.

"It could be the Mojave Desert, but that's just a guess. Regardless, there's nothing special about this place," Jay said.

"Is Terra normally this... dry and empty?" Angela asked.

"Nah," David said. "There are all kinds of different environments out there. It kinda sucks that we didn't end up near a city or town or anything. That woulda been pretty awesome to show you three."

Angela nodded. "I must admit, I am disappointed that we did not get to see a Terran city."

"We are here for the Wind Crystal, not sight-seeing," said Elfekot.

"Speaking of..." David took another look around. "Where's the Wind Chamber?"

"Down here," Jay answered. She had wandered away from the group to the top of a nearby hill. The Restorers climbed the mound to meet her. The other side of the hill declined sharply into the valley below. Opposite the hill was a tall cliff, and at the bottom of the cliff was a large stone panel, tinted green.

"That must be it!" said David. He darted down the hill and to the stone panel. The rest of them caught up.

There were etchings in the panel. The top section contained three lines of text. The characters were similar to the ones on the Scrolls. In the center was a circle cut slightly deeper than everything else. There were three wavy lines that curled at the end in the middle of the circle. It was the symbol for Wind.

Jay pulled out a small notebook from her pocket. "This must be the door," she said as she hurriedly copied down the foreign text.

Elfekot nodded at David. "Go ahead."

The Dijenuk took a couple of steps closer. He undid the latch and the box and opened it. The three Scrolls of Gales floated into the air. They inched towards the door as they moved into a triangle formation. The symbol on the door glowed green. The Scrolls did likewise. In an instant, the Scrolls vanished and the glow on the symbol disappeared. The door slowly lifted.

David shut the box triumphantly. "We're in."

He stepped inside first. The Restorers entered a spacious, albeit empty, room. It was entirely made of the same green-tinted stone as the door. The ceiling, held up by pillars, was high. There were three large entryways on each wall leading elsewhere. A statue of a robed woman occupied the center. She had both her arms raised at diagonals. Her face depicted a subtle intensity. The room overall reminded them of a castle. They were pleased to discover that the interior was well-lit, with plenty of torches along the walls.

"Woah. This place is huge. Echo!" he shouted. His voice echoed.

"Sh," said Elfekot. "It is probably best that we remain quiet."

"Oh, yeah. Sorry!" he whispered. David approached the statue. "Who's this?"

"If I had to guess, it is the Wind Elementian," Angela answered.

"When were these Chambers built?" David asked.

Elfekot shrugged. "We only know that they are quite ancient and precede even the nation of Light Elektia."

"More importantly, *why* were the Chambers built?" Jay

added.

"Perhaps the answer will reveal itself as we go on. Or perhaps not." Elfekot surveyed the entryways. "We might need to split up after all."

"I dunno. Isn't it dangerous? There's five of us, but three different directions. Assuming I did my math right, someone's gotta go alone," David pointed out.

"I'll do it," Jay said.

"Are you sure, sis? No offense, but… you're not super great with magic right now."

"Just worry about yourself, David."

"But…"

"Look," Elfekot interjected, "it would simply be more efficient if we searched the place by splitting up. If something goes wrong… well, you can always run."

"Come on, Elfekot. That's way too risky," David said. "Hold up… Jay, what about your powers or whatever? Didn't you sense one of the Scrolls of Gales in the tunnels back in Hegortant?"

Jay rested a hand on her chin. "Hm… I had to hold another scroll to do that. And, frankly, I would like to avoid using my Visionary abilities."

"What? How come?" David questioned.

She didn't answer.

"Can we please just go already?" Angela said. "I am tired of standing around."

Elfekot tapped his foot as he stared at his companions. "Let us see…"

The Restorers split into three groups, with Jay on her own as she set off to the left.

"Please be safe!" said David.

Jay stopped in place for a second. "You too."

Angela and Elfekot took the right path, while David and Clove made their way to the center path. They encroached on a lengthy hallway. It was several meters wide and filled with suits of armor that ran along both sides of the entire wall. The armor was all rusty. Most of these stands were knocked down and incomplete.

"Well, this is kinda cool," David said as they walked. "This kinda reminds of me a castle or somethin'. Weird, huh?"

Clove nodded.

"You don't talk much, do you?"

She shrugged.

"That's okay. Sometimes I worry I talk too much, actually." He paused. "You know, Jay used to be quiet, too."

"Really?"

"Yeah. Eventually, she started coming out of her shell. Then one day… she became quiet. She said nothing for over a whole month. When she spoke again, she was *way* out of her shell."

"What happened to her?"

"No one knows. Except for Jay, I guess. In my opinion, deep inside… she's just sad. I dunno about what, though."

"Huh."

The two of them made it to the end of the hallway. A set of

large, double metal doors awaited them. David rolled his shoulders in preparation. With considerable effort, he pushed them open.

"Do you need help?" Clove asked as he heaved.

"No... I got it." He shoved one of the doors open just wide enough for them to fit through. "What the...?"

The room they found was somewhat smaller than the first. Almost all of it was filled with large pieces of debris. Most of the walls were concealed as a result. The ceiling was gone, and so the terrain's red rock was exposed. While a vast majority of the floor space was covered, a tiny path was carved out in the debris. It led to a sizeable hole in the middle of the room.

"Jeez. I thought it'd be way nicer than this," said David.

The two of them approached the hole in the floor. Through it, they could see another room.

"It looks like a safe drop. I'll go down first," David said. "I'll let you know if it's safe."

Clove nodded.

He dropped down. As soon as his feet touched the ground, a deafening roar emerged. It was a heavy wind. "Woah... Come down here!"

Clove tentatively followed. She landed on a platform inside a long, spacious room. A ferocious wind ravaged this interior. It violently shook an extensive rope bridge that connected two platforms. On the other side was a door. It was the only exit they could see. Strangely enough, the wind had no visible source.

David peeked down. There was no bottom in sight. He could

only see a dark void. "I'm gonna be honest here… I think we're screwed."

≺∘≻

After making her way through a mess of debris, Jay found a spiral staircase leading downwards. She only traveled one story before being stopped by a blockade of rubble. With no other option, she took the door next to her.

Inside was a small, cluttered chamber. It was filled with dusty, broken furniture like chests, shelves, and drawers. On the other side was a short, narrow hallway that led to another door. As quickly as she could, Jay searched the room. She made sure to make as little physical contact as possible as to avoid the heavy dust. Most of the containers were empty. One of the chests, however, contained a mess of broken equipment such as swords, staves, brooms, and torches. Something at the bottom caught her attention. She pulled it out.

It was a silver metal rod about fifteen inches long. The shaft tapered until the end, where it formed a small, arrowhead-like tip. Its bottom segment was intricately wrapped in hide. Jay assumed it was a handle.

"*Clono.*"

The dust that covered the object disappeared, revealing its shine. Jay studied it for a few seconds. Unsure as to its purpose, she slid the object into her boot and continued onwards. As she walked, she found it slightly uncomfortable housing her sheathed dagger in one boot and the mysterious silver object in the other.

Jay reached the door. Just as she placed her hand on the bronze doorknob, she felt a subtle, unnatural vibration in her core. It was a feeling she had come across before. *That buzz. It's a magical presence*, she thought. She pressed an ear against the door. There was a faint whooshing sound. She retreated from it. *It is likely a trap.*

Back in the same room, the girl more carefully examined her surroundings. A light spilled out from underneath one of the tall dressers. Jay dropped down to the floor to examine the light. There, she spotted an opening in the wall. She hopped back up. Despite the fact that it was empty, Jay had difficulty moving the dresser. She took a few steps back. The girl clutched her amulet and pointed a palm towards it with her fingers somewhat curled.

"*Unés dyelgé.*"

A light grey projectile of light fired from her hand. When it made contact with the dresser, it briefly shone with the same light. She tried moving the dresser again. The object was significantly lighter. As such, she easily pulled it away from the wall.

With the dresser gone, a narrow tunnel was revealed. Its lighting was much dimmer than the rest of the Wind Chamber, but it was enough, and the walls were more polished. Jay followed the tunnel. It took her downwards for a while. Eventually, the slope led back up. After a short walk, she met a dead end.

There is no way that this is it, she thought. Jay examined the wall, but she found nothing suspicious. There was only the sound of a rushing wind. It was louder than what she'd heard through the door from earlier.

"I'm gonna be honest here… I think we're screwed," said a familiar voice. It came from the other side of the wall. Jay pressed a hand against the stone.

"*Téléneh.*"

Jay disappeared and instantly reappeared on the other side between two people. It was David and Clove. They jumped at the sight of her.

"Jay?! Where did you come from?" David asked.

"I followed a tunnel and teleported through this wall behind us," she answered. The violent wind made it difficult for her to see as her hair blew over her face.

"What?" He couldn't hear her over the heavy gusts.

"I teleported through the wall," she repeated with a louder voice.

"Oh. Huh. Did you find anything?"

"No."

"Well… we found this." David pointed a thumb at the swaying bridge before them. "I don't think we can cross it. The wind's too heavy."

"Hm… There must be a deactivation mechanism."

"But where, though?"

"I see something," said Clove. She pointed at the other side of the bridge. David and Jay squinted. Next to the door appeared to be a small button in the wall.

"What?!" David said. "We need to cross the bridge in order to… cross the bridge? How do we do that?"

Jay and Clove were silent.

David stared at the violently swinging bridge. "I guess I gotta try."

Jay nodded. Clove faced David. "Huh? But… it's—"

"Dangerous, I know," David finished. "But this looks like the only way. We can try to wait for Elfekot and Angela, but they might be in a worse position then we are. They might even be in danger. Who knows? But we can't waste time."

Clove nodded.

"Just go for it… and be careful," said Jay.

David took a deep breath. He sprinted. His balance was constantly challenged as the gusts shook the bridge. His running only made it more unstable. David made sure to keep both his hands near the rope rails. He approached the midpoint, where the wind was worse. He had to stop and clutch the railing with both hands. He took a few seconds to find his balance. He then continued his sprint.

The bridge flipped over. David yelled as he fell with it. He caught the rope railing with one hand. He threw his other arm up to grab the rope. The bridge returned to its upright position, although it was still rapidly swaying. David pulled himself back up.

He returned to his run, this time even faster. He was nearing the other side. The bridge flipped over again. David leaped. He landed right on the edge of the platform. Once he made it back to his feet, he threw both arms in the air in celebration.

"Press the button," Jay yelled.

"Oh, yeah." David pushed in the large stone button behind him.

The wind calmed. The bridge became normal. They could hear themselves think again. Wasting no time, Jay and Clove crossed.

"I have to be honest... That was impressive, David," Jay said.

"You know, I think that's the nicest thing you've said in a long time."

"Tch."

David opened the door. The room on the other side was the largest yet. A wide set of stairs before them led down to a square chamber. In the middle of it sat a step pyramid about the size of the Dijenuk House. It was made of the same green-tinted stone as everything else. The steps near the bottom were smaller, like stairs, but the rest were so large that they had to be climbed. There were two more doorways at the bottom: one to their left, and one to their right. The left one was caved in. The trio began their descent down the stairs.

"I think I see something," said David.

They looked to the highest point of the pyramid. There sat a grey, stone pedestal with something green sitting on top of it.

"That's it! That's *gotta* be the Wind Crystal, yeah?" David began to run.

"David, you idiot, be careful," said Jay.

Before any of them could reach the bottom of the stairs, the door on the right slammed open. Two figures dashed into the room.

David stopped running. "Elfekot? Angela?"

"Landor... He's here!" Elfekot yelled.

David, Jay, and Clove drew their staves. "What? How?" David questioned.

The Restorers regrouped near the base of the step pyramid.

"He could not have followed us. That is impossible," said Elfekot.

"Then he knew about the location," Jay inferred.

"And portal crystals," Angela said. "He *did* possess the three Scrolls of Gales. Perhaps he acquired the location from that."

Jay shook her head. "It was a very brief amount of time. When I got to them, it appeared as though no one was studying them. He must have already known, but... how?"

A group of dark-clad soldiers burst inside. King Landor stepped in last. They counted about twenty of them.

David gasped. "The Crystal!" He sprinted up the small steps of the pyramid as the others engaged in combat. Landor transformed into his Dark Flight form and zoomed up.

"No!" David twirled his staff and thrust it forward. A rope of white energy lashed out and wrapped itself around the pedestal at the top. He retracted it and effectively flew to the pyramid's peak.

Landor ended up just a few feet away from David. The pedestal remained multiple pyramid steps away. The two of them stared each other down.

"I was wondering when you'd show your face, Landor."

The king's armored robes were torn, and his hair was ruffled.

"And you're already a wreck. What, did I kick your ass in advance or something?" the Dijenuk said.

"Tch. Your strange words are meaningless, Dijenuk. You were lucky back in the forest. You will not be so fortunate this time."

The Dijenuk and the Landor continued to glare at each other. Finally, Zecatsu fired. David pivoted to dodge the attack. He fired back. Landor ducked underneath it. He fired again. It struck David in the legs, and he fell.

Landor twirled his staff before sending forth a beam of white energy. It collided with David's magical shield as David remained crouched. A high-pitched sound rang throughout the entire chamber as the brilliant white light of the beam crashed with the softer light of the barrier. Landor continued the pressure. David's body strained against it, his entire being vibrating. He managed to stand, then moved towards the king. His steps were slow as the beam's pressure increased.

David stopped. He took a few quick breaths, then charged forward. He tackled Landor. They fell over, tumbling down a few of the steps.

They both groaned as they moved to stand. Not yet on their feet, David fired a quick blast of energy. Zecatsu did the same. They slid across the length of the step.

Landor rose first. He scrambled up the large steps and

towards the pedestal on the top. David thrust his staff forward. A rope of white energy manifested and wrapped itself around the king's leg. David pulled his staff down, tripping Landor over and yanking him back.

Zecatsu raised his staff. "You are quite tenacious, boy. I admire it, but it will only get you so far."

David clenched the grip of his staff. "I don't give a damn about what you think, Landor. You're gonna pay!"

He jabbed his staff forward and sent a charged blast of energy. Landor shifted his feet. The projectile struck the distant wall behind him, sending bits of stone into the air.

Landor frowned. "It ends here, Dijenuk."

He fired consecutive orbs of dark energy. Each of them was blocked by David's shield. Landor pointed his staff slightly away. The next projectile hit a step. It bounced off and struck David in the side.

A numbing yet suffocating feeling enveloped his body like a poison. He gasped as his lungs were robbed of their air. His clothes weighed on his body, and even his staff became difficult to hold, like it was suddenly made entirely of metal. He fell to a crouch.

Landor raised his staff again. "You perhaps could have stood a chance had you not faced me alone, but no." His eyebrows lowered. "You Dijenuks will risk anything for a sense of pride, even if it means death, even if it means leaving your son without a father."

David sprinted towards him, screaming. Zecatsu fired

another orb of darkness. It stopped the boy in his tracks, and he once again choked for air.

Landor threw his arms forward. Two tendrils of dark energy lashed out. David raised his staff. The dark magic hit David's shield, but Landor continued the pressure. As he floated a couple of feet into the air, he sent forth more dark tendrils. They felt around the shield, looking for the edge of it.

Still weakened from the previous attacks, David knew his shield wouldn't last long. It was already waning. He found that taking steps back alleviated some of the pressure, but he soon met the edge of the large stair. One of the tendrils made it over the rim of his shrinking shield. David craned his neck as it reached for his face. He glanced at his feet. They were already hanging over the edge.

Meanwhile, the other Restorers were defending themselves from the onslaught of Landor's soldiers. Elfekot sent forth a large magical fist. It plowed through three of them. Angela fired a charged blast of energy. It knocked one out cold. Jay cast a sleeping spell to knock out another. Clove hid behind them, unsure what to do.

"Clove, do something!" Angela yelled as she ducked under a projectile.

The girl's eyes darted left to right. She tightly clutched her staff. "Um…"

The fighting suddenly ceased. They each felt the same presence. It grew stronger. At the same time, a bout of wind was picking up. They slowly lowered their staves and glanced about.

The gusts grew in strength. On the set of the stairs, something invisible was picking up the dust and bits of stone. It swirled around like a miniature tornado. The wind in the room concentrated and took form. A giant, humanoid figure emerged, with only the tiny debris and dust it picked up giving away its shape, for it was made of wind itself.

"Run!" Elfekot barked.

The four Restorers dispersed as the giant threw down its enormous arms. Several pillars of wind emerged and sent some of Landor's soldiers rocketing into the ceiling.

"What the hell is that?" Angela asked.

"If I had to guess… it is a guardian of the Chamber: a Wind Giant," Elfekot answered.

The Wind Giant slammed its arms down again. An explosion of gales launched the four of them in separate directions. Jay groaned as she stood. She looked at the Wind Giant.

"I assume it is intangible. If it is… I don't believe we can defeat it."

As Elfekot deflected projectiles with his longsword, something else caught his eye. Near the top of the step-pyramid, David was struggling against Landor's onslaught of dark magic.

"Jay!" he called. "Your brother might need help."

She looked where David was. He was about to fall off.

Multiple tendrils were now reaching for him, all less than an inch away. David gripped his staff, then fell. He hit the next step down as the dark magic flew over him. David took a moment to breathe.

Guessing that Landor would beeline for the Wind Crystal, David returned to his feet. As he expected, Landor was climbing back up the steps.

David created another magical rope, attaching himself to the pedestal. He retracted it, letting himself fly again to the top. As he did so, he threw his legs out and swung himself through the air. He kicked Landor in the chest, knocking him down further.

Before he could turn to the pedestal, a ferocious gust of wind knocked both Zecatsu and David over. They felt each and every step that they hit on the way down. By the time David smacked into the bottom, his pain had turned into irritation.

David groaned. His body hurt too much to move. "No… can't… let it end like this," he said, forcing himself his to his feet.

He looked over at Landor. He was struggling to stand. Before the king could fully recover, David let out a yell and thrust his staff forward, launching a beam of energy.

Landor reacted. He crossed his arms in an X. A shield generated in front of him, and the beam collided with it. Like Landor had done, David continued the beam's pressure.

To his horror, however, Landor's shield would not wane. It remained in its brilliant, white translucency. David yelled again. The beam's thickness increased. Eventually, the beam thinned, until it became nothing.

David exhaled. His muscles ached as his blood burned. He had the urge to vomit.

"Are you done, Dijenuk?" Landor said. "Surely your limits

aren't that pathetic."

He fired a blast of energy. David raised his staff. Nothing happened. The projectile struck his thigh. There was a loud *crack*. David fell backwards, screaming in pain.

"Hmph. It is over, Dijenuk."

David couldn't find the strength to stand. Even if he did, he knew that his leg wouldn't let him. "No... not yet!" He raised his staff. "Huh?" The soft warmth that had once run through the staff was gone. "No..." he gasped.

Landor pointed his staff at the ceiling. He was floating again. A ball of dark energy charged at the tip. As it ballooned in size, Landor wore a serious, almost grim, expression. The sphere, already larger than Zecatsu, continued to grow. It cast a shadow over David as the light in the entire room dimmed. The magical buzz emanating from it rivaled that of the Wind Giant on the other side.

It finally stopped, now over three times Landor's size in its diameter. Landor glared at the boy below him, still unable to stand.

"This is the end of your family's cursed legacy!"

Landor threw his arm down, and, with it, the giant sphere of darkness. It fell slowly, dimming the room even further as it moved. David managed to sit up just in time to watch the pulsating black orb descend upon him.

"*Téléneh!*" said a voice.

Just before David closed his eyes, a red light flashed before him. He heard a grunt, then felt the magical buzz vanish. He opened his eyes.

Jay was on her knees in front of him. She was shivering. Jay struggled to stand as she moved her hand to her head, groaning.

Get up, said a voice in David's head.

Jay? How did you do that?

His dark magic is mostly ineffective against me.

Oh, right! Although he didn't shiver, David felt the same overwhelming cold that Jay did. The void of emotions that he had detected last time remained, but he knew not to explore it again.

Landor's jaw clenched. "Of course," he muttered.

I see your problem. I feel it, rather. Jay touched her amulet and pointed two fingers at his leg. "*Kanba eht gri.*"

A jet of white light outlined in gold hit his leg. There was a brief warmth before the pain was gone, as though it was never there.

Get up, Jay repeated.

"Now this is something exciting," Landor said, louder this time, his lips curling into a devilish smile. "King Zecatsu Landor versus the end of the Dijenuk family tree."

"We've already been in this situation, Landor," David replied as he stood. He spit some blood. "And we all know what happened then." *You can do that green thingy again, right?*

No, Jay's voice responded. *But, if we use our brains, we can overcome this, anyway.*

"Yeah, together," David said aloud, moving to stand next to her.

Jay paused. "Right."

As Landor moved to raise his staff, David sent another thought. *Wait! My staff is dead.*

Of course. That's what you get for putting everything into an attack you already know is being blocked, like the absolute idiot that you are. Take mine.

As they jumped of the way of Landor's energy blast, Jay tossed him her staff.

Pelt him with energy; force him to shield, Jay's voice said.

David caught the staff and fired a volley of blasts. The simple action alone put further strain on his body. Landor ran to his right to dodge the attacks, as Jay ran to his left in search of an opening.

He's not staying still!

I can see that. Jay put a finger gun to the side of her head. "*Téléneh!*"

A jet of red light erupted through the other side of her skull, like a bullet. Jay disappeared in that same red light, then reappeared next to Landor. She threw a punch. Landor's head snapped to side, spit and blood flying out. Jay punched again. The king doubled over. Before he could do anything, Jay grabbed him, holding him in front of her.

The moment she did so, David fired another volley of energy. Each blast struck Landor in the chest. Bits of metal and cloth flew off with each projectile. There were audible cracks. Landor gritted his teeth as he was pelted and struggled against Jay's hold.

Eventually, he wrestled one of his arms free. He threw it downwards. Jay was sent skidding across the ground. Teeth still bared, Landor twirled his staff as he dashed towards David.

He engaged his Dark Flight form and flew faster than David could react. Landor returned to his normal form. He tackled David. And he dragged him across the floor with his momentum, his hand gripped to his collar. A ball of dark energy charged at the tip of the king's staff. It was pointed at David's face.

"Swani nostro!"

A pale-red jet of light struck Landor in the back. He disappeared. Jay took his place. Landor was on the other end of the room, where Jay had been a second ago.

David stood. Landor was flying back. *What do we do? I don't think we can get the Crystal without stopping him first.*

I disagree. Keep in mind that he could easily fly up and take the Crystal, but he's choosing to engage us, so—

We split up? I can fight him, and you can get the Crystal. Like a distraction.

Almost. He'd notice something like that. And he wouldn't let it happen.... I have an idea, but the right opportunity needs to strike. Just stay in my head. For once.

In the short time that the siblings had spent communicating in their own heads, Landor had stopped his flight just a few meters away. He moved his staff. Before he could do anything more, a sudden gust of wind nearly knocked them off their feet. Their Restorer companions yelled in panic from elsewhere in the room.

While the two siblings were distracted, Landor fired a blast of energy. Jay flew into the side of the pyramid. The stone cracked from the force. David raised his own staff. He created an energy barrier. It blocked Landor's beam of dark energy.

Jay groaned. "The Wind Giant... it might kill our teammates," she said as she returned to her feet.

"Then you need to save them!" David replied, his voice strained under the pressure of Zecatsu's magic.

"No. You can't take Landor by yourself."

He looked at her. "Trust me, Jay. Just... trust me."

"Alright... fine. Don't die." Jay sprinted to the other side of the room.

David's knees buckled. He continued to hold up the shield. *Do you think that convinced him?*

We shall see, Jay's voice replied.

"This is the end, Dijenuk!" Landor yelled. "You may carry powerful genetics, but it is not enough. Once you die, your sister is next. And your family line will end. *That* is my promise!"

David was on his knees. His shield was shrinking. His teeth were clenched as he resisted the magical beam. "You don't understand, Landor.... I made my own promise! And you're gonna pay for what you did!"

David's magical barrier was nearly gone. It was a quarter of his size. Landor lowered his staff. The beam stopped. David almost collapsed.

"It was a fun road. But everything has to end eventually... everything." Landor raised his staff into the air. Like earlier, a large orb of darkness charged above him. "Goodbye."

He threw the orb down. It collided with David's being. The darkness exploded. The entire room quaked. When the darkness subsided, David was crouched, his mother's staff in hand. The greysteel section of the shaft glowed.

"What...? Again?!" Zecatsu's fist curled. He pointed his staff. "I said... goodbye!"

David acted first. The grey projectile launched with so much force that David fell to his back. Landor raised a barrier. The projectile met it, and the shield shattered. Landor's chest armor exploded, and he rocketed backwards. He crashed into the wall on the other side and slid down it.

David let out a breath of relief. "Thanks, Mom."

Meanwhile, a projectile of energy struck Jay in the shoulder. It launched her several meters away and over one of the pyramid's corners. Her shoulder throbbed. It was like something had hit her there with a heavy object. Jay moved to stand. The soldier fired again.

Jay cried out in pain. The energy blast had struck her squarely in the chest. She groaned. Noticing that the soldier was approaching, Jay grasped at her amulet.

"*Cintria excata!*"

Nothing happened. She looked down at the necklace. The amulet was shattered. There were tiny glass pieces on the floor beneath her. She looked back up at the soldier. There was a confident sneer on her face.

Jay blinked. A warm sensation had run through her leg when

452

she said the incantation. Realization struck. She reached into her boot and drew the silver object. The girl pointed it at him.

"*Cintria excata!*"

A green jet of light fired from the tip of the device. The soldier conjured a shield, but the spell passed right through it. He shot violently into the wall behind him. The force was enough to crack both the stone and a few of his bones.

At the same time, the other Restorers continued to fight Landor's minions. Half of them were taken out.

"We have to do something about this thing!" said Angela. The Wind Giant was still ravaging the battlefield.

"None of our attacks work!" said Elfekot. "It has no physical form. It is almost like… pure energy."

"Pure energy…" Clove echoed. She drew something from one of her leather boots. It was a greysteel rod, identical to the ones Sir K had given David and Jay back on Terra. She sprinted towards the Wind Giant.

"Clove, stay back!" Elfekot called.

She pressed the rod's button and tossed it at the magical creature. After a flash of light, the Wind Giant was gone. The greysteel rod dropped to the ground. Elfekot and Angela looked to her with astonished expressions.

"Um… I saw it lying around back at the house and thought it could come in handy," she explained.

"Are you guys alright?" said a voice.

David jogged towards them. He wore severe exhaustion.

"Landor's soldiers spent most of their effort fighting the

Wind Giant," Elfekot said. "Now that it is gone, however…"

The Landorians, now regrouped, were charging towards them.

"What about Landor?" Angela asked.

"We shouldn't have to worry about him," David replied.

"Good," Elfekot said. "Then get the Wind Crystal. We will hold off his men."

Jay? David thought as his companions engaged the soldiers. There was no immediate response. *Jay!*

Something near the ceiling caught the siblings' eyes. Landor was flying back to the top of the pyramid.

"Damn it, we are too late!" Elfekot said as he deflected a blast back at a soldier, knocking him out cold.

"David, catch!"

"Huh?"

David turned around. From the other side of the room, Jay dashed towards him. She threw something. It was a green, glistening crystal. David raised his arms to catch it. The crystal landed several meters away. From the corner of his eye, he spotted one of Landor's soldiers. She was the same distance away from the crystal, if not closer.

The Dijenuk put all his might into running as fast as he could. The other soldier was nearing the crystal. David couldn't catch up. The soldier gasped horribly and fell forwards. Angela's spear had stabbed through her leg. David jumped and snagged the crystal.

As soon as the crystal came in contact with his skin, an

overwhelming buzz ran through his body. He immediately felt more energized and alert. David took a second to examine the object. It was a bright-green crystal carved in the shape of a tornado. It fit well in the palm of his hand.

"If you have it, then we can leave. Come on!" Elfekot yelled.

As the Restorers ran to the stairs, Landor and his soldiers were closing in. The buzz from the Wind Crystal persisted. Instinct struck. The Dijenuk turned around and waved Jay's staff horizontally in a sweeping motion. A powerful blow of wind ravaged through his opponents. They were knocked down and away like bowling pins. He turned back and continued running with the Restorers.

Halfway up the stairs, a horrifyingly familiar energy manifested nearby, and they all felt it. Another Wind Giant materialized at the top. It blocked the door.

"Do we have another one of those rods?" Angela asked. She had retrieved her spear.

"I think that was our last one," said Elfekot.

David dropped the staff in his hand and swapped it for the one on his back. He read the name etched in the red wood one more time: *Sarah Griggs*. The Wind Giant raised its massive arms. Without any further pause, David ran and threw his mother's old staff like a javelin. It pierced the creature. In an instant, the Wind Giant vanished. It was absorbed into the staff's greysteel section. The staff hovered in the air momentarily before exploding into pieces with a near-blinding flash of light. With their way clear, the Restorers continued. David picked up the staff he had dropped and caught up with them.

Angela quickly glanced behind them. "They are still following!"

From the top of the stairs, David scanned the battlefield. Bodies littered the ground. Another Wind Giant was attacking the soldiers. The magical instability was so great that large chunks of the ceiling were falling on top of them.

"Do not let them escape!" said Landor's voice.

"David, what are you doing?!" Elfekot said, halfway across the bridge. David was standing next to the button on the wall.

"I need to buy time!" he said to them. "Just get to the other side!"

He glanced back at the room. The soldiers were just about to reach him. He ducked a couple of incoming blasts of energy. He then looked to his companions. They had just reached the other platform. With Jay's staff in his right hand and the Wind Crystal in his left, David pressed the button with his elbow. The wind engaged, and the bridge rocked violently.

A split second after pushing the button, David pointed his staff at the wall. The soldiers had reached him. The Dijenuk fired a powerful, continuous billow of wind. The force was enough to send David backwards. He was hovering over the pit. It was just enough for him to make into onto the platform.

Elfekot set a portal crystal down and pointed his staff at it.

"Wait!" David said, yelling over the sound of the wind. "Jay, quick, what's their capitol called?"

"Dark's End. Why?"

David turned towards Elfekot. "I need a portal crystal. You have two, yeah?" He spoke with urgency.

"David, we need to leave. Now!" Elfekot said. The soldiers were staring at the bridge, yelling amongst themselves.

"I..." David looked directly at him. "No. We can't just leave them to die here. They're innocent people!"

"David Dijenuk, follow my orders!" Elfekot barked. "They are our enemy!"

"Landor is! But the soldiers aren't."

"Damn it, David, *I* am the one in charge here. You need to respect that!"

"Yeah, and I disagree with you! Jay was right. I don't need to do everything you say." He took a step closer to the captain. "So give me the damn portal crystal."

Elfekot huffed. "Fine."

"Make sure to use the 'Kingdom of Landor' name," Jay added as Elfekot handed David a portal crystal just as the soldiers found the button on the wall.

The wind calmed, as did the bridge. The soldiers ran towards them again, firing projectiles. David tossed the portal crystal across the bridge as Angela pointed her staff down at the crystal next to them.

"They cannot escape!" yelled the king from the doorway. He entered his Dark Flight form. The ceiling split, the cracks in the stone like rivers.

"To This Place: Dark's End, the Kingdom of Landor!"

"To This Place: Light's Source, Light Elektia!"

CHAPTER IX:
A GATHERING STORM

"WE... WE MADE IT?" David stood and took a quick look around. Jay, Elfekot, Angela, and Clove had made it through. The Wind Crystal was still in his hand. A group of soldiers ran towards them with weapons drawn. When they saw that it was just the Restorers, they slowed their approach and put back their weapons. They had ended up right in front of the Council's castle. It was still morning.

"We have arrived with the Wind Crystal. Please notify the Council," said Elfekot to the soldiers.

One of them nodded and hurried inside. The rest murmured amongst themselves.

The Restorers gathered around David. They all stared at the Wind Crystal in his hand.

"Normally, no one is allowed to see any of the Crystals. They keep the Grand Shrine quite secure. I would not doubt it if this Council in particular has never seen them either," Elfekot explained.

"We truly are special," said Angela with a grin.

"We did it," Clove said quietly.

"Eh, not yet, technically. We still gotta put the Crystal on the shrine. *Then* we can say we did it," David pointed out.

Angela shrugged. "I think it is fair to say our fight for this Crystal is over."

David frowned. "Landor heard what Angela said when she activated the portal, though. What if he comes to Light's Source?"

"Relax, David. We are safe," Elfekot said. "Landor would not dare to attack the capitol of Light Elektia. Weakened we may be, but this place is secure."

Jay narrowed her eyes. "Landor managed to follow us to Terra. How was he so aware of our location? How did he reach Terra in the first place? He may even be aware of portal crystals, too."

"It is like we theorized. Landor planned all of this from the start. Who knows what kind of tricks he has up his sleeve," said Elfekot.

Jay shook her head. "Hm…"

The front doors opened. "You may enter," announced the guard.

"Let's go!" David had to restrain himself to a walk. His body was jittering with excitement.

The Restorers navigated through the grand entrance hall and into the Council's main chamber just as before. All eight Councilmen watched them approach from their oversized chairs.

"Welcome back, Restorers of the Elements," greeted Pralicriyus. The Council as a whole was less tense than last time, and they didn't wear as many scowls. A few of them even leaned back in their chairs.

The Restorers bowed, with Jay again being the exception.

"We have the Wind Crystal," said David as he held it up high dramatically.

"I see that. Well done, all of you. I had no doubts that you would complete this mission. Now, I believe it would be the most appropriate if Fhrlinti were to guide you to the Grand Shrine." Pralicriyus indicated towards the man in the first chair. His collar was trimmed with green. Fhrlinti nodded and stood. "Once you have finished, please return here," Pralicriyus instructed.

"Right. Thank you," David said.

"Follow me, please," Fhrlinti said. He was a skinny man with a coarse voice and a small nose. His thin brown hair was messy, and it was tied back like every other Light Elektian's.

The Restorers followed Fhrlinti through a metal door on the right. He led them through a hallway. Its gold carpeting well-accented the white, marble material of the walls and floor. Light beamed from the windows on the right side. At the end of the hallway was a spiral staircase. They took the staircase and made a lengthy trip to the top.

Through another metal door, Fhrlinti led the Restorers back outside. They were on a fenced section of the roof, from which they could see a large portion of Light's Source. In the middle of this area was a glass dome the size of an average dining table. It was completely opaque.

The group peeked over the edge. A crowd had gathered in the courtyard below. They were eagerly looking up at them. A

460

few waved. David and Angela waved back.

Fhrlinti pressed his fingertips against the glass. "Elementians, heed my call," he said quietly. "Allow us our power; allow us our gift. Elementians, heed my call."

An instant later, the glass disappeared as though it were never there to begin with. Fhrlinti stepped back to reveal the Grand Shrine. It was a circular, smoothly cut, dark-grey slab with eight pedestals sticking out from it. Etched along the edge of the circular slab were undetailed figures dressed in robes.

"Go ahead, Master Dijenuk. Place it on its pedestal," Fhrlinti said.

The cylindrical pedestals stuck out about three feet high. Seven of them were on equidistant points along the edge of the circle. The eighth pedestal rose from the center. They were topped with a thin layer of silver metal. Cut into the middle of each cylinder was a different symbol. One of them had its symbol missing, and there was a small recess instead.

The Dijenuk turned and held up the Crystal for all to see, and the civilians below cheered. David then walked towards the Shrine. He took a deep breath. Holding it with two hands, David slowly set the Wind Crystal on top of its respective pedestal: the one with the symbol for Wind. It stuck to the silver like a magnet.

The moment that the Wind Crystal made contact with its pedestal, a brilliant green light flared from both the Crystal and the symbol. David and Jay gasped. Their insides vibrated, and a pleasing warmth temporarily pulsed through their bodies. The crowd cheered again.

David turned to face his teammates. He wore a big grin. "We did it."

He then pulled out the staff Jay had given him. His face scrunched up as he concentrated. A few seconds later, a gentle gust of wind ran through them, ruffling their clothes and hair.

They all turned to face Jay. They stared at her expectantly. She sighed. "Fine." Jay took her staff back from David and raised it. Nothing happened. "Come on…" she muttered, raising it slightly higher. Again, the wind blew. She moved her bangs out of her eyes. "There. Satisfied?"

"I am certain that the two of you are excited to try your newfound power, but do not forget that Pralicriyus wishes to have another word," Fhrlinti reminded them.

"Huh?" David was distracted by the Grand Shrine. Its glass dome had just reappeared. "Oh, yeah. Let's go, then."

"Actually, before we return…" Fhrlinti approached the door and looked up at a golden plaque on the wall above it. "I imagine that this will help to clear some things up." He stepped aside to allow the others to see it.

Elfekot read it aloud. "'There will come a day in this Cycle of the Universe where *The Legends*, a Sacred Tome of Knowledge, will be improperly opened. *The Legends* itself, upon the Opening, will then release a horrible curse upon the universe with multiple components: The curse will first target the physical area around which *The Legends* was opened. Elemental Giants will wreak havoc upon this area, combined with shakings of the earth, violent storms, and rampant instability of magical energy. The curse will then teleport all Elemental Crystals, wherever they may be, to their respective Elemental Chambers.'"

"Wait, is this the prophecy?" David said.

Elfekot nodded before continuing. "'The curse will need to be countered. The counter for this curse will be a group of magicals called the Restorers of the Elements. The Restorers will be composed of five talented individuals. First, a young male Dijenuk with golden brown eyes who will eventually lead the Restorers and become the most powerful in all of Elektia. Second, a young female with green eyes, close to the eventual leader, who will focus on spellcasting and lead the group intellectually.'" He sighed. "'Third, a young adult male energy mage with grey eyes, captain of the local guards of Fort Dijenuk, who will guide the younger group members. Fourth, a young female fire mage residing in Fort Dijenuk with orange-red eyes and red hair. Fifth, a young female water mage residing in Fort Dijenuk with blue eyes and silver hair.'"

David, Elfekot, and Angela looked at Clove. She took a step back, mouth hanging open as they stared at her.

"So, it is true…." Angela muttered.

"That's good, right?" David said.

"There is more." Elfekot cleared his throat. "'The Restorers of the Elements will, alone, locate and access all of the Elemental Chambers and from them retrieve the Elemental Crystals to return them to the Grand Shrine, which will in turn restore the Element respective to the Crystal one by one, beginning with Wind and going clockwise according to the Dijenuk family emblem. This group will then become the saviors of Elektia. A few exact details of this quest are known: The Opening will be marked by a brief flash from Elektia's sun, Elepta. The male energy mage will find two of the Restorers, including the Dijenuk, outside Fort Dijenuk soon after the Opening. There will be hostile intervention outside and inside the Chambers from various sources. One of the Restorers is a Visionary...' That is all it says."

David scanned over the prophecy. "This is kinda creepy. Someone predicted all of this? They even got our appearances down."

"Is this the entirety of the prophecy?" Angela asked.

"No, but we believe it is most of it," Fhrlinti answered. "There are various pieces scattered across Elektia, some more known than others and some overlapping with each other as people copy down what they find, but this is the most complete version out there."

"Well, if this says we're gonna win, that means it has to happen, right?" David asked. No one answered. He looked at Jay. "Sis?"

She was looking away, her arms crossed. Her jaw was clenched, and the muscles in her face twitched. "I hope you're happy, David," she said with a low, almost bitter voice.

"Huh?"

"Never mind. Are we done here?"

"Yes. Let us return," Fhrlinti said.

The Restorers followed him back inside through the metal door. As the others continued, Jay stopped at the doorway and turned around to face Clove.

"I am sorry for earlier," Jay said.

"Huh?"

"At the Dijenuk House yesterday, I was vocally aggressive to you without needing to be. I just needed to make a point."

"Oh, um, that's okay."

With the other arm still crossed, Jay put her left index finger to her chin. "A reserved nature, the ability to interpret Ancient Elektian at least partially, and a correct prediction as to what the Secret Keeper would tell us, and, of course, you don't seem to be a complete imbecile…. That makes you quite the interesting person, Clove."

Clove's face reddened, and her heart skipped a beat. "W-What?"

"You are still a mystery and, like I said, no mystery escapes me." She turned around. "You, um, don't have to be so quiet, though… if you don't want to…. It doesn't matter to me." Jay continued onward.

Clove spent a few seconds standing there, dumbstruck, before following.

-<o>-

"Restorers of the Elements… I must congratulate you again," said Pralicriyus.

Fhrlinti returned to his chair. "Thank you. All of Light Elektia is grateful."

"Yes, they are. We all are. However..." Pralicriyus leaned forward. "I would like to remind you of our discussion regarding portal crystals."

"It was a mistake," said Elfekot immediately. "The Dijenuks are very new to this. They mixed up the incantation and took us to Fort Dijenuk instead of the Dijenuk House. We apologize."

Pralicriyus leaned back. "Hm... The Council will discuss this matter further. Expect to hear from us in a few days. Now..." The man clapped. His expression reverted from serious to pleased. "You five are very busy people. You are heroes, after all. I will not take up any more of your time. Feel free to return to us for either aid or when you acquire the next Crystal. We are here to serve. Farewell for now, and good luck. May the Elementians continue to bless your journey."

"Thank you," said David.

Two guards escorted the Restorers into entrance hall. David looked out through the open doors. Remnants of the crowd from earlier eagerly waited outside. "So... the Fire Crystal is next, yeah?"

"Yep!" Angela said.

"It would be wise to assume that Landor will only step up his game from here. I reckon that this will only grow more difficult," Elfekot warned.

David frowned. "Jay and I have Wind now... but Landor does, too, huh?"

Elfekot nodded. "So is the nature of things."

"There are still too many questions unanswered," said Jay. "The Wind Chamber mysteriously moved between entire planets, I have this magical green light that appears from me sometimes, and the true origin of our magic remains undiscovered. As for the last one, it surprises me that no one seems to know. At the very least, it gives me the opportunity to be the first. And I *will* be the first."

Elfekot sighed. "Good luck with that."

"Tch. You underestimate the intelligence of Jay Dijenuk," she said. "Actually…" Jay turned around just before they got to the exit. "Wait for me here."

"Where are you going?" David asked.

"I need to ask Sir K a few more things." Jay reentered the Councilmen's chamber. They were already gone. She turned to a nearby soldier. "Could you lead me to Sir K's study? I need to see him."

"I apologize, sir, but no one is allowed without the Council's permission."

"How come?"

"It does not matter. The Council's word is final."

Jay narrowed her eyes. "I understand." Jay sped past him and to the left door. It was the one that Sir K had approached yesterday.

"Hey, wait!"

Jay shut the door and took a quick look in both directions. It was exactly like the hallway on the other side. After finding it devoid of anyone else, she drew the silver rod from her boot and took a few steps down the hall.

The soldier burst inside. "You are trespassing. You need to leave. Now." He approached her.

Once he was away from the door, Jay waved the silver object. "*Dyermé.*"

The air that outlined the man rippled, and he stumbled forward, blinking a few times. "Hey!" He reached for his staff.

"Damn it. *Dyermé.*"

The soldier collapsed to the ground.

Jay slipped the object back into her boot and shouted, "Help! Someone help!"

A few seconds later, a pair of soldiers from the upper floor entered from the staircase.

"This man. He was leading me through here, and he just… collapsed!" Jay's voice had gone up in pitch, and she flailed her arms as though worried. Her facial expressions were exaggerated, with large eyes, raised eyebrows, and a gaping mouth.

They rushed to the sleeping man and knelt beside him. "Hey, are you alright?"

Jay left them and took the stairs up. The hallway was similar to the previous one, only it contained four doors along the wall. Jay scanned the wooden plaques next to them and knocked on the door labeled "Sir K."

"Huh? You may come in."

Jay hastily entered and closed the door behind her.

The room was small, and the large, wooden desk and

bookshelves stacked to the ceiling made for a cramped space.

"Jay Dijenuk? How did you get in here? The Council—"

"I need to ask you a couple things." Jay took a step forward and accidentally crushed a sheet of parchment.

The white floor was littered with books and sheets. The same went for the man's desk. Sir K was sitting in his chair and had turned to face Jay. His left eye was red and swollen, and the lens over it was cracked.

He sighed. "I already told you more than enough."

"You gave me a year yesterday. What does it mean?"

Sir K bit the inside of his cheek. "Someone could be listening…"

"And if someone were, rest assured, they would wish they never did."

Sir K made a low exhale as he massaged one of his temples. "I should not have ever said anything."

"And if *you* continue to remain quiet…" Jay took a step closer. "Then you would also wish you never did."

He looked at her. "Is that a threat?"

"Tch. I would do much worse than whatever the Council did to your face, so use that brain of yours, Sir K. It happens to be marginally larger than that of every other mindless slave of the Council. You seem to have a grasp on reality, so tell me…" Her eyes narrowed at him. "That year. 708. What does it *mean*?" she asked slowly.

Sir K let out a shaky breath. "Miss Dijenuk, I-I never said anything about such a year!" he said, adding a fake laugh.

"I always get what I want, Sir K." Her fist closed. "Always."

He muttered a low curse. "Fine! The Council did something that year, something big. I do not know exactly what, but... it may be the answer to that portal dilemma you brought up. I never found such an answer myself, so perhaps you—"

"Oh, believe me, I will. And what do you know about *The Legends*?"

He groaned. "As much as I hate the thing, I know it is very valuable. Not monetarily, of course, but in the immense amount of knowledge it contains. I imagine you are interested in finding it, but I fear that the Council will try to confiscate it. Seeing as I have the Council breathing over my neck, I figured that taking it would be a bad idea, even if I had the strength to."

"Hm. Is that all?"

His eyebrows lowered as his gaze became more intense. "If you find *The Legends*, Jay Dijenuk, you may end up finding what you need to turn this world upside down, in turn revealing the truth."

Jay made a hollow, unsmiling chuckle. "I already intend to do such a thing. I appreciate the confirmation, though. There is more I would like to ask, but I cannot spend too much time here. I will be going now."

"Wait! One more thing, if I may."

"Make it quick."

"I meant to ask you this sometime back on Terra, but you were never around long enough in the classroom... What happened to you?"

Jay crossed her arms. "Excuse me?"

"When you were in my debate class, second semester of your junior year, you were very... soft-spoken. Then, the next year, you are in my class again, and you are like a completely different person." His voice had become gentle, and his gaze drifted off. "If I recall, you had this one friend, but, in September, she—"

"I simply discovered my true self; my *better* self. Never bring this up again." She moved to the door.

"Everyone needs someone special, Miss Dijenuk, even if it is just a friend."

"I would rather die than have anything like that again." Before Sir K could respond, Jay exited.

"Hey, are you supposed to be here?" asked a soldier. He walked towards her from the staircase.

"I am. The Council gave me permission; worry not."

"I need certainty, sir."

"If I didn't have permission, how would I have even gotten here?"

The soldier stared at her for a second. "Fair point. Just make your exit quick."

Jay made her way back to the entrance hall with the soldier following. The other Restorers were still lingering.

"Finally," David said, moving away from the pillar he was leaning against.

"Can we go now? We need to step up our training and get to the Fire Chamber as quickly as possible," Angela said.

Elfekot nodded, and the Restorers walked to the entrance

again. "You know…" Elfekot faced his comrades. "I did not expect to make it this far. I honestly expected us all to die horribly before even reaching the first Crystal. You did a really good job, David. Perhaps you kids are not as helpless as I thought," Elfekot admitted as he walked outside.

"For the billionth time, Elfekot, I'm not a kid. I'm *technically* an adult on Terra. Well, kinda, 'cause I can't drink and stuff, but…" David followed him as he continued to ramble.

"Pralicriyus called us heroes," Angela said as she looked at the remnants of the civilians in the courtyard. "*They* call us heroes." She paused. "I like the sound of that." She joined David and Elfekot outside.

Jay turned and met Clove's blue eyes, and Clove's body tensed. Jay's green eyes were cutting. It was like they stared into one's very soul. At the same time, it was nearly impossible to read them. It didn't help that a tuft of her bangs covered one eye. The two were silent for a couple of seconds. Clove broke the eye contact and looked at the ground as she shuffled towards the exit. Jay remained where she was.

She stopped next to her. Clove carefully placed a hand on Jay's upper arm. "I, uh, I forgive you, and um, you did a good job, too, Jay." She hurried outside.

It was then that Jay briefly did something she hadn't done in months, not since the night of the party last June. For the first time in a long time, Jay smiled.

END OF BOOK 1

ABOUT THE AUTHOR

Solber Martinez, born November 25, 2000, is a Mexican-American from Salem, Oregon, USA. He has an obvious passion for writing, but also for music and tabletop gaming. He wrote the lyrics to the song "Stone Arch" by No Other Option, writes other songs and poems in his free time, and likes to write and run *Dungeons & Dragons* campaigns for himself and his friends.

With his background also in choir and theatre, Solber Martinez's calling for the arts and performance is clear, and the Under the Stone Arch series is the prime example of that.

For more on Solber Martinez, Under the Stone Arch, and other works—including the song "Stone Arch"—visit www.solbermartinez.com

You can also follow him on Instagram: @solbermartinez